John Nichols

The History and Antiquities of Hinckley

In the County of Leicester

John Nichols

The History and Antiquities of Hinckley
In the County of Leicester

ISBN/EAN: 9783337330491

Printed in Europe, USA, Canada, Australia, Japan

Cover: Foto ©Andreas Hilbeck / pixelio.de

More available books at **www.hansebooks.com**

THE

HISTORY and ANTIQUITIES

OF

H I N C K L E Y,

IN THE COUNTY OF LEICESTER;

INCLUDING THE HAMLETS OF

STOKE, DADLINGTON, WYKIN, AND THE HYDE.

WITH A LARGE APPENDIX,

CONTAINING

Some Particulars of the ancient Abbey of LIRA in Normandy;
Aftronomical Remarks, adapted to the Meridian of HINCKLEY;
and Biographical Memoirs of feveral Perfons of Eminence.

By JOHN NICHOLS, F. S. A. EDINB. *Correfp.*
and PRINTER to the SOCIETY of ANTIQUARIES of LONDON.

MDCCLXXXII.

To Mr. John Robinson, of Hinckley.

My good Friend,

TO what Patron is this Hiſtory intended to be inſcribed, is a queſtion you very naturally have aſked me: but I ſee not that any Dedication is neceſſary. If it were, I ſhould perhaps, when treating of Local Antiquities, look up either to the Society of Anti-quaries of London, to whom I can boaſt of a profeſſional relation; or to that of Edinburgh, which has done me the honour to enroll my name amongſt its Correſponding Members. But my reſearches, whilſt they have convinced me that there is ſcarcely a Village in the King-dom but could furniſh materials for the Hiſtorian, either as having been the ſeat of a battle, the peaceful reſidence of ſome religious ſociety, the birth-place of an eminent individual, or for ſome event which poſte-rity would wiſh to know, have led me to more ambitious views.

When I contemplate the dignity ſuſtained by a Town which furniſhed the Kingdom with an Hereditary Lord High Steward, I am naturally led to conſider the preſent amiable Representative of ſo high an Ho-nour, the Sovereign of the Britiſh Empire. To HIM, therefore, to the Father of his People, as Hereditary Baron of Hinckley, I have every inclination to offer up this humble tribute of dutiful reſpect, but have not the preſumption to requeſt the neceſſary permiſſion.

As a hearty Well-wiſher to the proſperity of your native Town; you will live, I hope, to ſee it reſtored to no ſmall portion of its primi-tive ſplendour. Whilſt there are ſo many blooming Branches of the Royal Stem, we may indulge the pleaſing expectation of ſeeing the Barony revived in the perſon of a Prince, and this ancient and loyal Borough again diſtinguiſhed by the privilege of ſending Repreſentatives to the Great Council of the Nation.

b 2

For

[vi]

For the active part you have taken in this History, accept my best thanks. The reader will easily perceive the advantages it has received from your accurate drawings and judicious communications.

I am Sir, with great truth,

Your obliged and faithful friend,

Nov. 1, 1782.

J. NICHOLS.

References to the PLAN of HINCKLEY.

1. The Church.
2. Presbyterian Meeting House.
3. Quakers' Meeting House.
4. Independent Meeting House.
5. Roman Catholic Chapel.
6. Methodist Meeting House.
7. The Ancient Priory, or Hall House.
8. The Vicarage.
9. Town Hall.
10. The Round Hill.
11. Free School.
12. The House of William Hurst, Esq., on the Spot where the Ancient Castle stood.
13. The Canal at the Foot of the Hill.
14. Building struck by Lightning (see p. 85).
15. Mr. Nicholas Hurst's Summer House.
16. Serpentine Garden, where, under the Summer House, is a subterraneous Passage.
17. The Lovers' Walk.

18. Cherry Orchard.
19. Gardens planted with Fruit Trees.
20. Hurst's Bowling Green.
21. } The Canals.
22. }
23. The Repository for the Fire Engines.
24. Gardens planted with Fruit Trees.
25. Well Lane.
26. } The Horsepools.
27. }
28. Pinfold.
29. Duke's Lane.
30. Westminster Yard.
31. Parish Workhouse.
32. House of Correction.
33. Mr. Robinson's House, where the Astronomical Observations were made.
34. New Methodist Meeting-house, now building (1782).

The variation of the magnetic needle from the meridian at Hinckley, the beginning of 1782, 16° 30' West.

HINCK-

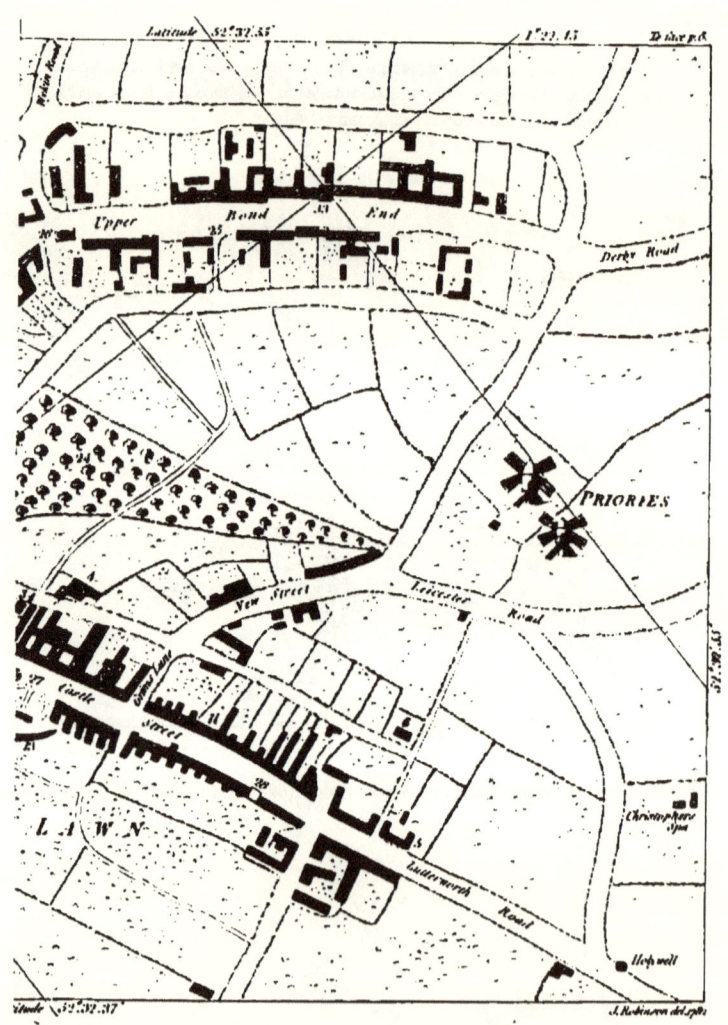

H I S T O R Y

O F

H I N C K L E Y.

HINCKLEY *, the fecond market-town in the county of Leicefter, is part of the hundred of Sparkenhoe, and is fituated (according to accurate aftronomical obfervations made on the fpot by Mr. John Robinfon) in latitude 52°. 32′. 46″. The difference between its meridian and that of the Royal Obfervatory at Greenwich is 5′. 31″. of time to the weft, and therefore its longitude is 1°. 22′. 45″. Weft of Greenwich.

The parifh, including its dependent villages of *Stoke Golding*, *Dadlington*, and *Wykin*, and the little hamlet of *The Hide* (each of which will be particularly treated of hereafter) is of very confiderable extent. It is bounded on the Eaft by Barwell and Burbach; on the Weft by Nuneaton and Higham; on the North by Stapleton and Barwell; and on the South by Burbach and Sketchley.

The town, which is built on rifing ground, ftands nearly upon the borders of Warwickfhire, from which county this part of Leicefterfhire is feparated by the Watlingftreet road. The entrance from the Coventry road is the loweft part of the town; and from thence, to the other extremes of Bond End † and Caftle Streets, the rifings are confiderable; and thefe ftreets enjoy a pure and healthful air ‡.

* A fpecimen of the various modes in which this name was antiently fpelt may be feen in the lift of Priors, p. 31. 32. The word is moft probably derived from the name of *Hinck*, fome Saxon proprietor, and *iey*, a field.—Two fmall ftreets in Birmingham are known by the names of *The Old Hinckley* and *The New Hinckley*. In one of thefe, till 1730, the only theatre of that town was fituated.

† Latitude obferved at the church, which is the South part of Hinckley, 52 32 37
———— at the Bond End, the North part of the town, 52 32 55
Mean, as above, 52 32 46
Thefe obfervations have been confirmed by the remarks of the Rev. W. Ludlam.

‡ It is fomewhat remarkable that, notwithftanding the populoufnefs of the town, eight weeks have elapfed (from Oct. 10, to Dec. 6, 1781) without a fingle funeral.

B   The

The limits of what is now called *The Borough*, were in its early days thofe of the town; from which the *Church* ftood at fome
diftance, and the *Caftle* (then the manfion of its lord) ftill farther. *The Bond End* (at firft confifting of only a few ftraggling
houfes, or rather huts *) in time became a ftreet; and was fucceeded by *The Caftle End*, *The Stocken Head*, and *The Duck Paddle*.
Hinckley is in the high road from Leicefter to Coventry, from
each of which towns it is diftant about thirteen miles, five from
Cleybrook †, and eleven from Lutterworth, through which two
                                                                    laft-

* " Thefe were built of timber, the interftices wattled with fticks, and plaiftered
" with mud, covered with thatch, boards, or fods, none of them higher than the
" ground ftory; the meaner fort only one room, which ferved for three ufes, fhop,
" kitchen, and lodging-room; the door for two, it admitted the people and the
" light. The better fort had two rooms, and fome three, for work, for the kitchen, and
" for reft, all three in a line, and fometimes all fronting the ftreet." I have given this
defcription very nearly in the words of Mr. Hutton, in his newly publifhed Hiftory
of Birmingham; and cannot but obferve, that there is a remarkable coincidence in
the early hiftory of the two towns, though Birmingham, once much inferior in confequence to Hinckley, has now got infinitely beyond it in the fcale of wealth and
commerce. The hollow roads round both towns are equal proofs of the antiquity
of each. " Some of thefe," fays Mr. Hutton, " no doubt, were formed by the
" fpade, to foften the fatigue of climbing the hill; but many were owing to the
" pure efforts of time, the horfe, and the fhowers. One of thefe fubterraneous
" paffages, in part filled up, will convey its name to pofterity in that of a ftreet
" called *Holloway Head*. *Dale End*, once a deep road, has the fame derivation.
" But the moft fingular is that between Derjtend and Camp hill, in the way to
" Stratford, which is even now many yards below the banks; yet the feniors of
" the laft age took a pleafure in telling us they could remember when it would
" have buried a waggon-load of hay beneath its prefent furface." Can any inhabitant of Hinckley defire a more faithful picture of *The Bond End?* I appeal alfo
to the memories of living perfons, whether *The Stocken Head* was not the counterpart
of *The Holloway Head* at Birmingham; and am not afraid of being contradicted
when I affert that *The Caftle End* was once a hollow road, filled up, like *Dale End*,
as trade and population have increafed. *The Duck Paddle* likewife of Hinckley has
more than an accidental refemblance of *The Digbeth* or *Duck's Bath* of Birmingham.
† The *Venona*, undoubtedly, of the Itinerary of Antoninus, near which, at *High-
Crofs* (fee p. 121.), two Roman roads, the *Watling ftreet* and the *Fofs*, interfect each
other ‡. Burton mentions feveral coins having been found near this crofs. Dr. Stukeley fays, Mr. Lee ‖ of Leicefter had a Roman urn, found here, 1717. In digging for
a vault in the church for Bafil earl of Denbigh, they met with a dozen urns covered
with Roman bricks. Foundations of houfes have been frequently dug up along the

‡ *Watling ftreet* rifes near Dover, and, running North Weft through London, Atherftone, and Shrep-
fhire, in the neighbourhood of Chefter, ends in the Irifh fea. The *Fofs* begins in Devonfhire, extends South
Laft through Leicefterfhire, continuing its courfe through Lincolnfhire, to the verge of the German ocean.
‖ Thomas Lee, an ingenious antiquary, and collector of curiofities. He died in 1776, aged 72.

                                                                    ftreet,

laſt-mentioned towns the direct road to London is one hundred miles *.

At the grand ſurvey †, begun by direction of William the Conqueror in 1080, and completed in 1086, *Hincbelie* was reported as part of the poſſeſſions of *Comes Albericus* [Aubrey de Vere, lord high-chamberlain], in the wapentake (or hundred) of *Gutlaciſlon* ‡.

After

ſtreet, all the way to Claybrook. Much *eubulus* grows here, ſought for in curing dropſies.

  * This road, " from Caſtle-Street, at the end of the town of Hinckley, to Lutter-" worth town's end," was amended, widened, and directed to be kept in repair, by an act of parliament paſſed March 24, 1762.—An act had been paſſed in 1760, for repairing the roads from Duck Paddle Street in the town of Hinckley, through Oſbaſton, Nelſton, Ibſtock, &c. to Derby.

  † " The king ſent his ſervants throughout all England, with power to enquire " how many hundreds were contained in each county, what lands and flocks in it " belonged to the king, and what ſubſidy it ought to pay yearly. He alſo autho-" rized them to take an account how much land belonged to the archbiſhops, bi-" ſhops, abbats, and earls, and in ſhort what lands and flocks belonged to each " Engliſhman, and the value thereof in money. He ordered them to ſurvey the " lands ſo diligently, that there ſhould not be a hide, nor even a yard of land, nor " indeed, which is ſhameful to mention, though he was not aſhamed to cauſe it to " be done, an ox or a cow omitted, but what ſhould be brought into the accounts, " and delivered to him in writing." Saxon Chronicle, ann. 1085, p. 186.

  ‡ Whence the hundred of Sparkenhoe was ſubdivided by Edward the Third, in 1347, for the more ſpeedy collecting of an aid levied for making his ſon the Black Prince a knight. Among the Harleian MSS. N° 6700, I find the " Auxilia in co-" mitatu Leiceſtriæ, Domino Regi Edwardo conceſſa, ad primogenitum filium ſuum " militem faciendum, anno regno xx°, A. D. 1347." In that remarkable levy, occurs this entry :

Hinckley, Stoke, Dadelington, Wychcoe, Vicar',	Procurações.	Taxações.	Denar' Sti Petri.	Patron'. Abbas de Lira het in pprios uſus.	Penſ'
	vii s vi d ob q.	lxiii mar'. v s.	v s.		...
		ix mar'.			

In reſpect to eccleſiaſtical juriſdiction, the *deanry* of Sparkenhoe is of much older date, being mentioned in the Matriculus of 1220, preſerved among the Cotton MSS. in the Britiſh Muſeum, and tranſcribed in our Appendix; and again in the Valor of Pope Nicholas IV. who granted the tenths of all eccleſiaſtical benefices to the King for ſix years, towards defraying the expences of an expedition to the Holy Land; and, that they might be collected to their full value, a new taxation by the king's precept was begun in the year 1288, and finiſhed 1291, by the biſhops of Lincoln and Wincheſter ; according

After an enumeration of feveral other lands of Earl * Aubrey in that wapentake, the record proceeds†,

> Ide.Co.tenuit *HINCHELIE*. Ibi sŧ.xiiii.cař trœ.In
> dñio sŧ.iiii.caŕ.7 viii.Servi.7 xlii.uilli cū.xvi.bord..
> 7 iii.fochis bñt.ix.caŕ 7 dim. Ibi jtū.vi.ᵭƺ in Ig..
> 7 iii.ᵭƺ lať..Silua.i.leu Ig.7 iii.ᵭƺ lať.
> Valuit.vi.lib.Modo.x.lib..

In Englifh thus,

The fame Earl held Hinchelie. In that place are xiv carucates ‡.
In the lordfhip are iv carucates; and viii fervants, and x lii villans ||,

to which, all church dignities and benefices were afterwards rated, and in many re-
fpeéts are valued at this day. The " Summa Taxacŭis decanatus de SPARKENHOE"
(taken in 1290, when Oliver [Sutton] was bifhop of Lincoln) was mxi li. ii ſ.
of which the proportions of the following towns ftood thus:

Ecclefia de *Afton*,	xx mar'.
Ecclefia de *Barwell*,	xxxvi mar' 11ŝ.11ᵭ.
Ecclefia de *Higbam* per penf',	xxii mar'.
Penf' abb' de Lyra in eadem,	iii mar'.
Ecclefia de *Hynáeley*, Cap. *Stoke, Dadelington*, &*Ilychene*, }	lxiii mar'..
Vicar' ejufdem,	ix mar'..

The abbats of Lira were patrons of the churches of *Afton*, *Bittefwell*, *Drayton*,
Hig!am, and *Sibbefton*; and had annual penfions from each. The original Valor
whence the above fums are extraéted (p..75. b.) is preferved among the Harleian MSS. N° 591. Of Pope Nicholas' Taxation-books, other originals are known
to be extant; one at the Tower, another among the archives of the dean and chapter
Canterbury, and another in the Bodleian Library.

   * Whence Aubrey had his title does not appear, for that of Oxford was
firft enjoyed by his grandfon, and Dugdale difputes his being earl of Ghifnes in
France. Bar. l. 188.   † Folio 231. b. col. 1.
   ‡ So called from *caruca*, a plough. A carucate is that quantity of land which is
fufficient to employ one plough. It is generally fuppofed to contain 120 acres, but
fometimes only 60. In Leicefterfhire 12 carucates (in fome other counties 18)
were a hide; and 48 carucates a knight's fee.
   || Villains, though above the rank of fervants, held their lands by tenure, and all
their property was at the will of the lord. Some judgement may be formed of their
condition by a reference to Plac. coram Rege apud Portefmouth, Trinit. anno 7° Rege
Johis, Rot. 6. where the abbat of Waltham maintains " that John le Tanur is his
" villain, having been purchafed by Walter his predeceffor for fixty fhillings."

                    with

with xvi bordarers*, and iii fochmen+, have ix carucates and a half. Meadow land vi furlongs in length, and iii furlongs in breadth. Wood i league‡ in length, and iii furlongs in breadth. It was worth [in the time of Edward the Confeffor] vi pounds; now x pounds ‖.

The moſt confiderable land-holder in the county appears to have been Sir HUGH de GRENTEMAISNEL (the fecond fon of a potent Norman baron), who came over in the train of the Conqueror in 1066; and ſo valiantly behaved himſelf, that the king not only rewarded him with many lordſhips in various counties §, but in two years after conſtituted him one of the affiſtants to Odo biſhop of Bayeux and William Fitz-Oſborn in the adminiſtration of juſtice throughout the whole kingdom; made him governor of Hampſhire in 1069; and upon the ſettling of ſuch garriſons as were thought fit to keep the ſubdued Engliſh in awe, he had Lei-ceſter committed to his charge, being alſo made ſheriff of the

---

* The Bordarers were peafants, hufbandmen, or cottagers; the conditions of whofe tenure were, to fupply the lord's table with fmall proviſions, and to perform his do-meſtic work, or even any lower offices he might require.

+ The focmen were properly free tenants, deriving great privileges and commu-nities from the nature of their tenure.

‡ *Leuva*, in the original, is a corruption of the Latin *Leuca*, which is three miles, and feems to be the extent of the pariſh on the South fide adjoining to Burbach; that is, from the Watling-ſtreet to the Lutterworth road, which probably was the wood in queſtion, and out of part thereof baron Hugo formed his park. The *Thorncy-crafts, Eaſt Woods, Out Woods*, and *Stocken*, will nearly ſhew the true fituation of the wood. A *leuva* is by fome faid to have contained 1500 paces, by others 2000. In the Monaſticon, vol. I. p. 313, it is 480 perches.

‖ A pound in that age contained three times the weight of filver that it does at prefent; and the fame weight of filver, by the moſt probable computation, would purchafe ten times more of the neceſſaries of life. Ten pounds, therefore, were equi-valent to three hundred.

§ In Northamptonſhire, it appears by Domefday-book, he had twenty lordſhips; in Bedfordſhire four, in Glouceſterſhire five, in Hertfordſhire one, in Suffolk one, in Nottinghamſhire one, in Warwickſhire five, and in Leiceſterſhire fixty-feven. He had alſo the manor of Lippard in Worceſterſhire, which he held of the church of St. Mary in Worceſter.

county;

county; and, befides thefe great trufts, the king richly married him
to Adeliza, a great inheritrix of noble family, and at the folemni-
zation thereof beftowed on him the honourable office of Lord
High Steward [a] of England (or Viceroy, for fo the word fignifies
in the Saxon), the firft great officer of the crown, and then for
the firft time made hereditary † in the family of Grentemaifnel.
Either as part of the dower of his lady ‡, or perhaps by the fortune of the field, or even by exchange or purchafe (for it appears
by Domefday that he had then been lately a purchafer), he added
the *honor* or *barony* of *Hinckley* to his other large poffeffions.

In 1079 he was one of the nobles who by earneft fuit endeavoured a reconciliation from the king to his fon Robert Curt-
hofe.   But in 1088, the firft year of the reign of Rufus ||, this
haughty Norman lord, in confederacy with many of his country-
men, appeared in arms againft their fovereign, and over-ran the
counties of Leicefter and Norfolk.   By the fpirited conduct of Rufus, this infurrection was fpeedily quelled; and Grentemaifnel,
after fuitable conceffions, was taken into ftill greater favour,
and became afterwards one of the moft ftrenuous oppofers of
Curthofe.

With a liberality proportionate to his more than princely fortune, he erected a ftately caftle, laid out a beautiful park, and caufed

---

* Of this important office a more particular account fhall be given in the Appendix.

† No more than two lords occur in our hiftorians, as having held this office earlier; Houclin was Steward to Edward the Confeffor; and William Fitz-Osborn,
who had been created earl of Hereford and lord of Wight in 1066, was made Lord
High Steward in '1067.   He married, 1. Adeliza daughter of Roger de Touey,
ftandard-bearer of Normandy; 2. Richildis, daughter and heirefs of Henault; and
died in 1072.   The baron of Hinckley fucceeded him in the office of High-Steward.

‡ Adeliza uxor Hugonis de Grentemaifnel occurs in Domefday as a landholder
in the counties of Leicefter, Warwick, Bedford, and Hertford.

|| " Hugo de Grente Maifnelo Legereeftriæ provinciam, Rogerus Bigot Eftang-
" ham depredati funt."   Diceto, inter X Script. col. 490.—" Rogerius Bigod apud
" Norwich, & Hugo de Grentemeifnil apud Legeceftre, fuis quifque partibus rapinas
" urgebant."   W. Malmsb. lib. iv. p. 68.

the

the parifh church to be built, the appropriation of which he granted to the abbey of Lira in Normandy; for whom he alfo founded* an alien priory †, or rather a cell, of two Benedictine monks, and erected a large and convenient houfe for their reception, on the fcite where the prefent hall-houfe (reprefented in plate II.) was afterwards built.

At the clofe of his life, being aged and infirm, he took upon him in 1094 the habit of a monk at St. Ebrulf's abbey in Normandy, which he had reftored‡; and dying fix days after, viz. 8 kal. Martii, was honourably buried in the chapter-houfe ‖, with this epitaph:

> " Ecce fub hoc tumulo requiefcit ftrenuus Hugo,
> " Qui viguit multos multa probitate per annos;
>   " Manfio Grentonis menilio dicitur ejus,
>   " Unde fuit cognomen ei multis bene notum.
> " Guillelmi fortis Anglorum tempore Regis,
> " Inter præcipuos magnates is claruit heros:

---

* By Tanner, in his Notitia, Robert de Blanchmaines is faid to have been the founder; by Dugdale, in his Baronage, vol. I. p. 86. the honour of it is given to Boffu his father; the Matriculus of 1220 afcribes it to Will. fil. Ofberti. Tanner has very properly fhewn the improbability of Dugdale's fuppofition, though it appears that in other refpects he was a benefactor to Lira. The Earl of Hereford was the original founder of the Abbey of Lira, not of its appendages in England. Blanchmaines, who married the daughter of a fucceeding baron of Hinckley, might poffibly confirm the donation; which indeed was frequently confirmed by fucceeding earls of Leicefter.

† An ingenious gentleman has obferved to me, that " it certainly was, and ought " to be called, a priory, for which reafon there muft be abfolutely three monks, the " prior and two others, becaufe three religious perfons, and not lefs, form a choir. " The profits of Wychen were to maintain two monks, and others the minifters of " the church, and to exercife hofpitality, which makes me think there were at leaft " five refiding in the priory, and the chaplains of Stoke and Dadlington fubject to " them.'

‡ To the monks of Thorney in Cambridgefhire he had alfo given one yard land in Wenge.

‖ Dugd. Bar. I. 425. & aut. ibi cit.

" Militiâ

" Militiâ fortis fuit & virtute fidelis,
" Hoftibus horribilis, & Amicis tutus herilis;
" Sumtibus Officiis augens, & pinguibus Armis,
" Cœnobium Sancti multum provexit Ebrulfi,
    " Dum Cathedram Sancti celebrabat plebs pia Petri,
    " Occidit emeritus, habitu Monachi trabeatus,
" Ecclefiæ cultor, largus dator, & revelator,
" Blandus egenorum lætentur in arce polorum. *Amen.*"

HUGH had iffue five fons and three daughters: *Robert*, who furvived him 28 years, but died, we are told, without iffue; *William*, a perfon of great confequence in the court of William Rufus, died in Apulia; *Hugh* died young; *Yvo* enjoyed his father's poffeffions in England, but engaging in a confpiracy againft Henry I. in behalf of Robert Curthofe, was difgraced and fined, and being unable to reinftate himfelf in Henry's favour, he mort-gaged his lands to the earl of Mellent, and undertook a journey to the Holy Land, but died by the way. It was previoufly fettled that his fon Yvo fhould marry the daughter of the earl of War-wick, and redeem the eftate. Hugh's fifth fon named *Alberic* was firft a fcholar, and then a foldier*.

Of Hugh's daughters, *Adeline* married Roger de Ibrci; *Hawife* died unmarried; *Roifia* was the wife of Robert de Curci; *Maud* of Hugh de Montpincon; *Agnes* of William de Say; and *Hawife* died fingle†.

· From Hugh's fon Yvo defcended another HUGH‡ *de Grentemaif-nel*, who had, it feems, great part of his anceftor's poffeffions reftored to him, viz. the honor of Hinckley, and the high-ftewardfhip of Eng-land. This Hugh had iffue two daughters, coheireffes; of whom *Pe-*

* Dugd. Bar. I. 425.
† In a pedigree of this noble family preferved in the Britifh Mufeum (Harl. MSS. 6160. fol. 17. b.) they are called " Earls of Leicefter and Hinckley."
‡ This Hugh and his grandfather are confounded by almoft all the old hiftorians.

tronilla

Ironilla *, married to Robert de Bellomont furnamed Blanchmaines, earl of Leicefter †, grandfon to Robert de Mellent, brought to her hufband the high-ftewardfhip and barony ‡. Her fifter *Alice* was married to Roger Bigot, father of Hugh, created earl of Norfolk in 1135.

* In a MS. written 1578 by Robert Cook Clarencieux, in Emanuel college library, and by another, a copy of it, written in 1589, in the poffeffion of the Rev. Mr. Cole of Milton, it is faid, that " Geoffrey earl of Hinckley was fo created by " William Rufus, of whom defcended Hugh Graunimaines earl of Hinckley, and " lord fteward of England, whofe daughter and heir called Pernell was married to " Robert Beaumont third earl of Leicefter, who, in her right, was lord fteward of " England." He gave for arms, Gules, a Pale, Or. Brook's Catalogue, 1612, p. 212. fays, Pernell was daughter of Hugh Grentmaifnel.
The fame Ralph Brook fays, That Robert de Bellomont or Beaumont, third earl of Leicefter, was called *Blanchmaines*, from his white hands: but query, if this title of Blanchmaines may not rather be derived from the white fcurf of the leprofy (then moft common in France and England), than from the beauty of his hands? efpecially as his fon William was fo infected with that malady, that he founded an hofpital for it in Leicefter. (Mr. Cole's MSS. vol. XXI. p. 218.) And more efpecially if we confider, that thefe fobriquets, or furnames, fo common in thefe times, were often impofed on imperfections or deformities; as William the Baftard, Robert Boffu earl of Leicefter, fo named, no doubt, from his crooked make, and many others eafy to be named if requifite : Edmund Crouchback, Henry Torto-Collo (Wryneck) duke of Lancafter.
" The mention of this hofpital," fays Mr. Cole, to whom I owe this note, " reminds " me of a particular which may be thought curious. Mr. Freeman, an ingenious " painter of Cambridge in 1776, brought me the impreffion of the feal of this hofpital, " the original brafs feal being then lately found at Saffron-Walden in Effex. It is of an " oval form of three inches depth, having the full figure of St. Leonard dreffed as an " abbat, with a fhort fquab mitre on his head, a crofier in his left hand, a book in " his right, and a pair of manicles or collar, and chains hanged from them to exprefs " the nature of his charitable employment in redeeming captives. Under an arch " below his feet is the half figure of one of the brethren of the hofpital praying to " him. The faint ftands under a beautiful Gothic canopy, and the whole is fur- " rounded with this legend in fmall Gothic characters:
Sigillu' roni'ume Magiftri et Fratrum Hofpital' Sc'i Leonardi Leceftrie.
" This hofpital at the diffolution fell into the hands of a perfon whofe name was Cat- " lyn. Now as a family of that name has long been fettled at Walden, it is not im- " probable that the feal and writings have been in that family, and the feal occa-, " fionally loft in that place."
† Dugd. ib.   ‡ Id. ib.

C   ROBERT

ROBERT BLANCHMAINES, earl of Leicefter, fon of Robert Boffu, and grandfon of Robert earl of Mellent and Leicefter, was
the man who laid his daring hand on his fword, and offered
to draw with the purpofe to have ftruck his fovereign king
Henry the Second, but was withheld from the attempt. He ad-
hered to prince Henry in his rebellion againft his father Henry II.
for which his town of Leicefter was taken and nearly deftroyed[*],
and himfelf and countefs coming from France with troops to re-
venge his lofs, were defeated and made prifoners 1173. After a
confinement of four years, he was reftored 1177 to all his lands
in England and France, except the caftles of Montforel in the
former, and Pavy in the latter. He furvived Henry II. and was
in great favour with Richard I. and dying 1190 on his return
from pilgrimage to Jerufalem, at Duras (the ancient Dyrrhachi-
um), was there buried[†]. He left three fons: 1. *Robert Fitz-Parnel*,
who fucceeded him. 2. *Roger* bifhop of St. Andrews in Scotland[‡].

3. *William*

---

[*] " The plan of Leicefter, as it ftood before this grand demolition, is eafily
" to be traced. In the heart of the town, on each fide the principal ftreet, are a
" number of large orchards; feparated not with one common fence as ufual, but
" a double fence; a wall belonging to each, with public ways between the two
" walls, called Back-Lanes. Thefe Back-Lanes were manifeftly the ftreets, and the
" orchards the fite of houfes and yards deftroyed, and never fince re-built. The
" traces of the town-wall and ditch are in many places plainly to be feen. Dr.
" Stukeley's plan of Roman Leicefter is fuppofed to be a meer figment. There
" are veftiges of two Roman works, and no more; the mount near the river
" (as was their cuftom), and the ruins of a bath near St. Nicholas's church. Two
" teffelated pavements have been found there; the lateft and largeft about 1750."
Mr. LUDLAM, MS.—To which may be added the Temple of Janus (fee Stukeley
It. Cur. vol. I. pl. 55.) now called Jewry Wall, in the place known by the name of
" Holy Bones;" of which a good reprefentation is given by Throfby, from a drawing of my ingenious young friend Mr. W. Bafi, to whom the prefent little work is
indebted for part of its embellifhments.

[†] His benefactions to Lira appear in the Appendix, N° IV. and V.; thofe of his
father Robert Boffu in N° III. and V.

[‡] His coufin William king of Scotland preferred him to be Lord High Chancellor of his kingdóm, and he was confecrated bifhop of St. Andrew's 1198. He
died

3. *William de Britolio*[*], a leper, founder of St. Leonard's hofpital at Leicefter: and two daughters, 1. *Amicia*, married to Simon de Montfort; and 2. *Margaret*, to Saher de Quincy †.

ROBERT FITZ-PARNEL defended Normandy from the inroads of the king of France during the captivity of Richard I. King John gave him all Richmondfhire; and he was alfo made earl of Maffonia in Sicily. He died after his return from the Holy Land, 1204, and was buried before the high altar at Leicefter abbey ‡. Leaving no iffue by his wife Lauretta, daughter of William de Braiofe, lord of Bramber in Suffex, his inheritance was divided between his two fifters Amicia and Margaret; Amicia, as eldeft fifter, retained as her moiety fuch lands as were fituated in the county of Leicefter, and with them the honor of Hinckley, and the high ftewardfhip which was not partable. The office was executed *jure uxoris* by SIMON DE MONTFORT; who, being created earl of Leicefter in 1206, became poffeffed both of the honor and high-ftewardfhip *pleno jure* ||. But taking part with the French againft king John, he was ftripped of his honours and eftates; and banifhed; and 2 or 3 Henry III. loft his life at the fiege of Touloufe under Lewis king of France **. His eftates were given to Randolph earl of Chefter ; but the high-ftewardfhip the king retained in his own hands, as annexed to the crown by forfeiture. " Now doth the power of the fenefcalcy," fays an ancient writer §, " fuffer an eclipfe, by being overfhadowed by the royal mantle of

---

died 1202, and was buried in the church of St. Rule. Keith's Cat. of Scotch bifhops, p. 9. & aut. ibi. cit.

* It appears by the Appendix N° VI. that Petronella countefs of Leicefter gave to the abbey of Lyra an annual penfion of eleven fhillings, out of her mills *de Britolio*, to celebrate the anniverfary of her fon William.

† Dugd. I. 87, 88. & aut. ibi cit.   ‡ Id. ib.
|| Id. ib. & Harl. MSS. 2194.
** Dugd. I. 712.
§ Harl. MSS. 2194.

" the

" the crown; a power next to the king's, and in some sort match-
" ing the Ephori of the Lacedemonians.

His second son SIMON was restored by Henry III; 1231, to his
lands in England, and to all his father's honours (the high-steward-
ship alone excepted, the king conceiving the power of that office to
be too great and exorbitant for any subject *). In 1238 this earl married Eleanor the king's sister, widow of William Marshal earl of Pembroke, and thus " raised himself to a degree of greatness hardly in-
" ferior to royalty, and of wealth superior to that of some of our mo-
" narchs. Nothing is more difficult than to form a just idea of the
" real character of this illustrious person, who was abhorred as a
" *devil* by one half of England, and adored as a *saint* and guardian
" *angel* by the other.   He was unquestionably one of the greatest
" generals and politicians of his age; bold, ambitious, and enter-
" prizing; ever considered; both by friends and enemies, as the
" very soul of the party which he espoused.   He was fierce and
" clamorous in the cause of liberty, till he arrived at power, which
" he employed in aggrandising and enriching his own family †."
After various discontents and various turns of the royal favour to and
from him, he engaged as principal in that grand rebellion against
his sovereign 1263, 47 Henry III. which, by his victory at Lewes,
gave him the absolute management of the kingdom till he was
defeated and slain with his eldest son Henry at the battle of
Evesham, in 1265 ‡.   It has been said of this nobleman, that he
was

* Coke, Instit. part IV. p. 58.
† This character is drawn by Dr. Henry, in the fourth volume of his " History
" of Great Britain, 1781," 4to.
‡ The king one day passing on the Thames, there happened a sudden clap of
thunder, whereat the king, somewhat affrighted, commanded to be set on shore at the
next landing-place, which happened to be at Durham-house, where this Montfort
then lay; who, seeing the king arriving, hasted down to meet him; and, perceiving
him troubled with the storm, said, " that he need not now to fear, the danger was past."
—" No, Montfort," quoth the king, " I do fear thee more than I do all the storms
" and tempests of the world!" The barons, under the conduct of this Montfort their
general,

was too great for a fubject; which had he not been, he might have
been numbered among the worthieft of his time, both for his valour, perfonage, and wifdom, as is implied in his epitaph:

" Nunc dantur fato, cafuque cadunt iterato
" Symone fublato, Mars, Paris, atque Cato."

After his death, his body was fhamefully abufed, and his wife
and children compelled to quit the kingdom.

With thefe ended the lineal defcent of the earls of Leicefter
and Hinckley.

King Henry III. in the 51ft year of his reign, beftowed all the
honours and rights which Simon had enjoyed on his fecond ED-
MOND, furnamed *Crouchback**, earl of Lancafter, and to his heirs,
for

general, bid the king battle near the town of Lewes in Suffex, in which battle the
king, the king of Almaine his brother, prince Edward his fon, with many others, are
taken prifoners. This kingly rebel, for that year and half another, carries his fovereign (as his prifoner) abour with him, to countenance his actions. But prince
Edward, efcaping the hands of his enemies, levies new forces, and being with his
army about Worcefter, the earl embattles in a plain near Hulfham; and noting how
the prince's army was approached, faid to thofe about him, " Thefe men come on
" bravely. They learned it not of themfelves, but of me;" and, feeing himfelf
likely to be fet and overlaid with numbers, advifed his friends Hugh Spencer, Ralph
Baffet, and others, to fhift for themfelves; which they refufing to do, " Then,"
faid he, " let us commit our fouls to God, for our bodies are theirs!" And fo undertaking the main weight of the battle, he perifhed under it.

His countefs Eleanor, a lady of eminent note, the daughter and fifter to a king,
nocent only by her fortune, from the coronet of miferable glory, betook her to the
vail of quiet piety, and died a nun at Montarges in France. *Henry*, their eldeft
fon, was with his father flain in battle. *Simon*, the fecond fon, was earl of Bygor,
and anceftor to a family of Montforts in thofe parts of France. *Almeric*, the third
fon, was a prieft, and treafurer of the cathedral church at York; afterwards a knight,
and valiant fervitor in the wars. *Guy*, the fourth fon, was earl of Angleria in Italy,
and progenitor of the Montforts in Fufkan, and of the earls of Campo Bachi in
Naples. *Richard*, the fifth fon, remained privily in England, and, changing his
name to *Wellefborne*, was anceftor to a family of that name. *Eleanor*, the only
daughter, was brought up in France, and afterwards was married to Llewelyn ap
Griffith prince of North Wales, the laft prince of the Britifh blood, who was flain in
1281. Harleian MSS. 2194.

* See " Charta Henrici III. Edmundo filio fuo honoris Leyceftriæ & al. terr. &c,
" dat.

for ever. On this man's perfon the great contention of Lancafter
and York was originally founded. He died in 1296; and was
fucceeded by

THOMAS his fon (by Eleanor queen of Navarre), who was beheaded at Pontefract, 1322. He was canonized; and his picture,
being fet up at St. Paul's, was greatly reforted to, till Stephen
Gravefend (bifhop of London 1319—1338) was fharply repre-
hended for permitting it.

HENRY of Lancafter, brothr and heir to Thomas, was reftored
to the earldoms of Lancafter, Leicefter, and Derby, with the office
of lord high fteward, 1 Edward III. He died 1345, and was fucceeded by

His fon HENRY of Monmouth, furnamed *Torto collo*, who was
created duke of Lancafter 1351, and died 35 Edward III.

His eldeft daughter's hufband WILLIAM *of Bavaria* fucceeded
to the earldom of Leicefter, and died without iffue 1360.

Edward III. created his fourth fon JOHN of *Gaunt* duke of Lancafter, earl of Leicefter, Lincoln, and Derby, 1361; and appointed
him conftable of France, and lord high fteward of England *; which
titles and high offices on his death, 1399, devolved to his fon

HENRY,

"dat. apud Scum Paul. Lond. 20° die Junii, anno regni quinquagefimo primo,"
among the Cotton MSS. Auguftus II. 129.
   * " After the death of Edward the Third, confultation being had about the folem-
" nity of the coronation of King Richard the Second; John king of Caftil and Leon,
" duke of Lancafter, appeared before the king and council, and claimed, as earl of
" Leicefter, the office of Senefchal of England; as duke of Lancafter, the right of
" bearing the principal fword called the Curtana, on the day of the coronation;
" and as earl of Lincoln, to cut and carve for the king, fitting at table on the day
" of his coronation. Diligent examination being made before certain of the king's
" council concerning thefe demands, it fufficiently appeared to the faid council, that
" to the faid duke, as holding by the law of England, after the death of Blanch his
" wife, appertained what he claimed. And it was confidered by the king and
" council, that the faid duke fhould exercife the faid offices, by himfelf or deputies,
" and receive the fees belonging thereto. On Thurfday before the day of corona-
" tion (which was the Thurfday following), by order of the king, he fat judicially,
                                                               " and

HENRY, afterwards king Henry IV*; whofe fon
HENRY V. was appointed to the office of lord high fteward;
till, falling into difgrace for having ftruck the chief-juftice, the
office was given to
THOMAS PLANTAGENET, the fecond fon of Henry IV. who was
earl of Aumarle, duke of Clarence, lord prefident of the council,
and, being a perfonage of fingular valour, conftable of the king's
army in France and Normandy, where he was flain, leaving no
lawful iffue.

ROBERT DUDLEY, fifth fon of John duke of Northumberland,
was created earl of Leicefter 6 Eliz. 1564, but died without
lawful iffue 1588. He was univerfally allowed to be the moft
ambitious, infolent, and corrupt perfon of his age.

James I. 1618, conferred this title on Sir ROBERT SIDNEY, fon to
Sir Henry; and it was fuccefflively enjoyed by his fon ROBERT,
grandfon PHILIP, great grandfon ROBERT, great great grandfons
PHILIP, JOHN, and JOCELINE, in which laft the title ended,
1743.

It was revived 1744 in the perfon of THOMAS COKE, who died
without iffue 1759.

" and kept his court in the Whitehall of the king's palace at Weftminfter, near the
" king's chapel, and there received the bills and petitions of all fuch of the nobility
" and others as, by reafon of their tenure or otherwife, claimed to do fervice at the
" new king's coronation, and to receive the fees and allowances therefore due and ac-
" cuftomed." Tranflated by the Author of an " Hiftorical Differtation" on the office
of Lord High Steward in England, 1776, 8vo. from a MS. in the Cotton library.
* In the laft year of this king's reign, Edward Courtney earl of Devonfhire was
appointed lord high fteward, pro hac vice, for the trial of John earl of Huntington.

Pedigree

Pedigree of Grentemaisnel.

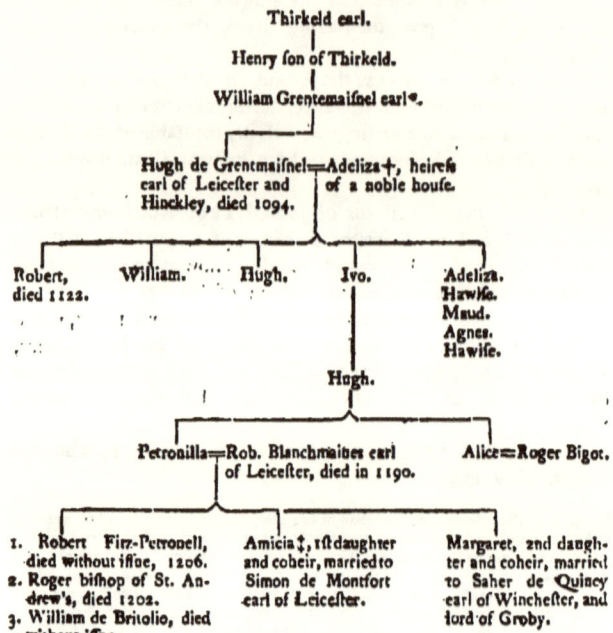

Thirkeld earl.
|
Henry fon of Thirkeld.
|
William Grentemaifnel earl*.

Hugh de Grentmaifnel=Adeliza†, heirefs
earl of Leicefter and   of a noble houfe.
Hinckley, died 1094.

Robert,   William.   Hugh.   Ivo.   Adeliza.
died 1122.   Hawife.
                                          Maud.
                                          Agnes.
                                          Hawife.

Hugh.

Petronilla=Rob. Blanchmaines earl   Alice=Roger Bigot.
of Leicefter, died in 1190.

1. Robert Fitz-Petronell,   Amicia‡, 1ft daughter   Margaret, 2nd daugh-
died without iffue, 1206.   and coheir, married to   ter and coheir, married
2. Roger bifhop of St. An-   Simon de Montfort   to Saher de Quincy
drew's, died 1202.   earl of Leicefter.   earl of Winchefter, and
3. William de Britolio, died   lord of Groby.
· without iffue.

* The three firft defcents are from a MS. Pedigree in a copy of Burton's Leicefterfhire.
† This lady, if a conjecture may be hazarded, was daughter of Edwin earl of
Leicefter. It is allowed fhe was an heirefs of a noble family; and the time of Edwin's death without iffue male (1071) agrees with the date of Grentemaifnel's marriage,
in 1072, the year in which the high-ftewardfhip was given to him on the death of
the earl of Hereford. (See above, p. 6.) On the death of Earl Edwin, his eftates
were granted to Hugh de Grentemaifnel; nor was there any other earl of Leicefter
till the difgrace of Yvo in 1103, when the title was beftowed on Robert de Bellamont,
the father of Robert Boffu, and grandfather of Blanchmaines.
‡ Who was a benefactrefs to Lira.

The

The Castle, Lordship, and Manors.

Hinckley Castle is traditionally faid to have been inhabited by John of Gaunt, fourth fon of king Edward III. and heir to the honors and eftates of the earls of Leicefter. The Lordfhip, as has been already fhewn, was undoubtedly his. From him it defcended to Henry of Bolingbroke (afterwards king Henry the Fourth) ; by whofe acceffion to the throne it paffed, with the Dutchy of Lancafter, into the poffeffion of the Crown. When it was alienated, or how long the Caftle has been demolifhed, is not with certainty known. If the hiftory of its demolition could be traced, it would moft probably appear to have been plundered, by the victorious Yorkifts, either in the reign of Henry VI. about the year 1460, the date of the battle of Northampton; or between that period and 1485, when by the death of Richard III. the civil contentions were clofed.

The battle of *Bofworth-field*, as it is ufually called, was fought, according to Burton, " in a large, flat, plain, and fpacious ground, " about four miles from Hinckley, and three from Bofworth, be- " tween the towns of Shenton, Sutton, Dadlington, and Stoke[a] ;" which plain comprehended part of thofe feveral lordfhips when uninclofed ; and this account, from an actual view of the fpot in September 1781, I have every reafon to believe is accurate.

[a] That the battle was fought on this fpot, " appeareth by many places remarkable; by a little mount caft up, where the common report is, that at the firft beginning of the battle, Henry earl of Richmond made his parænetical oration to his army: by divers pieces of armour, weapons, and other warlike accoutrements, and by many arrow-heads here found ; whereof, about twenty years fince, at the inclofure of the lordfhip of Stoke, great ftore were digged up, of which, fome I have now in my cuftody, being of a long, large, and big proportion, far greater than any now in ufe: as alfo by relation of the inhabitants, who have many occurrences and paffages yet frefh in memory, by reafon that fome perfons thereabouts, which faw the battle fought, were living within lefs than forty years, of which perfons myfelf have feen fome, and have heard of their difcourfes, though related by fecond-hand." Burton.

D   The

The plain is fpacious; and, being very nearly furrounded with hills and woods, has a beautifully noble appearance. The woods of Sutton Chainell and of Ambeime*, in particular, have a ftriking effect. " King Richard's Well," and " Crown Hill" where Richmond harangued his army, preferve the identity of the place. The head quarters of Richard were at Nottingham, whence his army, in its way to the place of action, muft have neceffarily paffed through or near Hinckley. Thofe of Richmond were at Coventry. Stanley, with a large detachment of the royal army, was pofted at Atherftone, not far from the expected field of battle, and foon after its commencement contributed to the decifion of the day, by declaring for the earl of Richmond. The flaughter was great; and many of the dead bodies were buried in the cemetery belonging to Dadlington chapel. Richard, it is univerfally acknowledged, performed prodigies of valour. Defperate perhaps at the laft, he rufhed furious into the thickeft of the fight, flew numbers, and among them the ftandard-bearer of Richmond, with his own hand; and fell at laft inglorioufly (if tradition may be credited) by a treacherous blow from one of his own followers. His body was thrown acrofs a horfe, and carried for interment to the Grey Friars at Leicefter†.

Leland, the earlieft recorder of Englifh Topography, who wrote in the time of Henry the Eighth, fays, " The ruines of " the caftelle of Hinkeley, now longging to the king, fumtyme to " the erle of Leircefter, be a V‡ myles from Leircefter, and in the " borders of Leircefter foreft, and the boundes of Hinkeley be " fpatius and famofe ther||."

---

* An ancient village, which in Burton's time " was altogether depopulated, not " one houfe remaining." In Sutton Chainell and in Ambeime Edward III, in the 21ft year of his reign, gave liberty of free warren to Aukeline de Houby.

† See in Peck's Defiderata Curiofa a view of the bridge of one arch, over which the dead monarch was carried.

‡ Now full XIII miles. || Leland's Itin. I. 24.

In

In Burton's time, 1622, the Caſtle was " utterly ruinated and
" gone, and only the mounts, rampires, and trenches were to be
" ſeen ;   and the fair and large Park* was then diſparked."
Camden, who wrote a little earlier (1607), deſcribes it in nearly
the ſame manner: " Ad Orientalem ſane partem templi foſſæ, &
" moles in eminentem altitudinem egeſta cernuntur, quod Hugo-
" nis fuiſſe caſtrum ferunt incolæ."   There is a tradition, that on
the *Prieſt Hill Headland* the cannon were placed which demoliſhed
caſtle.

The ſite of the caſtle had, beyond the memory of the oldeſt
inhabitant, been occupied as a gardener's ground; and the caſtle-
hill conſiderably lowered, by taking ballaſt from it for repairing
the roads ; when in 1760 it was purchaſed by *William Hurſt*, Eſq.
(high ſheriff of the county in 1779) who cauſed a handſome
dwelling-houſe to be built on it in 1770.   At this time the
foundation of a bridge acroſs the ditch which ſurrounded the
ancient caſtle, ſeveral large ſtones which had been part of the
caſtle†, a ball of ten inches circumference, and a piece or two of
ſilver coin, were found.

---

* In a very ancient MS. (Harl. MSS. 240. p. 25.) I find this entry:
" Hinckley, with Hinckley park, keeper of the woods, fees xxx s. iiii d."
The original ſituation of the park is eaſily to be traced.   *The Lawns*, ſtill ſo called,
which were a beautiful pleaſure-ground, divided it from the Caſtle, its Northern
boundary; on the South it extended to Burbach; on the Eaſt to the Faſt Woods,
the Stocking, and the Out-Woods; and on the Weſt to the borders of the pariſh.
David Wells, eſq. of Burbach, has an antler, dug up ſome years ago in a meadow of
his eſtate (called *Hell-Hole*), formerly part of the park, which is of an extraordinary
ſize; the diameter of the nutt next the head being near five inches, and the girth
of the ſtem above nine.   It is engraved in plate VII. fig. 1.

† After the demolition of the caſtle, it is the opinion of an ingenious friend, the
preſent ſteeple was built with part of the ſtones which came out of it.   The ſteeple is
evidently of modern date compared with the body of the church.   Some of the ſame
ſpecies of ſtone is diſcernible in the foundations of ſeveral houſes in Church-lane.   There
is alſo a conſiderable facing to the hollow-way in the Bond End ſtreet of the ſame ſort
of ſtone.

In

In a very ancient book* of the county of Leicester, being the Feodary's Account of that County, containing 84 quarto pages besides the Index, are the following extracts; which have been communicated by the Rev. Mr. Cole of Milton:

4 Edward III. William Turvill held lands in Hinckley, for which he paid an aid for making a knight of the king's eldest son.

Among the fees of Edmond earl of Leicester, Lancaster, &c. who died in 1296, for which he received scutage of the tenants,
Liberi Tenentes de Hynkeley tenent unam virgatam terre et dimidiam, et quartam partem unius virgate.

In a Feodary of 18 Edward II. the following persons are found to hold fees in the Baillywick of Hinkley.

In Balliva de Hinck'.
Joh'es Baseville tenet ibidem quartam partem unius feodi.

Duodecima pars unius feodi militis ibidem, pro qua Michell de Maynard tenet unum messuagium et dimid' rode terre.

Joh'es de Calby et X'ana [Christiana] uxor ejus, ut de jure uxoris sue, tenet unum mes. et 13 acras terre.

Will's Chapman, junior, tenet unum mes. et 7 acras terre.

Thomas Wake de Lydell tenet ib'm unum feodum militis.

Rich'us Chernelcs tenet ib'm, ut medius inter D'num Comitem et Joh'em Turvill, dim' feod' mil'.

Thomas Astelegh tenet ibidem tertiam partem unius feodi militis.

* The property of Dr. Farmer, the worthy and learned Master of Emanuel College, Cambridge; by whom, to accommodate my enquiries, it was kindly lent to Mr. Cole.

D'na la Botiller de Wemme, una her' Hug' de Herdeburgh, tenet, ut medius inter D'num Comitem et Thomam de Draiton, dim'
feodi militis.

Unum feodum militis pro quo Will's de Afshley et Chriftiana
uxor ejus ten', ut de jure dicte Chriftiane, capitale mef' Will' de
Stoke.

D'nus Joh'es de Segrave tenet ib'm, ut medius inter D'num Com'
et plur' Tenentes ib'm, quod quondam fuit Will'i le Botiller, unum
feodum militis.

In quodam antiquo rotulo de Feodis Leiceftr' continetur fic:
" Ces font le Feez del Honor de Leyc' doint mon Seigneur
" ad receu l'efcuage.
" Les Fraunc Tenauntes de Hinckley teignent une verge de
" terre et demy & la quarte part d'une verge.
" Nichol de Charnels demy fee en Hynkeley."

In an Inquifition in Edward the Third's time.

De Tenentibus terr' de Hynkley & Wykyn, que tenetur pro
12ᵐᵃ parte unius feodi militis, 18d.

De Will'o Chapman de Hynkley pro quarta parte 1 feod' mil'
in Wykyn, que quondam fuit Nich' Bertram.

Feoda D'ni Henrici Com' Lancaftr' in D'nis Com', de quibus
levari fecit rationabile auxilium ad primogenitum filium.
fuum militem faciend', anno regni Regis Edw. III. quarto.

Tenentes de Hynkle tenent 12ᵐᵃⁿ partem 1 feod' mil' in virgata.
terre et tribus quartern' terre in Hynkeley.

Nich'us Charnels tenet di' feod' in Hynkeley.

A° 2 Hen. V. Joh'es Happesford venit in curiam, et fecit ho-
magium pro certis terris et tenementis in Hynkeley et Whiken,
que tenentur de D'no Rege, ut de Ducatu fuo Lancaftr', per fer-
vicium 2od.

In:

In the printed Parliamentary Rolls, vol. IV. p. 187, col. a. " Villa & Manerium de Hynkeley" are mentioned in 1422, 1 Hen. VI. as part of Queen Catharine's dower. In the fame document " Hynkeley" occurs alfo as one of the " ballivæ forin" fecæ" belonging to the honor of Leicefter, which was included in the dower*. In vol. V. p. 118, a. in 1444, 23 Henry VI. " Manerium, Burgum, & Ballivæ de Hynkeley," appear to have been part of the dower of Queen Margaret.

The LORDSHIP of Hinckley comprehends two MANORS; one of which, containing " three parts in four equally to be divided," belonged formerly to Sir *Robert Cotton* of Great Connington in the county of Huntingdon and afterwards of Hatley St. George in the county of Cambridge, who was alfo poffeffed of lands and tenements to a confiderable amount, the greateft part of which, together with the manor and divers chief rents, after paffing from the Cottons through feveral intermediate hands, are now the property of *William Hurft*, Efq.

The other Manor, being one fourth part of the whole Lordfhip, has for time immemorial belonged to the inhabitants of the town ; for whom it is holden in truft by two nominal lords, whofe accompts are annually audited on St. Thomas's-day by two townmafters. The prefent lords in truft are Mr. *Thomas Sanfome* and Mr. *Jofeph Robinfon*. This portion was originally granted to the town by one of its early lords, with the refervation of a fee-farm rent. I have been told of a deed of feoffment in the time of Henry VIII. which was exifting within thefe few years, and which is faid to refer to deeds " fo old as to be beyond memory." On enquiring, however, for this inftrument, it was not to be found; but I have feen an original leafe † of 28 Eliz. fcaled with the Dutchy

---

* To this " balliva forinfeca" probably belonged the " foreign bailiff," who feen s to be fucceeded by the prefent mayor or bailiff. In fome of the deeds of feoffment the office of *Forrein Baillie* is enumerated among the grants.

† Of which an abftract fhall be given in the Appendix.

feal,

feal, which grants to feoffees, for the term of thirty-one years, 116 acres* of land, with gardens, houfes, &c. in Hinckley, and a fingle acre called *Earl's Acre*, in confideration of a prefent fine of fix pounds thirteen fhillings and four-pence, and an annual rent of fifty-four fhillings and four-pence.   By fubfequent grants from the crown, it has been continued uninterruptedly in the poffeffion of fucceeding feoffees to the prefent time.   The application of it will be noticed hereafter among the benefactions to the town. The fee-farm rent was alienated, it may be prefumed, by king Charles the Second, foon after the ftatute in the 22d year of his reign, which enabled him to fell.   It has fince been private property, and a crown-rent (as it is called) of 22l. 0s. 7½d. is regularly paid (deducting 4l. 8s. land-tax) to the ufe of lord Willoughby de Broke, Dr. Charles Mofs (now bifhop of Bath and Wells), and James Hayes, efq. truftees under the will of the late lord Feverfham †.

The Borough, as far as I can find, is the only part of the ancient property from which a chief rent is referved to the Crown in right of the duchy of Lancafter; and this fragment may perhaps foon be diffevered by lawful purchafe‡.   Of this rent, which is
collected

* 42½ acres were in the open field, which, at the inclofure in 1763, were augmented to 68 acres, 3 roods, 17¾ perches.

† Anthony Duncombe, who was created lord Feverfham in the county of Kent, and baron of Downton in Wiltfhire, June 27, 1747; and died June 18, 1763, when the title became extinct.

‡ By act of parliament, 20 George III. for fale of quit-rents, and making copyholds free, the terms upon which all perfons may difcharge their eftates from the payment of quit-rents belonging to the Dutchy of Lancafter are as follows :

    For rents not exceeding ten fhillings per annum, on payment of thirty years purchafe of the grofs rent;

    And for rents exceeding ten fhillings per annum, on payment of twenty-five years purchafe of the grofs rent.

In cafe the purchafe-money for any fingle rent doth not exceed 3l. 15s. then the fees for the grant will be only fifteen fhillings. If the purchafe-money exceeds 3l. 15l. and is under 10l. then the fees will be twenty-five fhillings ; and when it exceeds 10l. the fees will be thirty fhillings.   All perfons who apply to purchafe muft produce the laft receipt given for the rent.   The time of preference given by the act of parliament
to

collected by Mrs. *Hannab Ajbby*, and amounts in the whole but to
3l. 14s. 7½d. the sum of 1l. 0s. 1d. is paid for a small estate
now belonging to Mr. *Bonfor*, and described in old deeds under the
name of *The King's Bakehouse*.

There is also a chief rent of fifteen shillings paid to the *Chamberlain of Leicester*, which is collected by Mr. *Hurst*.

The *Dashwoods* of Oxfordshire are said to have formerly received
some chief rents in this town.

The other considerable land-owners at present are, *William
Burleton**, Esq. (lessee of the impropriate tithes); the Rev. Mr. *John
Gaunt*, *John Dyer†*, Esq. and Mr. *Paul* (who are possessed of the
glebe and priory lands); Mr. *Thomas Sansome* and Mr. *Joseph Robinson* (already mentioned as lords in trust for the town); *Nicholas
Hurst*, Esq. Mr. *Henry Brayrly*, Mr. *Thomas Cooper*, Mr. *William Brown*,
Mr. *Joseph Iliff*; Mrs. *Sansome* of *Loughborough*, Mr. *Farmer*, and
Mr. *Harper*. The writer of these pages has also a very small fragment; too small indeed to be here mentioned, unless as an excuse
for his attention to the history of a town where he has many
respectable friends, and which has every claim to his warmest
wishes for its prosperity.

In 1760, on a petition from the lords of the manor of Hinckley, and of the patrons, vicar, and incumbent, of the parish and
parish church, Mr. *Burleton* the impropriator of the great tithes,
and of the freeholders, leaseholders, and proprietors of lands and
commons, an act was passed for inclosing and dividing the open
and common fields.

to the present owners of estates charged with the quit-rents to purchase their rents, was
enlarged by the Dutchy-Court to the 12th day of April, 1781. The grants are made
out at the Dutchy of Lancaster office in Gray's inn, London, where Dutchy copyholders may enfranchife on reasonable terms." *Printed Advertisements.*
* The present worthy Recorder of Leicester, who for several years did honour to
the office of Major of the militia in this county.
† Son to the celebrated Author of " The Fleece;" of whom hereafter.

The

The BOROUGH and TOWN.

Under its original lords, the town of Hinckley certainly enjoyed the privileges of a borough; and not improbably fent deputies to the great council of the nation.   From their connexion with the Lancafter family, the inhabitants of courfe took a decided part in the civil contefts; and whatever their privileges were, they became forfeited to the conquering Monarch of the houfe of York.

The lordfhip, however, is ftill divided into the liberties of " The Borough" and " The Bond;" the former of which divifions hath its peculiar privileges.   The " Bond" is the *Bound* or outer-part of the town not within the liberties.

There is annually held, by Thomas Sanfome and Jofeph Ro-binfon, gentlemen, the nominal lords of the manor, a court leet and court baron; when three feveral juries are impaneled for difpatch of bufinefs; viz. the *Borough* jury, the *Bond* jury, and the *Foreign* jury, the latter being for the outlyers, confift-ing of the divers townfhips that pay fuit and fervice to the court at Hinckley.   At this court prefentments and amercements are made; and the peace-officers, (viz. the mayor, conftables, and headboroughs) are chofen and fworn into their refpective offices for the enfuing year.   The fteward of the court is Mr. William Norton, attorney.

The whole number of town officers is feventeen; viz.

For the Borough,   { The Mayor, or Bailiff.
                     One Conftable.
                     Two Headboroughs.

For the Bond,   { One Conftable.
                  Three Headboroughs.

E   Chofen

Chosen at Easter
at the church,
{
The Vicar's Churchwarden.
Another, elected by the Parishioners.
Two Overseers of the Poor.
One Town-master.
}

Chosen on St. Stephen's-day, Four surveyors of the highways.

The mayor, who must necessarily be an inhabitant residing within the borough, has authority to regulate the markets, examine the weights, and punish delinquents.

The town-master, in conjunction with his predecessor in that office, is empowered, as has been already mentioned in p. 22, to audit the accompts of the lords in trust.

The market on Mondays was in Burton's time " exceeding " good; and for trading in corn, cattle, horses, swine, and all " things vendable in a dry town, inferior to none in the whole " county. The old fair-day is upon the 15th of August *; and of " late divers new fairs have been purchased thereto. The town is " yet of good receipt; wherein (not many years since) the gene- " ral assizes for the whole county were kept."

The town gaol was situated on the spot now called " The Round Hill," which is that surrounding the present market-house. The old gallows stood near the gravel-pit at the end of the town leading to Derby; and in that spot, on inclosing the open field, many human bones were found in a state of petrifaction.

That the fair was of no small note, may be inferred from the mention of it by Shakspeare, in the Second Part of Henry IV. where Justice Shallow is asked by his man Davy, whether he means " to " stop any of William's wages, about the sack he lost the other day " at *Hinckley-fair?*"

* The Assumption of the Blessed Virgin Mary; to whom the church is dedicated.

The

The Monday market is ftill confiderable; and at the original fair (now changed by the alteration of the ftyle to Auguft 26), a great number of cattle are difpofed of. On the Sunday which follows* this fair-day an annual wake was long obferved, but has of late years fallen into difufe.

The *new fairs* mentioned by Burton were, 1. on the third Monday after Twelfth-day, for horfes and cattle; 2. on *Eafter-Monday*, of little confequence; 3. on *Club-Monday* † (the Monday before Whit-funday), which is ftill a large fair for cattle; 4. on *Whit-Monday*, when the millers from various parts of the country ufed to ride in proceffion dreffed in ribbands, with what they called "The King of the Millers" at their head. 5. A Cheefe fair in *November*.

A ftatute for the hiring of fervants is held in *September*.

" In 1717 there were 350 families in the town of Hinckley ‡."

Since Burton's Hiftory was publifhed, the introduction of the ftocking manufactory || has confiderably augmented the traffick of the town, which is now fuppofed to contain 750 houfes§, and about 4700 inhabitants.

* Wakes geneially *precede* fairs.

† *Callop* or *Colib* Monday is that before Shrove-Tuefday, or the firft Monday in Lent. See Brand's edition of Bourne's Antiquities of the Common People, p. 331. That at Hinckley is faid to have taken its name from a quarrel which happened at it, and occafioned a defperate fight with *clubs*.

‡ MS. note of Mr. Browne Willis, from Bifhop Gibfon.

|| The ftocking-frame was invented in 1589 by William Lee, of Woodborough, Nottinghamfhire, gent. (who was of St. John's college, Cambridge, and M. A.). Soon after he had completed the frame, he applied to Queen Elizabeth for protection and encouragement; but his petition was rejected. Defpairing of fuccefs at home, he went to France, and was patronized by Lewis the Twelfth; and after fome years refidence in that kingdom received an invitation to return to England, which he accepted, and the art of frame-work knitting foon became famous here. Lee had carried with him to France nine workmen; of whom feven returned to England, with their frames, early in the laft century.—This is the opinion moft generally received. The invention, however, has been alfo attributed to Mr. Robinfon, who was a Fellow of St. John's college, Cambridge, and curate of Thurcafton in Leicefterfhire.

§ In 1768 the number was 697; which have fince been augmented by new erections, and by out-buildings in yards having been converted into dwelling-houfes.

E 2   The

The firſt frame was brought into Hinckley before the year 1640 by *William Iliffe*, and is ſaid to have coſt him ſixty pounds*, at that time a very conſiderable ſum; and with this ſingle frame, which by the aid of an apprentice he kept conſtantly working day and night, he gained a comfortable ſubſiſtence for his family.

The manufacture is now ſo extenſive, that a larger quantity of hoſe is ſuppoſed to be made here than in any town in England. Nottingham, it is allowed, has more frames; but many of thoſe being confined to the very fineſt ſorts of ſilk, cotton, &c. the number there made is leſs in quantity than at Hinckley, where the frames are generally employed on ſtrong ſerviceable hoſe of a lower price, in cotton, thread, and worſted. Kendal and Aberdeen are the towns moſt celebrated for knit hoſe.

It is generally allowed that there are not ſo many frame-work-knitters employed at Hinckley at preſent as there has been for ſome years paſt; the recruiting of his Majeſty's fleet and army, and thoſe engaged in the militia, having drawn off great numbers of the working hands. The manufacture, however, employs, as nearly as can be computed, the following number of working people:

Framework-knitters in the town,	—	1000
————————— in the villages adjacent,		200
Seamers,	— —	300
Woolcombers,	— —	55
Frameſmiths, ſetters-up of frames, &c.		30
Spinners, doublers, and twiſters,	—	1000
Total employed in the manufactory,	—	2585

The number of frames at preſent is computed at about 1000. There are alſo about 200 frames employed in the adjacent villages, many of them belonging to the maſters at Hinckley, and ſome of them the property of the workmen.

* The price of a good frame is now not more than fifteen guineas.

5   Populous

Populous as the town is, the places of worſhip are numerous in proportion. Beſides the pariſh churches of Hinckley and Stoke, and the chapel at Dadlington (thoſe of Wyken and Hyde being entirely demoliſhed), there is a chapel for the Roman Catholics, and four meeting-houſes, for Preſbyterians, Independents, Quakers, and Methodiſts.

Mr. Snelling mentions *Hinckley* among the towns where tradeſmen's tokens were ſtruck during the civil war, but gives no ſpecimen; nor had a ſingle one ever fallen within the notice of the principal collectors of that ſpecies of curioſity. But, on a diligent enquiry through the town, I have lately diſcovered one, which, by the favour of Mr. Baſs, is now my own, and is engraved in plate IV. fig. 1. It is inſcribed w.ᴵ.ᴅ. WILLIAM ILIFFE. Reverſe, IN HINCKLEY, 1662. It was the token of *William Iliffe** before-mentioned, and paſſed in circulation as a farthing. There were others, without doubt; but not many, as the manufacture of Hinckley was then in its infancy. A ſecond is recollected to have been ſeen a few years ago, iſſued by *William Gilbert*, at " The Eagle and Child."

The town-hall and old ſchool-houſe† ſtill remain, but are both in ſo ruinous a condition, that the gentlemen of the feoffment have it in contemplation to pull them down, and to build a new market-houſe with a ſchool and town-hall over it. Six large oak trees were bequeathed for this uſe‡ by the will of Mr. Joſeph Nutt, who died in 1775, and of whom a more particular account will be given.

Under the town hall were ſhambles, where the country butchers uſed on market-days to bring great quantities of meat; a practice long ſince diſuſed for want of proper accommodations. The ſpot is now employed as a warehouſe for dry goods.

* Of whoſe iſſue, ſee the pedigree of Cleiveland.
† Of Richard Vines, the celebrated ſchoolmaſter of Hinckley, ſome particulars ſhall be hereafter given.
‡ Which were to be forfeited if not uſed within ten years.

The

The PRIORY.

After the many various conjectures relative to the founder of this religious houfe, I have already ventured to controvert the very ancient claims of Blanchmaines and Boffu, by afcribing it to the elder Grentefmainell. William Fitzofbern earl of Hereford, the only competitor who can difpute with him that honour, is acknowledged to have been the founder of Lira, and beftowed on it many confiderable poffeffions in England. Grentefmainell alfo, as has been already fhewn, was famous both for his liberality[*] and piety; and in his latter days retired to a monaftery in Normandy.

This Priory had the fate of all the foreign cells, of being often feized into the king's hands during the wars with France, and at length wholly fuppreffed, in the parliament of Leicefter, 2 Henry V, 1414. It had been given for a time to the Carthufian priory of Montgrace[†] in Yorkfhire, by king Richard II. and was wholly

[*] To the benefactions mentioned in p. 7, may be added, that he founded, before the year 1081, at Ware in Hertfordfhire, a Benedictine priory as a cell to Utica. See Salmon, p. 247.

[†] Thomas de Holland, duke of Surrey, earl of Kent, and lord Wake, founded a Carthufian priory in the manor of Bordelby [at Montgrace de Ingleby, in the archdeaconry and deanry of Cleveland], and dedicated it to the Bleffed Virgin and St. Nicholas, about 20 Richard II. A. D. 1396, and not only endowed it with his manor of Bordelby near Cleveland, but alfo obtained for it of the fame king the lands and poffeffions of the religious at Hinckley in Leicefterfhire, of Warham in Dorfetfhire, and of Carefbrooke in Southamptonfhire, three alien priories belonging to the abbey of St. Mary in Normandy, to hold the fame as long as the war betwixt England and France fhould laft; but he dying foon after, in arms againft king Henry IV. before all the buildings were finifhed, the work was at a ftand; and the right of the monks to their poffeffions were queftioned, till king Henry VI. in 1440, confirmed in parliament all the duke's grants to them. After this, the buildings were foon compleated, and the monaftery flourifhed till the general diffolution; about which time the revenues of it were valued at 382l. 5s. 11d. per annum. in the whole, and at 323l. 2s. 1d. clear. See Burton's Monafticon Eboracenfe, p. 258.

annexed

annexed to the fame * by king Henry VI. After the diffolution of, Montgrace, the priory lands and church of Hinckley were granted, Aug. 5, 1482, 34 Hen. VIII. to the dean and chapter of Weftminfter †, who are the prefent impropriators and patrons.

The following lift of the Priors of Hinckley is extracted from a valuable and laborious MS. ‡ of bifhop Kennet, preferved in the library of the earl of Shelburne, and has been enlarged by the kindnefs of Mr. Bradley, regiftrar of the diocefe of Lincoln.

1. Ricardus de Capella prefentatus per abb. & convent. de Lyra ad procurac'oem domus de *Hingbel* nunc vacantem, anno 16 Hug. Well. [1225].

2. Joh. de Capella, monachus, ad prioratum de *Hincle*, vacantem per refig. Ric'i de Capella, 5 id. Octob. [1231]∥. Hug. Well. anno 22.

3. Frater Ric'us de Paceio ad prioratum de *Hinkel*, per refign. Joh'is de Capellis, ultimi prioris, anno 25 Hug. Well. [1234].

4. Fr. Petrus Lumbardus, monachus, prefentatus per Abb. et Conv. de Lira ad priorat. de *Hinkil*, vacant. per refign. fr'is Ric'i de Paceio monachi, quondam prioris, in dicto prioratu inftituti, in manus Rad. Ebroicenfis Ep'i, de gratia Ep'i Linc'. Reg. Rob. Grofthead, anno 2 [1236].

5. Fr. Will. de Aquila, monachus de Lyra, prefent. per Abb. & Conv. de Lyra ad prioratum de *Hynkel*, per refign. P. Lumbard quondam ejus loci prioris, anno 10 Rob. Grofthead [1244].

6. Fr. Hugo de Winton, monachus de Lyra, prefent. per Abb. et Conv. ejufd. loci ad prioratum de *Hynkel*, per refign. fr'is Will. de Aquila, anno 12 Rob. Grofthead [1246].

* See Appendix, N° X. p. 152. And fee Pat. 3 Hen. V. p. 2. m. 39. de prioratu alienigena de Hinckley.
† See Rymer, vol. XIV. p. 665.
‡ This MS. (which fills two volumes in a large Atlas folio) was intended for publication, under the title of DIPTYCHA ECCLESIÆ ANGLICANÆ, &c. See the Anecdotes of Mr. Bowyer, p. 532.
∥ *Peter clericus de Lira*, a monk probably of *Hinckley*, was before this period witnefs to a deed of Robert Fitz Parnell earl of Leicefter.

E 4   7. Gil–

7. Gilbertus.

8. Adam de Trungey pref. per Abb. et Conv. de Lyra ad prioratum de *Hinckley*, per mort. Gilberti, 17 kal. Maii, 1264. Reg. Ric. Gravefend, anno 7.

9. Fr. Ric. de Audreya pref. per Abb. et Conv. de Lyra ad prioratum de *Hynkele*, per refig. Ade de Trungeio, 11 kal. Maii, 1268. Ib.

10. 'Fr. Nich'us dictus Burnet ad priorat. de *Hinkele*, per refign. fr'is Ric'i de Aldereia, ordinem fratrum predicatorum tunc ingreffur'; admiff' 5 id. Aug. 1271. Ib.

11. Will. de Avena.

12. Francis Herveus * de Alneto pref. per procur. Abbatis & Conv. de Lyra ad priorat. de *Hinkele*, per refign. fr'is Will. de Avena, 12 cal. Dec. pont. 10. Rot. Ol. Sutton, 1289.

13. 8 cal. Oct. A. Dom. 1300, Herveus de Alneto refignavit d'cum Priorat. & Will'us Abbas de Lira prefent. Rayner de Jarieta ad d'cum prioratum; fuit admiffus 7 cal. Oct. anno fupradicto.

14. Mattheus de Puteo prefent. per Abb. et Convent. de Lira ad prioratum de *Hynkele*, vacantem per mortem Reynerii de Jarieta; per Dn'm Ep'um admiffus 3 cal. Martii, anno D'ni 1310.

15. Henricus de Pie, prefentatus per Abbatem & Convent. de Lyra ad prioratum de *Hinkele*, vacemtem per mortem Matthei de Puteo, admiffus 10 cal. Junii 1319.

The only priors of Montgrace that occur are,

1. Robert Tredewy †, the firft prior, in 1396.
2. Edmund ‡, 1399.
3. Robert Layton §, 142.
... John Wilfon, the laft prior ‖.

---

* Mr. Mores found him 25 E. I. 1295. MS. note to his Tanner's Notitia Monaftica; and he occurs in 1299 in Prynne, vol. I. p. 706.
† See Appendix, N° X. and Tanner, Not. Mon. p. 695.
‡ Ib. 21 R. II.
§ Reg. Teftament. p. 38, marked Dc.
‖ Rymer, Fœd. XIV. 605.

On a mantlepiece in the kitchen of the HALL-HOUSE (the manfion of the ancient priors, of which a South view is exhibited
in plate II. and the North fide of it in plate III. fig. A.*) is a
ftrange ornament, in a kind of baked clay, which tradition has erroneoufly called " the arms of three monks." A fecond tradition,
with more probability, calls them the figns of three houfes †, which,
whilft the priory exifted, were deftined to the relief of pilgrims
travelling through Hinckley, who were to receive a night's lodg-
ing, and fomething the next morning to help them forward on
their journey. And this perhaps was " the HOSPITALITY" to
which a part of the revenues of Wyken was to be applied.
A fketch of thefe ornaments may be feen in plate VII. fig. 4. :

The Hall-houfe was in the laft century the refidence of Sir
John Oneby, the only fon of the Mr. Oneby whofe pedigree at large
is here annexed, and whofe monument (engraved in plate VI.) remains in Hinckley church.

It came afterwards to *Peter Gerard* (fon of Mr. *Nathanael Gerard*,
who had married a fifter of Dame Mary Oneby). By Mr. Gerard
the middle part of the houfe was rebuilt in 1715, foon after the
battle of Prefton field; the wings are of much older date.

Mr. *Orton* was the next poffeffor of the houfe.

A fine row of old walnut-trees, which ftood between the
houfe and the church ‡, was cut down by Mr. *John Strong Enfor*,
the fucceeding owner, in 1740.

The houfe, now the property of the reverend Mr. *Gaunt*,
is inhabited by a ftocking-maker. The garden is let to Mr. *Hunt*
(the principal inn-keeper of the town), who has converted it
into a bowling-green.

* B. in the fame plate reprefents the vicarage-houfe; and C. a modern-built houfe
at the oppofite corner of the church lane.
† The Eagle and Child; the Rofe; and the Bull's-head.
‡ An eminent attorney, and fteward of the courts at Hinckley and Burbach. He
married a daughter of Mr. Purefoy, attorney, at Hinckley; but fome years before
his death he quitted that town, and refided in the neighbourhood of Newmarket.

F   The

The Church.

To the Church of Hinckley were annexed three Chapels[a];
1. *Stoke*[†] [now a parish church], which had power to adminifter
facraments, and paid fynodals as the mother church did, viz. 3s. 6d.
and had a refident chaplain provided by the prior.   2. *Dadlington*,
which had fervice performed in it three days in the week, by the
prior's appointment.   3. *Wyken* [fince demolifhed], which had
fervice but once a year, becaufe the revenues were ordered to
be expended at Hinckley, to maintain two monks there refident,
to fupport the parochial minifter, and to uphold hofpitality.

The vicarage (now belonging to the dean and chapter of Weftminfter) was formerly appropriated to the abbey of Lira.   It is
valued in the king's books at 9l. 9s. 9¼d.

" The church," fays Burton, " is very fair and large, having a
" very great and ftrong fpire fteeple, fo fpacious within
" that two rings of bells may hang therein together, and
" hath (for the better ornament thereof) a very tunable ring of
" five[‡] bells, and a chime;" to which a treble bell was added by
public fubfcription in 1777; and in 1779 the great bell was exchanged, which now renders them a complete fet[‖].

On

---

* Extract from the Matriculus Dom. H. [Wallis] Epifcopi Lincoln' de omnibus
ecclefiis in archidiconatu Leyceftric, anno Dom. MCCXX°, 5 H. III.

" Æcel' de Hynkel' patron' abb' de Lyre fins eam in pprios ufus de dono Willi
fil' Osbti ab antiquo, & fiet tres capellas, Stoke, Dadlington, & Wychen. Capella de Stokys fiba eft fins oia facramentalia, & redot fynodal' ut matrix ec-
clia III ʒ vi d, & fit capellan' refid' p porem miniftrant' ei neceffaria. Capella de
Dadelinton debet deferviri III diebz in ebd' p pcuracoem fioris. Capella de
Wychen non nifi femel in anno, & debet oia bona ill' eccle expd' ap⁴ Hynkel' ad
fuftentacoem duor' monachor' ibide refiden' & miniftr' ecclef', & hofpitalit' faciend',&c.

† An account of a fuit inftituted by the mother parifh for the recovery of taxes,
which was determined in 1627, will be given under the defcription of Stoke ; and
the proceedings on a tithe-caufe in 1747 under that of the hamlet of Hyde.

‡ The weight of the prefent great bell is 18cwt. 2qr. 20lb.

‖ " The peal of ten bells at St. Margaret's in Leicefter is fuperior to any in the
                                                                    " county,

North East Prospect of Hinckley Church.

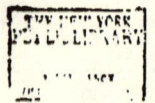

On the old bells is written,

COELORUM CHRISTE, PLACEAT TIBI, REX, SONUS ISTE.

In Englifh,

O Chrift, Heaven's King, be pleas'd with this ring!

On the new ones, the names of the vicar and churchwardens.

The parifh regifters, beginning in 1524, are preferved in feven books; the fecond of which contains the amount of the feveral briefs collected by Mr. Cleiveland from 1659 to 1663: among thefe, are

£. s. d.

0 12 2 for the Royal Fifhery.

2 0 10 for diftreffed Proteftants in the Dutchy of Lithuania.

3 15 8 for the town of Soulbay in Suffolk.

3 0 0 for the diftreffed town of Metheringham, in the parts of Kefteven, in the county of Lincoln.

On a brief for Mr. *Bowyer* the printer, after his lofs by fire in 1712-13, there was collected at Hinckley church 13s. 1d.; and at the Prefbyterian meeting-houfe 7s.

Two large chefts ftand in the chancel; one marked

"Hinckley Tow | Anno 1613. Nov. 4. | ne Cheft."

The other, "A Towne cheft given by Michael Meffinger, 1641; George Warren, William Keene, Churchwardens."

"county, or perhaps in England. I can fpeak with fome confidence, becaufe a "friend of mine, William Fortrey, Efq. of Norton by Galby, made it his bufinefs "all his life to enquire into thefe matters: he is poffeffed of all the anecdotes that "remain relating to the founder of that fteeple (Hugh Watts, once mayor of Lei- "cefter), and was himfelf the patron and director of Thomas Eayre, late of Ketter- "ing, the founder of the new bells in that fteeple. The two additional bells, and "a great part of the expence of new hanging the whole peal, was borne by Mr. For- "trey, who has alfo fince rebuilt the church and fteeple at Norton, and furnifhed it "with a peal of ten bells, clock, and chimes, at his own expence." Mr. LUDLAM, MS.

In the chancel was a beautiful large window, containing a great variety of arms, figures of faints, warriors, &c. on fmall panes of painted glafs; which darkening the chancel, it was changed for plain glafs in 1766, when feveral fragments of the old window were crowded together at the top of the window.

In another window at the end of the North aifle is a head of Chrift with thorns; and alfo portraits of the Virgin and of a bareheaded monk.

The king's arms (painted during the reign of Charles the Second) are preferved in the South aifle.

The gallery, with a convenient finging-loft, at the Weft end, was erected in 1723; John Carte, M. A. vicar; William Warner churchwarden.

In 1727, the church was beautified; John Iliff and Richard Good churchwardens.

In 1763, a faculty was granted to Thomas Brown and John Bolefworth, churchwardens, for new pewing the church, which was completed with great neatnefs in 1766; John Blair, LL.D. vicar; Jofeph Iliff and John Bolefworth churchwardens.

A fmall neat font of marble, cut out of a flab which had been part of an old monument, was erected in 1766, inftead of the old one then demolifhed. A beautiful ftep, of the fame marble, is placed at the chancel door.

In 1779, the Lord's Prayer, Creed, and Ten Commandments, were painted over the entrance into the chancel; John Cole Gallaway, M. A. vicar; John Turner and Thomas Sanfome, churchwardens.

In 1780 a compromife was made between Mr. Gallaway vicar of Hinckley and Mr. Gaunt leffee of the glebe land under the dean and chapter of Weftminfter, by which a rood of land was add.d to the vicarage-garden in lieu of a tithe of two guineas.

References

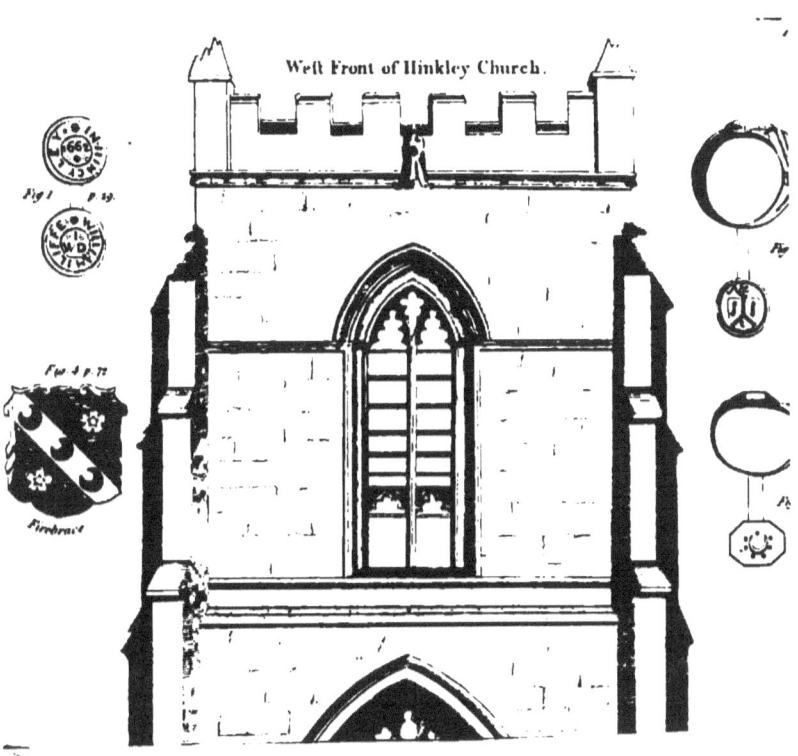

West Front of Hinkley Church.

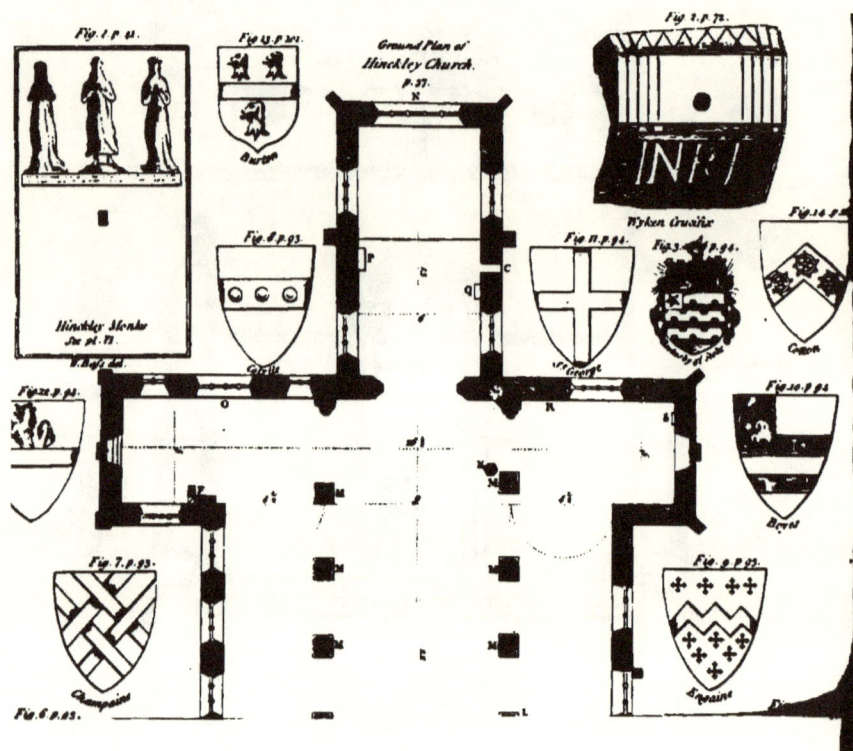

Fig. 1. p. 51.

Fig. 13. p. 101.
Barton.

Ground Plan of
Hinckley Church.
p. 57.

Fig. 2. p. 72.

Wyken Crucifix.

Fig. 14. p.

Hinckley Monks
See pl. 71.

W. Ross del.

Fig. 4. p. 93.

Fig. 11. p. 94.
St. George.

Fig. 3. p. 94.
Priory of Kent.

Green.

Fig. 12. p. 94.

Fig. 10. p. 94.

Byron.

Fig. 7. p. 93.

Champeine.

Fig. 6. p. 93.

Fig. 9. p. 93.

Knoaine.

References to the PLAN of the CHURCH. [See plate V.]

A. The belfry door.
B. The North door of the church.
C. The chancel door.
D. The Weft door.
E. Stairs into the Weft gallery.
F. Stairs into the North gallery.
G. Stairs into the bell-chamber.
H. Stairs into the fteeple.
I. An old ftaircafe blocked up.
K. The pulpit.

L. The font.
M. Pillars of the church.
N. Altar window, with painted glafs.
O. Window with portrait of Virgin, &c.
P. Mr. Oneby's monument.
Q. Dr. Morres's.
R. Mr. Savage's.
S. Mr. and Mrs. Allen's.
T. Mifs Watfon's.

From the chancel to the Weft door the church is 22 yards long; near the chancel it is 26¼ yards wide; in the body 18¼ yards. The chancel is 6 yards by 13. The roof is of beautiful old oak; and the beams fupported by large penient cherubim (like thofe in Weftminfter Hall) and ornamented with a number of grotefque faces, of which a fpecimen is exhibited in plate VI. fig. 1. The admirers of ancient architecture may rejoice with me on the mifcarriage of a barbarous attempt, which was made a few years ago, to hide this admirable roof by a modern cieling!

The age of the prefent church is only to be gueffed at from its appearance. The body of it is probably to be afcribed to the thirteenth century. The Weft door (plate IV.) refembles thofe of the reign of Edward I. or II. The window immediately over it is fuppofed to be an improvement made about the time of Edward IV. when windows were in general enlarged, and divided with four or five mullions. The upper window was alfo improved about that time, but was moft probably built in the time of Edward the Second, when they were generally divided in the middle by one mullion. The building of the fteeple (which is 40 yards high) may alfo be dated with probability in the reign of Edward IV.

I

m

In the Harleian MSS. Nº 2129, p. 121—123. are feveral Leicefterfhire epitaphs; among others, in *Hinckley* church,

" Orate pro bono ftatu WILL'MI WIYETMAN* et FRANC' ux'
" ejus."   A merchant's mark in the efcutcheon.
     " *Eft clarum certe claro de ftemmate nafci.*"

Notes taken in HINCKLEY Church, 1619, at the Vifitation† of
Sampfon Lennard Blewmantle and Auguftine Vincent Rougecroix, Purfuivants of Arms.

[Communicated (1782) by J. C. BROOKE, Efq. Somerfet Herald.]

" 1. Or, 3 lions paffant, guardant, in pale, Or. *England.*
" 2. The fame, with a file of three points Azure, each charged
    " with three Fleurs de Liz, Or. *Lancafter.*
" 3. *England* as before, a bordure gobonè Argent & Azure.
    " *Beaufort.*
" 4. Or, Fretty, Gules. *Verdon.*
" 5. Party per pale, indented, Argent and Gules. *(Old earls of*
    " *Leicefter.)*
" Alfo the effigy of a man kneeling on a cufhion in a gown and
    " ruff."

.. The above arms‡ and effigy (which probably is that of *Wiyetman*) are delineated in plate VI. fig. 2, 3, 4, 5, 6, 7.

* Of this family, fee more under the article of WYKEN. *John* occurs among
the benefactors to Hinckley.
† Seven different volumes of Vifitations of Leicefterfhire, containing pedigrees
and arms principally taken in 1619, and many of them merely duplicates, are among
the Harleian MSS. Nº 1180. 1187. 1189. 1369. 1431. 6125. 6283. I have examined them all; but they contain nothing relative to Hinckley.
‡ Another copy of thefe arms (but not of the effigy) as drawn in 1610 by Nicholas Charles Lancafter Herald, is preferved in a valuable volume of Church Notes
and Monuments, formerly the property of Mr. Henry St. George, afterwards of Mr.
Weft, and now in the library of the Earl of Shelburne.

                                                            Thefe

Fig.6.p.38.

Fig.7.p.38.

A Beam in HINCKLEY CHURCH.

Fig.1.

p.37.

W. Batts del. 1761.

Fig.10.p.71.

Fig.2.p.38.

Fig.10.p.71.

Fig.9.p.43

Fig.8.p.39.

H.S.E.
THOMAS MORRES D.D.

Fig.11.p.72.

There now (1782) remain :

1. On a monument in the chancel, with very aukward painted bufts, half length, of Mr. Onebye and his lady; under them, bufts of their 5 children; all in the drefs of the times; at top, their arms; (fee plate VI. fig. 8.)

" Hic jacet Johannes Onebye Ar. J'c^{tus},
Præcipuum ipfe (fiqua gratiis, fiqua virtuti præmia debetur)
fuiipfius monumentum.
Conjugem duxit Emmettam Humfredi Byard Gen. filiam.
Ex qua quinque liberos fufcepit;
Elizabetham, Dorotheam, Emmettam, Mariam,
& Johannem filium unicum.
Elizabetham matrimonio junxit Benjamino King Gen.
Dorotheam Ezekieli Wright, S. T. B.
Emmettam Richardo Mason, M. D.
& Mariam Thomæ Staveley J'c^{to},
pulchro forte confilio;
quippe qui primus artes in fe omnes, dein in natis maritavit.
Johannes denique Mabellæ
ex illuftri Ashbeiorum familia * locatus eft.
Tandem optimus fenex
cum Deo imprimis patriæ liberifque
longam at fructuofam vitam traxerat
velut Autumnus meffibus & ævo gravis
fere octogenarius quafi feffus,
fexto Februarii, A. D. 1662, obiit dicam vel fuccubuit."

2. On a flat ftone, underneath :
" Here lyeth interred the Body of
Dame Mercy Onebye,
Late wife to Sir John Onebye."

* The family of Afhby were then at leaft numerous. Mabell had five brothers and three fifters.

F 4   3. On

3. On two other flat ftones, near the altar :

" Mrs. Elizabeth Gerard, relict of Nathanaell Gerard, gent. and fifter to Dame Mercy Onebye, late of Hinckley, departed this life Aug. 31, 1706.

" Mrs. Frances Dudson, fifter to the late Dame Mercy Onebye, died May 5, 1719, in the 87th year of her age."

4. Oppofite Mr. Onebye's monument, on a beautiful tablet of white marble (fee plate VI. fig. 9.) is the following infcription, written by Dr. W. Freind, fometime Dean of Canterbury :

" H. S. E.
Thomas Morres, D. D.
Olim Collegii Hertfordienfis apud Oxonienfes focius ;
Sereniffimæ Augustæ
Principiffæ Walliæ Dotariæ
E facris Domefticis ;
Hujus Parochiæ cum Rectoria de Stoke conjunctæ
Vicarius.
Ne quid amplius pro meritis attigerit
(Si quid apud mortales meritis debetur).
Morte inopinâ præreptus eft.
Erat in illo
Ingenium liberale & prorfus virile,
Ad ftudia aptiffimum
Vel fua profequenda vel aliorum promovenda.
Erat, qui & in vultu quodammodo fpirare vifus eft,
Mirus animi vigor atque acies ;
In fecernenda diftinguendo fubtilitas penè fingularis ;
In meliora quæque feligendo
Judicium acre & fubactum ;
Diligentia accurata & indefeffa ;
Memoria tenax,
Omnes itaque Doctrinæ fontes, præfertim Græcos,
3   Avidè

Avidè haufit,
Philofophiæ Veteris & Novæ
Studiofus indagator.
Autorum etiam, qui Clallici habentur,
Ita gratiam illam & raram elegantiam
Sacris, queis fe dedidit, immifcuit literis,
Ut mirandus Idem fe præftaret
In colloquiis jucundiflimum;
In concionibus gravem, lucidum, difertum;
Paftorem denique fidelem, pium, ac verè Chriftianum,
Deceffit Mart. 16, 1761, natus annos 47,
Magnum fui defiderium relinquens
Amicis, quos habuit plurimos,
Uxorique præcipuè ANNÆ MORRES,
Quæ mœrens hoc pofuit
M. S."

5. In the body of the church, on a flat ftone, are three braffes,
(fee plate V. fig. 1.) with two lines of an infcription almoft obliterated:

" Hic . . . . us
. . . . quorum anim· Deus propic' . . ."

6. Near the above, on a flat ftone,

" PETRUS JAQUES, hujus Ecclefiæ Vicarius,
Gregi fui 22 annos perfpexit
Probus & pius, femper ftudiofus,
Laudabilem egit vitam,
Et tranquillus obiit
Oct. . . , anno falutis 1704, ætatis 56.
Pofuit uxor."

G   7. CATHA-

7. CATHARINE the daughter of Mr. JAQUES is buried near her father; but the greater part of the inscription is hid by the pews.

8. On a flat stone, in the North aisle:

" Here lyeth
The Rev. JOSEPH CARDALE, M. A.
Vicar of Hinkley※;
who dyed June 20, 1752,
aged 73 years."

9. On another:

" Here lieth the Rev.
WM. CARDALE, M. A.
Fellow of Pembroke Hall in Cambridge;
who died Nov. 12, 1756, aged 28 years."

10. On a small tablet of white marble, finely ornamented, at the top of the South aisle:

" In gratefull remembrance
of WILLIAM SAVAGE of Hinckley
Brafier, who dyed April the 3d
1731, in the 76th year of his age.
And also of FRANCES his
wife, who dyed May the 3d
1703, in the 44th year of her age.
Their son WILLIAM SAVAGE
erected this monument.
He died the 15th of January
1764, aged 74."

※ Mr. Cardale had before been vicar of Bulkington in Warwickshire.

11. On

11. On a neat white medallion, in the middle of a large tomb of black marble, in the North aisle:

" Near this place lieth the body of ELIZABETH the daughter of WILLIAM and MARY WATSON, of this parish, who died the 6th of April 1775, aged 18 years."

12. In the South East corner, on a large tablet of black marble, finely adorned:

" Near this place lie interred
The remains of THOMAS ALLEN *, Gent.
and ANNE his wife,
Daughter of JOHN FOSTER, Gent. 1761."

There are a few other flat stones in the body of the church, in memory of WILLIAM PUREFOY, Esq. of Woolvaston Hall, and JANE his wife, with ELIZABETH DAWES, their daughter; Mrs. MARY PRIOR relict of ROBERT PRIOR, late rector of . . . . . , aged 77; Mr. JOHN ELEY and THOMAS his son; Mr. JOHN SOUTHALL and JANE his wife; Mr. THOMAS REEVES and SARAH his wife, with her mother HANNAH BOLESWORTH; Mr. JOHN WOOD and ANNE his daughter; Mr. FRANCIS DAWSON, &c. &c.

---

* On opening his grave, a very ancient free stone was found, lying horizontally about two feet under ground, with a monumental infcription which is not diftinctly remembered. By one gentleman I am told it was " Robert Roe Rector," and the date either MLXXXIII. or MLXXXVII. By another report the name is faid to have been Thomas Potter, aged 67. The ftone was depofited in the belfry, where it lay fome years neglected, and is now loft.

In

In the Church-yard are several monuments of Swedeland slate [a], which are in general coloured with a fine black, and the workmanship bestowed on some of them is uncommonly good. A few of these were by the late Mr. Woodcock ; but most of them are by Mr. Bass, whose abilities and friendship I have already had occasion to mention, and whose premature death I now sincerely lament. The principal inscriptions are these :

13. " Here lieth the body of Anne
late wife of George Wood, senior,
who departed this life A. D. 1705,
in the 61st year of her age."

14. " Thomas Sansome changed this
life for a better, October 28,
in the year of { our Lord 1713,
{ his age 69.
Monarchici Regiminis,
Tam suo quam Avorum Genio,
Strenuus Assertor."

15. " Here lieth the body of Anne
late wife of Robert Paul, senior,
who changed this life in hope of a better, Jan. 31, 1717,
in the 44th year of her age."

16. " Nicholas Ward died Jan. 15, 1720, aged 87 years.
Elizabeth Ward died Nov. 1, 1729, aged 69 years."

* Tomb slates are common throughout the county. They are excellently written on by Christopher Stavely of Melton Mowbray.

17. " Here

17. " Here lieth the body of WILLIAM WARNER, who changed this life Feb. 18, 1721, aged 85 years.
Born at Wolvey;
and was a lover of the Church and Monarchy;
who, by his induftry, acquired a plentiful fortune,
and died in peace with all the world."

18. " Here lieth the body of JOHN STEPHENS, who departed this life Nov. 13, 1721, aged 38.
You readers all both old and young,
Your time on earth will not be long:
For Death will come, and die thou muft,
And like to me return to duft."

19. " Here lieth the body of RICHARD SMITH, who departed this life the 12th day of April, 1727, in the 20th year of his age.
A fatal halbert* this body flew,
The murdering hand God's vengeance will purfue;
From fhades terrene though Juftice took her flight,
Shall not the Judge of all the World do right?
Each age and fex his innocence bemoans,
And with fad fighs lament his dying groans."

20. " Here lieth the body of JOHN BRAYERLY, late of this parifh, who departed this life the 16th day of Auguft, in the year of our Lord 1729, aged 55.
Alfo near this place lieth buried
the body of MARY BRAYERLY, his wife."

* He was murdered by a recruiting ferjeant, whom he had affronted by a trifling joke.

21. " Here

21. " Here lieth, in hopes of a bleffed refurrection,
the body of John Robinson,
who changed this life Dec. 8, 1729, in the 33d year of his age."

22. " Here lieth the body of Hannah Maria Iliff,
who departed this life Dec. 27, 1738."

23. " Here lies the body of Robert Tompson, who changed this
life in hopes of a better, Feb. 1, 1739, in the 78th year of his age."

24. " Near this place were interred the bodies of
Elizabeth Warner, June 29, 1740, aged 84;
William Warner, Jan. 15, 1741, aged 43;
John fon of William Warner, Feb. 21, 1764, aged 37
Mary wife of John Warner, Oct. 12, 1762, aged 30.
Alfo William, Elizabeth, and Mary their children,
who died in their infancy ;
and Grace, daughter of William and fifter to John Warner,
who died Nov. 18, 1765, aged 35."

25. " In memory of Elizabeth the wife of Jonathan
Hurst, who departed this life the 24th day of Auguft, 1744, in
the 44th year of his age.   Near this place lie two of their children, Frances and Arthur, who died in their infancy."

26. " Here lie the bodies of two infants, the fons of Thomas
and Frances Cooper of this town ; viz. Thomas, who died Feb.
12, 1745; and William, who died the 7th of Auguft, 1753."

27. " Here lieth the body of Edmund Iliff,
who died Sept. 20, 1746.
Near it was buried the body of Mary Iliff his
wife, who died Jan. 13, 1741, aged 37."

3   28. " Here

28. " Here lieth the body of GEORGE WOOD, who departed
this life the 12th day of January, in the year of our Lord 1754,
aged 75."

29. " To the memory of
WILLIAM HURST,   ELIZABETH his wife,
who departed this life   who departed this life
February 19, 1756,   February 24, 1742,
aged 82 years.   aged 68 years.
            And fix of their children ; viz.
NATHANIEL who died in 1728, aged 21.
JOSEPH, BENJAMIN, WILLLIAM, } died in their minority.
    CHRISTIAN, and ELIZABETH, }

Thrown from life's battlements, behold
    How low in earth together lie
Captives of Death, both young and old,
    Sad ruins of mortality.
Yet know, vain Conqueror! that the hour
    Comes on apace, when thefe fhall rife
Triumphant o'er thy dreaded power,
    And claim their manfions in the fkies.
Whilft thou, the King of Terrors late,
    Thy fad captivity fhall mourn,
Sad without hope: Thy pomp and ftate,
    Once flown, fhall never know return."

30. " In memory of ELIZABETH the wife of JOHN BASS,
and daughter of WILCOX GREEN of Somerby in this county.
        She died Oct. 16, 1756, aged 45 years.
    Alfo two of their children, who died infants.
            Alfo of ANN their daughter,
        who died June 1757, aged 20 years."
                                    31. " Here

31. " Here lies the body of ROGER ASHBY,
who was 30 years clerk of this parish.
He died July 25, 1759, aged 71 years."

32. " In memory
of MARY the wife of JOHN POOLE,
who, by a sudden call of the Almighty,
was summoned in a moment
into Eternity,
the 20th of October, 1760, aged 43.
May that awful act of Providence,
which so suddenly removed her to a better world,
incline our hearts to say, *Thy will be done!*
Also of ANN his second wife,
who departed this life
the 28th of September, 1768, aged 47."

33. " To the memory of THOMAS BROWN,
who departed this life May 6, 1766, aged 66 years."

34. " Here lieth the body of CATHARINE PAUL,
who departed this life Aug. 20, 1768, aged 78.
Also here lies the body of ROBERT COOPER,
who departed this life June 18, 1771, aged 49."

35. " Here lie interred
the remains of THOMAS GREEN,
late of Somerby in this county, gent.
who departed this life the 10th day of June,
in the year of our Lord 1772,
in the 55th year of his age.
An honest man's the noblest work of God."

36. " In

36. " In memory of JOSEPH WALLIN, fen.
Whofe conduct through life
(the evening of which was a feries of pain,
which he bore with great patience and manly fortitude)
rendered him refpectable to all that knew him.
He died May 13, 1773, aged 73 years.
And ELIZABETH his wife, who died Dec. 9, 1762, aged 60 years.
Their fon JOSEPH died January the 5th, 1773, aged 40 years.
Alfo THOMAS fon of THOMAS and CATHARINE WALLIN,
who died in his infancy."

37. " To the memory of
MARY PARR, the relict of the Rev. ROBERT PARR,
late rector of Horftead and Coltifhall, in the county of Norfolk,
died the 5th of February, 1774, in the 61ft year of her age."

38. " Here lieth interr'd the body
of WILLIAM BURTON, Comedian,
who departed this life May 2, 1774, in the 42d year of his age.
Silence how dread, and darknefs how profound!
'Tis as the general pulfe of life flood flill
And nature made a paufe! an awful paufe!
Prophetic of her end!"

39. " In memory of JOHN POOLE, many years clerk of this parifh.
He departed this life January 27, 1775, in the 66th year of his age.
He was a ftudent and a lover of the fciences,
and delighted in viewing and contemplating
the works of the Almighty
in his difpenfations of creation and providence,
(viz.) the power, wifdom, and goodnefs of the Supreme Being.
The works of the Lord are great, fought out of all them that have
pleafure therein."

II   40. " To

40. " To the memory of
WILLIAM DODDINGTON WHALLEY, Surgeon,
who departed this life Sept. 24, 1778,
aged 69 years."

41. " To the memory of JOSEPH NUTT, apothecary,
who died October 16, 1775, aged 75 years.
The deceased was a great, correct, and pure claffical fcholar,
and a lover of learning;
whofe humanity and conftant practice in life was
to affift the poor and unfriendly with medicines and advice,
without any other profpect of reward,
than that heartfelt fatisfaction
which muft always accompany beneficent actions;
and whofe calm and philofophic mind
enabled him to guide the paffions in the paths of virtue,
and taught him through life
To enjoy the prefent hour, to be thankful for the paft,
And neither to fear nor wifh the approaches of the laft."

42. " In memory of THOMAS SANSOME,
who died Feb. 6, 1766, aged 80 years.
Of GRACE his wife, who died Auguft 29, 1776, aged 57 years.
Alfo of RICHARD and ELIZABETH, two of their children,
who died young."

43. " In memory of THOMAS BROWN,
who departed this life Auguft 3, 1776, aged 41 years."

44. " In memory of URSULA wife of JOHN ROBINSON,
who departed this life October 5, 1778.
Be ye ready; for ye know not the day nor the hour."

45. " To

45. " To the memory of WILLIAM BOLTON,
who departed this life October 4, 1780, aged 68 years;
Alſo of CATHARINE his wife,
who departed this life Auguſt 26, 1780, aged 62 years."

46. " Sacred to the memory of WILLIAM BASS;
who died Dec. 8, 1781, in the 26th year of his age.
If probity of manners, if modeſt worth,
If the practice of every duty which dignifies humanity,
Could have exempted from the grave;
Not a fairer example can be named
Than the Youth we now deplore.
Though born in humble life,
His merits were too conſpicuous to remain unnoticed.
He held near four years a commiſſion in the Leiceſterſhire militia,
Till, worn by a ſevere and lingering illneſs,
Which defied all medical aſſiſtance,
He retired to this his native town,
Where the ſuperiority of his genius was too late diſcovered
By the friend who inſcribes his tomb.
The laſt efforts of his pencil were Views of HINCKLEY Church,
Which will perpetuate his name
When this frail memorial is crumbled with his aſhes.
DEBORAH the wife of THOMAS BASS,
and mother to WILLIAM abovementioned,
died Jan. 25, 1781, aged 52."

There are alſo grave-ſtones to the memory of

NATHANIEL CALLIS, 1709; ROBERT COOPER, ROBERT ALLEN,
and THOMAS SMITH, ſenior, 1710; THOMAS SMITH, 1711;
WILLIAM and CATHARINE ASHBY, 1723; JOSEPH FISHER, aged
84, 1725; WILLIAM PAGETT, aged 79, 1729; JOSEPH ſon
of HENRY BURTON of Swannington, 1740; ROBERT BACON,

1741; John Dagley, and John Law, aged 82, 1744; Samuel Riley, 1751; Mary Nutt, aged 81, and Thomas
Reeve, 1758; John Nutt, aged 62, and Elizabeth Gent,
1762; Anne Preston, 1765; Thomas Ashby, 1768; Noble Reeve, and John King, 1769; Thomas Dash, Sarah
Nutt, and Hannah Rogers, 1772; Michael Kilborne,
1773; Mary Gent, 1775; Sarah Baines, 1776 (with two
of her children); Rebecca Stafford, 1779; Thomas and
Elizabeth King; Abraham and Elizabeth Farren; and several children of Thomas and Elizabeth Estlin.

In the burial-ground belonging to the Presbyterian meeting-
house (which is a large and good building, erected in 1722) are
the following epitaphs:

47. On a small brass plate, fixed in the side of an altar tomb:
" To the memory
Of the late Rev. Mr. Robert Dawson;.
Whose strong and elevated genius
Was richly improved with ancient Literature:
Well he loved and knew the Sciences,
Yet better loved and knew the Gospel;.
. Tempering his zeal for truth with meekness and charity.
His private character was unspotted,
His social virtues ornamental and attractive,
His piety solid and sublime.
He, as a Friend, was steady, wise, sincere;
As a Christian, adorned the doctrines of Christ;
As a Minister, resembled his great Master,
Whom he served many years with acceptance and success;
and was much lamented when suddenly removed
From his usefulness on earth to his reward in Heaven,
June 20, 1751, in the 66th year of his age."

48. " Here

48. " Here lieth the body of
MARY the wife of JOSEPH HARRISON,
who departed this life
Nov. 19, 1752, aged 70.

Here lieth the body of
JOSEPH HARRISON,
who departed this life
Jan. 2, 1755, aged 59.

It muſt be ſo; our father Adam's fall
And diſobedience brought this lot on all.
All die in him; how hopeleſs ſhould we be,
Bleſt Revelation! were it not for thee!
Hail, glorious Goſpel, heavenly Light, whereby
We live with comfort, and with comfort die!
Look through this gloomy ſcene beyond the tomb,
And ſee a hope of endleſs life to come.
Our bodies now deform'd again ſhall riſe
Refin'd and ſuited for immortal joys.
All tears be dried, each riſing ſigh ſuppreſt,
This is our entrance on eternal reſt.
Here, freed from pain and grief, and every ſin,
To live indeed the dead in Chriſt begin."

49. " To the memory of JOSEPH KEMP,
who departed this life March 24, 1758, aged 78.

*God, who is rich in mercy, for his great love wherewith he loved
us, even when we were dead in ſins, hath quickened us together with
Chriſt; and hath raiſed us up together, and made us ſit together in
heavenly places in Chriſt Jeſus.* Epheſians, chap. ii. ver. 4, 5, 6.

50. " To the memory of Mrs. SARAH BROOKS,
who departed this life Feb. 17, 1761, aged 67,

Soft is the bed, the ſlumber ſweet,
    And bright the proſpect of the juſt;
Jeſus, who led them to this ſafe retreat,
    Receiv'd their ſpirit, and will raiſe their duſt."

51. " In

51. " In memory of JAMES ESTLIN, fenior, hofier,
who departed this life the 20th of December, 1761,
aged 67 years.

A wif's a feather, and a chief's a rod;
An honeſt man's the nobleſt work of God.

Here lieth interred the body of ANN the wife
of JAMES ESTLIN, fenior, who departed this
life the 19th of December, 1757, in the 54th year of her age.
Stay, read, prepare, reflect, whilſt this you view
Who next muſt die, uncertain: why not you ?"

52. " *Tolle crucem, fi uis auferre coronam.*
[An angel holding a croſs and crown.]

In memory of Mrs. ANN GILBERT,
who departed this life the 18th of January, 1769,
aged 47 years.

Don't mourn for me; I'm gone to reſt
Where Chriſt and all his faints are bleſt.
Prepare yourfelves whilſt this you view,
The ſummons next may call on you."

There are alſo grave-ſtones in memory of

JOSEPH PONO, aged 65, 1751.
ANNE BURTON, aged 60, 1754.
NATHANIEL WARD, mercer, aged 61, 1759.
ANNE his wife, aged 67, 1762.

Inftitutions to the Vicarage of HINCKLEY in the County of
Leicefter and Diocefe of Lincoln, extracted from the Rolls
and Regifter Books * of the Bifhop of LINCOLN, at Lincoln.

Communicated by Mr. BRADLEY, Regiftrar.

Date of Inftitution.	Names of Vicars.	Patrons.
1238.	Rogerus Capellanus,	
1247.	Richardus de Fefkcham.	
1268, 15 kal. Nov.	Robtus de Heram.	
1289, 16 kal. Jan.	Willus de Stanford.	
1303, 4 id. Maii.	Simon de Hynkele.	
1330, 3 kal. Maii.	Michael de Gaygniaco.	
1334, Dec.	Nicholaus Gaynaire.	
1347, 5 July.	Maurice Barnabe.	
1349, 3 kal. Aug.	John Appelton.	
. . . .	Wm. de Hynkele.	
1352, 5 non. Julii.	John de Benefeld.	Abbot of Lira.
1353, 5 id. Nov.	John de Gowteby.	
1357, 7 id. Oct.	John de Smythefton.	
1359, 2 non. Dec.	Abel de Eton.	
1360, Dec.	Galfridus de Hale.	
1361, 6 id. Nov.	John de Loughburgh.	
1367, 5 Nov.	Adam Stephens.	
1370, 15 Sept.	Richard Waltham.	
1373, 6 July.	William de Thorneton.	
1402, 30 July.	John Berrarde.	
1409, 22 July.	John Berfton.	
1421, 11 June.	John Howys.	
1434, 8 June.	William Erlle.	
1435, 7 Feb.	Nicholas Tapurto.	Prior of Montgrace.
1438, 28 May.	Richard Kynthorpe.	
. . . .	Roger Jackfon.	
1490, 4 May.	Robert Tylton.	
1497, 25 June.	Richard Smith.	
1507, 11 Aug.	John Gudeyer.	Dean and Chapter of Weft-
1513, 8 Dec.	James Porter †.	minfter.
. . . .	Henry Sarfby.	
1558, 9 Nov.	Richard Brifloe ‡.	
1600, 6 Dec.	Jafper Griffith ‖.	

* The Archiepifcopal Regifters at Lambeth having been very kindly fearched on this occafion by Dr. Dt-
CAREL, Librarian there; it is extremely remarkable that not one prefentation to this vicarage is to be found
during any vacancy of the See of Lincoln.
† I have not a doubt but this is the perfon whofe monumental infcription has been fo imperfectly recol-
lected in p. 43; James Porter, vicar, died either in 1513 or 1537, aged 67.
‡ He was buried July 19, 1609. See p. 77.   ‖ Buried May 15, 1614.

In

In addition to the preceding Lift of Vicars from the Lincoln records, the Parish Registers of Hinckley have enabled me to complete the feries to the prefent time.

1614, Robert Elmunds (calls himfelf " Minifter").
1621, Thomas Cleiveland (1).
1652, John Barowes (2).
1 63, George Nailer (3).
1653, Peter Jaques (4).
1704, Samuel Parr (5).
1720, John Carte, Ll. B. (6).
1735, Jofeph Cardale, M. A. (7).
1752, Thomas Morres, D. D. (8).
1761, John Blair, LL. D. (9).
1771, George Thomas.
1775, William Hicks (10).
1773, John Cole Gallaway, M. A.

Patrons.
Dean and Chapter of
Weftminfter.

Among the benefactions to this parifh recorded in the following pages may be inferted, a filver patten given by Mrs. Wightman in 1639, and another patten with two flaggons given by the fame lady in 1639, with the arms of Wightman on each, as in plate VII. fig. 7. and thefe infcriptions :

On one patten, " In teftimony of the good will of CONSTANCE WIGHTMAN, late " wife of John Wightman, to the parifh church of Hinckley, 1639."

On the other, and on the flaggons; " The gift of CONSTANCE WIGHTMAN, late " wife of John Wightman, to the parifh church of Hinckley, 1659."

There are likewife two old pewter flaggons, marked $_W^S$K.

A painting of the Virgin prefenting the child Jefus to Simeon was given to the Vicar and Church-wardens of the parifh, in November 1782, by the Author of this Hiftory, as an ornament to be placed over their Altar; W. Green and W. Lee, Church-wardens.

P. 36. l. 2. r. "warriors, monks, &c." Among thefe is the effigies of a monarch, which I take to be that of Henry IV. the firft royal lord of Hinckley. It is engraved in plate VI. fig. 11. Fig. 12. in the fame plate reprefents one of the monks, and fig. 13. the head of fome animal which occurs more than once in the windows.

Ibid. l. 7. r. " two bare-headed monks ; and a figure nearly effaced, apparently " a bifhop or abbot, perhaps an abbot of Lyra."

(1) Buried Oct. 16, 1651. See memoirs of him, p. 134—141.
(2) Buried Feb. 16, 1662. See p. 77.   (3) Buried Feb. 17, 1683. See p. 77.
(4) See his epitaph, p. 41.   (5) Of whom, fee p. 180—185.
(7) See his epitaph, and that of his fon, p. 42.   (8) See memoirs of him, p. 185.
(9) See memoirs of him, p. 150—191.
(10) Now rector of Hunnington in Suffolk, near the elegant feat of his Grace the Duke of Grafton.

BENE.:

BENEFACTIONS to the Town of HINCKLEY.

1. At the head of this article, what is known by the name of
" THE GREAT FEOFFMENT" muft undoubtedly hold the foremoft
rank. For this noble benefaction the inhabitants of Hinckley
were originally indebted to one of their very early lords the dukes
of Lancafter. It contains, as has been already obferved, a fourth
part of the lordfhip, and comprehends the whole of the demefne
lands which in right of the dutchy of Lancafter became vefted in
the crown.

The earlieft traces that can now be difcovered are, that in the
reign of Edward VI. the demefne lands were leafed to *Thomas Gon-
fale*, in truft for the benefit of the town, which, as will hereafter
appear, had been greatly impoverifhed by fire. This leafe was
four times renewed by Queen Elizabeth (in the 2d, 9th, 27th,
and 45th years of her reign) to *Edward Wightman* and others.

King James was fcarcely eftablifhed on his throne, when a com-
miffion for charitable ufes was held at Leicefter, on the 4th of
October, in the firft year of that king's reign, by Sir Henry Har-
rington, knt. Sir Thomas Beaumont, knt. Sir Bafil Broke, knt.
John Chyppingdale, doctor in laws, John Stanford and Edward
Temple, efqrs. commiffioners authorized under the great feal,
Jan. 17, 1602-3. The leafe which had been granted by Queen
Elizabeth in 1586 was then confirmed; and the clear income
of it appropriated " to and for the difcharge, fuftentacion, and
"bearing of the charges and bufineffes impofed and happening
"to the town of Hinckley." This meafure feems to have
been preparatory to a grant (dated May 21, 2 James I.) by which
the whole of the demefne lands were given in fee to *Edward
Howard, James Trevor, William Jackfon*, and *Robert Bragg*, in truft

3   for

for *Charles earl of Nottingham**. From that powerful nobleman they were purchafed in fee by the inhabitants, fubject
to the chief rent of 22l. 0s. 7¼d. which ftill continues to be
paid. And from this period the manor has uninteruptedly been
held by nominal lords, under fucceffive deeds of feoffment. By the
inclofure of the common field in 1760, a confiderable addition ac-
crued to the income; the grofs amount of which is now on an average about 115l. a year†. From this income the chief rent and other
neceffary expences are deducted; and on St. Thomas's-day a confiderable fum is annually given to the induftrious poor, a falary
paid to the town-fchool-mafters, and the reft of the revenue is
regularly applied to the public fervices of the town, fubject to the
audit of the two town-mafters. When the number of feoffees is
greatly reduced, the vacancies are fupplied by a new deed of feoffment, the laft of which bears date December 14, 1776, when
the following gentlemen were appointed to the truft:

Mr. Thomas Sanfome, fenior.	Mr. William Brown.
Mr. Jofeph Robinfon.	Mr. Jofeph Iliff.
Mr. Thomas Cooper.	Mr. John Cooper.
William Hurft, Efq.	Mr. Thomas Sanfome, maltfter.
Mr. Henry Bryerly.	Mr. Thomas Robinfon.
Mr. Robert Thompfon.	Mr. Thomas Sanfome, junior.

Receiver, Mr. Thomas Robinfon.

* This nobleman (eldeft fon of the firft lord Howard of Effingham) at various
periods of his life filled many important offices in the ftate. He was employed in
an embaffy to France, 1559; was elected a knight of the fhire for the county of
Surrey 1562; a general of horfe in the rebellion of 1569; knight of the garter and
lord chamberlain of the houfhold 1574; lord high admiral of England 1585; a lord
commiffioner for trying the queen of Scots 1586; had a penfion granted him for his
fervices in 1588; was commander in chief at fea when Cadiz was taken in 1596, in which
year he was advanced to the title of earl of Nottingham, and conftituted juftice itinerant of all the forefts South of Trent; lord high fteward on the coronation of king
James, under whom he continued to hold the office of lord high admiral and other
great employments. He died Dec. 14, 1624, in his 87th year.
† This was the receipt in 1779. In other years it has been a little more or lefs.

2. The

2. THE LESSER FEOFFMENT, which, as well as the greater, is of so old a date as to be beyond memory, was also, like the other, the donation of an early ducal lord; and was probably included in the purchase made by the inhabitants from the earl of Nottingham. It has been for time immemorial holden in trust for the town by successive feoffees; whose number being reduced to five, a new deed of feoffment was executed December 14, 1776, by which eight new feoffees were admitted to the trust of " all and singular the messuages, lands, outhouses, edi-
" fices, and buildings, with the appurtenances, situate, standing,
" and being in the borough of Hinckley, called *The Roundhill*, for-
" merly an inn, and called sometimes by the name of *The Bull*
" *Inn*, and compassed about on all sides with the king's highway
" or common street in Hinckley aforesaid, now consisting of the
" several buildings or tenements after mentioned, viz. *The Town*
" *Hall*, commonly called *The Drapery and Butchery*; four mes-
" suages or tenements*, &c.; together with all and singular edifices,
" buildings, out-houses, barns, stables, gatehouses, yards, ways,
" paths, passages, easements, commons, and common of pasture,
" emoluments, advantages, hereditaments, and appurtenances
" whatsoever, to the said messuages or tenements and premises be-
" longing, or in any wise appertaining, &c. To have and to
" hold, &c.; in trust to apply the rents, issues, and profits, to and
" for such uses, intents, and purposes, and in the same manner,
" as the same were originally given, granted, devised, and pur-
" chased for." The feoffees are empowered to lease the premises for a term not exceeding twenty-one years, for the best rent that can be obtained; to elect a receiver from among themselves

* By the side of these is a passage called *The Dale's Lane*, and close adjoining is *The King's Bakehouse*, mentioned in p. 23.—Of the crown rent there also mentioned, 5s. 4d. is paid for the Greater Feoffment; 2s. 1½d. for the Lesser Feoffment; 1s. 8d. by the bailiff of Hinckley, for licence to appoint a deputy; and 9½d. by the dean and chapter of Westminster.

I

yearly

yearly on the feaft of St. Thomas, on which day an account of
all receipts, payments, difburfements, and allowances, is to be produced; and the receiver is reftrained from expending in any one
year any fum exceeding fix fhillings on any one particular bufinefs, without the confent of the major part of the feoffees then
living. The " original intents, ufes, and purpofes, defigned and
" appointed in the applications and difpofition of the faid rents,
" iffues, and profits (until they fhall be more fully and plainly
" difcovered by infpection of the ancient deeds, charters, and writ-
" ings, relating to the faid premifes, for long time loft* or mif-
" placed)" are directed to be " hereafter guided and directed by
" the ufage, applications, and difpofition of the faid premifes,
" rents, iffues, and profits, which by the feoffees, or the major
" part of them for the time being, have been ufed, accuftomed,
" applied, and difpofed of, for the fpace of 70 years † and upwards.*

The whole of the Leffer Feoffment is now let to one tenant at
the yearly rent of 24l. 10s.; which is applied in aid of the general
public purpofes of the other feoffment.

The prefent truftees are,

William Hurft, Efq.	Mr. Jofeph Robinfon.
Mr. Thomas Sanfome, fenior.	Mr. Thomas Robinfon.
Mr. William Brown.	Mr. Jofeph Prefton.
Mr. Henry Bryerly.	Mr. Robert Bains.
Mr. William Applebee.	Mr. John Samuel Parr.
Mr. Jofeph Iliff.	Mr. Thomas Sanfome, junior.
Mr. John Cooper.	Receiver, Mr. W. Applebee.

* It is highly probable, that all the town records were confumed by fire in the
reign of King Henry VIII. The prefent church-regifter begins in 1524. The
grant for the market, which is dated January 20, [1550] 4 Edward VI. exprefsly
fays, that there had been no market held for feveral years, by reafon that their old
charter had been burnt " by mifadventure of fire." The leafe mentioned in p. 55,
is dated May 14, [1550,] 5 Edward VI. .

† This is merely an indefinite law term, to denote that they had been *at leaft* fo
long in poffeffion; " 300 years" would have been nearer the true period.

3. Sir

3. Sir WILLIAM ROBERTS, of Sutton Cheney, knight, gave 30l. to be lent yearly on bond with good fureties to fix tradefmen of this parifh, having moft need, and being good hufbands, by the minifter, churchwardens, and overfeers of the poor, at the intereft of 10d. per pound; which on *Good-Friday* fhall in equal fhares be diftributed betwixt the poor of Hinckley and the parifh of Barwell.

4. JOHN WIGHTMAN, late grocer and citizen of London, bequeathed in the year 1636 to this parifh 50l. the intereft of which is annually to be diftributed to the poor; fince which, a clofe called Studford Clofe, in Earl Shilton, in this county, was purchafed with the faid 50l. and now lets for 40s. a year, which is appropriated as above, for the ufe of the poor, on Good Friday. John Turner, Thomas Sanfome, 1779, churchwardens.

5. Mifs DOROTHY NOEL, of Hinckley, gave
To the church of Hinckley,　　　　40s.
To the poor there,　　　　—　　40s.
To mend wells and caufeys,　　　40s.
Bridges and ways in the lordfhip,　40s.
To purchafe lands,　　　　—　　40s.
Of which lands the yearly rents fhall be employed towards the education of three poor children of this town, chofen by the minifter, churchwardens, and overfeers of the poor, in the fchool there, by paying for the teaching and buying books for them, till they are able to be apprentices.

6. SARAH FARREN, of Hinckley, fpinfter, left January 3, 1734, five pounds to the vicar and churchwardens of this parifh, in truft, that the intereft thereof might be laid out upon a gown to be annually given on St. Thomas's-day to a poor widow of this

I 2　　　　　　　　　　parifh:

parish: and by the legacy being unpaid for several years, the principal is now increased to ten pounds, so that two gowns will be henceforth annually given to the proper objects. Sept. 26, 1763.

7. 1741. SAMPSON WOODLAND, gent. left to the poor of this parish 40l.; 10l. of which was disposed of amongst them; the other 30l. with 10l. more given by Richard Woodland, late of Leicester, brother to the said Sampson Woodland, purchased a close called the Stocking Close in this town, the yearly rent of which is annually distributed amongst the poor of this parish on Good Friday, by the overseers thereof. N. B. The present rent is 3l. 14s.

8. ELIZABETH FITCH, of Burbach, in the county of Leicester, did by her last will bequeath " to the poor of Hinckley, and to " repair the borough-street and causeys there, the sum of three " pounds and ten shillings, yearly and every year for ever; that is " to say, forty shillings to the poor, and thirty shillings to the re- " pair of the said street and causies, to be paid and distributed out " of my toll in Hinkley."

A true copy from the last will and
testament of the abovementioned
    ELIZABETH FITCH,
    Thomas Sansome, }
    John Turner,   } Churchwardens, 1781.

NATURAL

Plate VIII.

NATURAL HISTORY OF HINCKLEY.

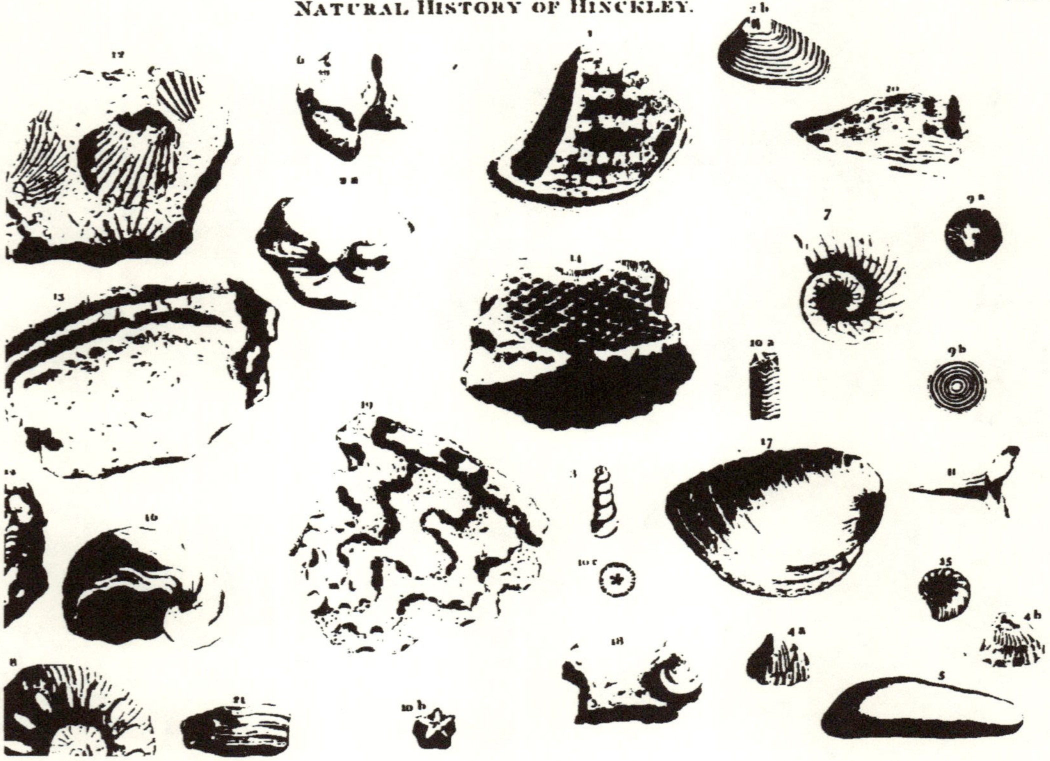

NATURAL HISTORY, MINERAL WATERS, FOSSILS, &c.

A tradition remains at Hinckley, which should not have been here recorded but that it is confirmed, not only by the particular relation of my intelligent friend Mr. John Robinson inserted at large below *, but also by other respectable testimonies which accompany it. In harvest-time, in the year 1672, a number of men, being at work in Hinckley field, were alarmed by a rumbling noise in the air, which they apprehended to be thunder at a distance, till one of them, who had been a seaman, asserted that it was assuredly the

* " I have often heard my late uncle Mr. Thomas Sansome (whose epitaph is " printed in p. 50) relate, that, being, when a young man among the harvest " in Hinckley field, a very particular noise was heard at a distance. Most people " concluded it to be thunder; but the day was fine and calm, and no appearance " of any such thing. It was much listened to on account of the harvest; the farmer, " when engaged in this business, being always attentive to the weather. There " happening to be a man at work in the field who had been engaged in sea affairs " some years before, he declared it to be the firing of great guns or cannon, and laid " himself upon the boggy ground, listening with much attention, and frequently de- " clared that and that, &c. were broadsides, which put them into some consterna- " tion; and soon after they heard of the sea engagement that was fought on that day."

History affords many instances of news of battles being carried so incredibly quick, that it is usual to suppose that it was only a groundless rumour, but which proving true was thought worthy to be recorded. Had the event been otherwise, we should never have heard of it. But there is a traditional story at Cambridge, which shews, that in later times at least, something very extraordinary in this way may happen, and yet be accountable for in a perfectly natural way. Sir Isaac Newton came into the hall of Trinity college, and told the other fellows, that there had been an action just then between the Dutch and English, and that the latter had the worst of it. Being asked how he came by his knowledge; he said, that, being in the observatory, he heard the report of a great firing of cannon, such as could only be between two great fleets, and that as the noise grew louder and louder, he concluded that they drew nearer to our coasts; and consequently that we had the worst of it, which the event verified. At the last siege of Ostend, the noise of the artillery was heard so plain on the Norfolk coast, that those who had been used to them could distinguish between the discharges of cannon and mortars.

2.

noise

noife of " broadfide to broadfide." However incredible this tradition may appear, the Rev. Mr. Jones, (F. R. S. and rector of Pafton in Northamptonfhire), in his valuable " Phifiological Difquifitions, or " Difcourfes on the Natural Philofophy of the Elements," p. 299, exprefsly fays, " It was commonly affirmed, and I heard it fpoken " of when I was young, that the great engagement between " the Dutch and the Englifh at fea in 1672, was heard by the " people who were out at work in the fields to the very centre of " England: Mr. Derham fays, it was heard 200 miles." It was heard at London; but that is not fo furprizing, as it is much nearer, the engagement having been off Southwold Bay in Suffolk.

On the road to Lutterworth, within a few yards of Hinckley town, is a fpring called " The Holy Well," originally dedicated to the Virgin Mary,. and once known by the name of " Our La- dy's Well," the water of which is exquifitely clear and good.

At Cogg's Well, Chriftopher's Spa, and the Prieft Hills, are alfo good mineral waters.

In a laige gravel-pit about a mile from the town, in the turn- pike road to Derby, a great variety of curious foffils has within thefe few years been difcovered. Many of thefe, by falling into the hands of the incurious, have perifhed; but a good collection is preferved in the cabinet of David Wells, Efq. of Burbach, and another has been formed by Mr. John Robinfon of Hinckley. Both thefe collections having been kindly fubmitted to my in- fpection, fome of the moft picturefque fubjects are accurately de- lineated in plate VIII*; and an explanation is here fubjoined.

* N° 1—18. were found at Hinckley; 19—22 at Burbach. N° 13—18, is Mr. Robinfon's; N° 22 is my own (the gift of the Rev. Mr. Norton); all the others belong to Mr. Wells, who has a fine duplicate of N° 16.

I. Con-

1. *Conchitæ Oftreolypoliti*; a fhell of the oyfter kind.

2. *a.*
2. *b.* } Bivalve fhells of the *Cardium* or cockle kind.

3. A fpecies of the *Turbo*, or fcrew-fhell.

4. *Pectinites*; both fides, *a* and *b*.

5. The Mufcle.

6. *Fungites*; this is fuppofed to be a mufhroom* petrified.

7. *Ophiomorphites*; the Snake-ftone; a fpecies of the *Cornu Ammonis* or *Nautilus*.

8. A fragment of another fpecies of the *Cornu Ammonis*.

9. *Fibulares Echiniti*; the Button-ftone; both fides, *a* and *b.*

10. *Afteriæ*, or *Aftroites*; Star-ftones. Two varieties, *a* and *b.* Of the radiated fort there are great numbers.

10. *c.* A fragment of an *Entrochus*, or St. *Cuthbert's* head.

11. *Gloffopetra* (fo called from its fomewhat refembling a tongue); a fhark's tooth.

12. *Lapis megaricus pectinites*; a congeries of fhells of the *Pecten* or fcallop kind. Of this clafs various forts are found, with different kinds of fhells cluftered together.

13. Large fragment of a *Cornu Ammonis*, curioufly marked.

14. A ftone that has evidently received a ftrong impreffion from the fcales of a large fifh.

15. Another fpecies of the *Cornu Ammonis*.

16. The oblong *Concha* perfect. This is the *Anomia Gryphus* of Linnæus, and is one of the foffils which moft abounds at Hinckley ; but they are feldom found perfect ; the greater part of them wanting the lid, which is frequently found feparated from the fhell, in which ftate it is often miftaken for a petrified oyfter-fhell, which it greatly refembles.

17. *Chamites longiufculus undulatus, feu Conchæ longæ latæque* Lifteri, p. 170.

* Mr. Wells has another mufhroom, which is apparently mineralifed.

18. A

18. A species of the *Trochites*, or Top-shell, accidentally fastened to the corner of a stone.

19. *Ichthyolithi*; the petrifaction of the vertebræ of a fish.

20. }
21. } *Corallitæ*; petrified sea plants.

22. A species of caterpillar mineralized.

Besides what are here engraved, Mr. Wells has shewn me the following articles:

1. *Anthropolithi*; the petrifaction of human bones.
2. *Lithoxyla*, petrified wood; of which various fragments are found.
3. *Carpolithi*; petrified fruit; particularly a pear.
4. *Zoolithi*; the teeth of an animal petrified.
5. Petrified horn.
6. *Belemnites*, or thunderbolts; so called from their resemblance to an arrow-point. The *Belemnite* belongs to the testaceous part of the animal kingdom, and to the family of the *Nautili*.
7. Two pieces of semi-metal, supposed to be Cobalt; some are entire and much larger. They are composed of sulphur, and a metallic substance, which first flies off in fusion.

Of these the four first were found at Burbach; the others at Hinckley.

Mr. Wells has likewise some small particles of native cinnabar and copperas stone; with quantities of yellow, brown, and red ochre; and Mr. Robinson has a great variety of the Asteriæ, Conchites, Belemnites, Markasites, Plum-pudding-stones, &c.

The head of a bird (with the bill or beak) mineralised, and the stones called Bufonites, have been found in the parishes of Hinckley and Burbach.

Of the plants growing fpontaneoufly in the environs of Hinckley (communicated by Mr. Robinfon) the following lift would
have been much larger, if I had not rejected from it fuch as are
very common in moft parts of this kingdom.

Amara dulcis. Solanum *Dulcamara*. Woolly Nightfhade, or bitter-
 fweet; in wet hedges: not uncommon.
Agrimony. Agrimonia *Eupatoria*; in margins of fields frequent.
Alexanders. Smyrnium *Clufatrum*; in ditches.
Ladies bed-ftraw. Gallium *verum*; in dry fields.
Betony. Betonica *officinalis*; banks, fields, and hedges; common.
Briony. Bryonia *alba*; in groves and hedges.
Butcher's broom. Rufcus *aculeatus*; on heaths and woody places.
Butter bur. Frequent in Leicefterfhire, but fcarce elfewhere in
 England. Tuffilaga *bybrida*, long ftalked Coltsfoot or
 Butter bur.
Burnet. Poterium *fanguiforba*; in mountainous meadows.
Centaury. Gentiana *Centaureum*; in dry and barren paftures.
Coltsfoot. Tuffilago *farfara*; in damp places.
Water-creffes. Sifymbrium *Nafturtium*; in watery places.
Devil's bit. Scabiofa *fuccifa*; in dry fields and woods.
Flower-de-luce. Iris *pfeudacorus*; in wet meadows and rivers
 frequent.
Hemlock. Conium *maculatum*; in hedges, &c. frequent.
Liverwort; Lichen *caninus*. Afh-coloured ground Liverwort,
 on heaths, &c.
Melilot. Trifolium *Melilotus officinalis*; in corn fields and hedges.
Moneywort. Lyfimachia *nummularia*; in wet meadows and
 paftures.
Saint Peter's-wort. Hypericum *quadrangulum*; in wet woods and
 hedges.
Meadow Sweet. Spiroea *Ulmaria*; in wet meadows and banks
 of rivers.

    K   This

This being the middle and perhaps the higheft part of the earth's common furface in England, my readers will not be difpleafed to fee a few remarks on that fubject, in the words of Mr. Robinfon, an intelligent obferver of the works of nature.

" The walks and views about the town are pleafing and ex-
" tenfive. From the Derby turnpike road near the Bond end is a
" diftant view of King Richard's field, Charnwood foreft, and the
" adjacent country; and from Beacon hill the woods extending
" from Burbach on the South, and the oppofite fields towards
" Barwell, form a pleafant rifing. Between thefe the ground finks
" into a deep valley, which, gradually opening and rifing towards
" the horizon, forms a moft delightful and very extenfive profpect,
" including a view of 50 churches*, with many gentlemen's feats, &c.

" A lift of Churches with their diftance.

		Miles.			Miles.
" Hinckley,	—	1	" Market Bofworth,		6
" Burbach,	—	1	" Claybrook,	—	6
" Barwell,	—	1	" Frolefworth,	—	6
" Afton Flamvil,		2	" Narborow,	—	6
" Elmifthorpe,		2	" Leir,	—	7
" Stapleton,	—	2	" Cofby,	—	7
" Earl's Shilton,	—	3	" Broughton Aftley,		7
" Stoke Goldingham,		3	" Whetfton,	—	7
" Shanford,	—	4	" Blaby,	—	8
" Sapcot,	—	4	" Ratby,	—	8
" Stonyftanton,	—	4	" Countifthorp,	—	8
" Thurlafton,	—	4	" Nelfton,	—	9
" Kirkby Malory,	—	4	" Dunton-Baffet,	—	9
" Croft,	—	5	" Glenfield,	—	9

* A remarkable fight, and perhaps not to be paralleled at any place but in Holland, where, on a rifing ground in the neighbourhood of Utrecht, more than 70 churches and villages are to be feen, and a dial is erected with their names and diftances.

" Afhby

	Miles.		Miles.
" Aſhby Magna,	10	" Bruntingthorp,	13
" Great Wigſton,	10	" Fleckney, —	14
" Gilmorton, —	11	" Saddington, —	15
" Lutterworth, —	11	" Ilſton on the Hill,	17
" Ailſtone, —	11	" Kibworth, —	17
" Markfield, —	11	" Theddingworth,	18
" Peatling, —	12	" Weſt Carlton,	18
" Orton on the Hill,	12	" Laughton, —	18
" Church over,	12	" Scraptoft, —	18
" Evington, —	12	" Naſeby, —	20
" Kimcot, —	12	" Norton, —	22

" SEATS.

	Miles.
" Aſton Hall, *Edmund Cradock Hartop*, Eſq. —	2
" Wykin, *William Burleton*, Eſq. ———	2
" Kirkby Malory, Lord Viſcount *Wentworth*, ———	4
" Boſworth, Sir *Wolſtan Dixie*, ———	6
" Oldbury, *Rowland Oakover*, Eſq. ———	8
" Gopſhall, *Aſsheton Curzon*, Eſq. ———	10
" Stretton Hall, Sir *George Robinſon*, ———	17
" Weſt Carlton, Sir *John Palmer*, ———	18
" Scraptoft, Mrs. *Wigley*, ———	18
" Quenby, *Shuckburgh Aſhby*, Eſq. ———	22

" HILLS and WOODS.

	Miles.		Miles.
" Croft hill, —	5	" Burrow hills, Nor- }	30
" Charnwood foreſt,	11	" thamptonſhire, }	
" Mereval wood,	11	" Peak hills, Derbyſhire,	40
" South Killworth wood,	16		

" From *The Lawns* and from *Prieſt Hill* Coventry is diſtinctly
" ſeen, with part of Warwickſhire.

K 2 " By

" By comparing my barometer journal for feveral years paft
" with thofe made in London during the fame years, I find à
" very confiderable difference in the excefs of the rifing and fall-
" ing of the mercury; for at London it rifes upon an average
" $\frac{1}{1}\frac{1}{1}$ of an inch higher than with me at Hinckley, but does not
" fink fo low at London by a like difference of $\frac{1}{15}\frac{1}{1}$; if therefore
" we fuppofe the fall of the mercury $\frac{1}{10}$ of an inch, very near
" equivalent to 98 feet of perpendicular height, then the above
" $\frac{1}{12}\frac{1}{1}$ will give 539 feet for the difference in height between
" Hinckley and London. Thefe computations cannot be fup-
" pofed to be entirely exact and accurate, yet they may be fuf-
" ficient to juftify the above conjecture.

" Some of the principal rivers in the ifland, the Trent, Se-
" vern, &c. take their rife in and about this neighbourhood *.

" The parifh of Hinckley contains a variety of earths or foils,
" as clay, gravel, fands, and a variety of mixed foils of all thefe;
" alfo peat-earth and marle, with very good brick clay. The
" brick made here is confiderable; and fome of it, if properly ma-
" naged, might be good potter's clay. There is alfo a variety of
" water, moftly good and wholfome, and fome of it excellent.
" There is a confiderable variety of timber trees; the oak, afh,
" and elm, &c. grow very well, but at prefent the elm is moft
" planted. The ftronger foils bear very good wheat and beans,
" and the lighter ones peafe, barley, and oats, in great plenty.
" Large quantities of land are at prefent employed in pafturage,
" being very good for the dairy and feeding cattle, and alfo for
" fheep. The moft barren land is in the extremities of the parifh,
" which parts were formerly much covered and overgrown with
" furze, but have been improved, and there is little of it now
" remaining. Moft of the land produces good crops of turnips,
" and the different varieties of graffes."

* The *Scare*, anciently called *Leire*, takes its rife near Hinckley; and, after com-
paffing Leicefter on the Weft and North fides, dividing part of this county from Not-
tinghamfhire, and enlarging itfelf with the *Wreke*, the *Dene*, and the *Snite*, unites with
the *Trent* a little beyond *Radcliffe upon Scare*.

ANTI-

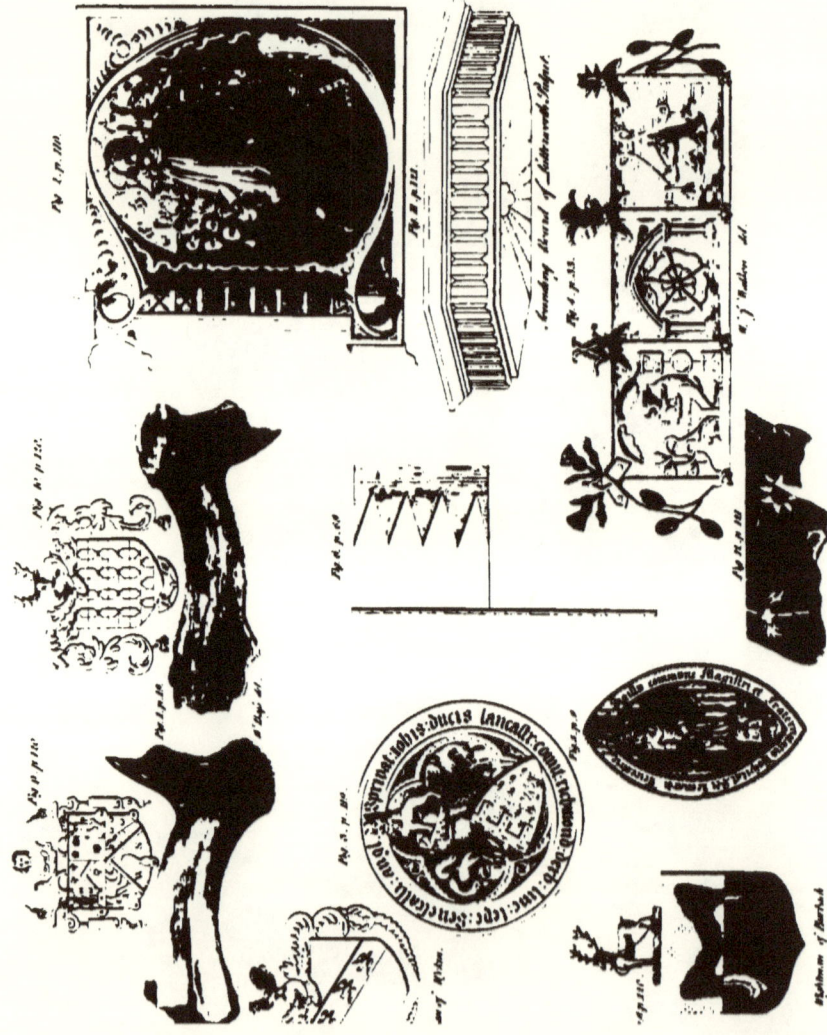

ANTIQUITIES.

In a valuable volume of Records belonging to the office of the Dutchy of Lancafter is the blazonry of the ducal arms, accompanied by the banners of the various lordſhips which centered in that diſtinguiſhed title.   Among theſe is the banner borne by the *old earls of Leiceſter* in right of their HONOUR OF HINCKLEY, viz. Party per Pale indented, Argent and Gules, as in the arms engraved in plate VI. fig. 7.   The banner itſelf is alſo delineated in plate VII. fig. 4.   For the ſight of this curioſity, and for the communication of many other particulars relative to the early part of the Hiſtory of this ancient Town of Hinckley, I am indebted to the politeneſs of Francis Ruſſell, eſq. ſolicitor to the Dutchy of Lancaſter.

In a field about a mile from Hinckley, on the road to Leiceſter, ſtood formerly a Beacon*.   The ſpot is ſtill called " Beacon Hill," Another was on the tower of the church† (as may be ſeen in

---

* Before the reign of Edward III, Beacons were but ſtacks of wood ſet up on high places, which were fired when the coming of enemies was deſcried ; but in that reign pitch-boxes were ſet up inſtead of theſe ſtacks.   Such is the deſcription of a Beacon as cited from lord Coke, by Profeſſor Ward, in the Archæologia, vol. I. p. 3; where it appears, p. 6, that there were formerly three beacons in Warwickſhire, which, when all lighted, would convey notices to ſix adjacent counties; that at *Burton-Daſſet* into Glouceſterſhire and Oxfordſhire ; that at *Bickenhill* into Staffordſhire and Worceſterſhire ; and that at *Monkſkirby* into Leiceſterſhire: whence the *Hinckley* beacon (ſituated almoſt in the centre of the kingdom) would extend the intelligence into the counties of Derby, Nottingham, Rutland, and Northampton.

† Dr. Ducarel has obſerved in very many of our churches, particularly thoſe in Kent and Suſſex, that where you ſee a tower of a church in a high ſituation, and that the preſent pinacles are not alike, although of ſtone (as is the caſe at Hinckley), the difference ariſes, as he thinks, from there having formerly been a beacon placed on the ſaid ſteeple.

plate

plate II), near the stone chair on the battlements, commonly called
" The King's Chair *."

In one of the windows of Mr. Green's house in Castle-street are
the arms engraved in plate V. fig. 15. viz. 3 boars heads on a
fess Sable (Query, if *Bethell, Evans,* or *Warner?*), with three eagles
Or, displayed, in a field Vert, *Wynne.*

Mr. *Wells* of Burbach has seven Roman copper coins of Claudius
Gothicus and Constantine, which were found on the Watling-
street road, near the Roman camp at Mancester, near Hinckley.
On some of them, IMP. CLAVDIVS.—Rev. PROVIDEN. AVG.
On others, VICTORIA EXERCITVS, &c.—Rev. Romulus and Re-
mus with the Wolf.

In a field near *The Holy Well* were found, in 1755, six nobles
of Edward III. of fine gold, struck probably in 1353. Two of
them, in good preservation, remain in the possession of Mrs. *Whalley*
of Hinckley, and exactly answer the description given by Mr.
Folkes †.

> EDWARD DEI GRA REX ANGL DNS HYB ET AQT. The king
> standing in the centre of the ship, on the right side armed,
> with his sword drawn in his right hand, and in his left his
> shield, on which his arms, quarterly, 1. 4. France semé de
> lys, 2. 3. England three lions passant guardant. Over the
> ports appear the lion of England as in the arms, and fleur
> de lys alternately; below are spikes projecting between them.
> A flag bearing St. George's cross is flying at the stern.

* The vestige of some forgotten custom may here be traced. On Shrove Tuesday
the sexton has an ancient privilege of admitting as many persons as he pleases on the
leads and battlements, and to examine the bells; which is considered as an annual
holiday to the children of the town.
  † See his valuable Table of English Gold Coins, plate I. N° 4. Some similar coins
were mentioned in the news-papers of that year to have been found on *Finchley* common; an error of the transcriber, possibly, for *Hinckley.* See Gent. Mag. 1755, p. 234.

ICH

IHC AVTEM TRANSIENS PER MEDIVM ILLORVM IBAT. In a double treffure of eight arches with trefoils in the outward angles, and a fleur de lys and crown over the lion of England alternately within a crofs fleury voided; in the centre a rofe with four leaves pointed with as many trefoils faltirewife, including the letter E.

Mifs *Cooper* of *The Afhwoods, Hinckley*, has a filver groat of Henry V. (ftruck by the Conqueror of France in his mint at Calais) which was found in a field between Hinckley and Burbach. It is accurately engraven by Mr. Folkes[*], and may be thus explained: HENRIC DI GRA REX ANGL ET FRANC. In a double treffure a full face and open crown fleury, with an annulet on each fide the neck; marked on both fides with a crofs pierced. VILLA CALISIE in the inner limb; POSVI DEVM ADIVTORE MEVM in the outer. Crofs fleury to the edge; on each quarter of the inner circle three pellets; an annulet joining the three pellets in two tranfverfe quarters, and one after the word POSVI.

Mr. *Edward Warden*, of *Nuncaton*, has a curious coin of Philip king of Spain and Mary of Portugal (his fecond queen) not dated. It was found June 16, 1773, in an old box belonging to *William Efford* of *Higham* [†], is exactly the fize of the Angelet defcribed by Mr. Folkes[‡], and weighs 52 grains. Though totally unconnected with Englith hiftory, as it was found in the neighbourhood of the town I am writing about, a reprefentation

---

[*] In his table of filver coins, plate IV. fig. 9.

[†] Several other gold and filver coins were found at the fame time. Among the gold coins (43 in number) were fome of Edward VI. and feveral of Elizabeth; the Britifh gold crown of James I. (fee Folkes, plate XI. N° VII.) and fome of Charles I. Of the filver, I have no other account than that 5 (about the fize of a fhilling) were not dated; two large fiege pieces were marked V° and two fmaller pieces dated 1673 and 1676.

[‡] In his ninth plate of Gold Coins, fig. 6.

of

of it is given in plate VI. fig. 10. On one fide are the heads of
Philip and Mary, facing each other, both crowned*; infcribed
PHLS. DEI. GRAT. HISPANIAR. REX.
Reverfe, the arms of Caftile and Leon, quartered,
DVCATVS. ORDI. TRANVA. HISP.
Mint-mark, a caftle.

Mr. *Skardon* of Colman-ftreet Buildings has a large filver feal
ring (the impreffion of it a merchant's mark) which was found
by a fervant of Mr. Binley in the road between Smockington an
Little Wigfton. It weighs 18 dwts. 12 grs. and is engraved in
plate IV. fig. 2.
The third figure in the fame plate is a brafs feal, with a fardo-
nyx, found in Bofworth field by the late Mr. Thomas Green †
of Somerby, and now in the poffeffion of his daughter Mrs. *Morris* of Weft Smithfield.
In the fourth figure are the arms of *Firebrace* of Stoke; of
which family a farther account will be given in the Appendix,
p. 157.

In plate V. fig. 2. reprefents the top of an old ivory crucifix
found in the garden at *Wykin Hall*, and now in my poffeffion.
The arms in fig. 15. (taken from a window at the top of the
Upper Bond End Street) are thofe of *Thomas St. Nicholas* of
Afhe, near Sandwich in Kent, Efq. and *Dorothy* his firft wife,
daughter of —— *Tilghman* of Kent ‡.

---

* Only two Englifh gold coins of Philip and his firft queen Mary occur in Mr.
Folkes's plates; neither of which has any effigies. And where this king and queen
are reprefented together on their Englifh coins, a fingle crown is fufpended between
their heads.
† See his epitaph in p. 48.
‡ They had iffue Thomas St. Nicholas, Efq. of Afhe, barrifter at law, living
1663. Vide H. 2—85, and D. 18—138. b. in Coll. Armor. Timothy Nicholas,
Efq. was fheriff of Leicefterfhire in 1737.

RECORDS,

Withlaf king of Mercia, by his charter to Croyland abbey dated in 833, as recited at large in Ingulphus, p. 10, confirms to that abbey " donum *Normanni* quondam vicecomitis in *Sutton juxta* " *Bosworthe*, duas carucatas terræ, & unum molendinum ventri- " cium. Item donum ejusdem Normanni in *Stapilton*, viz. ma- " nerium, & duas carucatas terræ. Item donum ejusdem in " *Badby*, viz. quatuor hidas terræ cum appendiciis." Q. Whe- ther *Normanton Turvile* was not the residence of this Norman, and took its name from him? There is another Normanton and Sutton near Belvoir castle, on the edge of Lincolnshire.

Haraldus was in 1060 steward to Edward the Confessor; and was succeeded in that office by *Houelin* (mentioned in p. 6).

Henry Beauclerc, son to William the Conqueror, was high steward in 1072, between the death of William Fitz-Osborn and the appointment of the elder GRENTESMAINEL; in whose person, about the year 1090, the HIGH STEWARDSHIP and the HONOUR OF HINCKLEY became HEREDITARY.

In 1205, Petronilla countess of Leicester gave 3000 marks to have the county of Leicester with its appurtenances, together with the fees and domains belonging to the HONOUR OF GRENTESMAINEL as well within the county as without, as her right and inheritance; provided that all the lands of the Normans holden of the same fee belonged to the king; and that the house of Witewich should be committed to whomsoever the king would, the party giving surety that he would faithfully serve the king. Mag. Rot. 1205, 6 Joh. 17. b. Warw. & Leic. Madox, Hist. Excheq. 338. There is a liberty or franchise within this county called *The Bishop's fee.*

---

* The reader will readily see that the greater part of these articles relate imme- diately to the town of Hinckley; and the very few that are not so are con- nected with the subject, as relative to the county at large.

At

At the coronation of queen Eleanor in 1235, Simon de Montfort earl of Leicester claimed the office of high steward: his
claim was then controverted by Roger Bigot earl of Norfolk, as
being his right; but it appeared that the same contention having
arisen about the coronation of king John, it was compromised in
favour of the earl of Leicester, on his giving ten knights fees to
the earl of Norfolk, who thereupon released his claim.   Ex Lib.
Rubro Scaccarii, ut transcribitur in MS. Cotton. Claudius, C. IV.

In 1289, Oliver Sutton bishop of Lincoln quitted claim to
Edmund earl of Leicester of all pretensions to the *lordship of
Hinckley.*

Hinckley mill and fines occur 1326, in a roll de Banco, Trin.
19 Edward II. Rot. 153.

Search being made in the Exchequer, 1351, for the reliefs due
from Henry earl of Lancaster, son and heir of Henry earl of Lancaster, it was found that his father had been charged with the relief
of fifty pounds for the HONOUR [OF HINCKLEY], with the town and
castle of Leicester, formerly belonging to Simon de Montfort; to
wit, for the moiety of the inheritance formerly belonging to Robert
de Melan, earl of Leicester. Com. Hill. 25 Edw. III. Rot. 4. ex
parte Rem. Thef. & Hill. 6 Ed. IV. Fines.

William de Clown, abbot of Leicester, being summoned to parliament by writ dated Nov. 15, 1351, 25 Edw. III. petitioned the
king that he might be excused from that attendance, alledging that
his abbey was founded in frank almoigne by *Robert Fitz-Robert
of Melan, earl of Leicester,* and that the advowson or patronage
thereof came into the hands of king Henry III. by the forfeiture
of Simon de Montfort then earl of Leicester; and that the said
abbot neither held of the king any lands by barony or otherwise,
whereby he was obliged to come to parliament; and that none of
the preceding abbots were summoned, after the forfeiture of the
said Simon, before the 49th year of Henry III. in which year all
the

the abbots and friars throughout England were voluntarily fum-
moned. The truth of thefe allegations appearing upon fearching
the records, the king granted the abbot a patent, dated Feb. 15,
whereby he difcharged him and his fucceffors for ever after from
coming to parliament; and accordingly we find in the fummons to
parliament, in Dorf' Clauf', part 1. 25 Ed. III. n. 5. Dorf. the name
of William de Clown abbot of Leicefter is cancelled, and this
written againft it: " Abbas Leyceftriæ cancellatur, quia habet
" cartam regis, quod non compellatur venire ad parliamentum."
In the fummons 27th year of the fame king to a great council,
the abbot of Leicefter is among the reft; but in that of his 29th
year the abbot of Leicefter's name occurs again, with the fame
words written again it as in the 25th year. Dorf' Clauf' 29 Edward III. m. 28.

In 1377, at the coronation of king Richard II. John king of
Caftille and Leon, duke of Lancafter, claimed the office of fteward
of England as earl of Leicefter and lord of the HONOUR OF
HINCKLEY; which claim was allowed by the commiffioners, he
being tenant by the law of England after the death of Blanch
his late wife, to whom the faid office had belonged*.

In 1399, at the coronation of Henry IV. the earldom of
Leicefter and HONOUR OF HINCKLEY, to which the office of fteward
belonged, being in the king by defcent from his mother Blanch;
the king committed that office to be executed by his fon Thomas†.

In 1412, at the coronation of king Henry V. Richard Beau-
champ earl of Warwick was conftituted fteward of England for
that purpofe‡.

The *keeperfhip of Hinckley park and warren* were granted,
1466, 6 Edward IV. to *William* Lord *Haftings*, in tail male.

* Clauf. 1 Ric. II. m. 45. And fee above, p, 14.
† Roll of Services; and fee Selden's Titles of Honour, part II. ch. 3. p. 655.
‡ Ibid.

May

May 14, 1550, king Edward VI. in right of the dutchy of Lancaster, leafed to *Thomas Gofnale*, or rather *Gofnold*, for the term of 31 years, the whole of the DEMESNE LANDS OF HINCKLEY, at the rent of 5l. 15s. 8d. Thefe lands, according to the fpecification of the leafe, comprehended 136 acres, with houfes, gardens, and the caftle-ditch [*domibus, gardinis, & foffat' caftr'*,] lately in the tenure of *John Haftings*, and by him leafed out to divers fub-tenants; a parcel of land called *Heartewell Stocking*, otherwife *Tipping Stocking*, containing 40 acres, lately in the oc-cupation of *John Robyn, William Jonfon, Roger Adam*, and *Thomas Rawfon*; a fingle acre called *Earl's Croft*; a clofe called *Culver-croft*, or *Cukve croft*, held by *James Smytbe*; three clofes called *Slody* or *Sludy Meadow*, held by *John Woodham*; the herbage of the manor and caftle, leafed to *Robert Woodham*; and an agiftment in *Shedley*, demifed to the bailiff [*præpofitus*] of Hinckley at the yearly rent of feven fhillings.

On the 20th of January following this benevolent young mo-narch granted a commiffion for a MARKET to be kept in the bo-rough of Hinckley every Monday in the year; it having been made appear that the market of late days had been decayed and not ufed nor kept, for that the charter for the liberties of their faid market was burnt by mifaventure and cafualty of fire.

The earlieft Regifter of this parifh now exifting* began in 1554, with the title of

" HINCKELEY. The Regefter Booke trewly taken
" out of the olde Regefter accordinge to the Lawe made."

The

* By the kindnefs of the Rev. Mr. Gallaway, the prefent vicar of Hinckley, I have been indulged with a perufal of the early Regifters; which appear to have been very exactly kept as far as relates to baptifms, marriages, and funerals; but are extremely barren of hiftorical information. A few extracts are here tranfcribed, of families occurring in this little Hiftory.

The earlieft mention of the name of *Wightman* is November 5, 1568, when *Va-lentine Wghtman* of Wykin married *Margaret Laxton*. I begin with this name, as he is the earlieft *known* benefactor to the town, and one of the lords in truft in their feoffments. *Thomas Wightman* was buried March 30, 1570; another *Thomas Wightman*

The firſt entry is, " Bartholomeus Laxton, filius Joh'is Laxton,
" baptizatus fuit vicefimo fexto die Martii, anno Dom. 1554;" and
this

Wightman was churchwarden in 1611; and a third *Thomas Wightman* was *buried*
in woollen, January 26, 1678-9 [*]. The family was numerous during the greater part
of the laſt century; and on the ſecond of June 1657, by the marriage of *Thomas San-*
ſome ſenior with *Sibbil Wightman,* became united with the family which have ever
ſince that period taken the lead as lords in truſt. They are frequently mentioned
under the deſcription of *Sanſome of the Hill,* and *Sanſome of the Town's End.*

Richard the ſon of *John Ownebe* was baptized Sept. 25, 1563.

Richard Briſtoe, who had been vicar 43 years, was buried July 19, 1600..

Jaſper Griffith vicar, and *Robert Peylton,* his clerk, were both buried on the ſame
day, May 25, 1614.

Jane Vynes daughter of *Richard Vynes,* clerk, and *Katharine* his wife, was buried
March 13, 1639.

Thomas Cleiveland vicar was buried October 26, 1652.

John Oneby and *Mabell Aiſhbey* married September 2, 1659.

Mr. *John Barowes,* miniſter of Hinckley, was buried February 16, 1662.

Madam *Emmet Onebye,* buried October 6, 1674.

Mr. *George Nayler,* vicar, buried February 17, 1683, in the 84th year of his age.

Frances daughter of *John Robinſon,* of *The Tavern,* buried May 25, 1658.

The account of the briefs, in p. 35, was printed from memory. The following liſt
includes all that occur between the periods there mentioned:

		£.	s.	d.
1659, Aug. 14.	Town of Southwould, al. Soulbav, Suffolk,	3	15	8
Mar. 14.	Diſtreſſed inhabitants of Metheringham, in the parts of Keſteven, Lincolnſhire,	3	0	0
1660, Dec. 30.	Inhabitants of Wilnhall, Staffordſhire,	1	10	7
Feb. 3.	———— Mount Sorill, Leiceſterſhire,	1	5	5
Oct. 1.	———— Fakenham, Norfolk, —	2	2	10
1661, April 4.	———— Ilmiſter, Staffordſhire,	2	4	8
May 14.	Church of Dalby Chalcombe, Leiceſterſhire,	0	18	0½
June 30.	Pontefract, Yorkſhire, ————	0	14	2
July 14.	Inhabitants of Milton Abbas, Dorſetſhire,	0	14	0
21.	———— Scarborough, Yorkſhire,	0	13	10
Aug. 4.	Given to George Heine of Loughborough,	0	2	6
11.	Inhabitants of Great Draiton, Silop, —	0	11	0
Sept. 22.	———— Watchett, Somerſetſhire,	0	10	2
29.	Bullingbrooke, Lincolnſhire, ————	0	9	4
Oct. 20.	———— Heden, Yorkſhire, ————	0	10	6
27.	———— Elmſley Caſtle, Worceſterſhire,	0	12	8
Nov. 10.	Diſtreſſed Proteſtants in the Dukedom of Lithuania	2	0	10
11.	Inhabitants of Eaton, Leiceſterſhire, ————	0	5	6
	Rebuilding Ripon church, Yorkſhire,	0	8	0
18.	Given to Zachary Harris of Melton Mowbray,	0	2	6

[*] Several entries of this ſort occur in 1678 and 1679; but none earlier or later.

1662,

this feems to have been an after-infertion, the common entries beginning with the marriage of Anthony Harris and Alice Ward,
3 Eliz. June 16, 1560; from which date the regifter is regularly
continued; and hence to 1575 every leaf is figned by *Richard
Brifloe* vicar, and *John Swift* and *John Barloe* churchwardens;
thence to 1585 by *Richard Brifloe* vicar, only.   From the beginning, to 1602, appears to have been a copy of an older regifter*, kept probably on detached flips of parchment or paper.

Book II. begins April 14, 1650; and in 1653 occurs this memorandum: "I do hereby certify that I allow *Calebbe Cafe* † of
" Hinckley to be Regifter.   FRANCIS SHUTE ‡."

1662, Jan. 16. For the Royal Fifhing,   ——   0 12 2
       Aug. 10. Rebuilding Market Harborough church, Leicefterfhire, 0 8 0
Each of the preceding articles is figned by " THO. LEADBETER, Minifter;"
and the four following ones by " GEORGE NAILER, Vicar."
1663, May 17. Diftreffed inhabitants of Walton in the Club, Salop,   0 11 3
       July 29. Inhabitants of Hexham, Northumberland, (collected } 0 12 7½
                 through the town, Aug. 7, by Tho. Underwood), }
       Nov. 15. ——— ——— Heighington, in the parifh of Wafhing-} 0 10 0
                 brough, in the parts of Kefteven,   }
       Mar. 20. ——— ——— Eafthendred, Berks,   —   0 9 7
I make no apology for copying this lift: it contains all entries of the kind that are in
the books; and if not of ufe, is at leaft a curiofity. The variety of religious perfua-
fions in this parifh renders any comparative ftate of births and burials here in the
higheft degree uncertain.
   * The earlieft public injunctions for keeping parochial regifters were made in
1538, by the direction of Cromwell, then vicar general; which in 1547 were confirmed by Edward VI, with a penalty on the minifter for neglect. By a canon of
1603, regifters are directed to be made up from *the law's firft taking place*, and more
particularly fo from the firft year of Queen Elizabeth. See Mr. Juftice Barrington's
Preface to " Propofed Forms of Regifters for Baptifms and Burials, 1781," 4to.
   † Caleb Cafe, the parifh clerk, was married to Anne Willday, February 9, 1657-8.
He had feveral children; and was buried Sept. 19, 1665.
   ‡ By an act paffed in 1653, a Regifter was directed to be appointed for every parifh, who was to publifh the names, &c. of the parties intending to be married three
feveral Lord's-days, at the clofe of the morning exercife ; or, if defired, in the mar-
ket-place next adjoining, on three market-days in three feveral weeks, between the
hours of eleven and two ; which being done, they were to go before a juftice of
peace, who was authorized to compleat the ceremony. An abftract of this act is printed
in the Parliamentary Hiftory, vol. XX. p. 214.

In

. In 1559 a common oven* was leafed to William Scale, and another to H. Raynefcroft.

A decree was iffued in 1587, to enable the *clerk of Hinckley markets* to enforce the payment of tolls.

In 1588 a grant was made to the corporation of Leicefter, which entitles them to the chief rent mentioned in p. 24. And in the fame year a commiffion was iffued for the furvey of Hinckley wood; after which, Hinckley wood and Attwood were leafed to Peter Houghton for 31 years.

In 1589, a writ was iffued to conftitute Lifley Cave " Cuftos " bofcorum infra manerium de Hinckley, alias vocat. Hinckley " parke, in com. Leic. durante beneplacito."

In 1590 a common oven was leafed to Richard Boothby.

In 1594 the Priory Stockings and Moore Furlong were leafed to Robert Younglove.

In 1599 the tolls of the markets and fairs were leafed to William Okes.

In 1600 a licenfe was granted to B. Laxton, to erect a windmill on the Stockings.

In 1603 Queen Elizabeth, not long before her death, gave all the trees growing in Hinckley wood to Sir John Stanhope.

In 1609 another decree was iffued, giving farther powers and authority to the clerk of the markets.

In 1666 the great plague, which had raged in London the year before, found its way to Hinckley; the particulars of which are thus related by Mr. Robinfon: " The ficknefs is faid to have been brought to this town in the following manner. An inhabitant of Hinckley had a near relation in London, whofe daughter died of the plague. After her death they fent a fine

* At this time all the tenants of the Dutchy of Lancafter were compelled, under a heavy penalty, to bake only at the Royal bakehoufe. The King's baker at Leicefter appears, from feveral inftances, to have been a perfon of confequence.

coat-

coat-body as a prefent to their friends at Hinckley, who had a daughter about the fame age. When they had received it, being fearful of the infection, and yet pleafed with the prefent, they concluded to give it a thorough airing, which was attended to during all the winter feafon, and fometimes without-doors. After this precaution, thinking it quite fafe and free from infection, they ventured to put it upon their daughter, who foon fickened and died. After this, it fpread in the town; but, by the extreme care and caution of the inhabitants, it was not fo fatal as might have been expected. They had an hofpital for the fick at the bottom or further part of the Aftwoods. Moft people (as is generally the cafe in fuch calamity) kept as much to them-felves as poffible. As an inftance of this, upon the ceafing of the ficknefs, they found the pavements of the ftreets overgrown with grafs. Some of the inhabitants retired to their friends in the villages free from infection *. An anceftor of mine, whofe wife had near relations at Stony Stanton, retired thither, on the approach of the ficknefs, with the young family, the hufband remaining at home; but, on the increafe and near approach of the ficknefs, he thought it prudent to go to a fo-litary building on his own land at a diftance from fociety, leaving his houfe and bufinefs to the care of a trufty fervant, who fre-quently vifited him, bringing him what neceffaries he wanted, and giving him information of the progrefs of the ficknefs. From this dreary retreat he walked every morning to Mill Pit, about a poft-mile from Hinckley ; for it was cuftomary about ten o'clock to give as many tolls on the great bell as there were perfons dead of the plague. Here he continued till the town was free from

* No memorandum of this remarkable occurrence is to be found in the parifh regifter; unlefs the neglect of entries in that year may be fo deemed.
In 1665 the regiftered baptifms were 37 ; the burials 30.
In 1666 ————— 16; ——— 18.
In 1667 ————— 50; ——— 35.

4   infection.

infection. I think it is worth notice, that during the ſickneſs there often was a very great calm ; the bell being generally heard very diſtinct at Mill Pitt, alſo at Stony Stanton, nay very fre- quently at this laſt place they could hear the church clock ſtrike the hour."

" Sept. 5, 1728, a ſudden and terrible fire about noon de- ſtroyed the brewhouſe of Anne Woodward, widow, and the houſes, barns, ſtables, outhouſes, goods, wool, and harveſt produce, ſtock- ing-frames, and ſhop-goods, of William Abbot, William Alwey, Samuel Allen, Thomas Brown, Joſeph Evans, Thomas Hurſt, Jo- ſeph Lawrence, Sarah Paul, William Savage, Marmaduke Stanley, Anne Tomſon, Richard Gore, Joſeph Hurſt, Joſeph Harriſon, Han- nah Goode, Eleanor Stanley, Job Burde, Richard King, junior, Joſeph Kemp, and John Bagott; and of 80 other perſons; the whole loſs, upon a low and the ill-judged computation of 12 regu- lators, was 3434l. to the great detriment of thoſe people, and of all the town." *Pariſh Regiſter*, *temp. J. Carte*, M. A.

After this fire, an engine was given to the town (the firſt they ever poſſeſſed) by the lady NOEL. There are now four, which are kept in tolerable order. It were to be wiſhed, however, that they were more frequently examined into, ſo as to be always ready for immediate uſe.

In 1766 a fiery meteor and a large fire-ball were obſerved at Hinckley by Mr. Robinſon ; phænomena not unuſually thought worthy of being recorded in the Philoſophical Tranſactions, and which therefore the reader will not be diſpleaſed to ſee deſcribed in the words of the ingenious obſerver :

" October 26, 1766, at half paſt five in the evening, after a " violent ſtorm of wind and rain, being in the open air, I obſerved " a fiery meteor. Its direction was from North Weſt to South " Eaſt, nearly in a horizontal direction ; it paſſed very near to " me, and was of an elliptical form ; its motion about 40 degrees " in two or three ſeconds of time. It was very bright and lucid " to appearance, like the paleſt lightning ; and emitted ſparks

M " continually'

" continually, which formed a kind of tail towards the North
" Weft, which feemed to be extinguifhed at the diftance of two
" or three degrees from the body; there was a fmall portion that
" parted from it. The cohefion of matter was fo great, that it
" drew a thread of confiderable length from the body before it
" broke from it. During the paffage there was a kind of hiffing
" noife much like to what we hear from the electrical machine
" when the electric matter is running away, or as when it is efcap-
" ing from a full charged jar.

" December 2, 1766, being in the open air at half paft 10
" o'clock at night, it being clear and fine, except a few fcattering
" dufky clouds near the zenith, there fuddenly appeared a large
" fiery ball proceeding from the clouds before mentioned, with a
" great and glaring light, and brifk but unequal motion. The
" fparks flew from it very copioufly; its direction was towards the
" fouth, being nearly at right angles with the horizon.. This
" fire-ball was fomewhat larger than the fiery meteor mentioned
" above, being to appearance more than half a degree in diame-
" ter *."

A

* " When phænomena of this kind make their appearance in the higher parts of
" the atmofphere, they then make what are generally called *footing* or *falling-ftars*,
" which before the late improvements in electricity were not very intelligible to the
" philofopher.
" That thefe are electrical appearances, I think, Beccaria makes very evident; and
" the fact which he relates as a proof of it is exceeding curious and remarkable.
" He informs us, ' that as he was fitting with a friend in the open air an hour after
" fun-fet, they faw what is called a falling-ftar directing its courfe towards them,
" and apparently growing larger and larger till it difappeared not far from them,
" when it left their faces, hands, and cloaths, with the earth and all the neighbour-
" ing objects, fuddenly illuminated with a diffufed and lambent light, attended with
" no noife at all. While they were ftanding up ftaring and looking at each other,
" furprized at the appearance, a fervant came running to them out of a neighbour-
" ing garden, and afked them if they had feen nothing, for that he had feen a light
" fhine fuddenly in the garden, and efpecially upon the ftreams which he was
" throwing to water it.' What has been faid of thefe appearances in the air, is alfo
" applicable when they appear rolling upon the furface of the earth or water; and
" I fhall relate one, as it bears evident marks of electricity, made by Mr. Chalmers
" when be was on board the Montague, under the command of Admiral Chambers.

" On

A remarkable aurora borealis was obferved by Mr. Robinfon, at Hinckley, on the evening of October 24, 1769. "Thefe illuminations" he fays, "began to fhew themfelves as foon as the evening twilight would permit, their firft appearance being near the horizon. They feemed to proceed from dufky light clouds, as they frequently do, ftreaming upwards towards the zenith; thofe from the weftward, after fome time, began to be tinged with red, and continued alternately to exhibit great varieties of that colour, which fucceeded each other by quick fucceffions, being fometimes of a wan light red, then approaching by degrees to a full dufky red, and fometimes a full blood-colour, and even the colours of pink and light fcarlet were afterwards nearly reprefented. The illuminations from the other quarters of the heavens had nearly their ufual appearance, except from the north-eaft, which were of a remarkable pale bright filver colour for a confiderable time; at near feven o'clock they likewife began to be a little tinged with red, which increafing, and intermitting, at length came to exhibit the fame appearance as thofe in the weft, it being now near half paft feven o'clock; and the different ftreams of light arifing

"On the 4th of November, 1749, in lat. 42° 48' long. 9° 3', he was taking an "obfervation on the quarter-deck, about ten minutes before 12, when one of the "quarter-mafters defired he would look to the windward; upon which he obferved a "large ball of fire with a blue appearance rolling on the furface of the water at or "about three miles diftance from them. They immediately lowered their top-fails, "&c. but it came down upon them fo faft, that before they could raife the main-tack "they obferved the ball to rife almoft perpendicular, and not above forty or fifty "yards from the main chains, when it went off with an explofion, as if hundreds of "cannon had been fired at one time, and left fo great a fmell of brimftone that the "fhip feemed to be nothing but fulphur. After the noife was over, which he be- "lieved did not laft longer than half a fecond, they found their main top-maft fhat- "tered into above a hundred pieces, and the main-maft rent quite down to the heel. "There were fome of the fpikes which nail the fifh of the main-maft drawn with "fuch force out of the maft, and they ftuck fo faft in the main deck, that the car- "penter was obliged to take an iron crow to get them out. There were five men "knocked down, and one of them greatly burnt by the explofion. They believed "that when the ball, which appeared to them to be of the bignefs of a large mill- "ftone, rofe, it took the middle of the main top-maft, as the head of the maft above "the hounds was not fplintered."

from

from moſt parts of the horizon, ſeemed to be in their full ſtrength, directing themſelves towards the zenith, where they formed a corona, or point, which appeared and diſappeared frequently, and was ſometimes partial and broken. This point near the zenith was frequently ſurrounded by a kind of radii, the points of which at this time were tinged of a light red colour; the ſtrongeſt appearance was from ſeven to eight o'clock. It was obſervable that the corona, or point, was not exactly in the zenith; it appeared and diſappeared frequently; but always formed itſelf a few degrees towards the ſouth; nor was it exactly in the meridian, but inclined a little towards the eaſt[*]."

On the 21ſt of September, 1775, a dreadful ſtorm of thunder and lightning, which began about ten in the morning at *Leeds* in *Yorkſhire*[†], after ravaging the intermediate counties, entered

Leiceſter-

[*] "That this is an electrical appearance," Mr. Robinſon thinks, "is evident, from the good repreſentations given at the electrical machine with the aurora borealis tube, &c. It is now ſuppoſed by many modern philoſophers and electricians, with good reaſon, that earthquakes are not owing to ſubterraneous winds, fires, vapours, or any thing that occaſions exploſions, and heaves up the ground (as was formerly ſuppoſed), and the concluſion is ſupported by a variety of circumſtances. The impreſſion made by an earthquake by land and water, to the greateſt diſtances, is obſerved, as far as could be judged, to be inſtantaneous, and only to be effected by electricity, the motion of which is ſo inſtantaneous as hardly to admit of the leaſt ſenſible tranſition of time in its paſſage even to the moſt diſtant parts. It is not upon the principle of any ſubterraneous exploſion that we can in the leaſt account for the manner in which ſhips, far from any land, are affected during an earthquake, which ſeems as if they ſtruck upon a rock, or as if ſomething thumped againſt their bottoms; even the fiſhes are affected by an earthquake; this ſtroke therefore muſt be occaſioned by ſomething that could communicate motion with unſpeakably greater velocity than any heaving of the earth under the ſea, by the elaſticity of generated vapours; this could only produce a gradual ſwell, and could never give an impulſe to the water, ſo as to make it feel like a ſtone."
To illuſtrate the above, Mr. Robinſon has made the following experiment with the electrical machine: place a veſſel of water ſo as to let each extremity of its ſurface communicate with a wire or chain; then let the perſons preſent put their hands, or even a finger into the water; and when an electrical flaſh is paſſed over its ſurface, they feel a ſudden concuſſion given to them, exactly like that which is ſuppoſed to affect ſhips at ſea during an earthquake.
[†] The eldeſt daughter of Mr. Car of Leeds was ſtruck dead in an inſtant, as ſhe ſtood between the fireſide and the window; as was likewiſe a maid ſervant to a
farmer

Leicesterfhire about twelve hours after, and early next morning
fpent its force on the barns and ftables of Mr. *Watfon* of Hinckley,
fituate about 200 yards to the South-Eaft of the church. A particular account of this accident was taken at the time by Mr. Robinfon, and accompanies this narrative.

In

farmer near Topcliff, in the North Riding, much in the fame fituation. Several other
perfons were ftruck dead in the fame ftorm, which extended to a great diftance.
See the Gentleman's Magazine, 1775, p. 496, 498.

* " This ftorm, which was very extenfive, was perceived to be coming on by thofe
in the fields near Hinckley, about ten o'clock in the evening. Few in the town knew
any thing of it; but about midnight moft of the inhabitants were awaked by the loud
peals of thunder. There was likewife at that time a more diftant thunder rolling.
The diftance between the flafh and claps of thunder I obferved to be from four to
feven or eight feconds of time, except a particular one at the diftance of two feconds
nearly, which was a very great clap. I fuppofed it to be between one and two
o'clock in the morning. After fome time, the thunder became more moderate, and
removed to a diftance, and I flept till day-light. In the morning of September 22,
I heard the thunder at a great diftance. At the affembly at Leicefter (it being the
firft race-day, and the day of chufing the mayor), the lightning glared in, to the
great terror of the ladies; and from other parts it was reprefented as very terrible.
The morning after the ftorm Mr. Craven came to me, defiring my company,
with Mr. Robfon and himfelf, to view Mr. Watfon's buildings in the fields (now the
property of Mr. Nicholas Hurft), part of which had been ftruck by the lightning
the preceding night. We examined them in the afternoon. There are two ranges
of buildings nearly of the fame height, the one to the North, the other to the South;
on the Eaft are lower buildings; on the Weft a wall and gates; thefe inclofe the
farm yard. The part ftruck was the Weft gable-end of the South range, from the
ridge to the wall-plate; the tiles were broken all the way down about three feet wide,
and the greater part of them driven off the roof; the wall below the wall-plate was
fplit and fhattered about two feet. On each fide the North-Weft corner to the floor
of the chamber the wall was double brick, i. e. a nine-inch wall; the outfide half
of the wall was divided from the other, and the bricks thrown about. Under this
chamber is the ftable; in the North-Weft corner was a bing about three feet high,
and from it to the cieling a clofet for gears, &c.; the cieling about the top of this
clofet was burft, and a fmall ftream of the lightning had run along a row of lath-
nail heads, and fplit the plaiftering from the lath about four feet, and loofened and
left it hollow much farther; but the greater part burft the cieling, and ftruck the
upper joint of the clofet door, burnt the wood black, fplit off the door, and made its
way to the gears, which were thrown down, and a little melted in feveral places; one
place in particular was as if that part of the chain was in fufion, and fomething
about the bignefs of a quill had been preffed in a little way; round this hole the
fufed metal had formed a fmooth regular collar of the melted iron, as though iron;
a hand-faw in the fame place it had touched, and melted a little fuperficially. The
bing

In 1781 the lands and houses throughout the parish of Hinckley were new qualitied ; and the parochial levies proportionably ad-
justed.

On

binn under this closet was of brick, with a wooden cover, which was scorched, and
the brick-work cracked perpendicularly in two places. The horses were in the
stable ; and one of them, a bay one (whose place in the stable was next the closet),
had his tail singed on that side next the closet. This was not perceived till the horse
was brought to Mr. Watson's house, where I saw it. The horse being very gentle, I
examined him, and found that the strong long hairs of the tail, especially those on
the outside, were singed off; the stumps of hair as to colour and form much the same
as in common singing; also upon the thigh on that side it had touched several places,
and raised the hair; they were about an inch in diameter, but did not appear singed.
Upon applying the hand, they were hot and feverish, compared with other parts
of the body, much like a burn or a scald. Mr. Watson soon after sent a mason to
repair the damage in the building; and at the same time sent to let me know that, if
I pleased, I might examine again before they made any alteration. I went accordingly. We had before been much crowded with people, but were now quite free ;
and the mason's ladders gave a good opportunity. The top side of the wall-plate
was burnt black ; and as masons, especially in out-buildings, when they build double
brick walls, generally perform the work by building two single walls and joining them
together in a few places with a brick laid across, so that in the middle of these walls
there is often a cavity ; upon examination, the lightning appeared to have passed
through this cavity, and so burst out the outer wall; the marks of it were very evident on the bricks of the inner wall, especially about the corner, where they appeared of a rusty ash colour; also the outer wall on either side was sprung and left
hollow, and some of the tying bricks broken, especially on the West. Being desirous
to know how it came to the closet, the mason taking off the loose bricks to begin his
work, we found that it passed directly through the wall, especially through a cavity
by a joist, and at several of the open joints in the inner wall. We then went into
the chamber, to examine the inside, where lay a quantity of wheat straw in bottles,
which we removed, but saw no appearance of it there. We then took up a board
in the floor over the closet, and found that it entered between the boards of the floor
and the cieling; it had scorched the underside of the board we took up, and the bricks
where the principal part of it passed were melted on the outside, and turned of a
dark grey and blackish, like the bricks that run in the kiln ; some of these I brought
home with me, and they are worth viewing with a magnifying power, their surface
being melted, and by the vitrification changed into glass of a dark and greyish
colour. The part of the cloud that the lightning descended from was, I suppose,
very low; or probably it might have directed itself to other objects. In this situation,
being within striking distance, it passed down the roof of the building; and, by the
stroke and velocity, broke the tiling: being more collected at its passing into the
cavity of the wall, it is not at all strange that it burnt the wall-plate black ; the cavity of the wall being small, the impetuosity of the lightning split or burst out the
outer

On the 7th of February, 1782, a petition was prefented to the Houfe of Commons, fetting forth, " that, by a furvey lately made, " it

outer part of the wall. Had it made its way through the chamber to the clofet, it would moft probably have fet the ftraw in a blaze, and have hurnt the building. If there had been no gears or other good conduflor in the clofet, a chain or wire of a proper fize might have carried the lightning in an horizontal direction in the fame manner it paffed the lath-nail heads, and have conveyed it fafely out of the room, efpecially if the lower end communicated with water or moift earth. This is a common experiment in electricity. But, finding the lath-nail heads but a weak conductor, and having communication with the chains in the clofet, it returned back to the beft and ftrongeft conduftor in its defcent to the earth. By this defcription it is eafy to conceive, efpecially to thofe a little verfed in electricity, that, by a proper apparatus, the whole of the lightning might have been fafely conducted to the earth without doing any damage. As to the very particular clap of thunder heard by many perfons when it was fuppofed the building was ftruck, thofe in the Caftle-ftreet in general agree that it immediately followed the flafh, or if there was any fpace of time it was very little. As to feconds or parts of feconds, no one could give a very exact account except Mr. Robfon, who faid it was about half a fecond; and I have already obferved that I myfelf heard the fame at the diftance of nearly two feconds. From thefe data (according to Dr. Derham, who, from better inftruments and advantages than many others, Phil. Tranf. N° 313, concludes the velocity of found to be fuch, that it moves ordinarily 1142 feet in a fecond of time), the diftance of the building or thunder-cloud from my houfe is 2284 feet, or 761 yards, which I fuppofe is very near the true diftance : by Mr. Robfon's obfervation, he was at a quarter of this diftance. And here it may be ufeful to give fome account of the elementary fire or lightning, as it may be applicable to the ftorm juft recited as well as to what may follow, efpecially as of late years fuch ample difcoveries have been made by electrical experiments, that we find it an univerfal agent appointed by the great Creator in almoft every phænomenon of nature. It is therefore an opinion of modern philofophers, that falling ftars, lightning, *aurora boreales*, fire balls and other meteors, hurricanes, whirlwinds, water-fpouts, &c. and even earthquakes, are fuppofed to be effects of this grand agent the electrical fire. That water-fpouts have an electrical origin, I think, may be concluded from feveral circumftances. They are generally faid to appear in months fubject to thunder-ftorms, and commonly in calm weather. The fea feems to boil, and fend up a fmoke under them, rifing in a hill towards the fpout. Perfons who have been near them have heard a rumbling noife. The form of a water-fpout is that of a fpeaking trumpet, the wider end being in the cloud, and the narrower end towards the fea. Their fize is various; in the fame fpout the colour is fometimes inclining to white, and fometimes to black, whitcifh, or yellowifh. Flafhes of light have fometimes been feen moving about them with prodigious fwiftnefs. Their pofition is fometimes perpendicular to the fea, and fometimes in the form of a curve. Their continuance is very variable, fometimes difappearing as foon as formed, and fometimes continuing a confiderable time. That electricity has a very great influence on water, appears very evident; for water that but juft drops from a fmall hole, upon being electrified, fuddenly fpouts out with great velocity. Another thing in favour

" it appears that a canal for the navigation of boats and other vef-
" fels may be conveniently made, from or near a place called Griff,
" in the parifh of Chilvers Coton, in the county of Warwick,
" through the parifhes of Buckington, Wolvey, and Burton Haf-
" tings, in the faid county of Warwick, and through the parifhes
" of *Burbach, Hinckley, Higham, Stoke Golding, Dadlington, Sutton*
" *Cheney, Shenton, Market Bofworth,* Carlton, Congerfton, Shack-
" erftone, and Snarefton, in the county of Leicefter, and through
" the parifh of Meafham, and the lordfhips of Oakthorpe and De-
" nifthorpe, in the county of Derby, to Woodlands Farm, on Afh-
" by Woulds, in the faid county of Leicefter, whereby a fafe and
" eafy communication will be opened with the coal mines at
" Meafham, Oakthorpe, and Afhby Woulds, and with the
" towns and villages adjacent to the faid intended canal, and alfo
" with the Oxford and Coventry canals ; and that the whole courfe
" of the faid intended canal lies open upon a dead level, fo that
" there will not be occafion for any lock to be made thereupon,
" unlefs it be one to regulate the water ; and that the want of
" coal for fuel, and lime for the manure of land, is feverely felt
" by the inhabitants who refide in and about feveral parts of the
" counties of Leicefter, Warwick, Northampton, Buckingham,
" and Oxford ; and, by the making of fuch navigable canal, the

favour of electricity is, that they have fometimes been difperfed by prefenting to
them fharp-pointed knives and fwords; this at leaft is the common practice of mariners
in many parts of the world. It is very probable, that what water-fpouts are at fea,
the fame are fome kinds of whirlwinds and hurricanes by land; for they have fometimes been known to tear up trees by the roots, to throw down buildings, and to fcatter
the materials in every direction, and many times attended with a prodigious rumbling
noife. We have fometimes in the fummer months whirlwinds in our harveft fields,
very fimilar to the water-fpouts; for they generally happen in calm weather, and
fometimes whirl up the hay and other light bodies in the form of a fpiral to a confiderable height in the air; and thefe, like the water-fpouts, are generally of fhort
continuance, and commonly attended with a murmuring noife. Thefe, as to their
effects with us, are generally very mild and moderate. In fome parts of the world
whirlwinds and hurricanes are moft terrible. Dreadful have been thofe of late in
the Weft India iflands, which are fubject to them from the climate; from which
Great Britain and moft other parts of the world are happily exempt."

3   " con-

" conveyance of coal and lime, and alſo of divers goods, wares,
" and merchandizes, as well to the Coventry and Oxford canals,
" as to the towns and villages adjacent thereto, in the ſeveral
" counties aforeſaid, will be greatly facilitated, and the ſame will
" be of public utility."

A bill was ordered to be brought into parliament for this purpoſe, which is now depending [*April* 18, 1782] and in its con-
ſequences may be highly beneficial to the pariſh of Hinckley.

Hinckley is celebrated for good ale; and by the following old
verſe we may ſuppoſe that formerly it was no leſs famous :

> *Higham* on the hill,
> *Stoke* in the dale,
> *Wykin* for butter-milk,
> *Hinckley* for ale.

Thus modernized by a friend :

> From *Higham* looking down we view
> *Stoke* in the vale below ;
> And *Wykin* claims the milking pail,
> As plenteous dairies ſhew ;
> *Hinckley* diſtils the malted grain,
> Whence health and vigour flow.

I ſhall conclude this ſection of my Hiſtory by obſerving, in the
words of Mr. Robinſon, " that it may be ſaid of Hinckley, as
" of other improved places, as learning advances, ridiculous
" credulity retires. Superſtitious tales and traditionary legends
" loſe credit daily, and wear away very faſt. The inhabitants in
" general are an induſtrious ſett of people, and of much more po-
" lite and gentle addreſs than formerly."

STOKE,

S T O K E,

NOW commonly called *Stoke Golding, Goldenbam,* or *Golding-
ton*[a], and mentioned in a subsidy roll of the year 1505 under the name of *Stoke Manfield,* is one of the townships which pay
suit and service to the court at Hinckley. The history of this town,
any further than as included in that of Hinckley, is comprised in
Burton's account of its early lords, which shall therefore be transcribed: "The moiety or one half of this manor was the ancient inheritance of *Rafe* Lord *Baffet* of *Sapcoate* in the time of King *Edward*
the first, who held the same of *John* Lord *Haftings* (whose issue
was after Earl of *Pembroke*) as of his manor of *Dadlington.* From
Dadl.... (by an heir general) it came to *Moton,* and in like manner from *Moton* to *Harington,* all which did appear for the said
land at the Court Baron of the said manor of *Dadlington,* and
performed their suits and services for the same; as is apparent
and to be proved by divers ancient Court Rolls belonging to
the said manor; and also by Inquisitions and Records. The other
moiety, or one half of this manor, was belonging to the family of
Champaine, whose heir general was married to [Edmund Boug;
by whose daughter and heir it came to] *Turvile*† ; from *Turvile*
(by alienation made) it came to *Harington.* Sir *John Harington,*
after Lord *Harington* of *Burley* in the County of *Rutland,* was
seised of the whole, and (not many years since) sold it to the tenants ;" the families, probably, of *Firebrace, Trymnell,* and *Brokesby.*

* Compare the pedigrees of Champagne and Turvile in Burton's Leicestershire.
    † There is a *Stokerston,* in old records called *Stokerften,* in the hundred of Gar-
tree in this county; where, by licenfe of Edward IV, " Tefte Rege apud Staunford,
" XXII die Januarii, MCCCCLXV," an hofpital was founded by *John de Heivile,* for a
chaplain and three alms-men to pray for his foul for ever; who were made a body
corporate, had a common feal granted them, and were empowered to purchase lands
to the amount of ten pounds a year. I mention this particular (as it is unnoticed by
Burton) from Peck's Monafticon Anglicanum, MS. in the British Mufeum, and Tanner's Notitia Monaftica, p. 247.

3   The

The whole lordſhip is now the property of *William Hurſt*, Eſq. by whom it was purchaſed in 1772.

In the matriculus of 1220, Stoke is deſcribed as part of the pariſh of Hinckley, having a free chapel, with a reſident chaplain who had power to adminiſter ſacraments, and paying 3 s. 6 d. ſynodals in the manner of the mother church.

The chapel was pulled down very early in the fourteenth cen-tury by Sir Robert de Champaine, who, having married the daughter and heirefs of Sir Roger de Stoke, became poſſeſſed of a moiety of the manor. By this gentleman the church which ſtill remains was founded * in or about the year 1304, and dedicated, in honour of his lady, to St. *Margaret*. The following memorial I tranſcribed in September 1781 from a ſtone ſtill remaining againſt the wall in the North aiſle of the church:

ROBERT¹ DE
CAMPANIA
MIL¹ ET MARGARE-
TA VXOR EIVS
FILIA ROGERI
DE STOKE MILI-
TIS FVNDAVE-
RV̄T HANC EC-
CLESIÃ IN HO-
NORE S. MARG-
ARETE VIRGI-
NIS TEMP'E ED. I.

From this period Stoke is to be confidered as a ſeparate pariſh, though the rectory has been conſtantly annexed to the vicar-age of Hinckley. That it is however perfectly diſtinct as to parochial rates was determined by a cauſe tried regularly at the Lent aſſizes for the county in 1627, and confirmed the ſame year by a ſolemn determination of the court of King's-bench.

The circumſtance is thus related in an old MS. belonging to Mr. Hurſt: " There was lately a controverfy between Hinckley

* The like was performed by Sir Thomas Welch in the reign of Richard II. for *Wanlip*; who, of a chapel, made it a parochial church, building a new fabrick from the ground. *Peckleton* was in 1220 a chapel belonging to Kirkby Malory, but was made a pariſh church in 1349. So *Angodeſthorpe*, which 5 Hen. III. was a chapel belonging to Whittick, is now a pariſh church; and others might be pointed out.

N 2   " and

" and Stoake.   Hinckley-men contended to have Stoake to be a
" hamlet or member of Hinckley, and like only a chapelry, and
" within their parish.   But at Lent affizes in the fecond year of
" King Charles, upon good evidence fhewn, a fpecial verdict was
" given by the jury with Stoake, who found it to be no member or
" hamlet of Hinckley, and to be an abfolute parifh of itfelf. Upon
" which, judgement was given accordingly⁹."

* This cafe is reported by Sir *Richard Hatton*, in his Reports, 1656, fol. 93.
Hilton verfus *Paule*.   Hil. 2 Car. Rot. 565.   " Richard Hilton brought an action
" of trefpafs againft Robert Paule, for the taking of a faddle at Stoke Goldenham;
" and upon Not Guilty pleaded, the Jury gave a Special Verdict, viz. ' That the
" parifh of *Hinkley* was *de temp. dent memorie &c.* and yet is an ancient Rectory and
" a Church Parochial ; and that the town of *Stoke Goldenham* is an ancient town,
" and parcel of the Rectory of Hinckley ; and that from the time of Henry the Sixth,
" and afterwards until this time, there hath been, and is, in the town of Stoke Gol-
" denham, a Church, which by all the faid time hath been ufed and reported as a
" parifh ; and that the inhabitants of Stoke Goldenham by all the faid time had had
" all parochial rights, and churchwardens; and that the town of Stoke Goldenham
" is diftant two miles from Hinkley.' And the verdict concluded, ' If it fhould feem
" to them that Stoke Goldenham is a parifh for relief of poor, within the ftatute of
" 43 Eliz. cap. 2. then they find for the Plaintiff; if not, for the Defendant'.——
" And this cafe was argued by Serjeant Buckley; and he vouched Linwood, fol.
" 89; and faid, that there is *Ecclefia major & minor*, and a dependant church upon
" the principal and another church, and which is found to be ufed and reputed :
" *ergo* it is not a Parifh ; and that the exception of the Chapel of Fownes, which
" by the ftatute is made a Parifh, proves that Chapel and Parifh are not within the
" ftatute.   He vouched 4 Edward IV. 39. and 5 Edward IV. to prove that divers
" Towns may be in a Parifh.   And the Lord Richardfon faid, that it is a clear cafe
" that this is a Parifh, within the intent of the ftatute of 43 Eliz. for the relief of the
" poor ; and that the Churchwardens and Overfeers of Stoke Goldenham might
" affefs for the relief of the poor.   And though it be found that, after the time of
" Henry the Sixth, and until now, it had been ufed as a Parifh Church, that doth
" not exclude that it was not ufed fo before.   And a reputative Chantry is within
" the ftatute of Chantries, 1 Edward VI. And this ftatute being made for the relief
" of the poor, and that they might not wander, therefore the intent of the ftatute is
" to eafe the relief to parifhes then *in effe*, and fo ufed.   And every one of the
" Court delivered their opinion, and concurred ; and fo judgement was given for the
" Plaintiff."

The

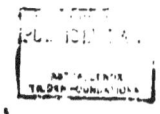

The Church

hath at the Weft end a good fpire fteeple, 30 yards high, fupported by ftrong abutments, and containing four bells.   The top of this fteeple is faid by Burton to have been fhaken down by an earth-quake* in 1580.   The fouth fide of the church has been by the architect finely ornamented in the windows and on the roof, which gives it a pleafing and folemn appearance ; but if it had been raifed higher, it would have been more majeftic. Compared with the fteeple, and the ground it ftands upon, it is rather low, but yet makes a good appearance, as the reader may judge by the fketch of it from the pencil of Mr. Robinfon, which accompanies this Hiftory. [See plate IX.]   The view of the chan-cel from the Eaft bears the character of gravity and veneration ; on the North it is finifhed in a plainer manner, and fupported by ftrong abutments of good ftone and mortar, which appear har-dened by ftanding in the air ; at leaft the corroding hand of Time has made but little impreffion on them in almoft five centuries.

The infide confifts of two ailes, one of them confiderably widened near the chancel ; and in 1619 contained the following arms (delineated in plate V. fig. 5—12. from a book in the College of Arms communicated, 1782, by J. C. Brooke, Efq. Somerfet Herald) :

Gules, three lions paffant, guardant, Or, a label of France. *Earls of Lancafter.*

Gules, a lion rampant, Arg.   *Mowbray* †.

Or, a frett Sable, *Champaine* ; the founder of the church.

Or, on a fefs Gules. 3 plates.   *Cokvile.*

Gules, a fefs dancette between 10 crofslets Or. *Engaine.*

---

* In 1571 there had been a remarkable earthquake at Marcle-hill in Hereford-fhire ; and in 1575 part of Ruthin Caftle in Derbyfhire was fhaken down by a fimilar calamity.

† The Mowbrays had large eftates in Leicefterfhire, by marriage with the heirefs of the baron Segrave.

Argent,

Argent, 2 bars, and a canton Gules. *Boyes.*
Argent, a plain Crofs, Gules. *St. George.*
Or, a fefs Azure, from which a Lion naifant, Gules.

There now remain (1782) feveral fragments of old painted glafs ; the moft perfect of which are two fmall heads of Apoftles. There is alfo an octagon font, with rude figures on feven of the fides, expreffive of the feven deadly fins, but almoft obliterated ; and an old dial, dated 1620, from which the hand has long been broken off.

The town cheft, preferved in the church, is marked
" Stocke Cheft,
w. b. c.   1636.   w. t. o.
The king's arms were new painted in 1775, John Prinfep churchwarden.

The prefent rector of Stoke is the Rev. Mr. Gallaway, vicar of Hinckley ; his curate, the Rev. Mr. Brown.

Of the epitaphs, which are not numerous, the principal ones are here tranfcribed :

1. In the South Eaft corner of the church (where it is highly probable that there was formerly a chantry) on a very fmall, but neat, brafs efcutcheon, ornamented with the arms engraved in plate V. fig 3.

" In piam memoriam
FRANCISCI BROKESBY, vici hujus gen.
Qui licet
Profapiâ ortus honeftâ,
Uxore felix unicâ,
Prole lætus pulchrâ,
Vicinis gratus, viciffim amatus ;
Aliam tamen,
Sperandi præpofuit fortem,
Spirandi adhibuit normam,
Refpirandi contigit metam,

Gratiam

Gratiam in terris, gloriam in cœlis.

Pofuere

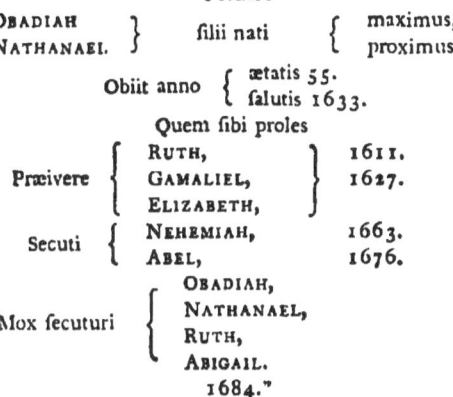

OBADIAH } filii nati { maximus,
NATHANAEL. } { proximus.

Obiit anno { ætatis 55.
{ falutis 1633.

Quem fibi proles

Præivere { RUTH, } 1611.
{ GAMALIEL, } 1627.
{ ELIZABETH, }

Secuti { NEHEMIAH, 1663.
{ ABEL, 1676.

Mox fecuturi { OBADIAH,
{ NATHANAEL,
{ RUTH,
{ ABIGAIL.
1684."

2. On a moft elegant monument of white marble, on the South fide of the altar, is the following infcription (effaced by time, but preferved in the "Baronettage, 1741," vol. IV. p. 76.)

"Hic juxta fitus eft
HENRICUS FIREBRACE, Miles,
Vir ortu vitâque fplendidus,
Pervetuftâ a Normannis ufque familiâ,
Fide ad pofteros memorabili;
Quam Carolo I°. per res fuas difficillimas,
Non gratam magis quam utilem præftitit,
Cum a Cubiculo Regis fub cuftodiâ habiti nufquam difcederit;
Nifi ad procuranda ipfi negotia, quæ varia
Domi forifque tam publica quam privata
Capitis cum difcrimine expedivit;

Stu-

Studioque in eum tam conftanti quam fortuna odio,
Ad extremum malorum & vitæ terminum perduravit.
Prævalentibus deinde Rebellium armis & conftitutâ Tyrannide,
Ruri fe continuit feré in hoc viculo,
Donec Deo communibus omnium votis favente
Defideratiffimus rediret in patriam Carolus :
Tum in hofpitio Regio munera obivit
Sine periculo honorifica,
Ubi domefticis rebus adminiftrandis præfuit,
Inter principales de Tapete Viridi (ut vocant) Officiarios,
Faciliori jam Fortunâ ufus, pari diligentiâ
Triginta propé annos vixit in Curiâ ;
Innocentiffimis moribus fuâque integritate,
Carolo & Jacobo auguftis fratribus femper carus,
Quorum altero naturæ cedente, Fortunâ altero
Amifsâ tum demûm Aulâ ut fervaret Fidem,
Cum in hunc notum fibi receffum & antiquum perfugium reveniffet,
Non ita diu poft vitam cum morte commutavit
Die 27 Januarii, 1690, anno ætatis fuæ 72°."

Of this faithful fervant to his prince, I fhall collect fome parti-
ticulars from the Baronettage before cited, and other fources ;
which the reader will find among the anecdotes of eminent men
who were natives of, or connected with, Hinckley.

3. " Here lies the body of WILLIAM TRYMNELL of this town,
gent. whofe loyalty and courage were very memorable during the
late unhappy wars. He ferved king Charles I. in the quality of
captain of horfe; and in feveral gallant and dangerous expeditions
fignalized himfelf. His other more private virtues, his integrity,
candour, humility, and eafinefs of converfation, made him juftly
beloved of all while living, and lamented when dead. He departed this life in the year of our Lord 1693, of his age 67."

4. " Here

4. " Here lies interred
JOHN BLACKWALL, gentleman,
REBECCA his wife,
ELIZABETH their daughter,
and ANNE OSBORNE, fifter to the faid REBECCA.
JOHN BLACKWALL was the fon
of the Rev. ANTHONY BLACKWALL [*], M. A.
late mafter of the Grammar-fchool
in Market Bofworth in this county.
He died the 5th of July, 1763,
in the 56th year of his age.
REBECCA BLACKWALL and ANNE OSBORNE
were the daughters of the Rev. JAMES OSBORNE, M. A.
late vicar of Leek in the county of Stafford.
The former died the 25th of Auguft, 1763,
in the 54th year of her age ;
The latter died the 4th of October, 1763,
in the 53d year of her age.
ELIZABETH BLACKWALL died the 14th of May, 1760,
in the 17th year of her age."

There are a few other flat ftones, for the families of WYAT,
TRYMNELL, WRIGLEY, JOHNSON, SAUNDERS, KING, MOULTON,
and BENSKIN.
In the church-yard are none worth copying.

[*] Author of " An Introduction to the Claffics," &c. and of " The Sacred Claf-
" fics defended and illuftrated," &c.   A more particular account of him will be
given in the lift of eminent men at the end of this little volume.

DADLINGTON

CONTINUES, as it was defcribed in 1220, to be a hamlet containing a chapel dependent on the town of Hinckley.   In the
collection of parochial rates, however, it is, like Stoke, diftinct.

The manor, as appears from *Burton* [*], who was himfelf lord of
it, was anciently the inheritance of *William de Haftings*, lord fteward
of the houfhold to king Henry the fecond, from whom lineally
defcended Henry Haftings, created baron Abergavenny in right of
Joane his wife, daughter and heir of William de Cantelupe lord
Abergavenny, from whom defcended lineally Lawrence created
earl of Pembroke; whofe grandchild John earl of Pembroke dying
without iffue, all his lands, manors, and tenements defcended and
came to Reginald lord Grey of Ruthin, as coufin and next heir to
the faid John earl of Pembroke by Elizabeth grandmother of the
faid Reginald, who was daughter of John Haftings lord Abergavenny, and great great aunt to the laft John earl of Pembroke :
Philip the widow of this laft John earl of Pembroke was married
to Richard earl of Arundel, and was endowed with part of this
manor.   Thefe lord Haftings (long before the ftatute of *Quia em-
ptores terrarum*,made the 13th of Edw.I.) gave certain lands within
the faid manor to divers perfons, to be held of the faid manor by
feveral tenures.   The abovenamed Reginald lord Grey of Ruthin
gave this manor, with the manor of Barwell and other lands in
the county of Leicefter, to Sir John Grey his younger fon.   John
Grey of Barwell, Efq. defcended lineally from the faid Sir John
Grey, in the reign of queen Elizabeth fold this manor with the
court leet thereto belonging to my father Rafe Burton of Lindley,

* Of whom, and his brother, an account will be hereafter given.

Efq.

Efq. and it is now the inheritance of me William Burton fon and heir of him the faid Rafe Burton."

Mr. Hurſt has in his poſſeſſion the court rolls from 1272; and a curious MS. drawn up by Burton, under the title of " Antiqui- " tates de Dadlington manerio com. Leic. five Exemplificatio Scrip- " torum, Cartarum veterum, Inquiſitionum, Rotulorum Curiarum, " Recordorum, 8: Evidentium probantium Antiquitates dicti ma- " nerii de Dadlington, & hæreditatem de Burton in dicto manerio " de Dadlington, quæ nunc funt penes me Will'mum Burton de " Lindley com. Leic. modernum dominum dicti manerii de Dad- " lington. Labore & ſtudio mei Will'mi Burton de Lindley, " Apprenticii Legum Angliæ, & Socii Interioris Templi Londini : " nuper habitantis apud Falde com. Staff. nunc apud Lindley, " 25 Aug. 1625, æt. 50."

John of Bolingbroke occurs in this MS. (temp. 18 Ed. II.) as Eſchaetor domini regis. After that time, the *Greys* appear to have been lords till 1585, when it was purchaſed by the *Burtons*. Mr. *William Cox* was owner in 1659; *Joſhua Grundy*, Eſq. in 1742; and in 1772 it came to *William Hurſt*, Eſq. and *Nicholas Hurſt*, Gent. the preſent owners.

It appears from Burton's MS. that the manors of *Higham* and *Dadlington* were united under one lord; and in all the court rolls, from the reign of Edward the Second to the preſent time, the in- quiſitions, &c. have been taken for the manors of Dadlington and Higham; and by an antient roll we learn that the inhabitants of Higham were fined at Dadlington court, for not providing bows and arrows.

Dadlington is ſituated on riſing ground, in a good and health- ful air, about one mile from Stoke, in the road to Boſworth, near the ground where the memorable and deciſive battle was fought between the houſes of York and Lancaſter *.

In

---

* The account already given of this remarkable event in Engliſh Hiſtory may be illuſtrated by the following ſhort narrative of facts : Richmond, landing at Milford
O 2   Haven,

In the field still known by the name of " Crown-hill," whence

Haven, passed through Haverford West; and, crossing the Severn, came to Shrewsbury, and thence through Litchfield to Tamworth, where his army arrived late in the evening; but he himself, following in the rear with about twenty horsemen, missed his road, and passed the night solitarily at a little village three miles distant.   Early on the 25th, after shewing himself at Tamworth to his army, he had an interview with his father-in-law lord Stanley at Atherstone, when measures were concerted for the operations of the next day: and in the evening he was joined by Sir John Savage, Sir Bryan Sanford, Sir Simon Digby, and many other experienced warriors.   Richard, meantime, despising the supposed weakness of his adversary, yet desiring effectually to crush him, led his army in great regal state from Nottingham castle to Leicester, through which town he passed in open pomp, the crown-royal on his head, on Sunday evening, and thence came to a hill called *Arme Beame*, in the parish of Bosworth, where " he pitched his field, refreshed his soldiers, and took his rest."   The next morning early, bringing all his men out of the camp into the plain, he ordered both horsemen and footmen to be drawn up in a length of line, that their numbers might appear as large as possible.   The archers were placed in the front, under the command of the duke of Norfolk and his son the earl of Surrey.   This long vanguard was followed by Richard himself with a chosen band, supported on each side with wings of horsemen.   The whole number exceeded 16,000.

The army of Richmond, which amounted not to 5000, was proportionally arranged by their gallant leader.   The archers, in a narrow front, were led by the earl of Oxford; the right wing was entrusted to Sir Gilbert Talbot, the left to Sir John Savage. Richmond himself reserved a good company of horse, and a small number of foot.

On each side the leader addressed his troops with a spirited oration; " which was " scarcely finished," says an old historian, " but the one army espied the other. Lord! " how hastily the soldiers buckled their helms, how quickly the archers bent their " bows, and brushed their feathers, how readily the billmen shook.their bills and " proved their staves, ready to approach and join when the terrible trumpet should " sound the bloody blast to victory or death ! Between both armies there was a great " morafs, which the earl of Richmond left on his right hand for this intent that it " should be on that side a defence for his part, and in so doing he had the sun at his " back, and in the faces of his enemies."   The first conflict of the archers being over, the armies met fiercely with swords and bills; and at this period the Earl was joined by lord Stanley, which determined the fortune of the day.   In this battle above a thousand persons were slain on the side of Richard; and amongst them the duke of Norfolk, the lord Ferrars of Chartley, Sir Richard Ratelyffe, and Sir Robert Brackenbury lieutenant of the Tower.   Of Richmond's army scarcely one hundred were slain, among whom the principal person was Sir William Brandon his standard-bearer.   The victor was crowned in the field by Sir William Stanley, with a crown of ornament which Richard wore in the battle, and which was found among the spoils.   The battle, which lasted little more than two hours, was fought on the 22d of August, 1525; and hence, by the way, may be pointed out a palpable mistake in Cibber's additions to Shakspeare's tragedy, where Richard in the eve of the battle smells " the ripe harvest of the new-mown hay."

4

gravel

gravel is fometimes fetched to repair the highways, Mr. Robinfon informs me, there have been dug up many human fkeletons,
which are faid to be very common on breaking frefh ground.
From this fpot is a fine and extenfive view along the vale towards
Bofworth, being the celebrated ground commonly called King
Richard's Field. A tradition remains, that the crown was fe-
creted on this hill or fpot, which is but juft without the town.

The foil at Dadlington is of a gravelly mixed nature, and is
fruitful in corn and grafs, and excellent for orchard fruit, efpecially for the nonpareil, and others of a choice kind. The *ab-
fintbium* or wormwood grows here fpontaneoufly in great plenty.
That fcarce and tender bird the nightingale is here more common than in any other parts of the country, and frequently in
the fummer feafon ferenades the benighted traveller.

The CHAPEL

is appropriated to the dean and chapter of Weftminfter, who allow
20l. a year to the minifter (payable by the leffee of their glebe)
for ferving this cure. The prefent chaplain is the Rev. Mr.
Gallaway, vicar of Hinckley; his curate the Rev. Mr. Brown.

In 1622 the following arms remained in this chapel:

Or, a maunch Gules.   *Haftings.*

Barry of 6, Arg. & Az. 3 torteauxes in chief, quartered with
  Haftings and *Valence.*   *Grey.*

Quar- ⌠ Azure, femé d' Eftoiles a crefcent Arg. ⌡ *Burton*.
terly ⌡ Azure, a fefs between 2 talbots heads erafed Or. ⌠

The chapel bears evident marks of great antiquity; and, by
fome late repairs, makes a decent appearance. It has a fmall
wooden turret with two bells. There was within memory a
large old door on the North fide, now ftopped up. Part of the

* See plate V. fig. 13.

arch

arch remains, filled up with modern brick-work.   But a better
idea of it may be taken from the South-west view of it in plate
X. which my readers owe to the kindness of Mr. Robinson.

In the inside is a very old town chest, without date.

The Lord's Prayer, &c. were new painted in 1773; Thomas
Eames churchwarden.

There are the remains of an old monument of the *Cottons*, but
not one letter legible.   The arms (viz. Azure on a Chevron Arg.
3 Katharine wheels Gules, see plate V. fig. 14.) are barely difcernible on an old pane of painted glass.

Within the chapel there is not one monumental inscription;
and in the burying-ground which surrounds it there are but few,
amongst which the family of BALLARD is most conspicuous.
The following epitaph is remarkable only for its simplicity:

" Here lieth interred the late THOMAS BALLARD of Drayton, who
departed this life the 16th of October, 1765, in the 84th year of
his age.

> I lov'd my honour'd parents dear,
> I lov'd my wife and children dear,
> I lov'd my brothers and sisters too,
> And hope in Heaven to meet them there;
> I lov'd my uncles, aunts, and cousins too,
> I pray to God to give my children grace the same to do."

" ELIZABETH BALLARD, late wife of Thomas, died Sept. 28,
1761, aged 77."

There are also monuments to three of their children; and one
in memory of

" JOHN EVERARD, who died Jan. 3, 1726, aged 40."

WYKIN

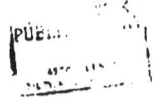

W   Y   K   I   N

IS a fmall hamlet or village (as the name implies) in the
parifh of Hinckley, where formerly ftood a chapel, which,
fo far back as 1622, had been " long fince decayed and gone."
It was a very fmall edifice, in which fervice was performed only
once a year; and its revenues were originally appropriated to the
maintenance of two monks refiding at Hinckley, to fupport the
parochial minifter, and to uphold hofpitality. It is now entirely
incorporated with the mother parifh, and pays a proportionable
fhare in all levies.

The manor of Wykin was granted by Robert Boffu earl of
Leicefter to the monaftery of Nuneaton in Warwickfhire, which
was founded by Amicia his wife, daughter of the earl of Montfort. Priorefs *Ouldton*, Sept. 5, 1540, furrendered up the whole
monaftery of Nuneaton, together with Wykin, and all other lands
and tenements thereto belonging, to K. Henry VIII. who, on the
firft day of May, 1544, granted the manor of Wykin to *Edward*
lord *Clinton and Saye*, and to Sir *Robert Terwbit*, knight, and to
their heirs, to be held *in capite*, by the hundredth part of a
knight's fee. By them it was fold, on the 10th of May following,
to *William Wightman*, whofe heir continued to hold it in 1622.
The lordfhip and by much the greater part of the land are now
the property of *William Burleton*, efq; LL. D. recorder of Leicefter.
The Rev. Mr. *Hunt* and *John Simpfon*, efq; have alfo eftates in
this hamlet. A South-eaft view of Wykin-Hall is engraved in
plate X. from a drawing of Mr. Robinfon.

* The fame, probably, whofe effigies and epitaph were placed in Hinckley church.
See p. 38 ; and fee the arms in plate VII. fig. 5.—Of this family was one Wightman ·
of Burton upon Trent, a notorious heretick, who publifhed himfelf to be the Holy
Ghoft, holding " that the Holy Ghoft was different from God, and that he was a
" creature." He was convened before divers grave and learned men ; but, refo-
lutely perfifting in his herefy, was burnt at Litchfield about 1610.

THE

THE HYDE.

THIS little hamlet, though fituated in the county of Warwick, is part of the parifh of Hinckley.

"It is now," fays Sir William Dugdale[*], "a depopulated place;
but had anciently a chapel † appertaining to *Hinckley* in *Leicefter-
ſhire*, whereof (doubtlefs) it was not long fince a member, in regard it appears to be of the fee of Winchefter by *Quincy* earl of
Winchefter's intereft in the honour of *Leicefter*. As for the fig-
nification of the names, I fhall refer you to the Gloffary of the
learned Sir H. Spelman, where may be feen the various accep-
tations thereof; conceiving that in this place it was firft impofed
to exprefs a certain quantity of land fufficient for one plough to
manage. But the firft mention that I have met with of it is in
3 Joh. where *Will. Marefchall* and *Ralph Mallore* levied a fine of
two yards of land here to the ufe of *Richard Fitz-Robert.* To
which *William* fucceeded *Thomas*, who in 55 H. III.‡ held half
a knight's fee in this place and Eton (now Nun-Eaton) with Sap-
cote in Leicefterfhire. After which I have not feen any thing
confiderable relating thereto, till 20 E. III. that *William Moton* an-
fwered‖ for the 8th part of a knight's fee here, held of the ho-
hour of Winchefter, whofe title therein devolved, as it feems, to
Richard Grey of *Codnoure* and *Laurence Dutton.* For 11 Richard II.
the half knight's fee before fpecified lying here and in Eaton, was
certified § to have been held by them of Henry lord Ferrars of
Groby; from which time till 1 Mary I can difcover no more thereof;

* Warwickfhire, 2d ed. p. 52.   † Rot. de nonis garb. &c. in Scac.
‡ Efc. 55 H. III.   ‖ Rot. penes S. Clarke bar.
§ Efc. 11 R. II. n. 26.

but

but then it was found that Sir Walter Smith, of Sherford in Burton Haftings in the county of Warwick *, died feifed of three parts of this manor, as alfo 300 acres of pafture, 60 acres of meadow, and two fhillings rent, lying here and in Hinckley, purchafed of John Leake and Richard Aftell, leaving Richard his fon and heir 22 years of age, which Richard, 35 Elizabeth, being poffeffed of two parts, fettled them upon *William Littleton* in marriage with Margaret his daughter, in the fame manner as he did Sherford; fince which it hath accompanied the poffeffion of that lordfhip."

Mr. Thomas adds, " there is only one houfe ftanding here, near which are yet to be feen the veftigia of this depopulated village."

Sir Walter Smith was murdered by a young wife, who was afterwards executed for it; and his fon Richard juggled out of this and the reft of his eftate by Sir John Littelton of Frankley, in the county of Worcefter; whofe third fon William was married to Mr. Smith's only daughter. The management of the writings had been imprudently trufted to Sir John; and at the time of execution Mr. Smith was drawn off after a brace of bucks, and hurried to fign them before they were read throughout. But the artful knight had made fuch provifion for his own family in the fettlement, that, on the death of his third fon without iffue, the eftate was to devolve to his heir, which was his elder brother *Gilbert*; and his third brother George married the widow. Mr. Smith fued Gilbert's fon John for recovery of his eftate, which, on the attainder of John for adhering to the earl of Effex, 42 Eliz. came to the crown. Muriel, his widow, petitioned James I. to have it reftored, and obtained her requeft. But, to avoid further fuits with Mr. Smith, fhe fold it to Serjeant *Hele*, a great lawyer; who, likewife confidering on what foundation

* Efc. 1 Mary.

P   Littelton's

Littelton's title was at firft built, difpofed of it between his five fons, Sir Warwick, Sir Francis, Nicholas, Walter, and George. But fuch, fays Sir William Dugdale *, is the fate that follows thefe poffeffions, that for want of a public adverfary, thefe brothers are now at fuit among themfelves for them ; and as none of the line of Gilbert Littelton, to whom they fo defcended by force of the before-fpecified conveyance, doth enjoy a foot of them, fo it is no lefs obfervable, that the fon and heir, by George and Mary, viz. Stephen Littelton of Holbeach, in Staffordfhire, was attended with a very hard fate, being executed, and his eftate forfeited, for being concerned in the Gunpowder Treafon.

This lordfhip of Sherford did not long continue in the family of Hele ; for by an heirefs it paffed to —— Hook; whofe fon Sir Hele married Hefter daughter of —— Underhill, citizen and grocer of London, and died 1712, without iffue, leaving his three fifters coheirs ; the elder married —— Groves, gent. the fecond —— Dyer, gent. and the third John Hammond, efq; who, with his relict, afterwards the wife of Dr. Lifley, owned it in Dr. Thomas's time †.

The Earl of Stamford is now the owner of the lordfhip ; which appears, by an admeafurement taken in 1781, to contain in the whole but 431 acres, of which the principal land-holders are Lady Grefley, Sir John Dyer, Mr. Hawkins, Mr. Ball ‡, Mr. Stokes, and Mr. Talkington.

* Ib. p. 56.
† Ib. p. 56.
‡ The Cafe of Carte, adminiftrator of the late Vicar of Hinckley, verfus Ball & al. (as reprinted in Atkyns, vol. III. p. 469, Cafe 170), will be given hereafter, under the life of the Rev. John Carte.

APPENDIX.

N° I.

Some Particulars of the Abbey of LIRA, and of its Possessions in this Kingdom.

LIRA, or LYRA, is a Benedictine abbey, in a town of the same name, in the diocese of Evreux, on the river Rille in Normandy, founded about the year 1045, and taxed to the apostolical chamber at 300 florins of gold for annates. Its annual income is 20090 livres, with a right of presenting to 30 churches. William Fitz Osbern, kinsman to duke William, afterwards king of England, a powerful man, and commendable for his endowments both of body and mind, founded two monasteries in honour of the blessed Virgin Mary; the one at *Lira*, in which he afterwards buried Adelina, the daughter of Roger de Toene, his wife; and the other at *Cormeille*, where he was himself interred. This William was also earl of Hereford, allied to the Dukes of Normandy both by father and mother; for his father *Osbern* was son to Herfast, brother to the countess Gunnora, wife to Richard the first duke of Normandy; and his mother was the daughter of Rodolph earl of Ivry, which Rodolph was brother, by the mother's side, to the above-named duke Richard.

Thomas Becket, archbishop of Canterbury, resided at Lira for some time.

This abbey was possessed of six churches (among the rest that of Carisbrooke), and some manors and lands, in the isle of Wight. Tanner, p. 159.

Abbatia S MARIÆ de Lire ht in insula de Wit. VI. æcclas.

quibʒ ptin . II . hidæ 7 II . virgʒ træ 7 dim . 7 in plurilʒ ꝏ hnt
. v . uillos qui ten . I . hid 7 dim . qrtã parʒ uni v min.

Decimas hnt de omitʒ reddditionibʒ regis . Tot qd hi apꝓciat
xx . lib . Geld redd de . II . hid 7 dim v træ.   Domesday, *Hantesshire.*

A grant or release from the abbey at Lira, to the abbey of Quarere in the Isle of Wight of tithes there, in Arreton, Haseley, Luccomb, Tidlingdham, and Scaldecumb, is printed in Madox, Form. N° cccxcvii.

The priories of Hinkeley and Minting in Leicestershire were cells to this abbey. The author of Neustria Pia, besides these two, names the monastery of Lankywan in Wales; but this is a mistake; for the Monasticon has no such monastery; but in vol. II. p. 989, takes notice that the manor and parish church of Languian in Monmouthshire (where, according to Tanner, Not. Mon. p. 330, was a cell of black monks) belonged to the abbey of Lira.

The manor of Ocley, or Lyre Ocle, in Herefordshire, belonged to this abbey. Tanner, p. 175.

After the Conquest, one or more of the churches in the town of Wareham in Dorsetshire, with some lands in the neighbourhood, being given by Robert Bellamont earl of Leicester, temp. Hen. I. to the abbat and convent of Lira in Normandy, they sent over and settled here a cell of their own Benedictine monks, which was dedicated to the Virgin Mary. Ib. p. 101.

Henry II. by charter sans date, confirmed to this abbey the churches of Wareham, and one hide of land in Wareham of the gift of William de Warmuta, and one

P 2   ounce

ounce of gold in præpofitura de Warham. Dugd. Mon. II. 906. inter addit. ex reg'ro abb. de Lyra, Hutchins's Dorfet, I. p. 80. They had alfo the churches of St. Martin, St. Michael, St. Peter, and St. Mary here. Hutchins, Ib. p. 29—38.

N° II.

Lift of the ABBATS of LYRA, from Neuftria Pia, p. 538. 539. 540.

1. *Robert*, a monk of that place; faid to have been an anchorite in the vale of Chalet, a mile from thence, and to have been admonished from Heaven, as he was hunting a flag, to procure the founding of a monaftery there.

2. *Erfaft*, or *Herphaft*,
3. *Birno*,
4. *Erard*,
5. *Hildebert*,

} monks of St. Evroul.

6. *Giftebert*, *Guillebert*, or *Gilbert*, monk of the fame place; governed almoft ten years, much improved the monaftery, and died about 1100.

7. *William*, monk of the fame place.

8. *Ralph*, monk of Bec, reformed the order.

9. *Helder*, *Hilder*, or *Hildier*, monk of St. Evroul. He obtained from the Arch-bifhop of Rouen, 1145, a confirmation of all their poffeffions.

10. *William* the fecond, monk of the fame place.

11. *Ofbert*, or *Ofbern*, brother to the former, had all the poffeffions of the abbey confirmed by Pope Alexander the third, in 1171. He died in 1177.

12. *Walter*, brother to the laft mentioned; a thing fcarcely ever known, that three brothers fhould fucceed each other in the government of the fame church, as thefe did. In his time, in 1188, the monaftery was burnt.

13. *William* the third, whofe name occurs in deeds of 1266 and 1214.

14. *Geffry*, chofen in 1221, when, his predeceffor being dead, the monks immediately fent to Philip Auguftus II. king of France, for his licence to choofe an abbat, which he gracioufly granted, and Geffry was accordingly elected.

15. *John de Almenefebis* occurs in 1237, 1238, and 1241.

16. *Gilbert* the fecond lived in 1247.

17. *Robert* the fecond died between 1269 and 1274.

18. *Ralph* the fecond; who, growing fickly, refigned the charge of this abbey to Nicholas bifhop of Evreux, in 1288, when he had governed the fame very commendably.

19. *Geffry* the fecond, In whofe time, 1293, Pope Celeftine IV. confirmed all the poffeffions of this monaftery.

20. *William* the fourth; of whom mention is made in deeds from 1301 to 1326.

21. *Aftorgius*, or *Euftorgius*. He earneftly folicited the apoftolical fee that the monks of this monaftery might lay afide the white habit they wore, and ufe black, and quite banish this relaxation from the order of St. Benedict, and obtained the following indulgence:

Bulla Clementis VI. papæ, ftatuens quod monachi Lirenfes habitu nigro utantur, et non albo.

"Clemens, epifcopus, fervus fervorum Dei, ad perpetuam rei memoriam. Ad ea libenter dirigimus ftudia mentis noftræ, quod ecclefiarum & monafteri-
orum,

orum, ac aliorum locorum ecclesiasticorum, & personarum in eis degentium, præfertim sub regulari habitu Domino famulantium, statum, in eo maximè, ut tam in capite, quàm in membris, habitu se conforment, respicere, dinoscimur. Exhibita
siquidem nobis, pro parte dilecti filii Astorgii, abbatis B. Mariæ de Lira, ordinis S.
Benedicti, Ebroicens. diœcef. petitio continebat, quòd in dicto monasterio, à funda-
tione ipsus, temporibus plurium abbatum eiusdem monasterii, qui fuerunt pro tempore abbates, ipsi, ac monachi dicti monasterii, vestes et habitu nigri coloris mona-
chales gestaverunt ; et quod priores & monachi prioratuum ac membrorum, à dicto
monasterio dependentium, in Anglia existentium, vestes & habitu nigri coloris prædicti ex tunc gestaverunt, prout gestant de præsenti: quodque omnium eorundem
abbas dicti monasterii, qui de monasterio de Becco Helluini, dicti ordinis, Rothoma-
gens. diœcef. (in quo, per abbatem, & monachos ipsus monasterii de Becco Heloini,
vestes & habitus albi coloris geruntur & habentur) in abbatem dicti monasterii B.
Mariæ assumptus fuit, vestes & habitus nigri coloris, qui in dicto monasterio B.
Mariæ, ut præmittitur, gerebantur, in vestes & habitus albi coloris, commutavit : &
ex tunc in dicto monasterio B. Mariæ abbates & monachi ipsus, exceptis prioribus
& monachi prioratuum, ac membrorum prædictorum duntaxat, album habitum gestaverunt, & similiter vestes albas: et quod de præmissis, dicto monasterio B. Mariæ
est publica vox & fama. Quare, pro parte dicti Astorgii abbatis nobis extitit sup-
plicatum, ut quod de cætero vestes & habitus nigri coloris in dicto monasterio B.
Mariæ de Lira gerantur, statuere & ordinare de benignitate apostolica dignaremur.
Nos, hujusmodi divisionem amputare, ac vestes & habitum monachorum monasterii
B. Mariæ prædictorum, ad pristinum colorem reducere cupientes ; hujusmodi sup-
plicationibus inclinati, authoritate apostolica statuimus, & etiam ordinamus, quod
abbas, qui nunc est, & successores sui abbates, priores, & monachi prædicti monasterii B. Mariæ, tam in capite, quàm in membris, habitu, & vestibus albi coloris penitus rejectis, habitum & vestes nigri coloris portare perpetuo teneantur : quemad-
modum per monachos ipsus monasterii in Anglia existentes à fundationis tempore
ipsius monasterii est fieri consuetum. Nulli ergo omnino hominum liceat hanc pa-
ginam nostræ constitutionis & ordinationis infringere, vel ei ausu temerario contraire :
si quis autem hanc attentare præsumpserit, indignationem omnipotentis Dei, & BB.
Petri & Pauli, apostolorum eius, se noverit incursurum. Datum Avenioni, Calendis
Julii, pontificatus nostri ann. 10."

22. *Thomas.*

23. *Richard.*

24. *Simon.*

25. *Edward.*

26. *William* the fifth, who flourished in 1450, 1453, and 1457, performed much in
the monastery, and was at length bishop of Avallon.

27. *Lewis de Harcourt* patriarch of Jerusalem and bishop of Bayeux, about 1460,
died 19 cal. Jan. 1479.

28. *Benedict,* lived in 1483.

29. *John* the second, *de Cadillat,* 1506.

30. *Renée de Prye,* cardinal, bishop of Bayeux, died in 1516.

31. *Ambrose le Veneur,* bishop of Evreux, died 7 id. Aug. 1543.

32. *George.*

32. *George.*

33. *Hippolyte d'Este,* cardinal of Ferrara, occurs 1556, and 1559.

34. *Stephen.*

35. *James Davy du Perron,* born Nov. 5, 1556. In 1587 he pronounced the funeral oration on Mary Queen of Scots, as he had in 1586 that of the poet Ronfard. After the murder of Henry IV. of France, Perron laboured ſtrenuouſly in the converſion of the Reformed, and his labours were crowned with that of Henry IV. who nominated him to the biſhoprick of Evreux, and afterwards made him grand almoner of France, and archbiſhop of Sens, and obtained for him in 1604 the dignity of cardinal. After the murder of Henry IV. Perron devoted himſelf entirely to the court and ſee of Rome. In 1615 he was one of the preſidents of the aſſembly at Roan; ſoon after which he retired to his houſe at Rognolet, where he employed himſelf wholly in reviſing his literary works, and eſtabliſhed a printing-office that they might be printed under his own inſpection. He died at Rouen Sept. 5, 1618; and his works were publiſhed, in three volumes folio, 1620—1622.

36. *James le Noel du Perron,* nephew to his predeceſſor, abbat of Lira and of St. Taurinus at Evreux, counſellor of ſtate to the king of France, and high almoner to the queen of England, ſiſter to Lewis XIII.

37. *Lewis le Barbier de la Riviere,* biſhop and duke of Langres, made abbat in 1650.

N° III.

Ex vetuſto Lirenſis coenobii regiſtro, penes Franciſcum Du Cheſne, illuſtriſſ. Galliar. regis hiſtoriographum, ann. 1648. (Dugd. Mon. Ang. I. 986.) Carta Roberti comitis Leiceſtriae donationem Amiciae uxoris ſuae de una uncia auri confirmans.

R. Comes Legerceſtriae Ernaldo de Boſco conſtabulario ſuo, et omnibus baronibus et hominibus ſuis de honore Britolii et Pontis Sancti Petri ſalutem. Sciatis quia benevole et optime concedo, quod Amicia comitiſſa Legerceſtriae uxor mea dedit in eleemoſinam perpetuam Deo et beatae Mariae de Lira et conventui ejuſdem loci unam unciam auri, quam habebat in ponte Sancti Petri, quare volo &c. Teſtibus Simone comite, Iſabella uxore ſuo, Radulfo pincerna, Reginaldo de Bordign, Ricardo Mall, Ricardo clerico, Godefrida nepote Ernaldi. (n. 23.)

N° IV. Carta Roberti comitis de Leiceſtria.

Robertus Comes Legerceſtriae omnibus hominibus &c. Sciatis me conceſſiſſe &c. pro ſalute animae meae et Petronellae comitiſſae uxoris meae et Roberti comitis Legerceſtriae patris mei et Amiciae comitiſſae matris meae &c. omnes donationes quas Willielmus filius Osberti et Robertus comes Legerceſtriae pater meus et alii predeceſſores mei dederunt Deo et eccleſiae beatae Mariae de Lira &c. Teſtibus Petronella comitiſſa uxore mea, Willielmo et Roberto filiis meis, &c. (Ib. n. 8.)

N° V. Carta Roberti comitis Leiceſtriae.

Univerſis &c. Robertus comes Legerceſtriae ſalutem. Noverit univerſitas veſtra me conceſſiſſe et hac mea carta confirmaſſe Deo et Sanctae Mariae de Lira, et monachis ibidem Deo ſervientibus, omnes donationes quas Robertus pater meus fecit eis; (vid. ſ. et,) eccleſiam de Hinkelai cum capellis de Stoke et Daldiutone,

Daldintone, ecclefiam de Ettona eum capella de Afhleburge et aliis pertinentiis fuis, ecclefiam de Sibefdefdune cum capellis de Widredeffcy, et de Atreton, et de Huptone, et de Draitone, ecclefiam de Heccham, cum capella de Lindlay. Concedo et confirmo quoque praedictis monachis decimam denariorum meorum de foka de Hinkeley, et plenariam decimam de dominicis carucis meis de Hinkelay, et de Etona, et de Sebedefdune, et in porcis et in ovibus, et in omnibus illis unde decimae debent exire. Confirmo quoque eis duas uncias auri, fcilicet duas marcas argenti quas comitiffa Amicia mater mea habebat in villa de Hinkeley, et xvi fol. et viii denar' de unciis, quas habebat in Wikeingefton, in fcambium pro decimis nummorum de Etona, et pro decimis pecud' totius dominii, et omnium aliarum rerum, exceptis garbis. Confirmo etiam praedictis monachis unum hofpitium liberum in Leigr', et xx folidat' terrae, quas Rog' de Canford dedit eis in Watone. Teft' Petronilla com' Legerc', Rog' electo Sancti Andreae et Rob' fratre ejus, Ernaldo de Bofco, Hug' de Alneto, Rog' de Hum, Gilberto de Charneles, Euftachio de Herlemvilier, magiftro Hugone, &c. (Ex eod. reg'ro. Dugd. Mon. Ang. I. 603.

Nº VI. Carta Petronillae comitiffae Leiceftriae, de xl s̃. annui redditus pro anniverfario filii fui. Ex eod. reg'ro, n. 7. (Dugd. II. 985.)

Univerfis &c. Petronella comitiffa Legereeftrae falutem &c. Noverit &c. me dediffe &c. Deo et fanctae Mariae de Lira &c. xl s. in molendinis meis de Britolio annuatim perfolvendos &c. ad faciendum anniverfarium Willielmi de Britolio filii mei &c. Teftibus Willielmo Buffaio, &c.

Nº VII. Carta Amiciae dominae Montis fortis de xv s̃. fterlingorum annuatim. Ex eod. reg'ro, n. 29.

Sciatis &c. quod ego Amicia domina Montis fortis dedi &c. Deo, beatae Mariae, et monachis Lirenfibus, fexaginta folidos Andegavenfes, vel quindecim fterlingorum annuatim de maritagio meo, pro anima patris mei Willielmi de Bertolio, in liberum et perpetuam elemofinam, &c. Hiis teftibus, fratre meo Rogero Sancti Andreae electo, Willielmo facerdote de Bertolio, &c.

Nº VIII. Confirmatio Regis Henrici Secundi, &c. Chartae Antiquae, n. 3. Mon. Ang. I. 604.

Henricus Dei gratia rex Angliae, dux Normanniae et Aquitaniae, comes Andegaviae, archiepifcopis, epifcopis, abbatibus, comitibus, baronibus, jufticiariis, vicecomitibus, et omnibus miniftris et fidelibus fuis, Francis et Anglis, totius Angliae, falutem. Sciatis me conceffiffe et praefenti carta mea confirmaffe ecclefiae fanctae Mariae de Lira, et monachis ibi Deo fervientibus, donationem quam Robertus comes Leyceftriae eis rationabiliter fecerat fuper hiis quae fubfequens litera declarat; fcilicet, de ecclefia de Hinchelai, cum ecclefiis eidem ecclefiae adjacentibus, et cum capellis omnibus, et cum decima denariorum de foka de Hinckelai, et cum plenaria decima de dominicis carucis fuis de Hinckelai, et de Hartunc, et de deftone, et in porcis, et in ovibus, et in omnibus illis unde decimae exire. Praeterea de omnibus decimis dominico fuo de Suptwica et de Kingellune, et et foenis, de lanis, et de agnis, et cafeis, et de porcellis, et de omni infta fuo. Quare volo et firmiter praecipio quod praefata ecclefia, et monachi

7

ecclefiae, habeant et teneant omnia haec praedicta, cum omnibus pertinentiis fuis, ita bene, et in pace, libere, et quiete, et plenarie, et integre, et honorifice, ficut cartae Roberti comes Leyceftriae quas inde habent teftantur. Teftibus, Gaufrido archidiacono, Johanne decano Sarum, Reginaldo * archidiacono Sarum, comite Willielmo de Maudevilla, Reginaldo de Curteney, Reginaldo filio Urfi. Apud Chinon.

N° IX. Carta Regis Henrici Secundi, donatorum conceffionem recitans et confirmans.
Ex vet. reg'ro Lirenfe fupra citato, n. 3.

Henricus rex Angliae, &c. Sciatis me conceffiffe et in perpetuam elemofinam confirmaffe ecclefiae Lirenfi, et monachis ibidem Deo fervientibus, quicquid eis rationabiliter datum eft, et tenementa fua, et quicquid jufte et rationabiliter poffederunt tempore regis Henrici avi mei, et tempore avi mei.

In Epifcopato Ebroicenfi, in loco qui Vetus Lira dicitur, ex dono Will' comitis, terram de eadem villa quam tenebat in dominico, et duo molendina in eadem villa, et quartam partem Novae Lirae &c.
    In Anglia, in Epifcopatu Wigorniae &c.
    In Epifcopatu Herefordiae &c.
    In Epifcopatu de Landaff &c.
    In Epifcopatu Wigorniae &c.
    In Epifcopatu Salefburiae &c.
    In Epifcopata Lincolniae Ecclefiam de *Hinkelai,* cum pertinentiis fuis, &c.
Teftibus Philippo Bajocenfe Epifcopo, et Ernulfo Luxorienfi Epifcopo, et Roberto. Comite Legerceftriae, et al.

De prioratibus alienigenis de Hinkley, Warham, et Carefbroke, huic domui [Mount-gracenfi coenobio in agro Eboracenfi] conceffis.

N' X. Pat. 22 R. II. part. 3. m. 11. (Dugd. I. 968.)

Rex omnibus ad quos &c. falutem. Sciatis quod de gratia noftra fpeciali, et ad fupplicationem cariffimi nepotis noftri Thomae ducis Surriae, conceffimus dilecto nobis Edmundo priori domus de Mountgrace ordinis Cartufien. per praefatum ducem de novo fundatae, et commonachis ejufdem loci et fucceffibus fuis, prioratum de Hinkele in comitatu Leyc' alienigenam, prioratum de Warham in com' Dorfet alienigenam, et prioratum de Caresbrok in comitatu Sutht' alienigenam, ac omnia alia terras, tenementa et polieffiones ad abbatiam beatae Mariae de Lira in Normannia alienigenam pertinentias, cum omnibus maneriis, cum fuis pertinentiis, ac cum aliis terris, tenementis, redditibus, poffeffionibus, advocationibus ecclefiarum, vicariarum, et cantfariarum, portiones, penfiones, parvas porciones aliarum ecclefiarum, elemofinas, et ecclefias appropriatas, cum quibufcunque poffeffionibus &c. ad praedictos prioratum de Hynkele &c. pertinentiis &c. Qui quidem prioratus de Hynkele &c. ad manus noftras occafione guerrae inter nos et illos de Francia noftrae devenerunt &c. Habendum &c. praefato Edmundo priori &c. et fucceffibus fuis a festo fancto Michaelis abhinc praeterito quamdiu praedicta guerra duraverit &c. T. Rege apud Haverford in Wallia xii Maii.

Ratificatio fundationis per Regem Henricum VI. Cart. 19 H. VI. m. 22. (vid. Dugd. I. 964.)

* Mafe Bifhop of Lichfield and Coventry in 1173.

N°

Nᵒ XI. On the Office of HIGH STEWARD of ENGLAND.

From Hearne's Curious Difcourfes *.

Here is fhewed who is the High Steward of England, and what his Office is.

The Senefchalcye, or High Stewardſhip of England, belongeth unto the Earl-dom of Leicefter, and of old tyme did thereunto appertayne; and it is to be under-ftood that it is his office, under and immediately after the king, to overfee and go-vern the whole kingdom of England, and all the officers of juftice within the faid kingdome, in tymes boeth of peace and war, in manner following:

" The manner how and when the Lord High Steward ought to exercife his " office by duty and the oath of fealty is fuch : whenever man or woman ſhall " come unto the king's court, in whatfoever court it be, and poffibly unto the " king himfelf, to feek for redrefs againft injury done unto them, and he or ſhe not " being able in due feafon to obteyne remedy, then the high fteward of Eng-" land ought, and is bound to receive their petitions and complaynts, and to keepe " them until the next parliament thereafter to be holden, and to affign unto fuch " complaynants, if he think fit, a day wherein they may exhibit and profecuto " their petitions ; and in full parliament, in the prefence of the king, to reprehend " or blame that officer, or thofe officers, whoever they bee, that foe have fayled " in doing of juftice, and thofe thereof to call to account, unto whom in fuch " cafes every one throughout the kingdome is bound to anfwer, the king onely ex-" cept. If the chancellour of England have fayled of making original remedy " and amends, and the juftices, treafurers, barons, and chamberlaines of the ex-" chequer, fteward of the king's houfe, efcheatours, coroners, fheriffes, clearkes, " bayliffes, and other officers, of what place or records foever they be, in their " proceffes, judgements, executions of judgments, and juftice to be made to the " favour of one, and lofs of the other party, for gifts, bribes, or other procure-" ments, ſhall fyle or give over at the leaſt ways ; if any jufticiar, when as both " parties pleading before them ſhall ftand in judgment, ſhall by fuch falfe pro-" curements deferr judgment, contrary to juftice, and the laws and cuftomes of " the land; if then the chancellour of England, or any other of the king's offi-" cers, in fuch cafe, ſhall alleadge in parliament, and fay for their excufe, that " in that cafe fuch hardnefs and doubtfullnefs of the law and right did arife when " the fame was heard and propoued before them, that neither he nor the court " of chancery, or any other courts wherein he is an officer, were able or knew " how to attaine unto the fafe determination of the right, then ſhall he declare " and open the fame ambiguity and doubt in parliament; if then it be found that " the law was doubtful in that cafe, the chancellour or other officers ſhall be " held accufed, and then ſhall the high fteward of England, togeather with the " conftable of England, in the prefence of the king, and other of the parliament, " make choice of five and twenty perfons more, more or leffe, according as the " cafe ſhall require, togeather with fuch other cafes in the parliament rehearfed;

* In the Britiſh Mufeum is a Latin copy of the above piece ; it is much damaged and imperfect, and feems to have been written about the time of Henry VI. Cott. MSS. Nero D. VIII.

Q

" amongft

" amongſt whom ſhall be earles, barons, knights of the ſhire, citizens, and bur-
" geſſes, who there ſhall ordaine, agree upon, and eſtabliſh remedye by law in
" all ſuch caſes, for ever after to endure. And thoſe laws ſhall be recited, writ-
" ten and allowed in full parliament, and ſealed with the great ſeal, and delivered
" forth to all places of law and juſtice from thenceforward to be holden for laws,
" and in public places where it ſhall be thought expedient they ſhall be pro-
" claimed and divulged, whereas all other common laws, and chiefly ſtatute lawes,
" throughout the whole kingdom ought to be publickly proclaymed.

" If it ſo happen that there was in ſuch like caſe either common law or ſtatute
" law, ſoe that the king's ſteward and others of the parliament may underſtand
" and perceive that ſuch defaults and delays in proceſſes and judgments do hap-
" pen by ſuch officers, when as the deceit and malice of ſuch officers hath openly
" and often before been apparent, then ſhall he be removed out of his office, and
" ſome other officer fit ſhall be put in his place. If they ſhall preſume againſt the
" juſtices and officers, or, by excuſing themſelves, ſhall ſay that they have not
" heretofore known themſelves, and the courts whereby they are in ſuch caſes to
" be deliberate and take adviſement, then ſhall they be admoniſhed by the ſteward
" on the behalf of the king and parliament, to ſtudy and ſearch better the com-
" mon laws, that noe ſuch ignorance nor negligence be found in them in the like
" caſes afterwards. If they ſhall happen to offend in the like againe, they then
" ſhall be put out of their offices, and other diſcreter and more diligent perſons
" ſhall, by the king and his council, be appointed in their roomes.

" Likewiſe it is the ſteward's office (if the king have evil councellours about him
" that adviſe him to doe things tending openly and publickly to his diſhonour, or
" to the diſinheriting, and public hurt of his people) for the ſteward of England,
" taking with him the conſtable and other great eſtates, and others of the commu-
" nalty, to ſend to ſuch a counſellour, forbidding him in ſuch ſort to leade and
" counſel the king, and of ſuch his evil counſel he ſhall make rehearſall, enjoining
" him to depart from the king's preſence, and longer not to abide with him to his
" diſhonour, and the public hurt as is aforeſaid; which if he ſhall not doe, they
" ſhall ſend unto the king to remove him from him, and to give no more ear unto
" his councell, for that amongſt the people he is eſteemed to be an evil councellour
" between the king and his ſubjects. If hereupon the king do not put him away,
" againe and often ſhall they ſend, as well unto the king as unto him: if at the
" laſt neither the king nor ſuch councellours of his have regard unto the meſſages
" and requeſts made unto them, but ſhall refuſe to doe thereafter, then, for the
" weale publick, it is lawfull for the ſteward, conſtable of England, noblemen, and
" others of the communalty of the realme, with banner in the king's name diſ-
" played, to apprehend ſuch councellour, as a common enemy to the king and
" the realme, to commit his body to ward until the next parliament, and in the
" mean time to ſeyze on all his goods, lands, and poſſeſſions, till judgment be pro-
" nounced of him by adviſe of the whole kingdom in parliament, as it happened
" unto Godwyn the earle of Kent, in the days of king Edward the Confeſſour,
" next predeceſſour to William duke of Normandy, conquerour of England, who,
" for ſuch evil acts and councells of his, was deprived of his earldome, which eſ-
                                                        " cheated

" cheated to the aforefaid king: notwithflanding, at the king's fuite, and by the
" noblemen's permiffion, Godwyn came again to England, and did after forfeit as
" before. And as it happened likewife to Hubert de Burgh, earle of Kent in the
" tyme of king Henry III. that was fon of king John, who for his evil deeds and
" bad councell was apprehended, and by the high fenefcha'l and other peers de-
" prived of his earldome by the allowance and confent of the whole parliament.
" So likewife did it befall unto Pierce of Gaveßon, who in the days of king Ed-
" ward the fon of king Henry, for fuch his evil acts and councells, was banifhed
" out of all the king of England's dominions, as well on this fide as beyond the
" feas, which Pierce afterwards by the king's meanc, and the permiffion of the no-
" bility, returned to England and had of the king's guift the earledome of Corn-
" wall; but was after that, for his evil deeds and councell, banifhed the realme
" againe by the nobles and commons, and had his faid earledome efcheated unto
" the king: but he returned afterwards without the noblemen's confent and leave,
" and did refort and affociate himfelf to the king, as before tyme he had done;
" which when the high fteward, conftable, and other of the nobility underftood,
" hee was by them apprehended and beheaded att Blacklow in Warwickfhire, as
" a public enemy to the king and the realme. Soe have you as much as in the
" fayd old boulc is to be feene touching the office of High Steward*."

N° XII. HIGH STEWARDS of England, from the Conqueft to the prefent Time.

1. Hugh de Grentemeifnel, baron of Hinckley; of whom fee p. 5.
2. Yvo de Grentemeifnel, baron of Hinckley; fee p. 8.
3. Hugh de Grentemeifnel, baron of Hinckley; fee p. 8.
4. Robert de Bellomont, earl of Leicefter and lord of Hinckley; fee p. 9.
5. Robert Fitz-Parnel, earl of Leicefter and lord of Hinckley; fee p. 11.
6. Simon de Montfort, earl of Leicefter and lord of Hinckley; fee p. 11.
7. Simon de Montfort jun. earl of Leicefter and lord of Hinckley; fee p. 12.
8. Edward Crouchbacke, earl of Lancafter, Leicefter, and Derby, and lord of Hinckley; fee p. 13.
9. Thomas earl of Lancafter, &c. and lord of Hinckley; fee p. 14.
10. Henry earl of Lancafter, &c. and lord of Hinckley; fee p. 14.
11. Henry duke of Lancafter, &c. and lord of Hinckley; fee p. 14.
12. William of Bavaria, earl of Leicefter, &c. and lord of Hinckley; fee p. 14.
13. John of Gaunt, duke of Lancafter, earl of Leicefter, Lincoln, and Derby, conftable of France, and lord of Hinckley; fee p. 14.
14. Henry duke of Lancafter, &c. and lord of Hinckley; afterwards king of England by the title of Henry IV.; fee p. 14.
15. King Henry V. fee p. 15.
☞ From this period the KINGS OF ENGLAND, as fucceffive LORDS OF HINCK-LEY, have granted the important office of LORD HIGH STEWARD to particular No-blemen only *pro hac vice*. See p. 116.

* Lord Chief Juftice Coke's Account of this high office, effentially differing from that here quoted, is given at large, and freely controverted, in a tract on " The Lord High Steward of England," printed in 8vo, 1776. " Great writers," fays the ingenious Author of this pamphlet, " frequently betray the dull- " nefs of common minds, in works looked up to by the world with admiration and awe."

Q 2   N° XIII.

N.º XIII. Lift of the Stewards of England, who have been appointed by Royal Commiffion for the Trial of Peers, with the Names of the Peers tried by them, and their Crimes and Sentences*.

Note, *Thefe Peers to whofe Names this mark* [†] *is prefixed, fuffered Death; thofe that have this mark* [*] *were condemned, but pardoned.*

HIGH STEWARDS.	PEERS TRIED.
Edward Courtney, earl of Devonfhire.	† John Holland, earl of Huntingdon, for high treafon, 1 Henry IV.
Humphrey duke of Gloceffer.	Thomas Courtney, earl of Devon, for high treafon, 37 Henry VI. *Acquitted.*
John Vere, earl of Oxford.	† John Tiptoff, earl of Worcefter, for high treafon, 10 Edward IV.
John Vere, earl of Oxford.	† Edward Plantagenet, earl of Warwick, for high treafon, 15 Nov. 15 Henry VII.
Thomas Howard, duke of Norfolk.	† Edward Stafford, duke of Buckingham, for high treafon, 13 Henry VIII. 1521.
Thomas Howard, duke of Norfolk.	Lord Dacres, for high treafon, 9 July, 26 Henry VIII. *Acquitted.*
Thomas lord Audley, chancellor of England.	† Edward Courtney, marquis of Exeter, and * Gertrude his wife, for high treafon, 30 Henry VIII.
William Paulett, marquis of Winchefter, high treafurer of England.	† Edward Seymour, duke of Somerfet, for high treafon and felony, 1 Dec. 5 Ed. VI.
Henry Fitz Alan, earl of Arundel.	† Henry Grey, duke of Suffolk, for high treafon, 17 Feb. 1 Mary.
Thomas Howard, duke of Norfolk.	† John Dudley, duke of Northumberland, for high treafon, 18 Aug. 1 Mary. † William Parr, marquis of Northampton, for high treafon. † John Dudley, earl of Warwick, fon of the duke, for high treafon, 18 Aug. 1 Mary.
George Talbot, earl of Shrewfbury.	† Thomas Howard, duke of Norfolk, for high treafon, 16 Jan. 14 Eliz.
Henry Stanley, earl of Derby.	Philip Howard, earl of Arundel, for high treafon, 18 April, 32 Elizabeth. *Guilty, but died in prifon.*
Thomas Lord Buckhurft, high treafurer.	† Robert Devereux, earl of Effex; and * Henry Wriothefley, earl of Southampton, for high treafon, 19 Feb. 43 Eliz.
Thomas Egerton, lord Ellefmere, chancellor of England.	* Lady Frances Carr, countefs of Somerfet, 24 May, 14 James I. 1616. * Robert Carr, earl of Somerfet, 25 May, 14 James I. 1616; both for murder.

* This and the following Lifts are copied from the pamphlet referred to in p. 115.

HIGH STEWARDS.	PEERS TRIED.
Lord Coventry, keeper of the great seal.	† Mervin lord Audley, earl of Castlehaven, for aiding in a rape on his own wife, and other heinous crimes, 27 April, 7 Cha. I. 1631.
Thomas Howard, earl of Arundel.	† Thomas Wentworth, earl of Strafford, for high treason, 24 March, 16 Charles I. 1641.
Edw. Hyde, e. of Clarendon, chancellor of England.	Thomas Lord Morley, for murder, 30 April, 18 Charles II. 1666. *Manslaughter.*
Heneage l. Finch, chancellor of England.	Philip Herbert, earl of Pembroke, for murder, 4 April, 30 Charles II. 1678. *Manslaughter.*
Heneage l. Finch, chancellor of England.	Charles lord Cornwallis, for murder, 31 Charles II. 1679. *Not guilty.*
Heneage l. Finch, chancellor of England.	† William viscount Stafford, for high treason, 30 Nov. 32 Charles II. 1680.
Lord chancellor Jefferies.	† Henry lord Delamere, for high treason, 1 Jac. II. 1685. *Not guilty.*
Thomas D'Anvers, marquis of Carmarthen, president of the council. The great seal was in commission.	Charles lord Mohun, for murder, 31 Jan. 4 Will. and Mary, 1692. *Not guilty.*
John lord Somers, chancellor of England.	Edward earl of Warwick, for murder, 28 March, 11 William and Mary, 1699. *Manslaughter.*
John lord Somers, chancellor of England.	Charles lord Mohun, for murder, 29 March, 11 William and Mary, 1699. *Not guilty.*
William lord Cowper, chancellor of Great Britain.	† James earl of Derwentwater : * William lord Widdrington : † William earl of Nithisdale : * Robert earl of Carnfath : † William viscount Kenmure : * William lord Nairn ; all for high treason, 9 Feb. 2 Geor. I. 1715.
William lord Cowper, chancellor of Great Britain.	George earl of Wintoun, for high treason, 15 March, 1 George I. *Guilty; but made his escape.*
Philip earl of Hardwicke, lord chancellor of Great Britain.	† William earl of Kilmarnock. * George earl of Cromartie. † Arthur lord Balmerino : all for high treason, 9 March, 21 George II.
Philip earl of Hardwicke, lord chancellor of Great Britain.	† Simon lord Lovat, for high treason, 9 March, 21 George II.
Robert lord Henley, ld. chancellor of Great Britain.	† Lawrence earl Ferrers, for murder, 16 April, 33 George II.
Robert e. of Northington, ld. chancellor of Gr. Britain.	William lord Byron, 16 April, 5 George III. for murder. *Manslaughter.*
Henry earl Bathurst, lord chancellor of Great Britain.	Elizabeth dutchess of Kingston, for bigamy, 15 April, 1776. *Guilty; but claimed, and was allowed, the benefit of clergy.*

N° XIV.

Nº XIV. High Stewards at Coronations.

Thomas of Lancaster, affisted by Thomas earl of Worcefter.	Henry IV. 13 Oct. 1399.
Richard Beauchamp, earl of Warwick.	Henry V. 9 April, 1413.
Thomas duke of Clarence.	{ Catharine, his queen, 14 Feb. 1421.
Humphrey duke of Gloucefter.	Henry VI. 6 Nov. 1429.
Richard earl of Warwick.	Edw. IV. 28 June, 1461.
(Nothing appears on the fubject).	Edward V. 1483.
John Howard, duke of Norfolk.	Richard III. 5 July, 1483.
Peter bifhop of Exeter.	
Jafper earl of Pembroke.	
John earl of Oxford.	
John earl of Nottingham.	Commiffioners at the Co-
Thomas lord Stanley.	ronation of Henry VII. 30
John lord Fitzwater, fteward of the houfhold.	Oct. 1485.
Robert Moften, keeper of the rolls.	
Thomas Brian, knt. ch. juftice of the King's Bench.	
Humphry Starkey, chief baron of the Exchequer.	
Richard Croft, knt. treafurer of the houfhold.	
Jafper duke of Bedford.	
John earl of Oxford, great chamberlain of England.	Commiffioners at the co-
Thomas earl of Derby.	ronation of Elizabeth, wife
William earl of Nottingham.	of Henry VII. 25 Nov. 3
John Radcliff, knt.	Henry VII.
John Sulyard, knt. juftice of the Common Pleas.	
John Hawes, juftice of the King's Bench.	
Earl of Surrey, treafurer of England.	Commiffioners at the co-
Earl of Oxenford.	ronation of Henry VIII. 24
Sir John Fineux, the chief judge.	June, 1509.
Sir Thomas Englefield, knt. &c.	
John lord Ruffel.	Edward VI. 20 Feb. 1547.
Edward earl of Derby.	Mary, 1 Oct. 1553.
Henry earl of Arundel.	Elizabeth, 15 Jan. 1559.
Charles earl of Nottingham.	James I. 24 July, 1605.
Sir Thomas Coventry, lord keeper.	
James lord Ley, high treafurer.	
Edward e. of Worcefter, keeper of the privy feal.	
Thomas earl of Arundel and Surrey, earl marfhal of England.	Commiffioners at the co-
	ronation of Charles I. 2 Feb.
William earl of Pembroke, lord chamberlain of the houfhold.	1625.
Edward earl of Dorfet.	
Sir Randoll Crew, ch. juftice of the Common Pleas.	

James

James Butler, duke of Ormond.

William Cavendish, duke of Devonshire.

Charles Fitzroy, duke of Grafton.
Lionel Cranfield, duke of Dorset.
William earl Talbot.

{ Charles II. 23 Ap. 1661.
James II. 23 April, 1685.
Will. and M. 11 Ap. 1689.
Anne, 23 April, 1702.
George I. 20 Oct. 1714.
George II. 11 Oct. 1727.
George III. 22 Sept. 1761.

N° XV. Explanation of the Figures in Plate VII.

Fig. 1. The antler of a large ſtag, found in the old park of Hugh Grentefmainell (ſee p. 19.)

Fig. 2. is a repreſentation of John of Gaunt duke of Lancaſter, hearing and determing the claims of thoſe who were entitled to any office at the coronation of Richard II. On his head is a circlet of gold and pearls; the ſame probably that Edward III. his father put on him, when he made him duke of Lancaſter in parliament, 13 Nov. 36 Edward III. A. D. 1362. This circlet is without the cap of fur, which Edward put on his head, at that ceremony, previous to the impoſition of the circlet. His hair is curled in the faſhion of that time. Round his neck is a rich collar of gold and flowers wrought. In one hand he bears the ſtaff of his office; in the other he has a roll, which he is delivering to a perſon below him, probably to Thomas of Woodſtock, his younger brother, conſtable of England; who, we may ſuppoſe, is receiving the inſtrument which confirms him in the office of conſtable, and authorizes him to act at the enſuing coronation. This perſon's outward robe or coat is half of a dark blue from top to bottom; the other half of a kind of reddiſh yellow. The other figures in the picture are deſigned probably to repreſent the high chamberlain, the mareſchal of England, and ſome other great perſon, who were petitioning the high ſteward to be allowed their reſpective claims. The ſeat is a ſort of ſtool painted and carved, with a green cuſhion. The ground of the piece is red. This picture is on vellum, and contained within the cavity of the letter D highly illuminated, being the initial of a record.

Fig. 3. is taken from a ſeal of red wax, appending to a deed now remaining in the Dutchy Office. dated 28 Jan. 39 Edward III. The workmanſhip of the ſeal is beyond any thing of the kind which hath been diſcovered previous to that time. In a ſhield hanging cornerways are his arms: France ſemé, and England quarterly, a label of 3 points, ermine. Upon his helmet, lambérquin & chapeau turned up, ermine, ſtands his creſt, a lion paſſant guardant crowned, and accolled with a label of 3 points, alſo ermine. "On each ſide this atchievement is placed an eagle ſtanding on a padlock, and eſſaying to open the ſame. It may be this John meaning thereby that although he wanted the key of right and title, to free him from this lock of ſubjection, yet would he, by the power of the eagle, that king of birds, force off his fetters: not willing patiently to expect, with Edmund duke of York, his brother, the freeing of his *falcon* from the *fetterlock* of ſervitude, till king Edward IV. his great grandſon opened it with the right key: but endeavours to cut. this Gordian knot, which he could not untie, making way to the crown for his ſon Henry earl of Derby, who uſurping it placed the ſame on the head of his royal eagle." Thus Sandford (p. 249) ingeniouſly gloſſes on this device on a ſeal of this nobleman's, of 49 Edward III. engraved by him p. 244. After all, theſe *eagles* and *padlocks* ſeem to be be nothing more or lefs than the *falcon* and *fetterlock*, the device or badge of the houfe of York, derived from this duke. Such a device on a feal, and fo curioufly executed, for John of Gaunt, the richeft and moft accomplifhed man of his time, ferves, at leaft, to denote that the age w.s improving in tafte and fentimen:. On the circumference of the feal are the following words abbreviated. *Sigillum privatum Johannis ducis Lancaftriæ, cemitis Richmondiæ, Derbia, Lincolnia, Leicestria, Senefcballi Angliæ.* We fee from hence he paid fome regard to the title (holden as lord of HINCKLEY) of High Steward of England: which however we do not find he made any ufe of till after the death of Edward III.

Fig. 4. The ornaments over the chimney at the old Hall-houfe (fee p. 33.)

Fig. 5. is the feal of St. Leonard's Hofpital at Leicefter, of which a particular defcription has been already given in p. 9; and an impreffion of which has fince been kindly conveyed to me by my worthy friend Mr. Cole.

Fig. 6. The banner of the LORDS OF HINCKLEY (fee p. 69.)

Fig. 7. reprefents the arms of the ancient family of *Wigbiman* of *Wykin*, fo frequently mentioned in this Hiflory (engraved from the communion plate); and fig. 8. thofe of another family of *Wigbiman* †, of great antiquity at Burbach.

Fig. 9. and 10. are arms remaining in a window near the old market-houfe.

N° XVI.   Abftract of the Leafe * referred to in p. 22.

HEC Indentura facta inter excellentiffimum Principem et Dominam Dominam Elizabeth', Dei gratia, Anglie, Francie, et Hibnie Reginam, Fidei Defenfor', &c. ex una parte, et *Edwardum Wigbtman, Thomam Bauduyn, Will. Sampfon, Johannem Hurft, Richardum Warde, & Johannem Ley* ex altera parte, Teftatur, quod cum prefata Dna Regina nunc, per aliam indenturam fuam figillo fuo Ducatus fui Lancaftr' figillat', gerent' dat' vicefimo nono die Junii, anno regni fui undecimo, concefferit, tradiderit, & ad firmam dimiferit, prefatis *Edwardo Wigbtman, Thomæ Bauduyn, Willielmo Sampfon, Johanni Hurft, Richardo Woodland,* et *Thomæ Smyth* (inter alios) centum triginta et fex acr' terre dnical' de HINCKELEY in com' Leic', cum uibus domibus, gardinis, et foffat' Cdftr' ibm, tunc in tenura *Johannis Hoftings,* et poftea dimiff' diverf' tenent' ibid': Necnon unam acr' terre vocat *Coves-acre,* als *Earl's-acre,* ibm: Que dia et fingula fimiffa tunc fuer' parcell' terr' dnical' dicti manerii de Hinckeley, et parcell' antiquar' terrar' et poffeffionu dci Ducatus Lancaftr' in dco com' Leiceftr' exift': Habend' et tenend' &c. a fefto Pafche ult' pterit' ante datum dce recitare indenture ufque ad finem termini viginti unius annor' prox' fequent'; Reddend' &c. Liv s. iv d. &c. Prefata Regina nunc, ₚ & in confideratoe fumme iv l. x111 s. iv d. noie finis ad manum gen' Receptor' Ducitus Laucaftr' fxl' p pfatos &c. fxl' cxxxvi acr' &c. reddend' L111 s. iv d. & ₚ Earl's-acre x11 d. ad term' xxxi ann' &c. Dat' apud palatium Weftm', fub figillo dci ducatus Lancaftr', xx11° die Novembris, anno regni dci dne Regine Elizabethe xxv111°.

Irrotulat' in officio Walteri Mildmay mil', v11° die Maii, anno regni R. Elizabethe xxv111°, p THEO. SADLER, Cleric' Audit'.

* The orig'nal leafe, now in the poffeffion of Mr. Sanfome, is fealed with the Dutchy Seal.
† *Thomas Wigbtman* de Burbach, Harl. MSS. 1113. p. 4. b. and ibid. 2198. 135. b —A beautiful alabafter monument for *Richard Wigbiman* and his two wives (ftill remains (1782) in Burbach church.

N° XVII.

APPENDIX, N° XVII.

HIGH CROSS.

ABOUT four miles from Hinckley, in the road to Cleybrook, is the famous fpot where formerly ftood a crofs erected by the Romans, which was fucceeded by a beacon; and where in Camden's time was a very high poft, with fupporters. " Here is a crofs," fays Dr. Stukeley (who has engraved a view of it, together with a plan of the antient *Benonis*, as he writes it, delineated Sept. 9, 1722, in his Itinerary, vol. I. p. 110.) " of handfome defign, but of a mouldering ftone, through the " villainy of the architect, one Dunkley, built at the charge of the late earl of " Denbigh * and the gentlemen in the neighbourhood. It confifts of four Doric co- " lumns, regarding the four roads, with a gilded globe and crofs at top upon a fun- " dial; on two fides, between the four Tufcan pillars that compofe a fort of pe- " deftal, are thefe infcriptions:

On the Weft fide,	On the North fide,
" Vicinarum provinciarum VERVICENSIS	" Si veterum Romanorum veftigia
Scilicet & LEICESTRENSIS ornamenta,	Quæras, hic cernas, Viator. Hic enim
Proceres patriciique,	Celeberrimæ illorum viæ militares,
Aufpiciis illuftriffimi BASILII	Sefe mutuo fecantes, ad extremos ufque
Comitis de DENBIGH,	BRITANNIÆ limites procurrunt. Hic
Hanc Columnam ftatuendam	Stativa fua habuerunt VENNONES, & ad
Curaverunt, in gratam pariter	Primum abhinc Lapidem Caftra fua;
Et perpetuam memoriam JANI tandem	Ad STRATAM & ad FOSSAM Tumulum
A Sereniffima ANNA claufi.	CLAUDIUS quidem Cohortis Præfectus
A. D. MDCCXII."	Habuiffe videtur."

The infcriptions, I am told, were written by Mr. George Greenaway, a fchoolmafter at Coventry. The prefent earl of Denbigh is very defirous of having the crofs repaired, and has offered a contribution for that purpofe; but the cornices are fo mouldered, that it has been declared impracticable. As far as I can judge however by a particular examination of it (in May 1782) a coat of ftucco would effectually anfwer every purpofe of reparation and beauty; which is the more to be wifhed, as the architecture and proportion are pleafing and juft. The number of letters cut on the fides of the pedeftal, by travellers who have left there the initials of their names, is almoft incredible. But the crofs being now inclofed by a neat little garden, encompaffed with a fine quick hedge, that nuifance would not be again likely to happen.

* Bafil, grandfather to the prefent earl. This noble earl gave to the church of Lutterworth their prefent font, on which is a model of a fpire 47 yards high, demolifhed by a ftorm in 1701. The founding-board of Wickliff's pulpit, and the cope worn by that reformer when rector of Lutterworth, preferved in the church as relicks, are engraved in plate VII. fig. 11, 12. I fhall here infert an epitaph on an anceftor of the Denbigh family, which I tranfcribed in May 1782 from a tomb in Lutterworth church: " Hic jacet Johannes Fildiug de Lutterworth, qui obiit xi° die menfis Octobris MCCCCIII, & Johanne " uxoris ejus, que obiit quinto die menfis Aprilis MCCCCXXVIII, quorum animabus propicietur Deus." Their effigies, carved in ftone, are ftill remaining. This lady (the daughter of Sir William Bellers) was his fecond wife. His effigies and that of Margaret Purefoy, his firft lady, are alfo preferved in brafs; and in the window are the arms of Fielding and Purefoy.

R   APPEN.

APPENDIX TO THE

APPENDIX, Nº XVIII.

MEMOIRS of EMINENT PERSONS;

Natives of HINCKLEY, or closely connected with that Town.

1. Sir ROBERT BRUCE COTTON [*].

This very eminent English Antiquary, "whose name," says Dr. Johnson[†], "must always be mentioned with honour, and whose memory cannot fail of exciting "the warmest sentiments of gratitude, whilst the smallest regard for Learning sub- "sists among us," was owner of three-fourths of the manor of HINCKLEY, as has been mentioned in p. 22. How much is it to be regretted that this truly great man did not supersede the present publication, by turning his thoughts to the history of a town in which he had so considerable a property, at a period when his researches would have been so much easier than they are at this distance of time!

He was the son of Thomas Cotton, Esq. descended from a very ancient family, and born at Denton in Huntingdonshire, January 22, 1570; admitted of Trinity College, Cambridge, where he took the degree of B. A. 1585; and, some little time after, went to London, where he soon made himself known, and was admitted into a Society of Antiquaries, who met at stated seasons for their own amusement. Here he indulged his natural humour in the prosecution of that study, for which he afterwards became so famous; and in the eighteenth year of his age began to collect ancient records, charters, and other manuscripts. In 1600 he accompanied Mr. Camden to Carlisle, who acknowledges himself not a little obliged to him, for the services he did him in carrying on and perfecting his "Britannia;" and the same year wrote "A Brief Abstract of the Question of Precedency between England "and Spain." This was occasioned by Queen Elizabeth's desiring the thoughts of the Society of Antiquaries upon that point, and is still extant in the Cotton Library[‡]. Upon the accession of King James I. to the throne, he was created a knight; and during this whole reign was very much courted, admired, and esteemed by the great men of the nation, and consulted as an oracle by the privy counsellors and ministers of state, upon very difficult points relating to the constitution. In 1608, he was appointed one of the commissioners to enquire into the state of the navy, which had lain neglected ever since the death of Queen Elizabeth; and drew up a me- morial of their proceedings to be presented to the king, which memorial is still in the Cotton Library. In 1609, he wrote "A Discourse of the Lawfulness of Com- "bats to be performed in the Presence of the King, or the Constable and Marshal "of England," which was printed in 1651 and in 1672. He drew up also the same year "An Answer to such Motives as were offered by certain Military Men "to Prince Henry, to incite him to affect Arms more than Peace§." This was

---

[*] The principal part of this life is copied from the "Biographical Dictionary;" and is in substance the same with the Latin Life by T. Smith.
[†] Preface to Harleian Catalogue, p. 1.   [‡] See Casley's Catalogue, p. 325.
[§] To an 8vo. edition of this track was prefixed the author's head, engraved by T. Cross, and inscribed
" ROBERTUS COTTONUS BRUCEUS.
" Æ sculapius hic librorum; ærago, vetustas,
" Per quem nulla poterit Britannum consumere chartas."

4   com-

composed by order of that prince, and the original manuscript remains in the Cotton Library. New projects being contrived to repair the royal revenue, which had been prodigally squandered, none pleased the king so much, as the creating a new order of knights, called baronets; and Sir Robert Cotton, who had done great service in that affair, was in 1611 chosen to be one, being the 36th baronet that was created. His principal residence was then at Great Connington, in Huntingdonshire; which he soon exchanged for Hatley St. George, in the county of Cambridge.

He was afterwards employed by King James to vindicate the behaviour and actions of Mary Queen of Scots, from the supposed misrepresentations of Buchanan and Thuanus; and what he wrote upon this subject is thought to be interwoven in Camden's Annals of Queen Elizabeth, or else printed at the end of Camden's Epistles. In 1616 the king ordered him to examine, whether the papists, whose numbers then made the nation uneasy, ought, by the laws of the land, to be put to death, or to be imprisoned? This task he performed with great learning, and produced upon that occasion twenty-four arguments, which were published afterwards in 1672, among "Cottoni Posthuma." It was probably at that time that he composed a piece, still preserved in manuscript in the Royal Library, intituled, "Considerations for the repressinge of the encrease of Preests, Jesuits, and Recusants, without drawinge of blood." He was also employed by the house of commons, when the match between Prince Charles and the Infanta of Spain was in agitation, to shew, by a short examination of the treaties between England and the house of Austria, the unfaithfulness and insincerity of the latter; and to prove that in all their transactions they aimed at nothing but universal monarchy. This piece is printed among "Cottoni Posthuma," under the title of "A Remonstrance" of the Treaties of Amity," &c. He wrote likewise a vindication of our ecclesiastical constitution against the innovations attempted to be brought in by the Puritans, intituled, "An Answer to certain Arguments raised from supposed Antiquity, and urged by some Members of the Lower House of Parliament, to prove that Ecclesiastical Laws ought to be enacted by Temporal Men." In the year 1621, he compiled "A Relation to prove, that the Kings of England have been pleased "to consult with their Peeres, in the great Councel and Commons of Parliament, of Marriadge, Peace, and War," which was printed first in 1651, then in 1672 among "Cottoni Posthuma," and then in 1679 under the title of "The Antiquity and "Dignity of Parliament." Being a member of the first parliament of King Charles I. he joined in complaining of the grievances, which the nation was said in 1618 to groan under; but was always for mild remedies, zealous for the honour and safety of the king, and had no views but the nation's advantage.

In 1619 the remarkable transaction happened, which gave rise to the following very curious particulars * :

Letter from Dr. Samuel Harsnett, Archbishop of York, to Sir Henry Vane, Ambassador at the Hague, dated London, Nov. 6, 1629.

"On Saturday in the evening there were sent Mr. Vice-Chamberlain and others "to seal up Sir Robert Cotton's library, and to bring himself before the lords of "his majesty's council. There were found in his custody a pestilent tractate, which

* See Gent. Mag. 1767, p. 335.

"he

" he had fostered as his child, and had sent it abroad into divers hands; contain-
" ing a project how a prince may make himself an absolute tyrant. This pernici-
" ous advice he had communicated by copies to divers lords, who, upon his con-
" fession, are questioned and restrained; my lord of Somerset sent it to the bishop
" of London; the lord Clare to the bishop of Winchester; and the lord Bedford
" I know not well to whom. Cotton himself is in custody *. God send him well
" out !   I am, &c."

The Same, to the Same, dated Nov. 9.

" Yesterday his majesty was pleased to sit in council with all the board, and
" commanded that devilish project found upon Sir Robert Cotton to be read over unto
" us. For my own part, I never heard a more pernicious diabolical device, to
" breed suspicious, seditious humours amongst the people. His majesty was pleased
" to declare his royal pleasure touching the lords and others restrained for commu-
" nicating that project; which was, to proceed in a fair, moderate, mild, legal
" course with them, by a bill of information preferred into the star-chamber, where-
" unto they might make their answer by the help of the most learned council they
" could procure. And though his majesty had it in his power most justly and truly
" to restrain them till the cause was adjudged, yet, out of his princely clemency,
" he commanded the board to call them, and to signify unto them to attend their
" cause in the star chamber. They were personally called in before the lords
" (the king being gone) and acquainted by the keeper with his majesty's gracious
" favour. Two never spoke a word, expressing thankfulness for his majesty's so
" princely goodness; two expressed much thankfulness, which were my lord of
" Bedford, and Sir Robert Cotton. St. John and James are still in prison; and
" farther than unto these the paper reacheth not in direct travel, save to Selden,
" who is also contained in the bill of information. I fear the nature of that conta-
" gion did spread farther; but as yet no more appeareth. I am of opinion it will
" fall heavy on the parties delinquent.   I am, Sir, &c.".

* This account (as was afterwards observed by a correspondent in Gent. Mag. p. 388) seems in some
respects doubtful, in others defective; for among some records in the Paper Office is a warrant for
the commitment of Sir Robert Cotton, so early as the year 1615, being suspected of a correspondence
with the Spanish ambassador, prejudicial to the affairs of Government. From this confinement, it is
however probable, he was soon released, and that he had his library, which was at that time shut up,
restored to him not long after his enlargement; but I have reason to believe, that after his last confinement in 1629, he never had his library restored; for I have seen a letter which mentions his death in
1631, in which it is said, " That before he died, he requested Sir Henry Spelman, to signify to the
" lord privy seal, and the rest of the lords of the council, that their so long detaining of his books from
" him, without rendering any reason for the same, had been the cause of his mortal malady; upon which
" message, the lord privy seal came to Sir Robert, when it was too late, to comfort him from the king,
" from whom the earl of Dorset likewise came, within half an hour after Sir Robert's death, to condole
" with Sir Thomas Cotton, his son, for his death, and to tell him from his majesty, that as he loved
" his father, so he would continue to love him.
" That Sir Robert had entailed, as far as law could do it, his library of books upon his son, who
" makes no doubt of obtaining the same; but for all these court holy-waters, says the writer, I, for my
" part, for a while suspend my belief."
From this it appears, that the government was in possession of Sir Robert's library at the time of his
death, and that it was even doubtful whether it would ever be restored to his posterity."

                                                                              Sir

Sir Symonds D'Ewes's account of this affair, in his manuscript life, written by himself, and still preserved among the Harleian manuscripts, will give further light to this very interesting fact.

"Amongst other books," says he, "which Mr. Richard James lent out, one
" Mr. St. John, of Lincoln's Inn, a young studious gentleman, borrowed of him,
" for money, a dangerous pamphlet that was in a written hand, by which a course
" was laid down, how the kings of England might oppress the liberties of their
" subjects, and for ever enslave them and their posterities. Mr. St. John shewed
" the book to the earl of Bedford, or a copy of it; and so it passed from hand to
" hand, in the year 1629, till at last it was lent to Sir Robert Cotton himself, who
" set a young fellow he then kept in his house to transcribe it; which plainly
" proves, that Sir Robert knew not himself that the written tract itself had origi-
" nally come out of his own library. This untrusty fellow, imitating, it seems,
" the said James, took one copy secretly for himself, when he wrote another for
" Sir Robert; and out of his own transcript sold away several copies, till at last
" one of them came into Wentworth's hands, of the North, now lord deputy of
" Ireland. He acquainted the lords, and others of the privy-council, with it. They
" sent for the said young fellow, and examining him where he had the written
" book, he confest Sir Robert Cotton delivered it to him. Whereupon, in the
" beginning of November, in the same year 1629, Sir Robert was examined, and
" so were divers others, one after the other, as it had been delivered from
" hand to hand, till at last Mr. St. John himself was apprehended, and, being
" conceived to be the author of the book, was committed close prisoner to the
" Tower. Being in danger to have been questioned for his life about it, upon
" examination upon oath, he made a clear, full, and punctual declaration, that
" he had received the same manuscript pamphlet of that wretched mercenary fel-
" low James, who by his means proved the wretched instrument of shortening
" the life of Sir Robert Cotton; for he was presently thereupon sued in the
" Star-chamber, his library locked up from his use, and two or more of the
" guards set to watch his house continually. When I went several times to visit
" and comfort him, in the year 1630, he would tell me, 'they had broken his
" heart, that had locked up his library from him.' I easily guessed the reason, be-
" cause his honour and esteem were much impaired by this fatal accident; and
" his house, that was formerly frequented by great and honourable personages, as
" by learned men of all sorts, remained now upon the matter desolate and empty.
" I understood, from himself and others, that Dr. Neile and Dr. Laud, two pre-
" lates that had been stigmatized in the first session of parliament, in 1628, were
" his sore enemies. He was so outworne, within a few months, with anguish and
" grief, as his face, which had been formerly ruddy and well-coloured (such as
" the picture I have of him shews) was wholly changed into a grim blackish pale-
" ness, near to the resemblance and hue of a dead visage. I heard it certainly af-
" firmed that the young fellow whom Sir Robert kept in his house, and had em-
" ployed to transcribe the said written tractate, was his bastard; which shews God's
" admirable justice, to cause the spurious issue of his fatal lust to prove the in-
" stru-

" ftrument of his final ruin. I, at one time, advifed him to look into himfelf, and
" ferioufly confider, why God had fent this chaftifement upon him; which, it is
" poffible, he did; for I heard from Mr. Richard Holdefworth, a great and lear-
" ned divine, that was with him in his laft ficknefs, a little before he died, that
" he was exceeding penitent, and was much confirmed in the faithful expectation
" of a better life."

This James, mentioned by Sir Symonds D'Ewes, was Richard James, fellow of
Corpus Chrifti College, in Oxford, born at Newport, in the Ifle of Wight, and
author of feveral fermons, both in Latin and Englifh. He died at the houfe of
Sir Thomas Cotton, bart. in the beginning of December 1636. Sir Symonds
D'Ewes gives a very fevere character of him; an atheiftical profane fcholar, but
otherwife witty and moderately learned; and he adds, that he had fo fcrewed himfelf into the good opinion of Sir Robert Cotton, " that whereas at firft he had on-
" ly permitted him the ufe of his books; at laft, fome two or three years before
" his death, he beftowed the cuftody of his whole library on him. And he being
" a needy fharking companion, and very expenfive, like old Sir Ralph Starkie
" when he lived, let out, or lent out, Sir Robert Cotton's moft precious manu-
" fcripts for money, to any that would be his cuftomers; which, fays Sir Symonds,
" I once made known to Sir Robert Cotton, before the faid James's face."

It may be neceffary, in order to elucidate this matter ftill farther, to take notice
that one of the articles in the attorney general's information againft Sir Robert
Cotton was, " that the difcourfe or project was framed and contrived within five
" or fix months paft here in England;" but Sir David Foulis teftified upon oath,
being thereunto required, that it was contrived at Florence, feventeen years before
by Sir Robert Dudley; upon which moft of the parties were releafed, and Sir Robert Cotton had his library reftored to him foon after.

The other works of Sir Robert Cotton, not already mentioned, are, 1. " A
" Relation of the Proceedings againft Ambaffadors, who have mifcarried them-
" felves, and exceeded their Commiffion." 2. " That the Sovereign's Perfon is re-
" quired in the great Councils or Affemblies of the States, as well at the Confultations as
" at the Conclufions." 3. " The Argument made by the Command of the Houfe of
" Commons, out of the Acts of Parliament and Authority of Law expounding the
" fame, at a Conference with the Lords, concerning the Liberty of the Perfon of
" every Freeman." 4. " A Brief Difcourfe concerning the Power of the Peers
" and Commons of Parliament in point of Judicature." Thefe four are printed in
" Cottoni Pofthuma." 5. " A Short View of the long Life and Reign of Henry
" III. King of England," written in 1614, and prefented to King James I. printed
in 1617, 4to. and reprinted in " Cottoni Pofthuma." 6. " Money raifed by the
" King without Parliament, from the Conqueft until this Day, either by Impofition
" or Free Gift, taken out of Records or Ancient Regifters," printed in the " Royal
" Treafury of England, or General Hiftory of Taxes, by Captain J. Stevens," 8vo.
7. " A Narrative of Count Gondomar's Tranfactions during his Embaffy in Eng-
" land, London, 1659," 4to. 8. " Of the Antiquity, Etymology, and Privileges of
" Caftles; 9. of Towns; 10. of the Meafures of Land; 11. of the Antiquity of Coats of
" Arms," all printed in Hearne's Difcourfes, pp. 166. 174. 178. 182. He wrote books
upon

upon feveral other fubjects, that remain ftill in manufcript: namely, "Of Scutage; "Of Enclofures, and converting Arable Land into Pafture; Of the Antiquity, au- "thority, and Office of the High Steward and Marfhal of England; Of Curious "Collections; Of Military Affairs; Of Trade; Collections out of the Rolls of "Parliament," different from thofe that were printed, but falfely, under his name, in the year 1657, by William Prynne *, Efq. He likewife made collections for the hiftory and antiquities of Huntingdonfhire; and had formed a defign of writing an account of the ftate of Chriftianity in thefe iflands, from the firft reception of it here to the Reformation. The firft part of this defign was executed by Archbifhop Ufher, in his book, "De Britannicarum Ecclefiarum Primordiis," compofed proba- bly at the requeft of Sir Robert Cotton, who left eight volumes of collections for the continuation of that work.

But, without intending to derogate from the juft merits of this learned and knowing man as an author, it may reafonably be queftioned, whether he has not done more fervice to learning, by fecuring, as he did, his valuable library † for the ufe of pofterity, than by all his writings. It is for this library that he is now moft famous; and therefore it may not be improper to be a little particular in the ac- count of it. It confifts wholly of manufcripts; many of which being in loofe fkins, fmall tracts, or very thin volumes, when they were purchafed, Sir Robert caufed feveral of them to be bound up in one cover. They relate chiefly to the Hiftory and Antiquities of Great Britain and Ireland, though the ingenious collector refufed nothing that was curious or valuable in any point of learning. He lived indeed at a time when he had great opportunities of making fuch a fine collection: when there were many valuable books yet remaining in private hands, which had been taken from the monafteries at their diffolution, and from our univerfities and col-

---

* See Preface to the 3d volume of Tyrrel's Hiftory of England, p. 9.

† I was almoft tempted to tranfcribe, from the excellent Preface to the Harleian Catalogue, a fhort hif- tory of the oldeft MS. Libraries in this kingdom; but it would have led me too far from my fubject. The character, however, of Sir Robert Cotton is too important to be omitted: "Bodley's great contem- "porary, Sir Robert Cotton, had been equally diligent in collecting ancient MSS. The ftudy of anti- "quities, particularly thofe of this kingdom, had engaged his attention, though he always fhewed a high "regard for every part of philological learning, in all which he was extremely converfant. He had "obferved with regret, that the hiftory, laws, and conftitution of Britain, were in general very in- "fufficiently undeftood; and being fully convinced, that the prefervation of fuch monuments of an- "tiquity, and other documents, as were conducive to render the knowledge of them, and their deduc- "tions from their primary ftate, more accurate and univerfal, would neceffarily redound to the advantage "of the public, he had, in an expenfive and indefatigable labour of upwards of forty years, accumu- "lated thofe numerous and ineftimable treafures which compofe the Cottonian Library, and now remain "an indifputable teftimony of his benevolent difpofition towards his native country. But, happily, thefe "patrons of literature lived in an age peculiarly favourable to the completion of their refpective purpo- "fes, and more efpecially to thufe of the latter. The laft general diffolution of religious houfes had "difperfed an infinite number of curious MSS. Many of thefe were fecured by the nobility and gen- "try; but no inconfiderable number falling into the hands of peafants, mechanics, and other perfons "ignorant of their importance, and totally inattentive to their prefervation, were eafily to be pur- "chafed. From this fource Sir Robert Cotton had fupplied his library with a multitude of rare "MSS. and to them Mr. Camden, Mr. Lambert, Dr. Dee, and Sir Chriftopher Hatton, had kindly "contributed their ftores."

leges

leges at their visitations: when several learned Antiquaries, such as Josceline, Noel, Allen, Lambarde, Bowyer, Elsinge, Camden, and others, died, who had made it their chief business to scrape up the scattered remains of our monastical libraries: and, either by legacy or purchase, he became possessed of all he thought valuable in their studies. This library was placed by Sir Robert Cotton in his own house at Westminster, near the house of commons; and very much augmented by his son Sir Thomas Cotton, and his grandson. Sir John * (who died in 1702, aged 71). In 1700 an act of parliament was made for the better securing and preserving that library, in the name and family of the Cottons, for the benefit of the publick; that it might not be sold, or otherwise disposed of and embezzled. Sir John, great grandson of Sir Robert, having sold Cotton-house to Queen Anne, about 1706, to be a repository for the Royal as well as the Cottonian library, an act was made for the better securing of her majesty's purchase of that house; and both house and library were settled and vested in trustees. The books were then removed into a more convenient room, the former being very damp; and Cotton-house was set apart for the use of the king's library-keeper, who had there the Royal and Cottonian libraries under his care. In 1712 the Cottonian library was removed to Essex house in Essex street; and in 1730 to a house in Little Dean's Yard, Westminster, purchased by the crown of the lord Ashburnham; where a fire happening upon the 23d of October, 1731, one hundred and eleven books were lost, burnt, or entirely defaced, and ninety-nine rendered imperfect. It was thereupon removed to the Old Dormitory belonging to Westminster school, and finally, in 1753, to that admirable repository, The British Museum, where they still remain.

It is almost incredible how much we are indebted to this library, for what we know of our own country: witness the works of Sir Henry Spelman, Sir William Dugdale, the Decem Scriptores, Dean Gale, Bishop Burnet's History of the Reformation, Strype's Works, Rymer's Fœdera, several pieces published by T. Hearne, and every book almost that hath appeared since, relating to the History and Antiquities of Great Britain and Ireland. Nor was Sir Robert Cotton less communicative of his library and other collections in his life-time. Speed's History of England is said to owe most of its value and its ornaments to Sir Robert Cotton; and Mr. Camden acknowledges, that he received the coins in the Britannia from his collection. To Mr. Knolles, author of the Turkish History, he communicated authentic letters of the masters of the knights of Rhodes, and the dispatches of Edward Barton, ambassador from Queen Elizabeth to the Porte; to Sir Walter Raleigh, books and materials for the second volume of his History, never published; and the same to Lord Verulam, for his History of Henry VII. The famous Mr. Selden was highly indebted to the books and instructions of Sir Robert Cotton, as he thankfully acknowledges in more places than one +. In a word, this

* Of whom there is a portrait, by Vandrebanc, from a painting by Kneller, inscribed,
JOHANNES COTTONUS BRUCEUS, φιλάρχων, φιλοανθρώπων, χ φιλοπάτρων.
  " Virtus repulsæ nescia sordidæ,
  " Intaminatis fulget honoribus;
  " Nec sumit aut ponit secures,
  " Arbitrio popularis auræ."
+ Dedicat. Analector. Britan. and of the History of Tithes.

Hon.

great

great and worthy man was the generous patron of all lovers of antiquities, and his house and library were always open to ingenious and inquisitive persons.

Two speeches of Sir Robert Cotton, it may be added, are printed in the Parliamentary History.

Such a man, we may imagine, must have had many friends and acquaintances, and indeed he was not only acquainted with all the virtuosi and learned in his own country, but with many also of high reputation abroad; as Janus Gruterus, Francis Sweertius, Andrew Duchesne, John Bourdelot, Peter Puteanus, Nicholas Fabricius Peireskius, &c. &c. He died of a fever, in his house at Westminster, May 6, 1631, aged sixty years, three months, and fifteen days *. He married Elizabeth, one of the daughters and coheirs of William Brocas, of Thedingworth in the county of Leicester, Esq. by whom he left one only son, Sir Thomas, the second baronet, who died 1662, and was succeeded by Sir John the third, and he, 1702, by his son John, who died in the lifetime of his father, 1681, leaving two sons, of whom the elder John succeeded his grandfather, and died without issue 1730-1. The title and part of the estate went to his uncle Robert, by whose death, at the age of 80, July 12, 1749, the title became extinct. He had one son, John, who died before his father, and one grandson John, who died of the small pox, on his return from his travels, in 1739.

2. WILLIAM BURTON †, Author of the HISTORY of LEICESTERSHIRE.

THIS eminent antiquary is connected with the subject of the present sheets as owner of the lordship of Dadlington, of which I have already said (p. 99) he drew up a particular account, which might easily be abridged into a valuable publication. He was the eldest son of Ralph Burton ‡, Esq. of Lindley, in Leicestershire, on the confines of Warwickshire; was born August 24, 1575, educated at the grammar-school of Sutton-Coldfield, admitted commoner or gentleman-commoner at Brazennose ||, 1591, at The Inner Temple May 20, 1593, B. A. June 22, 1594, and afterwards a barrister and reporter in the court of Common-pleas. But "his natural " genius leading him to the studies of heraldry, genealogies, and antiquities, he " became excellent in those obscure and intricate matters; and, look upon him as " a gentleman, was accounted by all that knew him to be the best of his time for " those studies, as may appear by his description of Leicestershire§." In 1602 he corrected Saxton's Map of that county, with the addition of 80 towns. His weak constitution not permitting him to follow his business, he retired into the country; and his great work, "The Description of Leicestershire," was published in folio,

* An original picture of Sir Robert Cotton by Van Somer, in the possession of the late Mr. West, was engraved by Vertue, at the expence of the Society of Antiquaries, in 1744. Another print of him has been already mentioned in p. 127; and there is a third, by R. White, from a painting by C. Johnson in 1629. Mr. Granger also mentions an original portrait of him at the late Duke of Queensbury's at Amesbury.

† Mr. Peck had collected materials for the life of Mr. Burton and his younger brother Robert, which are probably among the papers of the late Sir Thomas Cave, Bart. M. P. who bought the greater part of Mr. Peck's MSS. from his widow, on the suggestion of Mr. Ashby. The present article is chiefly compiled from Mr. Gough's "British Topography."

‡ One of his ancestors was esquire of the body of Richard I. and Lindley came into the family by marriage of his great grandfather with the heiress of John Hardwicke, who conducted the Earl of Richmond to the battle of Bosworth.

| He calls himself scholar there 1592, when Queen Elizabeth came to Oxford. Leicestershire, p. 68.

§ Wood, Athenæ Oxonienses, vol. II. p. 75.

1622. He tells his patron, George Villers, Marquis of Buckingham, that "he has
"undertaken to remove an eclipfe from the fun without art or aftronomical dimen-
"fion, to give light to the county of Leicefter, whofe beauty hath long been fha-
"dowed and obfcured;" and in his preface declares himfelf one of thofe who hold
that "Gloria totius res eft vaniffima mundi;" and that he was unfit and unfurnifhed
"for fo great a bufinefs; "unfit," to ufe his own words, "for that myfelf was bound
"for another ftudy, which is jealous, and will admit no partner, for that all time
"and parts of time, that could poffibly be employed therein, were not fufficient to
"be difpended thereon, by reafon of the difficulty of getting, and multiplicity of
"kinds of learning therein. Yet if a partner might be affigned or admitted thereto,
"there is no ftudy or learning fo fit or neceffary for a Lawyer, as the ftudy of Anti-
"quities." In concluding the book, he adds, "If there be any thing worthily done,
"which may give content or fatisfaction to the reader, it is what I defired: if any
"thing omitted, Bernardus non videt omnia; if any thing miftaken, erroneous, or
"fault worthy, I muft crave pardon; my intention was, that truth might be difco-
"vered; and that thofe clouds of darknefs and black mifts, wherewith this county's
"luftre hath long been fhadowed, might at length be difperfed, and that her fun's
"glorious rays, fo long eclipfed, might *rilucer*, fhine out to the view of every one;
"which now doth *rilumbre*, fomewhat clear appear, and by fome more happy genius
"and judicious pen may hereafter be better illuftrated. But where the fun's bright
"beams could not pierce into, I have to thofe *ofcure grotte*, dark caves and vaults,
"brought candle-light, my own conceit and conjecture, which (as they are) I fub-
"mit to the favourable cenfure of the more learned and judicious. And now hav-
"ing gone about and over the whole continent of this country, it is my good for-
"tune to end at the hithermoft angle [*Worthington*], next to mine own home, whi-
"ther I muft now retire myfelf; and having fpent all my viatical provifion in this
"my laborious journey, muft here furceafe, and with that ingenious *Macaronicall*
"poet conclude:

> "Nunc quia candela eft ufque ad culamen adufta,
> "Etiam confumpfit vacuata lucerna ftopino,
> "Multa per adeffo fcripfi, gis fcribere ceffo"

Merlino Coccaio Macaron. Phantaf. lib, xxiv. fol. 240.
He was affifted in this undertaking by his kinfman John Beaumont or Gvaredicu,
Efq. and Auguftus Vincent *, Rougecroix; but the church notes were taken by himfelf. He drew up the corollary of Leland's life, prefixed to the "Collectanea," with
his favourite device, the fun recovering from an eclipfe, and motto *Rilucera*, dated
Faledi 1612, from Fakle, a pleafant village near Tutbury, Staffordfhire, and a great
patrimony belonging to his family, and then to him. The county hiftory was dated
from the fame village, October 30, 1622. He alfo caufed part of Leland's Itinerary
to be tranfcribed 1631, and gave both the tranfcript and the feven original volumes
to the Bodleian library 1632; as alfo Talbot's notes †. To him the countryman
Thomas Purefoy, Efq. of Barwell bequeathed Leland's "Collectanea" after his death

---

* Of whom, &c fome particulars in the Anecdotes of Mr. Bowyer, p. 569. † Leland, III. 144.

1612. Wood charges him with putting many needless additions and illustrations into these "Collectanea;" from which charge Hearne defends him. Wood adds, he made a useful index to them, which, Hearne says, was only of religious houses and some authors. In 1625 he refided at Lindley, where, among other works, he compiled a folio volume under the title of "Antiquitates de Dadlington, &c." [See above, p. 99.] He died at Falde, after suffering much in the civil war, April 6, 1645, and was buried in the parish church thereto belonging, called Hanbury. He left several notes, collections of arms and monuments, genealogies, and other matters of antiquity, which he had gathered from divers churches and gentlemen's houses. Divers collections are mentioned in Gascoigne's notes, p. 53, probably by himself. In Osborne's Catalogue, 1757, was "Vincent on Brooke, with MS. notes by William Burton," probably not more than those on Cornwall, which Dr. Rawlinson had.—He was one of Sir Robert Cotton's "particular friends, and had the honour to instruct Sir William Dugdale. He was acquainted with Somner; and Michael Drayton, Esq. was his "near countryman and acquaintance," being descended from the Draytons of Drayton, or Fenny Drayton, near Lindley. He married, 1607, Jane, daughter of Humphrey Adderley, of Widdington, Warwickshire; by whom he had one son, Caffibelan, born 1609, heir of his virtues as well as his other fortunes, who, having a poetical turn, translated Martial into English, which was published 1658. He consumed the best part of his paternal estate, and died Feb. 28, 1681, having some years before given most, if not all, his father's collections to Mr. Walter Cherwynd, to be used by him in writing the Antiquities of Staffordshire. Several printed copies of Burton's Leicestershire, with MS. notes by different persons, are existing in various collections. Six or eight copies, with notes by the author and other persons (the natural history by Mr. Peck), are among the papers of the late Sir Thomas Cave. Mr. Gough has a copy, with numerous notes and many pedigrees, which once belonged to Robert Fisher, and afterwards to Mr. West. Another is in the Harleian library, with large additions by Peter Le Neve. Gascoigne's copy, with many emendations, is in Jesus College library, Cambridge; and Dr. Ducarel has another, with many notes by the late Dr. Vernon, Rector of St. George's, Bloomsbury. A copy of the same work, with MS. additions by Mr. Carte, was in T. Osborne's catalogue, 1756, vol. I. marked at five guineas.—"The reputation of Burton's book," as Mr. Gough justly observes, "arises from its being written early, and preceded only by Lambard's Kent 1576, Carew's Cornwall 1602, and Norden's Surveys; and it is in comparison only of these, and not of Dugdale's more copious work, that we are to understand the praises so freely bestowed on it, and because nobody has treated the subject more remotely and accurately; for Dugdale † says, Burton, as well as Lambard and Carew, performed briefly ‡. The present volume, though a folio of above 300 pages, if the unnecessary digressions were struck out, and the pedigrees

---

* Who had a considerable estate in Burton's neighbourhood. See the preceding article of these Memoirs.
† Dedication of Warwickshire, p. 1.
‡ He is called by his namesake, in his notes on Antoninus, p. 314, "the restorer of his own country "and the antiquities thereof in his exact description of Leicestershire." See a good abstract of it by Oldys, British Librarian, p. 187. Not above seven or eight families of note, mentioned by Burton, are now in being.

re-

reduced into lefs compafs, would fhrink into a fmall work. The typographical errors, efpecially in the Latin, are fo numerous, and the ftyle, according to the manner
of that time, fo loofe, that the meaning is often doubtful. The defcription is in al-
phabetical order, and confifts chiefly of pedigrees and moot-cafes. The author, fenfible of its defect, greatly enlarged and enriched it with the addition of Roman, Saxon,
and other antiquities, as appears from his letter to Sir Robert Cotton, dated Lindley,
June 9, 1627, ftill extant among Cotton's correfpondences, in his library, Jul. C.
iii. This book, thus augmented, was with other MSS. by the fame author, in the
poffeffion of Mr. Walter Chetwynd, of Ingeftry in Staffordfhire, whom Camden in
Staffordfhire calls *veneranda antiquitatis cultor maximus* ; and afterwards came to, or
was borrowed by, Mr. Charles King, tutor to Mr. Chetwynd, in whofe hands Brokefby[*] mentions it, and fays Mr. Chetwynd made confiderable additions to it[†]. He died
1693. Lord Chetwynd lent it to Sir Thomas Cave, in whofe hands Mr. Afhby faw
it 1763. It is continued to 1642. There are two copies of it, exceeding fair, and
a large folio with fome loofe drawings. That copy which Mr. Afhby faw was not
in Burton's hand-writing, but fair enough to be the work of a hired tranfcriber.—
Dr. Rawlinfon had the original manufcript [quere, if Gafcoigne's own writing ?]
with numerous notes and feveral pedigrees in MS. now in the Bodleian library.
Ames fays, Mr. Weft bought it for 2l. 12s. 6d. at Rawlinfon's fale 1750 ;" but query
if this be not the *printed* copy which Mr. Gough bought at Mr. Weft's fale 1773,
and which once belonged to Robert Fifher.

3. ROBERT BURTON,

YOUNGER brother of the Hiftorian of Leicefterfhire, was born at Lindley,.
February 8, 1576, educated at Sutton Coldfield, admitted commoner of Brazen-
Nofe college 1593, and ftudent of Chrift-Church 1599, under the tuition of Dr..
John Bancroft, afterwards Bifhop of Oxford. In 1616 he had, from the dean
and chapter of Chrift-Church, the vicarage of St. Thomas in Oxford (in which
parifh he always gave the facrament in Wafers), and from George Lord Berkeley
the rectory of Segrave in Leicefterfhire ; both which he held till he died at Chrift-
Church, January 27, 1639. " He was fuch a curious calculator of nativities,.
" that, the time of his death anfwering to his own predictions, it was whifpered,"
fays Wood, " that, rather than there fhould be any miftake in the calculation,
" he fent up his foul to heaven through a flip about his neck." He was a general.
fcholar and fevere ftudent, melancholy yet humourous, and figured in the pedan-
try of the times; but withal a man of great honefty, plain dealing, and charity.
He wrote " The Anatomy of Melancholy," which went through feveral editions.
in folio. On his monument in Chrift-Church is his buft, in ruff, gown, hair, and.
beard, with his nativity, as in the following fcheme :

* Francis, of whom fome account will be given among thefe Memoirs.
† Letter to Hearne, in Leland's Itinerary, VI. p. 96.

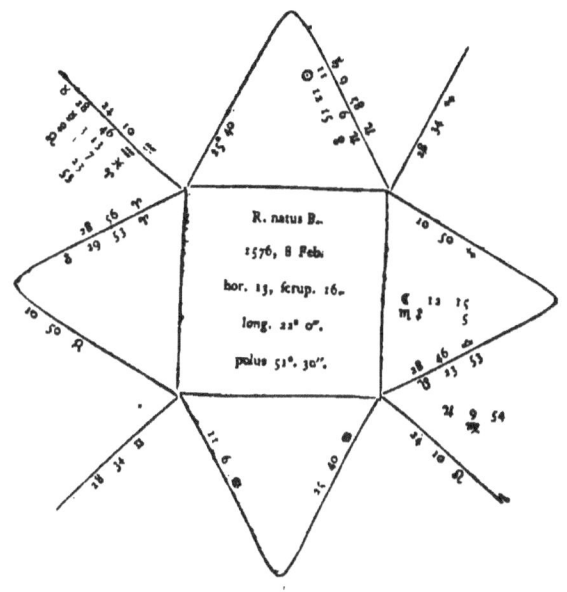

and on the middle of it this inscription by himself, put up by his brother :
" Paucis notus, paucioribus ignotus,
  Hic jacet Democritus junior,
  Cui vitam dedit & mortem.
  Melancholia.
      Obiit 8 Id. Jan. A. C. MDCXXXIX.
Arms : Az. on a bend O. between 3 dogs heads O. a crescent G. See plate V. fig. 12.
                                                                        H2

He left a choice library, part of which he bequeathed to the Bodleian, and 100l. to buy five-pounds-worth of books yearly for Chrift-Church library. It has been queried, whether the expreffion in the third line of the above epitaph favours Wood's fuppofition?—Burton, in his History of Leicefterfhire, p. 105, clofes his account of Anthony Faunt by obferving, that, " he fell into fo great a paffion of " melancholy, that within a fhort time after he died, in the year 1558. What " the force, power, and effect of melancholy is, I refer the reader to the Anatomy " of Melancholy, penned by my brother Robert Burton, bachelor of divinity in " Chrift-Church in Oxford."—Archbifhop Herring, in his 42d Letter to Mr. Duncombe, refers to a paffage in this work, with the following elogium : " I " mention the author to you as the pleafanteft, the moft learned, and the moft " full of fterling fenfe. The wits of Queen Anne's reign, and the beginning of " George the Firft's, were not a little beholden to him. Anthony Wood gives a " good account of him."

4. THOMAS CLEIVELAND, M. A. Vicar of HINCKLEY.

THE family of this moft worthy Divine came from Yorkfhire, and moft pro- bably from York, where fome of them were refpectable citizens for feveral genera- tions ; but their more early progenitors had confiderable landed property in the North-Riding of Yorkfhire, particularly in that diftrict or tract of country lying near Gilburne and Whitby, called now *Cleveland*, but anciently *Clivland*, whence they derived their name.

Thomas Cleiveland, who was a native of York, at leaft of that county, and ad- mitted of St. John's College in Cambridge, Nov. 5, 1605 ; a fcholar of Dr. Fell's foundation ; and taking the degree of M. A. 1614, was prefented to the vicarage of Hinckley, with the rectory of Stoke and chaplainfhip of Dadlington annexed, about the beginning of the year 1621. He had, by Elizabeth his wife, who died at Hinck- ley 1649 (where he himfelf was buried, Oct. 26, 1652), iffue fix fons and five daugh- ters, as appears at large in the genealogy annexed.

It appears, that the Vicar of Hinckley always wrote his name *Cleiveland :* which orthography was generally followed by his defcendants, but not univerfally, for fome of them wrote it *Cleveland* and *Cleaveland.* And in more early times, like that of all other ancient families, their name was written with every poffible variety of fpelling, viz. *Cliveland, Clyveland, Cliieveland, Cleivland, Cleaveland, Cleveland, Clevland,* and even *Clef* land.

What has occurred concerning their firft anceftors (who appear by their names not to be of Norman, but Anglo-Saxon defcent) will be feen in the following attempt towards

T H E G E N E A L O G Y

* *William Cleiveland fenex, pater Thomæ Cleiveland*, is the entry made by his son in the parish register.

** In Walker's *Sufferings of the Clergy*, fol. p. 111, we have the following character of Thomas CLEIVELAND, A. M. rector of Stoke, and vicar of Hinckley.

" He was a very great sufferer [for his loyalty and attachment to the an-
" cient constitution of church and state;] was father of the famous JOHN
" CLEIVELAND the Poet; and had at the time of his sequestration nine
" [eight] children (several of which, besides the Poet, were sufferers also)
" . . . . He was dispossest by the committee of Leicester; died in Oct.
" 1652; and was a very worthy person, and of a most exemplary life."

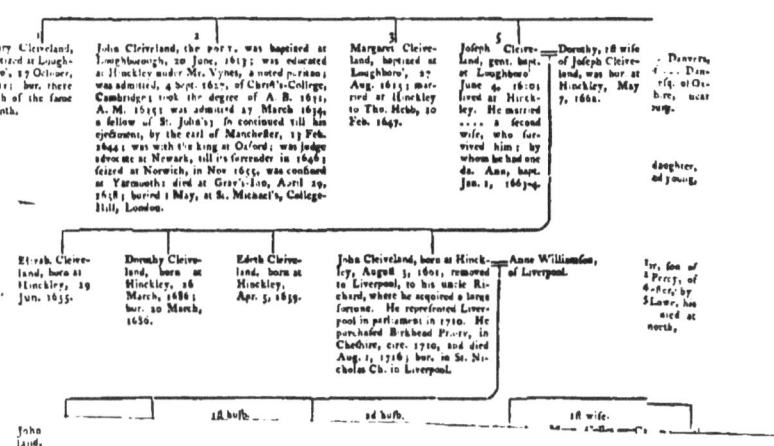

bed from the

1. M. 1614.
2. M. 1635.

3. M. 1681.
4. M. 1707.
5. M. 1715.

6. M. 1757.

THE MORE ANCIENT GENEALOGY of CLEIVELAND, or CLEVELAND.

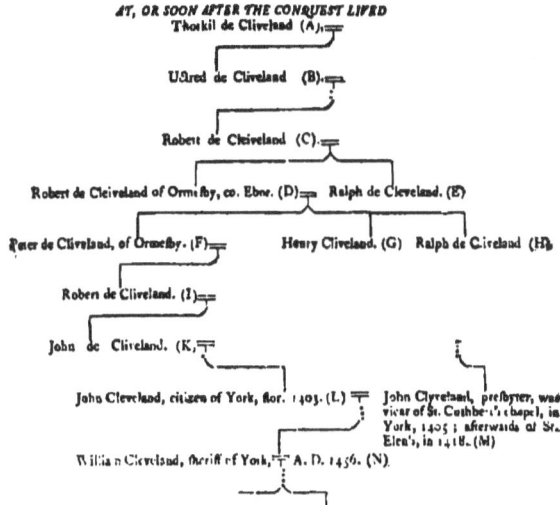

AT, OR SOON AFTER THE CONQUEST LIVED
Thorkil de Cliveland (A).

Udred de Cliveland (B).

Robert de Cleiveland (C).

Robert de Cleiveland of Ormesby, co. Ebor. (D)   Ralph de Cleveland. (E)

Peter de Cliveland, of Ormesby. (F)   Henry Cliveland. (G)   Ralph de Cireland (H)

Robert de Cliveland. (I)

John de Cliveland. (K)

John Cleveland, citizen of York, flor. 1405. (L)   John Cleveland, presbyter, was vicar of St. Cuthbert's chapel, in York, 1405; afterwards of St. Elen's, in 1418. (M)

William Cleveland, sheriff of York, A. D. 1456. (N)

FROM HIM WAS APPARENTLY DESCENDED
William Cleveland, father of the Rev. Thomas Cleveland, Eboracensis,
WHOSE DESCENDANTS SEE IN THE ANNEXED GENEALOGICAL TABLE.

(A) (B) Udred, son of Thorkil de Cliveland gave to Whitby Abbey two carucates of land, free from Danegeld, and the mill in Barneston (now Bernston, in Richmondshire,) co. Ebor. Vid. Mon. Ang. I. 74. (2r. b.) Charlton's Hist. of Whitby, 4to. 1779. p. 71.
(C) Robert de Cleiveland (so the name is spelt) gave to Whitby Abbey a piece of land in Ormesby. Mon. Ang. I. p. 72. (2r. b.) see also Charlton's Hist. of Whitby, p. 71. [This last writer has indicated his version of the old charters, by rendering the proper names too literally: thus Robert de Cleveland he translates Robert of Cleveland, &c. but we follow the original in the Monasticon.]
(D) (E) Ralph, son of Robert, granted and confirmed his brother's gift of lands to Whitby-Abbey, lying between the land which his father gave, and that belonging to the prior of Gisburne. Charlton, p. 130, 136.
(F) Peter de Cliveland gave to the church of Gisburn two bovates and four roads of land in Ormesby, and all his land in the valley of Marton, and all his land called Tunge, with other parcels of land enumerated in Mon. Ang. II. p. 151. (22. a.) He also confirmed the grant of his uncle Ralph (supra, E.) and his deed is annexed by Peter de Cleveland. Charlton's still. p. 136.
(F) (G) (H) These three brothers were benefactors to the priory of Gisburne or Gisburgh, in co. Ebor. See Burton's Monasticon Ebor . . . &c. p. 251. see also the same writer in the two generations (I) and (K).
(I) John Cleveland (verus . . .) is witness to a deed by which Richard Tekyll and Margaret his wife grant and convey to William Smythson, senior, and to his son William and his heirs, a tenement, with a croft in Dalton Norrays. Dat. 14 March, ano. 4 R. Hen. IV. The name herein is written by the scrivener copyist Clalland. (M) See Drake's History of York, fol. p. 343, 344; (N) Ibid. p. 303.

JOHN CLEIVELAND, the Vicar's second son, was born at Loughborough in Leicester-shire, as appears from the register of that parish, where his baptism is entered June 20, 1613. Having been educated at Hinckley under the Rev. Rich. Vines[*], he was admitted of Christ's College in Cambridge, September 4, 1627, and took the degree of B. A. in 1631. He thence removed to St. John's College in the same university, being elected Fellow, March 27, 1634, and became M. A. the following year, 1635. He continued for many years the delight and ornament of that house, in which he was one of the tutors, and, being excused from going into holy orders, became their rhe-torick reader, and was usually employed to draw up all epistles and addresses for that society, being much admired for the purity and terseness of his Latin style. He also became celebrated for his occasional poems in English, especially on the breaking-out of the civil wars, when he is said to have been the first champion that appeared in verse for the royal cause[†]. Afterwards, when the opposite party prevailed, he re-tired to the king at Oxford, and was in his absence ejected from his fellowship, April 8, 1644[‡]. On the fixing in Newark Castle that garrison which so long supported the King's declining cause, Cleiveland was appointed Judge-advocate there under Sir Richard Willis the Governor. After the surrender of that garrison in 1646, by the express-command of the King, then a prisoner with the Scottish army, Cleiveland followed the fates of distressed loyalty, living up and down concealed for some years, till in November, 1655, he was seized at Norwich, as a person of great abilities, ad-verse and dangerous to the reigning government[§], and was thence removed to Yar-mouth, where he lay many months in prison, till, addressing the Protector, he was by his order set at liberty. This petition (see p. 137.) is remarkable for the ad-dress with which the writer employs such moving topics as might neither do vio-lence to his conscience, nor betray his cause, and yet be effectual to procure his en-largement. At length removing to Gray's Inn, London, he was there seized with an epidemical intermitting fever, of which he died on Thursday morning, April 29, 1658, in his chamber in Gray's Inn, whence his body was brought to Hunsdon House, and on Saturday May 1. was interred in the parish church of St. Michael Royal on College Hill, London[¶]: his remains receiving the last honours, by the at-tendance of many persons eminent for their loyalty and learning, to whom his funeral sermon was preached by his intimate friend, the eminent Dr. Pearson, afterwards Bi-shop of Chester, and author of the celebrated exposition of the creed[**]. It does not appear that any monument was erected to his memory; but if there were, it was de-molished with the church by the great fire in 1666.

That kind and excellent antiquary Mr. Cole, in a letter on the subject of this memoir, says, "I have nothing more to add to the article of your relation Mr. John Cleiveland, than the following extract from a Weekly Journal in 1645, called " The Kingdomes Weekly Intelligencer," N° 101. p. 811. for Tuesday, 27, May, 1645.—" But to speak something of our friend Cleveland, that grand malignant of Cam-" bridge, we heare that he is now at Newarke, where he hath the title of advocate

* Of whom some account will be given in these Memoirs.
† Wood's Athen. Oxon. 2d Ed. ll. f. 274.   ‡ Walker's Sufferings, &c. part II. p. 149.
§ Thurloe's State Papers, vol. IV. p. 185.   ¶ Fuller's Worthies, in Leicestershire.
** Dav. Lloyd's Memoirs of Persons, who suffered for K. Charles I. 1668, fol. p. 617, 618.

" put

Plate XI

This I regard as now in the Possession of S. Knightley Esq. & c.

" put upon him. His office and employment is, to gather all the Colledge rents
" within the power of the king's forces in those parts, which he diftributes to fuch
" as are turned out of their fellowfhips at Cambridge for their malignancie. If the
" royal party be thus careful to fupplie their friends, fure it is neceffary to take
" fome courfe to relieve thofe who are turned out of their houfes and livings for ad-
" hering to the parliament."

From a collection of old pamphlets and journals during the great rebellion between
1639 and 1660, and forted by Mr. Carte, in Sir John Hinde Cotton's library at
Madingley near Cambridge.

" Mr. Granger and you," Mr. Cole adds, " agree in his being no clergyman ; fo
I have nothing more to fay on that fubject: but from his having a common place, or
fort of fhort fermon, or expofition, preached or pronounced in the College chapel,
and his old print * drefling him in a clerical habit, I was apt to conclude that he was
in holy orders; though I am aware that it is not unufual for laymen fometimes to
perform thefe fcholaftic exercifes, as well as that clergymen in thofe times of rebellion
and confufion were often obliged to lay afide their gown, and get their bread in other
profeffions as they could. Your dates are all accurate. He is allo mentioned in
Lloyd's Memoirs, edit. 1677, p. 261, 617." There are likewife fome notices of
him in Thurloe's " State Papers," vol. IV. p 184. It is there remarked, that
he was " a perfon of great abilities, and fo able to do the greater difervice."
Mr. Echard hath obferved, that " he was the firft poetic champion for the king."

Another worthy friend (the Rev. Mr. Kynafton, fellow of Brazen Nofe College,
Oxford) is fo kind as to fay, " Your obfervation concerning Cleiveland's ' Peti-
" tion to Cromwell' is exceeding judicious. I honour him for that petition †. It is a
" fine

* There are two other old portraits of our poet, one with a band, the other a buft crowned with laurel.
† The reader fhall judge of it for himfelf. Wood fays, " it was written in fuch towering language,
" and fo much gallant reafon, that upon the perufal of it Cromwell was fo much melted down with it,
" that he forthwith ordered his releafe."

" May it pleafe your Highnefs,
" RULERS, within the circle of their government, have a claim to that which is faid of the Deity,
' They have their centre every where, and their circumference no where.' It is in this confidence that
I addrefs to your Highnefs, as knowing no place in the nation is fo remote, as not to fhare in the ubi-
quity of your care; no prifon fo clofe, as to fhut me up from partaking of your influence. My Lord, it
is my misfortune, that after ten years of retirement from being engaged in the differences of the ftate,
having wound myfelf up in private recefs, and my comportment to the public fo inoffenfive that in all
this time neither fears nor jealoufies have fcrupled at my actions: being about three month fince at
Norwich, I was fetched with a guard before the commiffioners, and fent prifoner to Yarmouth; and if
it be not a new offence to make an enquiry wherein I offended (for hitherto my fault was kept as clofe as
my perfon), I am induced to believe, that, next to my adherence to the Royal party, the caufe of my confinement is the narrownefs of my eftate; for none ftand committed, whofe eftate can bail them. I only
am the prifoner, who have no acres to be my bonds. Now if my poverty be criminal (with reverence
be it fpoken) I implead your Highnefs, whofe victorious arms have reduced me to it, as acceffory
to my guilt. Let it fuffice, my Lord, that the calamity of the war hath made us poor; do not punifh us
for it! Who ever did penance for being ravifhed? Is it not enough that we are ftript fo bare, but it muft
be made in order to a feverer lafh! muft our fores be engraven with our wounds? muft we firft be made
cripples, then beaten with our own crutches? Poverty, if it be a fault, 'tis its own punifhment; who
pays more for it, pays ufe upon ufe. I befeech your Highnefs put fome bounds to the overthrow, and
do

T

" fine image of his soul. There is a nobleness of sentiment, and a dignity in the
" avowal of his principles in it, that would have done credit to Majesty itself. And
" at the same time a dexterity of ' address' as you remark, and a blameless finesse in
" the adopting of arguments proper for his purpose, that tyranny, the most steeled,
" could not fail to be soothed and conciliated by.—' The Rebel Scot' seems to be the
" utmost effort of Cleiveland's genius. And it is truly characteristic of it. His force
" was satire. Nature had endued him with a masculine strength of thought ; and
" the villainy of the times, co-operating with his own integrity and loyalty, made
" him direct that vigour of sentiment to the stigmatizing of the hypocrites of the age ;
" and the more forcibly to disburthen the forcibleness of his ideas, he laboured, in
" all the throes of an imagination on the full stretch, after a style that may not be
" improperly termed the gigantic, to express them in.——I greatly admire your
" print of Cleiveland. There is an abundant display of the *vis poetica* in the exte-
" rior at least. I admire too your distich that encircles his head. His distich on
" ' The Rebel Scot ' deserves it richly ; and, indeed, every eulogy in the satiric line.
" For nothing, surely, ever entered into the head of man, more happy, or more
" justly severe, on that traiterous crew, the Covenanters of the North of those days,
" than the celebrated couplet,

" Had Cain been Scot, God would have chang'd his doom ;
" Nor forc'd him wander, but confin'd him home."

do not pursue the chace to the other world. Can your thunder be leveled so low as our groveling condition ? Can your towering spirit, which hath quarried upon kingdoms, make a stoup at us, who are the rub-
bish of these ruins? Methinks I hear your former atchievements interceding with you, not to sully your
glories with trampling upon the prostrate, nor clog the wheel of your chariot with so degenerous a tri-
umph. The most renowned heroes have ever with such tenderness cherished their captives, that their
swords did but cut out work for their courtesies. Those that fell by their prowess, sprung up by their favour, as if they had struck them down only to make them rebound the higher. I hope your Highness,
as you are the rival of their fame, will be no less of their virtues. The noblest trophy that you can erect
to your honour is to raise the afflicted. And since you have subdued all opposition, it now remains, that
you attack yourself, and with acts of mildness vanquish your victory. It is not long since, my Lord, that
you knocked off the shackles from most of our party, and, by a grand release, did spread your clemency as
far as your territories. Let not new proscriptions interrupt your jubilee. Let not that your lenity be
slandered as the ambush of your further rigour. For the service of his Majesty (if it be objected) I am
so far from excusing it, that I am ready to alledge it in my vindication. I cannot conceit that my fidelity to my Prince should taint me in your opinion : I should rather expect it should recommend me to your
favour ; had we not been faithful to our King, we could not have given ourselves to be in your Highness ; you had then trusted us *gratis*, whereas now we have our former loyalty to vouch us. You see, my
Lord, how much I presume upon the greatness of your spirit, that dare prevent my indictment with so
frank a confession, especially in this which I may so safely deny that it is almost arrogancy in me to own
it ; for the truth is, I was not qualified enough to serve him ; all I could do, was to bear a part in his
sufferings, and give myself up to be crushed with his fall. Thus my charge is doubled ; my obedience
to my Sovereign, and what is the result of that, my want of fortune. Now whatever reflection I have
upon the former, I am a true penitent for the latter. My Lord, you see my crimes ; as to my defence, you
bear it about you. I shall plead nothing in my justification, but your Highness's clemency, which, as it
is the constant inmate of a valiant breast, if you graciously be pleased to extend it to your suppliant, in taking me out of this withering durance, your Highness will find that Mercy will establish you more than
Power ; though all the days of your life were as pregnant with victories as your twice auspicious third
of September. Your Highness's humble and submissive petitioner,   J. CLEIVELAND."

* It was translated into Latin by Thomas Gawen, of New College, Oxford, prebendary of Winchester, and rector of Exton, in the county of Hants, who afterwards turned Papist. (Ath. Ox. II. 758.)
It is printed in most of the editions of Cleiveland's Works.

In 1642, Mr. Cleiveland had the honour of fpeaking an oration before the King and Prince, at St. John's College, Cambridge, with which, Winftanley fays, the king was fo well pleafed, that he fent for him, gave him his hand to ki\`s, with great expreffions of kindnefs, and ordered a copy to be fent after him to Huntingdon, to which place he was haftening that night. When Oliver Cromwell was in election to be member for the town of Cambridge, as he engaged all his friends and interefts to oppofe it, fo when it was carried but by one vote, he cried out with much paffion, " that that fingle vote had ruined church and kingdom :" fuch fatal events did he prefage from the fuccefs of Oliver.

Mr. Aubrey informs us, that he went from Oxford to the garrifon at Newark ; where, upon drawing up certain articles for the royalifts, he would needs add this fhort conclufion, " And we annex our lives as a label to our truth." That gentleman adds, that after the king was beaten out of the field, he came to London, and entered himfelf at Gray's Inn, where he and Samuel Butler, of the fame fociety, had a club every night.

The correfpondence of Cleiveland, when at Newark, with a Parliament officer at Grantham, his anfwer to the Newark fummons; his epiftle to the earl of Weftmoreland, and thofe to the earls of Newcaftle and Holland, are equal proofs of the dexterity of his wit and the integrity of his heart.

During his ftay at Oxford he was venerated and refpected, fays Wood, not only by the great men of the court, but by the then wits remaining among the affrighted and diftreffed Mufes, for his high panegyrics and fmart fatires.

In Gataker's " Difcours Apologetical, 1654," 4to. our poet is mentioned under the appellation of " one Cleavland, a man to me, either by fight or hearfay, to rime " or pen, utterly unknown, further than his friend Lilie [in his Merlin 1654] gives " me notice of him, in fome fatyrical libel (it feems) is pleafed to term the late affem- " bly of Weftminfter (as he, who himfelf ftyles it Synod of Prefbyterians, as if " it confifted of none but fuch, relates) a flea-bitten fynod, an affembly brewed of " clerks, like Royfton crows, or friars of both orders, black and grey." I have not been able to meet with Lilly's Merlin for 1654, but in a fubfequent work (Hiftory of his Life and Times, p. 82. 2d edit. 1715) Lilly fays, " I had in 1652 and 1653, " and 1654, much contention with Mr. Gatacre of Redriff; a man endued with all " kinds of learning, and the ableft man of the whole fynod of Divines in the Oriental " tongues."

In 1662 was publifhed, " A Poem on the Fall of the South Side of St. Paul's " Cathedral. To which is added, A Satyre againft the Fanatick Boutefeus of thefe " Times; and a Memoriall offered up at the Tomb of the incomparable Mr. John " Cleaveland *. By T. P." In this memorial due honour is paid to the Rebel

---

* Soon after his death, Wood fays, (Faft. I. 274.) were publifhed feveral elegies on him, particularly that intituled, " Upon the moft ingenious and incomparable Mufophilift of his Time, Mr. John Cleaveland. A " living Memorial of his moft devotional Brother and cordial Mourner." Printed at London on the broad fide of a fheet of paper 1658. This elegy was written by *Phil-Cleaveland*; i. e. by a lover of Cleiveland (not by a brother Philip, as Wood erroneoufly fuppofed, for he had no brother of that name). It fhould have been Phile-Cleiveland; but the printer probably dropt the letter e. Wood alfo mentions " An Elegy upon the Death of the moft excellent Poet Mr. John Cleaveland," written by Francis Vaux, a fervitor of Queen's College, Oxford, and author of " A Poem in Praife of Typography," which was alfo printed on one fide of a fheet of paper in May 1658.

Scot,

Scot, the Rupertifmus, and feveral other poems of Cleiveland. On thofe to the memory of Edward King, the writer fays,

" Though to King's learned duft ftrict Fate allow'd
" Nor tomb nor trophy, but a watery fhrowd;
" Yet here his urn is fix'd, which fhall outvie
" Vain Cleopatra's marble pageantry."

Cleiveland's works were feveral times publifhed; 1647 *, 1651 †, 1658, 1659 ‡, 1660 1665, 1667, 1668, 1677, 1687, 1699; but the beft edition is that of 1687, 8vo. under the title of " The Works of Mr. John Cleveland, containing his Poems, Orati- " ons, Epiftles, collected into one volume, with the Life of the Author." This edition, which has his portrait in a clerical habit, was publifhed by Dr. Lake || (who pre- fixed to it " Clevelandi Manibus Parentalia") and Dr. Drake, under the initials J. L. and S. D. A Second Part was at the fame time printed, under the title of " John Cleveland's Revived Poems, Orations, Epiftles, and others of his genuine " incomparable Pieces, now at laft publifhed from his Original Copies by fome of " his entrufted Friends," (in which it is remarkable that fixty-five pages, viz. from p. 200. to p. 265. are literally copied from a book § intituled, Ex Otio Negotium, or Martiall his Epigrams Tranflated, with Sundry other Poems and Fancies by R. Fletcher. Lond. 1654," 8vo.) There is alfo in the fame volume a third part, called " The Ruftick Rampant, or Rural Anarchy affronting Monarchy; on the Infurrec- " tion of Wat Tyler, By J. C. Afperius nihil eft humili cum furgit in altum. Claudian."

Dr. Fuller gives him the character of " a general artift, pure Latinift, exquifite " orator, and excellent poet. His ftile was mafculine, his epiftles pregnant with

* This is a thin quarto, thus intituled, " The Character of a London Diurnal, with feveral felect " Poems by the fame Author. Optima & novifima editio. Printed in the yeare 1647." I have not met with any earlier edition.

† This edition was printed at London, " with additions." There is alfo printed " Clevelandi " Vindiciæ, or Cleaveland's genuine Poems, Orations, Epiftles, &c. purged from many falfe and " fpurious ones which had ufurped his name, and from innumerable errors and corruptions in the " true, &c. Lond. 1677." 8vo. before which is a little account of his life, wherein it is faid that Tho- mas Thurman performed the office of burial, and Dr. Pearfon, afterwards bp. of Chefter, preached his funeral fermon. The date of this edition (which Wood, Ath. Ox. I. Fafti 274. very properly fays muft be falfe) is probably a miftake for 1677.

‡ The editions of 1659 and 1660 contain what make the Second Part of the edition in 1687, and are thus intruled, " J. Cleaveland revived: Poems, Orations, Epiftles, and other of his genuine incompara- " ble pieces, never before publifht. With fome other exquifite Remains of the Wits of both Univerfities " that were his Contempo-a ies. Lond. 1659." 8vo. With a curious Preface by E. Williamfon, da- ted " Newark, Novemb. 21, 1658." The Editors of the edition in 1687, reprinting this volume with- out attending to the diftinction in the title-page, that it contained " fome other Remains," &c. of " emi- " nent Wits his Contemporaries," have publifhed as CLEIVELAND's, the additional Poems of John Hall, R. Fletcher, Jafper Mayne, Sir J. Denham, &c. &c. But the edition in 1677 (which makes the firft part of the edition in 1687) is all genuine; and fome few of the fecond part were evidently written by Cleiveland alfo.

|| " John Lake, D. D. (vicar of Leeds, and afterwards bifhop of Chichefter) was fent to St. John's " College, Cambridge, before he was complete 13 years of age; and committed to the tuition of the " famous Mr. Cleveland, for whofe memory he always retained a great reverence, and whofe poems, " orations, epiftles, &c. he and his friend Dr. Drake, vicar of Pontefract (1687) collected into one vo- " lume, to which they prefixed his life and parentalia, and dedicated them to Bifhop Turner, then maf- " ter of the college." Thorefby, Vicaria Leodenfis, p. 99.

§ See the Select Collection of Mifcellany Poems, 1781, vol. VII. p. 376. Other inftances of Poems falfely afcribed to Cleiveland are pointed out in p. 49. of the fame volume.

4   " me-

" metaphors; his lofty fancy seemed to slide from the top of one mountain to
" another, thereby making to itself a constant level of continued elevation. All
" his poems are incomparable, fo that to praise one, were to detract from the rest."
A copious specimen of them was printed, by the Compiler of this Memoir, in the
Seventh Volume of " A Select Collection of Miscellany Poems, 1781."

A portrait of him, painted by Fuller, during Cleiveland's attendance on the king
at Oxford, is now in the possession of the Bishop of Dromore; who has kindly permitted an engraving of it to accompany this History (see plate XI.) In this picture
he is reprefented holding a paper, on which is inscribed the title of his celebrated
poem; which, after all, is faid not to be meant for a satire on the Scottish nation in
general, but chiefly on that part of it then engaged in rebellion against king
Charles I. as the writer exprefsly excepts the valiant and loyal bands then enlisted
under Montrofe and Crawford, &c.

5. RICHARD VYNES,

A NATIVE of Blazon in Leicesterfhire, was bred in Magdalen College, Cambridge, where he continued till he commenced M. A. and was remarkable for his
fober and grave behaviour, not being chargeable even with the venial levities of
youth. From the univerfity he was elected (most probably at the recommendation of his contemporary Thomas Cleiveland) school-master of Hinckley; where he
entered into holy orders; and (as appears by the extract from the parifh-regifter
in p. 77.) married, and had at least one child, who was buried there in 1639.
After remaining some time in the faithful difcharge of his office at Hinckley-
fchool, he obtained the vicarage of St. Lawrence Jewry; and, being a good fpeaker
and an able divine, was chofen one of the Affembly of Divines that met at Weftminfter in 1644, to eftablifh the Prefbyterian government; which meeting his
own ideas, he was called their LUTHER, and was employed in the treaties of Uxbridge and the Ifle of Wight, where his conduct was fo fingularly refpectful and
proper to his Sovereign, that the King feldom fpoke to him without moving his
hat; a circumftance the more remarkable, as no other of the Parliament Commiffioners ever met with the fame token of attention. He came alfo with the
other London minifters to offer their fervices to pray with the king, the morning
before his execution [*]. Mr. Vynes, however, as Dr. Fuller tells us, was moft
charitably moderate to all that diffented from him, though conftant to his own
principles. He lost the mafterfhip of Pembroke Hall, Cambridge, because he
would not take the engagement. He was a very painful and laborious minifter,
and fpent his time principally amongft his parifhioners, in pioufly endeavouring
" to make them all of one piece, though they were of different colours, and
" unite them in judgements who diffented in affection." He died February 7,
1655, and was buried in the parifh church of St. Lawrence Jewry; which having been confumed in the general conflagration of 1660, no memorial of him
is there to be traced. Mr. Vynes preached the fermon at the funeral of Robert
earl of Effex, at Weftminfter Abbey, Sept 13, 1646, from 2 Sam. iii. 38 [†].

[*] Ath. Ox. II. 699.　　　　　[†] Ib. 95.

6. JOHN

6. John Onebye.

THIS gentleman, defcended from a family fituated in the fourteenth century at Newton Burguland in Leicefterfhire, firft took up his refidence at Hinckley about the middle of the fixteenth century; where he lived to a good old age, and died greatly refpected, leaving four fons, whofe defcendants will appear in the following Genealogy, compiled from the Parifh Regifters, Heraldic Vifitations, and other authentic Sources.

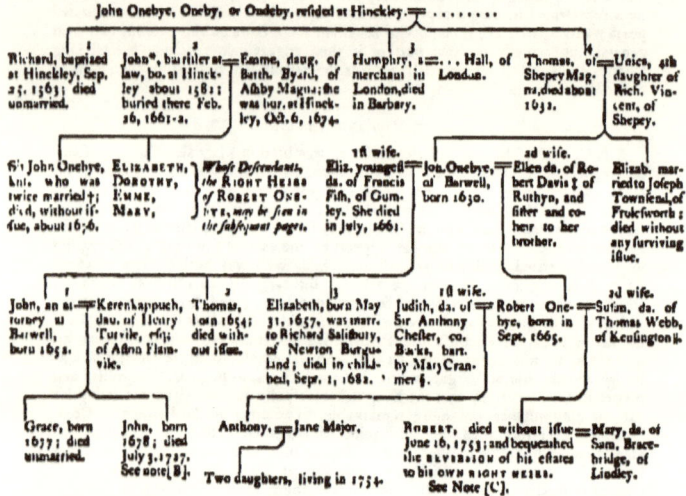

John Onebye, Oneby, or Ondeby, refided at Hinckley. ⚭ . . . .

1 Richard, baptized at Hinckley, Sep. 25. 1563; died unmarried.

2 John*, burfiler at law, bo. at Hinckley about 1581; buried there Feb. 26, 1661-2.⚭Emme, daug. of Barth. Byard, of Afhby Magna; fhe was bur. at Hinckley, Oct. 6, 1674.

3 Humphry, ⚭ . . . Hall, of merchant in London, died in Barbary.

4 Thomas, of⚭Unice, 4th Shepey Magna, died about 1651. daughter of Rich. Vincent, of Shepey.

1ft wife.

Sir John Onebye, knt. who was twice married†; d'd, without iffue, about 1676.⚭Elizabeth, Dorothy, Emme, Mary,

Whofe Defcendants, the Right Heirs *of* Robert One-bye, *may be feen in the fubfequent pages.*

Eliz. youngeft⚭Jon. Onebye, da. of Francis of Barwell, Fifh, of Gum-born 1630. ley. She died in July, 1661.

2d wife. Ellen da. of Robert Davis ‡ of Ruthyn, and fifter and coheir to her brother.

Elizab. married to Jofeph Townfend, of Frolefworth; died without any furviving iffue.

1 John, an at-⚭Kerenhappuch, torney at dau. of Henry Barwell, Turvile, efq; born 1652. of Afton Flamvile.

2 Thomas, born 1654; died without iffue.

3 Elizabeth, born May 31, 1657, was marr. to Richard Salifbury, of Newton Burguland; died in childbed, Sept. 1, 1682.

1ft wife. Judith, da. of⚭Robert One-Sir Anthony bye, born in Chefter, co. Sept. 1665. Barks, bart. by Mary Cranmer ‖.

2d wife. Sufan, da. of Thomas Webb, of Kenfington‖.

Grace, born 1677; died unmarried.

John, born 1678; died July 3.1737. See note[B].

Anthony, ⚭ Jane Major,

Two daughters, living in 1754.

Robert, died without iffue⚭Mary, da. of June 16, 1753; and bequeathed Sam. Brace-the reversion of his eftates bridge, of to his own right heirs. Lindley. See Note [C].

* Steward of the Court of Records at Leicefter.
† His firft wife was Mabell Afhby, as appears by his father's epitaph, p 39, and alfo by the parifh regifter, p. 77. The fecond (as appears from the laft vifitation of the county of Leicefter, now remaining in the Heralds Office, marked K, p. 84.) was *Mercie,* daughter of —— Dudion, co. Gloucefter; who, with two fifters, was buried in Hinckley church. See pp. 39, 40.
‡ Robert Davis married Dorothy, daughter and fole heir of Thomas Thelwall, 5th fon of John Thelwall of Llanrhydd, co. Denbigh.
§ Mr. Gough has a fine genealogy (on vellam) of " the ancient and worthy family of the Cranmers," taken in 1663, with maps of Elmefwell and Drenkefton in Suffolk, part of the eftates devifed by Robert Onebye's will.
‖ On whom, and his heirs, the reverfion of the eftates of Sir Henry Wood, of Loudham, in the county of Suffolk, was fettled; as will be more particularly mentioned in note [A], p. 145.

Genealogy of the FOUR DAUGHTERS of JOHN ONEBYE.

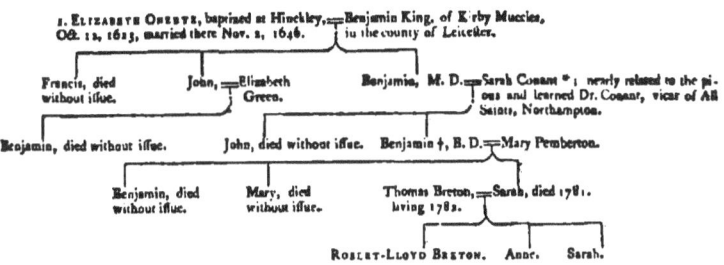

1. ELIZABETH ONEBYE, baptized at Hinckley, Oct. 12, 1623, married there Nov. 2, 1646.=Benjamin King, of Kirby Muxloe, in the county of Leicester.

Francis, died without issue.

John,=Elizabeth Green.

Benjamin, M. D.=Sarah Conant * ; nearly related to the pious and learned Dr. Conant, vicar of All Saints, Northampton.

Benjamin, died without issue.

John, died without issue.

Benjamin †, B. D.=Mary Pemberton.

Benjamin, died without issue.

Mary, died without issue.

Thomas Breton,=Sarah, died 1781. living 1782.

ROBERT-LLOYD BRETON. Anne. Sarah.

* This lady, with two brothers and three sisters, were all remarkable for longevity. The youngest of the six died at 82.

† Benjamin King, M. A. afterwards D. D. installed prebendary of Gloucester, Sept. 26, 1700. He was some time vicar of All Saints, Northampton, and of St. Mary de Lode, in Gloucester; on the south side of the chancel of which church he was buried, but has no memorial. He died in 1717 or 1718.

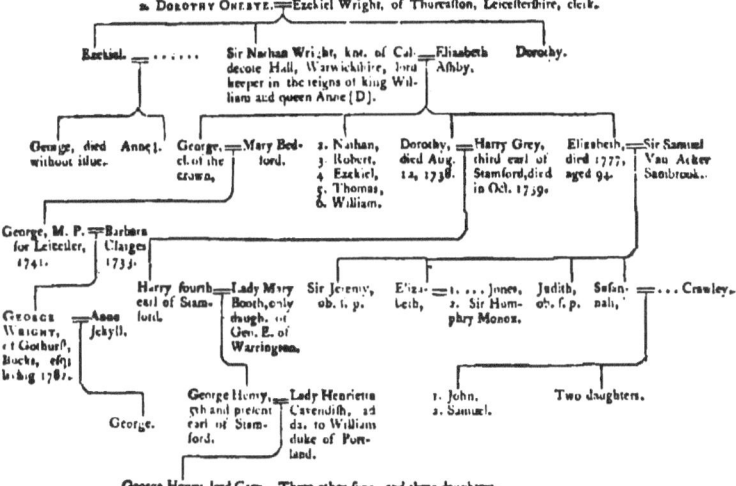

2. DOROTHY ONEBYE.=Ezekiel Wright, of Thurcaston, Leicestershire, clerk.

Ezekiel. . . . . . .

Sir Nathan Wright, knt. of Caldecote Hall, Warwickshire, lord keeper in the reigns of king William and queen Anne [D].=Elizabeth Ashby.

Dorothy.

George, died without issue.

Anne ‡.

George, clerk of the crown,=Mary Bedford.

2. Nathan, 3. Robert, 4. Ezekiel, 5. Thomas, 6. William.

Dorothy, died Aug. 12, 1738.

Harry Grey, third earl of Stamford, died in Oct. 1739.

Elizabeth, died 1777, aged 94.

Sir Samuel Van Acker Saabrook.

George, M. P. for Leicester, 1741.=Barbara Claiges, 1735.

Harry fourth earl of Stamford.=Lady Mary Booth, only daugh. of Gen. E. of Warrington.

Sir Jeremy, ob. s. p.

Eliza. Leib,=1. . . . Jones, 2. Sir Humphry Monox.

Judith, ob. s. p.

Susannali,=. . . Crawley.

GEORGE WRIGHT, of Gothurst, Bucks, esq; living 1782.=Anne Jekyll.

George Henry, 5th and present earl of Stamford.=Lady Henrietta Cavendish, 2d da. to William duke of Portland.

1. John. 2. Samuel.

Two daughters.

George.

George Henry lord Grey. Three other sons, and three daughters.

‡ Who was three times married. Her first husband's name was Mead; the second . . . . ; the third Fullerton.

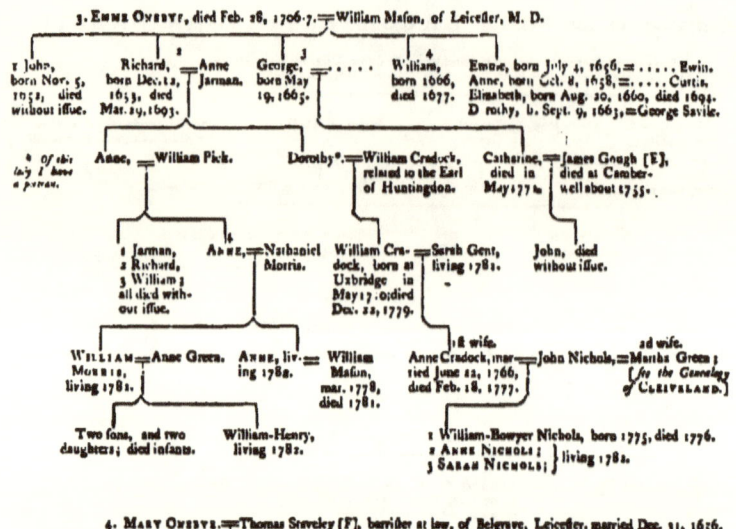

3. EMME ONEBYE, died Feb. 28, 1706-7.══William Mason, of Leicester, M. D.

1 John, born Nov. 5, 1653, died without issue.

Richard, born Dec. 12, 1655, died Mar. 14, 1693.══Anne Jarman.

George, born May 19, 1665.

William, born 1666, died 1677.

Emme, born July 4, 1656, ══ ..... Ewin. Anne, born Oct. 8, 1658, ══ ..... Curtis. Elizabeth, born Aug. 10, 1660, died 1694. Dorothy, b. Sept. 9, 1663, ══George Savile.

Anne,══William Pick.

Dorothy.══William Cradock, related to the Earl of Huntingdon.

Catharine,══James Gough [E], died in May 1774. died at Camberwell about 1755.

1 Jarman, 2 Richard, 3 William; all died without issue.

Abme,══Nathaniel Morris.

William Cradock, born at Uxbridge in May 17, 1751, died Dec. 22, 1779.══Sarah Gent, living 1781.

John, died without issue.

WILLIAM MORRIS, living 1781.══Anne Green.

ANNE, living 1782.══William Mason, mar. 1778, died 1781.

Anne Cradock, married June 22, 1766, died Feb. 18, 1777.══John Nichols,══Martha Green; [see the Genealogy of CLEIVELAND.]

Two sons, and two daughters; died infants.

William-Henry, living 1782.

1 William-Bowyer Nichols, born 1775, died 1776. 2 ANNE NICHOLS; 3 SARAH NICHOLS; living 1782.

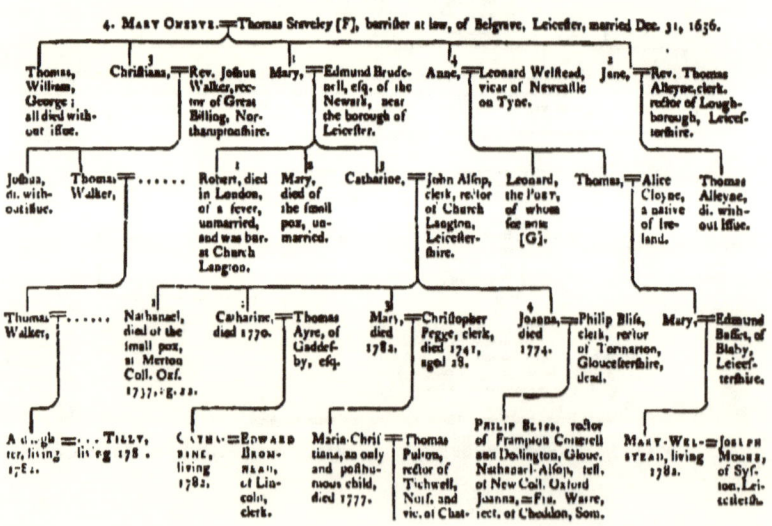

4. MARY ONEBYE.══Thomas Staveley [F], barrister at law, of Belgrave, Leicester, married Dec. 31, 1656.

Thomas, William, George; all died without issue.

Christiana,══Rev. Joshua Walker, rector of Great Billing, Northamptonshire.

Mary,══Edmund Brudenell, esq. of the Newark, near the borough of Leicester.

Anne,══Leonard Welstead, vicar of Newcastle on Tyne.

Jane,══Rev. Thomas Alleyne, clerk, rector of Loughborough, Leicestershire.

Joshua, di. without issue.

Thomas Walker.══.....

Robert, died in London, of a fever, unmarried, and was buried at Church Langton.

Mary, died of the small pox, unmarried.

Catharine,══John Alsop, clerk, rector of Church Langton, Leicestershire.

Leonard, the busy, of whom see more [G].

Thomas,══Alice Cloyne, a native of Ireland.

Thomas Alleyne, di. without issue.

Thomas Walker,══.....

Nathanael, died of the small pox, at Merton Coll. Oxf. 1737, æ. 22.

Catharine, died 1770.══Thomas Ayre, of Cadderby, esq.

Mary, died 1782.══Christopher Pegge, clerk, died 1741, aged 29.

Joanna, died 1774.══Philip Bliss, clerk, rector of Tarmarton, Gloucestershire, dead.

Mary,══Edmund Basset, of Blaby, Leicestershire.

A daughter, living 1781.══.... Tilly, living 1781.

CATHARINE, living 1782.══Edward Bromsell, of Lincoln, clerk.

Maria-Christiana, an only and posthumous child, died 1777.══Thomas Pulton, rector of Tilwell, Notf. and vic. of Chat-

PHILIP BLISS, rector of Frampton Cotterell and Dotlington, Gloue. Nathanael Alsop, fell. of New Coll. Oxford Joanna,══Fra. Warre, rect. of Cheddon, Som.

MARY-WELSTEAD, living 1781.══Joseph Mounr, of Syston, Leicester.

NOTES ON THE GENEALOGIES OF ONEBYE.

[A] Sir Henry Wood (son of Thomas Wood *, of Hickney, esq;) "Treasurer to the late Q_cen-
" Mother, and one of the council to Queen Catherine," married a daughter of the Rev. Michael
Gardiner, rector of Greenford, Middlesex, by whom he had one daughter Mary, who was married to
Charles Palmer earl of Southampton, afterwards duke of Southampton and Cleveland. I have in MS. a
copy of the original settlement † and last will of Sir Henry Wood, both made in 1671. The will is
dated

* Serjeant of the pastry to King Charles I. He married Susan, daughter and heir of ——— Cranmer, of London,
merchant; and died in May, 1649, aged 84; and his widow Oct. 17, 1650, aged 80. They were both
buried at Hackney, where there are inscriptions to their memory. This gentleman (son of Henry Wood, of
Hackney, esq; servant to Queen Elizabeth, and grandson to Thomas Wood of Burnley in the county of Lancaster) was lineally descended from le Sieur de Boys, dauphin in France; whose arms (a Lion rampant
Arg. in a field Gules) were granted to this Thomas by Sir Richard St. George, knight, Clarenceux, June 28,
1634. See Grants, vol. II. p. 664, in the College of Arms. I have in MS. an accurate pedigree of the
Woods.

† The substance of the settlement will appear by the following " Abstract of Sir Cæsar Wood, alias
" Cranmer's Case," which was heard at the Bar of the House of Lords, December 1, 1693.
   " SIR HENRY WOOD (the Appellant's Uncle) by lease and release, dated 22d and 23d of May, 1669, in
" consideration of a Marriage to be had between the Respondent (the now Duke of Southampton) and Ma-y
" Wood, his only daughter and child, and of 1000l. per annum in land, agreed (on behalf of the Duke) to
" be settled on Mary for jointure, did settle his whole estate, being about 4000l. a year, on trustees (his
" daughter being then about six or seven years old) in trust for himself for his life; and after his death, in
" trust to pay 450l. a year for his daughter's maintenance, till her age of twelve years, and 500l. a year, till
" her age of fifteen, or marriage; and to pay the residue of the profits after the Respondent's and Mary's
" inter-marriage (which would have been 1000l. and more if the same had taken effect according to Sir
" Henry Wood's appointment) unto the Respondent, which the Respondent was to have, though he should
" have no issue by Mary. If the marriage took effect (after Mary's age of sixteen years) and she should
" have issue male by the Respondent, then the trustees to stand seised of the estate, to the use of the Respondent
" and Mary for their lives, and after for the first and all their sons, and the sons of such sons, in tail male,
" and after for their daughters in general tail, and for want of such issue, for such persons as Sir Henry by
" his will should appoint; and in default thereof, for his right heirs. Sir Henry Wood, at the same time,
" makes his will, though dated the day after the settlement, and thereby devised his said estate, in case the
" marriage should not take effect, according to his appointment; or if there should be no issue, to Mary for
" life, and after to her first and all her sons, and the sons of such sons, in tail male; and after to her daughters
" in general tail, and after to the Bishop of Lichfield and Coventry, his brother, for life, and after to other
" persons (who are all dead), and then to the Appellant for life, with other remainders over. Sir Henry
" Wood died the next day after the making the settlement and will. The marriage between the Respondent
" the Duke and Mary was in other manner, and at other times, than was appointed by Sir Henry Wood;
" for Mary was first married at her age of seven years, and then again at her age of twelve years, when her
" father appointed it to be after her age of sixteen years; and the said marriage was had without the consent
" of such persons as were to have been present and consenting thereto. Mary afterwards (viz. in Novem-
" ber 1680) died, having never had issue by the Respondent the Duke. The Bishop of Lichfield and Coventry,
" upon such the decease of Mary, being next in remainder by Sir Henry's settlement and will (which makes
" but one conveyance) entered and enjoyed the estate for nine years and more, without any pretence of the
" Respondent's. The late King Charles the Second, the Respondent the Duke himself, acquiesced in the
" Bishop's entry, as satisfied that the Respondent's interest was determined by the death of Mary without
" issue: as an evidence that the said late King was satisfied therein, he was pleased to direct a treaty to be
" made with the Bishop for a marriage of one of his daughters to Mr. Charles Cranmer the Bishop's nephew.
" That the Respondent the Duke was so far then satisfied, that he made no pretence for nine years together,
" and in anno 1686, which was six years after Mary's death, the estate was sequestered (in a suit in Chan-
" cery, wherein the Respondent was plaintiff against the Bishop) for a contempt of the Bishop's, and upon
" the Bishop's electing the contempt, the sequestration was taken off by the court, and the Bishop let into the
" possession again. But in Michaelmas term, anno 1689, and not before (which was nine years after the
" death of Mary, and eighteen years after the settlement made, which was prepared and perused by great
" and eminent counsel on the Respondent's part, who, if it had been intended the Respondent should have
" had an estate for his life, though he had no issue, would not have used words of a contrary importance),
" the Respondent exhibited his bill in Chancery, and claimed the said estate for his life, though he never
" had any issue by the said Mary; and though there be no trust declared of the said estate for him the Re-
" spondent, but only on the precedent condition aforesaid, viz. ' But if the said intended marriage shall take
" effect after Mary's age of sixteen years, and the shall have issue male by the Respondent the Duke; Then
" for the better settlement of the premises upon such issue male, and for a more ample provision and mainte-
" nance of the Respondent and Mary his wife, and the longest liver of them, the trustees to stand intrusted
" for the said Respondent and Mary, for and during their lives and the survivor of them, and after their

U   " decease,

dated " May 24. 1671, after dinner," only one day before the death of Sir Henry Wood: " who was " buried, according to his will, after a fantastical way *, in the church near Lowdham-Hall," as Anthony Wood was told by Sir William Dugdale. He had three brothers, who all died before him; 1. John, a citizen of London. 2. Thomas †, bishop of Litchfield and Coventry 1671—1692. 3. William,

" deceased, in trust for their first son, &c. and for default of issue, for such persons as Sir Henry Wood should " appoint by his will.' Which is a plain precedent copulative condition, and being never performed for want " of issue, no trust of this estate could ever arise to the Respondent for his life; and yet, by a construction not " consistent with the positive words of the settlement, and which may be hereafter of ill precedent, and dan- " gerous consequence to deeds, settlements, and assurances, the court of Chancery hath decreed the estate to " the Respondent for his life. The Respondent (the Duke) by the settlement, was thus provided for : 1. If " the marriage did not take effect through the default of Mary, either by her refusal of him, or by marrying " another; or by her death before sixteen, he was to have 20000. to be paid him out of Sir Henry Wood's " estate. 2. If the marriage did take effect at Mary's age of sixteen, though there were no issue, the Re- " spondent the Duke was immediately to have the whole profits of the estate from the death of Sir Henry " Wood, which to Mary's age of sixteen would and did amount to more than 20000. which he hath had, " though nothing was settled on his part. 3. But if the marriage did take effect, and the Respondent the " Duke had issue male, then he was also to have an estate for his own life, but not otherwise; but by such " construction as before, an estate for life in the said estate is decreed to him, though he never had issue. " Therefore the said Appellant hath appealed from the said Decree, in the Right Honourable the Lords Spi- " ritual and Temporal in Parliament assembled." The decree, which had been made by the lords com- missioners of the great seal Oct. 31, 1691, was reversed by the house of peers.—At the time of making the settlement, which was honoured with the royal sanction, Sir Henry's daughter was not quite seven years old; and the marriage was to take place when she should be between sixteen and seventeen. In case of the Earl of Southampton's death before marriage, his right in the lady was to be transferred to his next brother, Lord George Palmer, son of Barbara Duchess of Cleveland. And in case of his daughter's death without issue, Sir Henry bequeathed his estates, after several intermediate settlements, all which became extinct, to his own right heirs.—Sir Cæsar Wood, alias Cranmer, was admitted in fee, as nephew and heir to Thomas Wood bishop of Litchfield, to two acres of copyhold at Dover Hedge, in Thelverton manor, January 21, 1694. Charles Wood was admitted in fee, Oct. 16, 1710, as only son to Sir Cæsar. In 1741. Henry Cockfedge, Gent. was admitted as receiver appointed for the heir of the above-mentioned Charles Wood then deceased, by the High Court of Chancery.—Nov. 11, 1745, a cause was heard in Chancery, Chapman and Chester versus Onebye, which is not reported by Atkyns, but which terminated in Onebye's being decreed heir at law to Charles Wood.—Sept. 16, 1765, it was resolved that Robert Onebye, Esq; was so decreed heir, and that Mr. Cockfedge and Mr. Onebye were both dead. Mr. Chapman was admitted for want of heirs, and paid a relief of four pence halfpenny. These extracts were transcribed from the court-book of Thelverton manor.

* This does not agree with the will; which says, " I desire my body may be buried in the parish-church " of I'Bond, in the county of Suffolk, in such decent and private manner as my executors shall think fit, with " as little cost as may be convenient."

† " Educated in the college school at Westminster, elected student of Christ-Church in 1627, or thereabouts, took the degree in arts, holy orders, and by the endeavours of Sir Henry Wood, his elder brother, was made chaplain in ordinary to King Charles I. being then but 20 years of age. In 1643 he took the degrees in di- vinity, by virtue of a dispensation for allowance of terms, and about that time was rector of Wickham in the bishoprick of Durham. In the time of the grand rebellion against King Charles I. he left the nation and his preferments, and travelled to Rome, and to other places in Italy, where he spent some years, and after his re- turn lived a retired life in the country. In the jubilee year of 1660 he was restored to his rectory, and, in reward of his sufferings, had a prebendship in the church of Durham conferred on him (installed therein Dec. 10 the same year;) and upon the promotion of Dr. William Paul to the see of Oxon, he was made dean of Litchfield in the latter end of 1663. In 1670 he was promoted to the see of Litchfield, on the death of Dr. John Hacket, by the endeavours of his said brother Sir Henry (whose daughter and heir was married to Charles Fitz-Roy Duke of Southampton, natural son of King Charles II.;) whereupon being consecrated on the second day of July (being the second Sunday after that of Trinity) anno 1671, (at which time Dr. Crew was consecrated bishop of Oxon) enjoyed that honour, though a person of no merit, unless it was for his preaching, to the time of his death. But so it was, that he not caring to live at Litchfield or Eccleshall (where is a seat belonging to the see) either for not being beloved, or to save charges, he retired to Hackney, and lived in the house where he was born, in an ordinary condition: whereupon Dr. Sancroft archbishop of Canterbury suspended him of his office. He died very wealthy at Astrop near King's-Sutton in Northamp- tonshire, where he had continued about two years for health's sake, on the 17th of April, or thereabouts, in 1692. He left several legacies to pious uses, among them 300l. to the junery masters of Christ Church, and an estate of 20l. per annum in Norfolk to the same matters." Wood, Ath. Ox. II. 1190.

When the cathedral at Litchfield was recovering after the Restoration, it appears from an authentic paper printed by Mr. Pennant [Journey from Chester, p. 424.] from the MSS. of Mr. Greene of Litchfield, that Bishop Wood, when Dean, gave   —   —   £. 50

And since Bishop   —   —   10

And promised (saith Dean Smallwood) more   —   100

clerk

clerk of the fpicery at Whitehall; and two fifters; 1. Mary *, married firft to Samuel Cranmer, fheriff of London in 1631; and fecondly to Sir Henry Chefter, of Luthington, Bedfordfhire, Knight of the Bath; 2. Elizabeth, married to Anthony Webb, father to Thomas, in whom the eftate fettled in remainder after the office of Sir Cæfar Cranmer. This Thomas had two daughters; 1. Sufan, married to Robert Onebye, efq. 2. Elizabeth, married to William Chapman, efq. who was knighted by King George I. in 1714, created a baronet in 1720, and died May 7, 1737; leaving two fons, fir John the late and Sir William the prefent baronet.

[B] This eccentric branch of a moft worthy flock was born at Barwell, in or about the year 1674. His grand-father, who poffeffed a plentiful eftate, was many years in the commiffion of the peace for Leicefterfhire; and his father was an attorney of unblemifhed reputation. John, the fubject of this note, after a liberal education, was placed as a clerk to an attorney of eminence; but his afpiring and haughty difpofition induced him to look much higher, and his parents foon found they had not properly confidered his inclinations.

The cuftody of the Great Seal being committed to his relation Sir Nathan Wright, application was made for fome genteel employment that would be more congenial to his high fpirit. Notwith-ftanding their affinity, nothing better happened to be then in the lord keeper's power than the employment of train-bearer, which young Onebye accepted, in hopes of fome future vacancy, his uncle being at the fame time employed as Sir Nathan's fecretary. Preferment not meeting his wifhes, he refolved to enter into the army; and a commiffion being obtained, he ferved in feveral campaigns under the duke of Marlborough in Flanders, and acquired much reputation, diftinguifhing himfelf on many oc-cafions, and received feveral wounds which remained vifible till his death.

He fought a duel at Bergen with a Saxon colonel, whom he killed; and, being tried by a court-martial, was honourably acquitted. And at Port Royal in Jamaica he afterwards fought lieutenant Tooley, where both were defperately wounded; but Tooley died, after having languifhed for eight months; in which time the antagonifts were perfectly reconciled.

After ferving feveral years in the army, and rifing gradually, by feniority, to the rank of major in Honeywood's dragoons, he found himfelf, by the peace of Utrecht, in the number of difbanded officers; and, returning to England, gained a fcandalous fubfiftence by dexterity at gaming. The frauds which this unhappy man is fuppofed to have committed were numerous, and difagreeable to relate; but the important event which occafioned his being tried at the Old Bailey, before Mr. Baron Hale and Sir William Thomfon, for the murder of William Gower, was thus drawn up at the time for the confideration of the judges, the jury having given in a fpecial verdict: " That the prifoner and the deceafed, with three other gentlemen (one of which was Mr. John Rich, then manager of Lincoln's-inn Theatre, and after-wards of Covent Garden), met at the Caftle Tavern in Drury lane, fupped together, and were good friends; that the company went to gaming: that the prifoner was difgufted at the deceafed's having jocularly fet another gentleman Three Half-Pence, inftead of Three Half-Crowns, faying it was impertinent. That the deceafed afked him, ' What he meant by impertinent?' ' You're an impertinent Puppy,' fays the pri-foner: To which the deceafed replied, ' The man that calls me Puppy is a Rafcal.' That the prifoner thereupon took up a bottle, and with violence threw it at the deceafed's head, which beat fome powder out of his periuig: who, in return, threw a glafs, or candleftick, at the prifoner, which did not reach him: That both rofe up together, and went to their fwords; that a gentleman ftepping between prevent-ed their fighting: that the company all fate down again, and drank for near an hour; when the de-ceafed, offering his hand to the prifoner, faid to this effect: ' We have had hot words, Major; you was the aggreffor; but let us be reconciled.' To which the prifoner anfwered, ' No, damn you, I'll have your blood.' That in about half an hour after the company broke up, when the prifoner hung his great coat upon his fhoulders; but, calling back the deceafed, faid, ' Hark ye, young gentleman, I have fomething to fay to you.' That they both re-entered the room, when the door was fhut violently, and fwords heard to clafh; and the deceafed received the wound of which he died. The Major alfo had received three flight wounds. That the deceafed being afked on his death-bed, if he had received the wound fairly? anfwered. ' I—think—I—did; but—I don't know what might have happened—if you had not come in.' This narrative is fubftantially confirmed by Raymond's Reports, vol. II. p. 1486. The Major, who had entertained ftrong hopes of coming off with a verdict of Man flaughter, was re-manded back to Newgate; where he continued tolerably eafy for about a year, being free from

---

* This lady's only fon, Cæfar Cranmer, of Aftwoodbury, Bucks, was afterwards knighted, and called himfelf Sir Cæfar Wood. He married Letis daughter of Simon de la Garde of Paris; inherited the Suffolk eftate, as nephew and heir to Bifhop Wood; and had two fons, Henry Cranmer, who died young, and Charles Cranmer, who took the name of Wood, and enjoyed the eftates. I have a copy of the laft will of Dame Mary Chefter, who furvived both her hufbands, was buried at Aftwood, and bequeathed to her fon all her right and title arifing from the fettlement or will of her brother Sir Henry Wood, to whom fhe was executrix. She had alfo a daughter, Mary, married to Sir Anthony Chefter, of Chichley, Bucks. By her fecond hufband, fhe had no child.

U 2

irons, and accommodated with the most commodious room in the prison: finding the prosecutor had taken no steps towards bringing on the hearing of the special verdict before the judges, he grew pretty confident it would be determined in his favour; and imagined the prosecutor was of that opinion: at length, having consulted some attornies and law-books, and judging too favourably for himself, he came to a resolution to move the judges of the King's Bench, for a *Certiorari* to be made for arguing the special verdict before that court. It was argued in the court of King's Bench about the end of Hilary term; and another argument being desired by the prisoner's counsel, the opinion of all the judges was taken, at Serjeants Inn Hall, May 6, 1727, near fourteen months after the trial; when he was found guilty of wilful murder by the opinion of 11 judges out of 12, and the day of execution was fixed for the 3d of July, 1727. Strong applications were made to the king for a reprieve; which not succeeding, on the evening of the 2d, which was on a Sunday, he went to bed as usual about 10 o'clock, a man being in the room with him, and another at the chamber-door. Mr. Clif—o came and took leave of him, as did his old friend Mr. Casslis, and then the man read several chapters from St. Matthew's Gospel to him, but he was not in the least affected with them. At four the next morning he called for a glass of brandy and water, and then for a pen and paper, when raising himself in his bed, he wrote as follows; viz.— " Cousin Turrile, give Ackerman the turnkey below stairs half a guinea, and Jack who waits in my room five shillings; the poor devils have had a great deal of trouble with me since I have been here." This being his last will and testament, and the last act of his life, excepting the dreadful one upon his own body, which soon followed, he then desired the man in the room and the other at the door to be still a-while, that he might compose himself against the coming of his friends. About seven his footman came into the room, when he falsely said, " Who is that, Philip?" After that, a gentleman, his relation, came to the bed-side, and calling, " Major, Major," and hearing no answer, drew open the curtains, when he was just expiring, and weltering in his blood. Mr. Green, a neighbouring surgeon, was instantly sent for, but he was departed. The razor with which he had cut through the great artery in his arm was found in the bed; and it was evident that he had been assisted in this horrible enterprize, the razor appearing to have been newly ground for the service. Only a six-pence, and three letters from some of his friends, were found in his pocket. This account is principally taken from " A true and faithful Narrative of the Life and Actions of John Onebye, Esquire; commonly called Major Onebye [1727.]" There was also published on this occasion, " The Weight of Blood; or, The Case of Major Onebye, &c."

[C] THIS is the last Will and Testament of me ROBERT ONEBYE*, of Lindley, in the County of Leicester, Esquire. And, after recommending my Soul into the Hands of the Almighty, and my Body to be decently interred in a private Manner; as to all my Worldly Estate, I dispose of the same in Manner following: I give, devise, and bequeath, all my Estate, Lands, Tenements, and Hereditaments, late belonging to Sir HENRY WOOD, and Bishop WOOD, and CHARLES CRANMER, alias WOOD, Esquire, or either of them, or to any other Person, in the County of Suffolk or elsewhere, and all other my Lands, Tenements, and Hereditaments, and all my other Real Estate, whatsoever and wheresoever, or whether in Possession, Reversion, Remainder, or Expectancy, and all Right and Title, Interest, Property, Claim, and Demand, of, in, and to the Premises, or to such or any other Real Estate as aforesaid, and not before settled by me upon my Heirs Male, or otherwise by me entailed, unto my Friends Thomas Boothby, of Marston, in the County of Leicester, Esquire, and Samuel Bracebridge, of Lindley, in the County of Leicester, Esquire, their Heirs and Assigns, up in the Trusts, and to the Uses, following; viz. That they shall, by Mortgage or Sale, felling Timber and felling the same, or otherwise, raise and pay such Sum and sums of Money as shall be necessary to defray my Debts, Legacies, Portions for Daughters and Younger Children, and Funeral Expenses; Then to the Use and Behoof of my loving Wife Mary Onebye, for and during the Term of her Natural Life, without Impeachment of Waste, subject to the Proviso hereafter mentioned; Then to the Use of the first Son of my Body, and every other Son, for Life, according to seniority, and the Heirs Male of such Son or Sons; And in case I should die without Issue Male, then to all and every Daughter and Daughters of my Body, and their Heirs, to take as Tenants in Common, and not as Joint-Tenants; And for Default of any Issue of my Body, then to the Use of William Chapman*, of Barton, in the County of Surrey, Esquire, for Life; Remainder to the said Trustees to preserve the contingent Remainders during his Life; and, after his Decease, to the first and every other Son of his Body, according to seniority, for Life, and the Heirs Male of such Son or Sons; And for Default, To the Use of William Brettey‡, of Barton as aforesaid, Esquire, for the Term of his natural Life; Remainder to the Trustees to preserve the contingent Remainders during his Life; and after his De-

* Mr. Onebye was high Sheriff of Suffolk in 1710.

† Born in September 1714; baptised at the church of St. Peter le Poor, Oct. 1, that year; and now 1781 (by the death of his elder brother) Sir William Chapman, baronet. He has been twice married, but has no issue, by either of his wives.

‡ Who died, without issue, *before* the testator.

3

ceafe, to the Use of his firft and every other Son, according to Seniority, for Life, and to the Heirs Male of fuch Son or Sons. And for Default, TO MY OWN RIGHT HEIRS. And in cafe I fhould leave any Daughter or Daughters, and more than one Son, my Mind and Will is, That my Truftees fhall have Power to raife out of the Premiffes, in Manner aforefaid, fuch Portion and Portions for fuch Daughters and Younger Children, as my Wife, by any Deed or Will, figned by her in the Prefence of Three Witneffes, fhall appoint: And for Default of fuch Appointment, my Will is, That the Sum of Ten Thoufand Pounds fhall be raifed out of the Premifes by my faid Truftees, and equally divided betwixt fuch Younger Children: Provided, and my Will is, That if I fhould die before my Wife, leaving a Son, or leaving her enceint with a Son, which fhall attain the Age of Twenty-one Years, Then the faid Life Eftate before devifed to my Wife in the Premiffes fhall be void and determined; and my faid Wife fhall releafe and furrender the faid Premiffes to fuch my eldeft Son at the Age aforefaid, who fhall take an Eftate for Life, or in Tail Male, as aforefaid; and in that Cafe, my faid Wife fhall have and receive one Yearly Rent Charge of Six Hundred Pounds *per Annum* from fuch my Eldeft Son, payable Quarterly, during her Life; and fhall have a Power to diftrain upon the Premiffes for the fame. And I give the faid Thomas Boothby and Samuel Bracebridge the Sum of Two Hundred Pounds apiece, for their Trouble in Execution of this my Will, befides Charges expended. And I give to Grace Seward *, of Bengworth, in the County of Worcefter, the Sum of Five Hundred Pounds, to be raifed as before. And I give, devife, and bequeath, all my Goods, Chattels, and Perfonal Eftate whatfoever, to my loving Wife Mary Onebye, her Executors, Adminiftrators, and Affigns. And I do hereby make her the faid Mary Onebye, Thomas Boothby, and Samuel Bracebridge, Executors and Executrix of this my laft Will and Teftament; and her the faid Mary Onebye Refiduary Legatee and Devifee. In Witnefs whereof, I have hereunto fet my Hand and Seal, this Third Day of December, in the Year of our Lord One Thoufand Seven Hundred and Forty-three. ROBERT (L. S.) ONEBYE.

Signed, fealed, publifhed, and declared to be the laft Will and Teftament of the faid Robert Onebye, in the Prefence of us, who have fubfcribed our Names as Witneffes, in his Prefence, and at his Requeft,

Anne Bracebridge,
Anne Johnfon,
Thomas Pundrill.

[D] Mr. Nathan Wright †, of Barwell, in the county of Leicefter, barrifter at law, was elected recorder of Leicefter in 1680 ¶; and was called, by writ, April 11, 1692, with thirteen other gentlemen, to take the degree of ferjeant at law ‡. He was knighted Dec. 30, 1696, and made king's ferjeant §; a point of preferment where, according to the concurrent teftimonies of his contemporaries, he ought, from his moderate abilities, to have ftopt. Accident, however, exalted him to a fituation to which his talents were very inadequate. On the refufal of the Lords Chief Juftices Holt and Trehy, and Trevor the Attorney General, to accept the Great Seal, which was taken from lord Somers, it was delivered to him, with the title of Lord Keeper, May 11, 1700 ‖. As he was raifed to this fituation by the Tories, fo he feems to have acted in conformity to the views of the party. Burnet ** fays, that many gentlemen of good eftates and ancient families were put out of the commiffion of the peace by him, for no other vifible reafon, but be-

* In 1760 a bill was filed in chancery, againft George Wright, efq; Mr. Thomas Breton, Mr. William Cradock, and the reft of Mr. Onebye's heirs at law, and alfo againft Mr. Boothby and Mr. Bracebridge as his executors, and Dr. Bracebridge as Mrs. Onebye's executor, by Sir John Chapman and Mrs. Roberts, formerly Mrs. Seward, for a debt of 360l. due to Sir John for the purchafe of a copyhold eftate by Mr. Onebye, and for Mrs. Roberts's legacy of 500l. by his will. By this bill the heirs at law were required to deduce and make out their pedigree to Mr. Onebye; and the bill was exhibited by the plaintiffs, in order to change the real eftate with the payment of this debt and legacy, in cafe Mr. Onebye's perfonalty fhould not be fufficient or liable to pay the fame.

† Richard and three John Wrights were rectors of Enhale in the county of Warwick, from 1650 to 1658. Q. if Sir Nathan's anceftors. Dugd. Warw. 339.

¶ He held that office till 1675, when the earl of Huntingdon was chofen by the new charter and continued about three years, when Mr. Wright was reftored, and held that office till he became king's ferjeant in 1696.

‡ Wynne's Mifcellanies, p. 310. § Ibid. p. 311.

‖ Ibid. "He received his appointment in 1700, unfortunately for him, as fucceffor to Lord Somers, " whofe precipitate dimiffion in favour of a Tory hardly allowed time for reflection on the impropriety of " the choice. Sir Nathan kept his place till the year 1705, when he was difmiffed, not without difgrace, " more through defect of ability than want of integrity, but contemned by both parties." Pennant's Journey from Chefter, p. 53f. He was one of the lords Juftices in 1700 on the King's going to Holland: Tindal. He became alfo officially one of the lords commiffioners for trade and plantations.

** Hiftory of his own Times, vol. IV. p. 55.

caufe

cause they had gone in heartily to the Revolution, and had continued zealous for king William; and at the same time, men of no worth nor estate, and known to be ill-affected to Queen Anne's title, and to the Protestant succession, were put in, to the great encouragement of ill designing men. He adds, that the lord keeper was " a zealot to the party, and was become very exceptionable in all respects: Money, " as was said, did every thing with him "; only in his court, I never heard him charged, for any thing " but great slowness, by which the Chancery was become one of the heaviest grievances of the nation. The same author likewise says, that the lord keeper " was fondly covetous †, and did not at all " live suitable to that high post: he became extreme rich, yet I never heard him charged with bribery " in his court, but there was a foul rumour, with relation to the livings of the crown that were given by " the great seal, as if they were set to sale by the officers under him." The Duchess of Marlborough, in the " Account of her Conduct," p. 114, says, " As soon as Queen Anne was seated on the throne, the " Tories (whom she usually called by the agreeable name of the church party) became the distinguished " objects of the royal favour. Dr. Sharp, archbishop of York, was pitched upon by herself to preach " her coronation sermon, and to be her chief counsellor in church-matters; and her privy council was " filled with Tories. My lord Normanby (soon after duke of Buckingham), the Earls of Jersey and " Nottingham, Sir Edward Seymour, with many others of the high-fliers, were brought into place; Sir " Nathan Wright was continued in possession of the great seal of England, and the Earl of Rochester in " the lieutenancy of Ireland. There were men, who had all a wonderful zeal for the church; a sort of " public merit that eclipsed all other in the eyes of the Queen." And in another place the duchess says, " I prevailed with her Majesty to take the great seal from Sir Nathan Wright, a man despised by all " parties, of no use to the crown, and whose weak and wretched conduct in the court of Chancery, had " almost brought his very office into contempt. His removal however was a great loss to the church, " for which he had ever been a warm stickler." This happened in May 1705; from which period Sir Nathan lived retired, and died at his seat at Caldecote Hall ‡, Warwickshire, Aug. 6, 1721. Macky ‖ describes him as a plain man both in person and conversation, of middle stature, inclining to fat, with a broad face, much marked with the small pox. A portrait of him was drawn and engraved from the life by R. White in 1700, in which the arms of *Wright* (viz. Azure, two bars Arg. in chief three Lopards faces, Or.) are quartered with those of *Oseby*; (see plate VI. fig. 14); and under it is written, " The Right Hon. Sir Nathan Wright, Knight, Lord Keeper of the Great Seal of England, and " one of his Majesties most honourable Privy Council, 1700 §." He left one son, George Wright, Esq; clerk of the crown, his heir, who purchased in 1704 the manors of Gothurst and Stoke Goldyngton, in the county of Bucks, with the advowson of both churches, which still remain in his family. The church of Gothurst was rebuilt in pursuance of his will. The figures of father and son face you as you enter; the first in his robes, the other in a plain gown; both furnished with enormous Parian periwigs ¶¶. George's son George, member for Leicester 1727—1741, married May 1733 Barbara, daughter of Sir Thomas Clarges, Bart ††. Sir Nathan's second son Nathan, a clergyman, married Anne only daughter and heir of lord Francis Pawlet, second son of John Pawlet fifth marquis of Winchester by his second wife, by whom he had a son, who died of the small-pox; and his widow, sister of the late Francis John Tyssen, Esq; lord of the manor of Hackney, who died 1781, married the late Governor Benyon, by whom she had Richard Benyon, Esq; now living, of Guldea hall, Essex. Her son Pawlet Wright died 1785. This branch of the family enjoyed the estate and manor house at Englefield, Berks, where the noble family of Pawlet lived and were buried. After the demolition of Balinghouse in the civil war, the late Mr. Wright's father greatly modernized this noble mansion, which on his death was leased out for a term of years. His son came to reside in it 1768, and further modernized it, taking away the two bow windows and a range of apartments behind the house. A lady who lived with him, and whom the public prints miscalled his widow, died 1782. Sir Nathan's daughter Dorothy married the third earl of Stamford, and died August 22, 1758, leaving issue two sons and five daughters. His other daughter Elizabeth married Sir Samuel Vanacker Sambrooke, and died in 1777 at the great age of 94. His sixth son, William, was recorder of Leicester from 1729 till his death in 1768.

---

† Swift says, he was very covetous. MS notes on Macky.
‡ Burnet, vol. IV. p. 122.
‡ Which he probably purchased at the same time with a moiety of the manor of Burton Hastings in the same county, 1714. Dugd. Warw. ed. Thomas, p. 52. 1097.
‖ P. 41.
§ There is a full length of him in his robes at Gothurst.
¶¶ Pennant, ubi sup p. 334. 338.
†† Baronetage.

PEDIGREE

PEDIGREE of WRIGHT,

From a Pedigree figned in 1681 by the LORD KEEPER, in the Heralds College.

John Wright *, of Kelvedon, in the county of Effex.

John, of Wrights-bridge, in the county of Effex, and of Gray's Inn, third fon, died 1644.

Robert, of Dinnington, in the county of Suffolk, fecond fon.

1	2	3	4	
Eufeby.	Nathan †, of London, merchant, died March 11, 1657, aged 66, married Anne Fleming of Warley Place.	Benjamin, knight.	Ezekiel, B. D. of Thurcafton c. Leicefter,	Dorothy, fecond daughter of John Onebye, coheir to her brother Sir John Onebye.

| | Jane Williams | Benjamin of Cranhamhall, c. Effex, created bart. Feb. 5, 1660. | 1. Sufan ‡. 2. Alice. 3. Mary. 4. Frances. 5. Jane. | |

4	5	6	7		
Abigail Tryft	Eliz. Bowater ; no iffue.	Elizab. Brage.	Anne Meyrick.	Nathan, bo. 1661, died October 16, 1717 ‡, and the baronetage extinct.	Benjamin.

| Samuel, married his only furviving heir. | Elizabeth, married General Oglethorp, 1744. | Benjamin, and another fon. | | | Elizabeth, fecond da. of George Afhby, of Quenby, co. Leicefl. efq. living 1681. | Nathan, of Barwell, c. Leicefter, barrifter at law, recorder of Leicefter in 1680, Lord Keeper 1700, died 1721 ¶. |
| | | Nathan, = ... Lawley. John. | | | | |

| .... | George, b. March 25, 1677, clerk of the crown; of Gothurft and Stoke Goldyngton, co. Bucks. | Nathan, b. Jan. 1, 1678, married Anne daughter and heir of Lord Francis Pawlet, of Englefield, co. Berks. | Robert, born Sept. 5, 1680. | Dorothy (fortune 12,000l.) married Harry third earl of Stamford. Died Aug. 11, 1738. | Elizabeth, married Sir Sam. Vanacker Sambrook; (fee p. 143.) |
| | | | | 2 fons and 5 daughters. | |

George, M. P. for Leicefter 1727—1741. (See p. 143.)	Pawlet, died of the fmall pox Jan. 6, 1741.	Aug. 16, 1737, Mary, daughter of Francis John Tylden, of Hackney, efq. remarried July 18, 1745, the late Richard Benyon, efq. of Guidea hall, Effex.
Son born Dec. 6. 1742; died Feb. 5, 1745.	Pauler, of Englefield, 9 months old at father's death, died 1751.	.... Richard, Daughter of Sir Edward Hulfe.
		Eleven or twelve children.

* See Morant, vol. I. p. 185.
† Who purchafed the manor of Cranham, in the county of Effex. See Morant, vol. I. p. 106.
‡ Married firft to Charles Potts, afterwards to Francis Drake, efq. She died July 15, 1664, aged 34. There is an epitaph for her in Cranham-church, and another for her father.
¶ He gave two alms-houfes in St. Mary Lane at Cranham. His relia Abigail was remarried to Herbert Try?, efq. who in his right enjoyed the eftate at Cranham till her death, Dec. 7, 1741. Another branch of this family was honoured with the title of baronet in 1680, which became extinct in 1681. See Morant, vol. I. p. 62.
¶ His brother Ezekiel (fee p. 142) died March 25, 1729.   ¶¶ This lady died Jan. 2, 1730-1.

[E] Son of James Gough, an exchange broker. He was put apprentice to an apothecary, but did not serve his time out; had a handsome fortune with his wife, which he lost in the South Sea bubble; and was afterwards dependent on Mr. Godfrey of Norton-court, who had married a sister of his, and of whom see more in the Anecdotes of Mr. Bowyer, p. 258.

[F] Thomas Staveley, esq. of Cossington in Leicestershire, after having completed his academical education at Peter House, Cambridge, was admitted of the Inner Temple, July 2, 1647, and called to the bar June 11, 1654. In 1662 he succeeded his father-in-law Mr. Onebye as steward of the records at Leicester. In 1674, when the court espoused the cause of Popery, and the presumptive Heir to the Crown openly professed himself a Catholic, Mr. Staveley displayed the enormous exactions of the court of Rome by publishing "The Romish Horseleech." Some years before his death, which happened in 1683, he retired to Belgrave near Leicester, and passing the latter part of his life in the study of English history, acquired a melancholy habit, but was esteemed a diligent, judicious, and faithful antiquary. Besides the "History of Churches," which first appeared in 1712. Mr. Staveley left a pedigree, drawn up in 1682, transcribed below *; and also some papers on the History and Antiquities of Leicester, to which

* William Staveley married Alice daughter and heir of Sir John Frances, Knight, by Isabella his wife, daughter and heir of Sir Henry Plesington, Knight. This William obtained great possessions by the marriage of his wife Alice, she being a very great heiress. He lived at Bygnell in Oxfordshire; and dying there in the year 1498, was buried at Bicester adjoining to Bygnell, on whose tomb or monument in the church there made of grey marble is his portraiture with this inscription in brass:
"Orate pro animabus Will'i Staveley armig. quondam D'ni de Bygnell, & Alicie uxoris ejus, filie &
"unice heredis D'ni Johannis Frances militis & D'ne Isabelle uxoris, filie & heredis D'ni Henrici Plef-
"syngton militis. Qui quidem Will's obiit decimo die Octobris A. D. MCCCCLXXXXVIII. Predicta
"vero Alicia obiit xx die Octobris A. D. MD. Quorum animabus propicietur Deus."
George Staveley was the son of William; this William having also issue two daughters: Mary, married to Thomas Gifford, of Twyford in the County of Buckingham, Esq. and Isabella, married to John Tansfield of Gayton in the county of Northampton. George Staveley married Isabella daughter of John Strelly, sister and heir of Sir Nicholas Strelly, Knight, by whom he had a large estate in Nottinghamshire.

John Staveley of Bygnell was the son of George. He took to wife Constance the daughter of Sir John Danvers, of Dauntsey in the county of Wilts, Knight, and by her had issue, Thomas Staveley, Edward Staveley, and Mary, married unto Edward Charrede, of Berkshire, Esq. This John was a very profuse person, and spent and sold almost all his estate, consisting of several manors and lordships, except what was settled in jointure upon his wife Constance, which, she surviving, descended to his heirs. This Constance proving in great a support to her family, her memory is gratefully preserved by her descendants, and her extraction was thus †. There was an ancient barony of the Latimers of Danby in Yorkshire, of which William the last lord Latimer of that name died without issue male in the reign of King Henry V. leaving one daughter Elizabeth, who was the wife of Ralph Lord Nevill of Raby, who by her had issue John Nevill. This John was summoned to parliament by the title of Lord Latimer from 9 Henry V. to 9 Henry VI inclusive, and died without issue; but divers of the lordships whereof he died seised, for want of issue of his body, being intailed upon Ralph Nevill, his elder brother Earl of Westmoreland, the same Ralph settled the same upon George Nevill one of his sons, who was thereupon summoned to parliament as Lord Latimer, which title and honour continued in his posterity until the twentieth year of Queen Elizabeth. John, the last Lord Latimer of this family, died without any issue male ‡; but by his wife Lucy, daughter of Henry Earl of Worcester, left four daughters his heirs, viz. Catherine wife of Henry Earl of Northumberland, Dorothy wife of Thomas Cecil Earl of Exeter, Lucy wife of Sir William Cornwallis, Knight, and Elizabeth wife of Sir John Danvers. Lucy, the wife of this John the last Lord Latimer, died 1583 §, and was buried in the north side of the chancel of the parish church of Hackney in the county of Middlesex, her epitaph specifying the marriages of her four daughters as above. Sir John Danvers, by his wife Elizabeth, had issue his eldest son Sir Charles Danvers, who lost his life, being attainted of treason for partaking with Robert Earl of Essex in his insurrection, in the 43d year of Queen Elizabeth; and Henry, who by especial act of parliament in the 3d year of King James was restored in blood, as heir to his father, notwithstanding the attainder of Sir Charles his eldest brother, and was afterwards created Earl of Danby and Knight of the Garter ‖. He was founder of the physic garden, which, with the wall about it, cost him about 5000l. He died unmarried. The daughter of Sir John Danvers, Constance, was married to John Staveley, as is said before,

Thomas Staveley, son and heir of John, took to wife Margaret daughter of John Baud, of Cossingham in the county of Essex, Esq. This family of the Bauds has been very ancient at Corsingham aforesaid, of whom we find this signal memorial. Sir William le Baud, Knight, in the third year of King Edward I. by his deed or grant gave to the deans and canons of St. Paul's church in London, a fat doe yearly in winter on the day of the Conversion of St. Paul, and a fat buck in summer upon the day of the Commemoration of the same Saint,

† Catalogue of Honour, under the Earls of Westmoreland, fol. 993.
‡ Camden. Annal. Eliz. fol. 224. Dugdale's Baronage, tom. I. fol. 313.
§ Stow's Survey of London, folio, 797. ‖ Ann. primo Car. I.

which he had more particularly applied his researches. These papers (which Dr. Farmer, who calls him *William* by mistake, proposed to publish) are supposed to be among the collections of the same

to be offered at the high altar there by the said Sir William and his houshold family, and then to be distributed among the canons resident. Which said doe and buck was so given by Sir William in lieu of 21 acres of land lying in the lordship of Westlee in the county of Essex, belonging to the said canons, and by them granted to him and his heirs to enlarge his park at Coringham. But about the time and formality of this offering there growing afterwards some dispute, Sir Walter le Baud, son and heir of Sir William, by his deed bearing date on the Ides of July, an. 30 Edward I. for the health of his soul, and for the souls of his progenitors and heirs, confirmed his father's grant, and did oblige himself and his heirs, and also his land and tenements for ever, that yearly on the day of the Conversion of Saint Paul in winter there should be a good fat doe brought by one of his or their hunting servants, and not the whole family, at the hour of procession, and through the midst thereof be offered at the high altar. And on the day of Commemoration of Saint Paul in summer a fat buck by some such servant, and so carried through the midst of the procession and offered at the high altar, the Dean and Chapter giving by the hands of their chamberlain twelve pence sterling to the person so bringing the buck. Unto which grant were witnesses Sir Richard de Rokell, Sir Thomas de Maunderville, Sir John de Rochford, with divers others. The reception of which doe and buck was, till Queen Elizabeth's time, solemnly performed by the canons at the steps of the choir attired in their vestments, and on their heads wearing garlands of flowers, the horns of the buck being carried on the top of a spear, as in procession found about the church with a great noise of horn-blowers, as is affirmed by Mr. Camden upon his own view. (Britannia, fol. 426.)

This Thomas Staveley, by his wife Margaret aforesaid, had issue Thomas and Henry; and this Henry left issue Ambrose and Charles.

Thomas Staveley, son and heir of Thomas, took to wife Margery daughter of Arthur Brook, of Okeley in the county of Northampton, Esq; and by her had issue five sons, Arthur, Thomas, Eusiby, William, and Charles; and four daughters, Catharine married to Thomas Rolt, of Milton in the county of Bedford, Esq; Anne to Thomas Stanford of Harkby in the county of Leicester, Esq; Elizabeth to Eustace Burneby, of the city of Coventry, Esq, and Temperance to William Bale, of Lodington in the county of Leicester, Esq.

Arthur, the eldest son of Thomas, married Lucy daughter and heir of Richard Edwick, Esq; and by her had issue two daughters, Margery married to Humphrey Adderley, of Weddington in the county of Warwick, Esq, who died without issue; and Mary twice married, first to Francis Stanton, of Bitchmore in the county of Bedford, Esq, and afterwards to Stephen Pheasant, of Upwood in the county of Huntingdon, Esq. Mary, by her first husband, had issue Staveley Stanton, who took to wife Elizabeth daughter of Sir Thomas Aston, of Odel in the county of Bedford, Bart. and by her had issue two sons, Staveley and Francis, and one daughter Elizabeth; and, by her second husband, Mary had issue two daughters, Susanna, who died unmarried, and Constance, who married John Overton, of Edington in the county of York, Esq.

William, the fourth son of Thomas, was a divine, and rector of Cullington in the county of Leicester. He took to wife Anne, one of the daughters of Thomas Babington, of Rothely in the county of Leicester, Esq; and by her had issue five sons, Thomas, William, George, Arthur, and Babington; and seven daughters, Catherine, Ann, Margery, that died young, Elizabeth, Martha, Mary, and Margaret.

Thomas, eldest son of William, took to wife (31 Dec. 1646) Mary, one of the daughters of John Onebye, of Hinckley in the county of Leicester, Esq; and by her had issue three sons, Thomas, William, and George; and four daughters, Mary married (1677) to Edmund Brudenell, Esq; Anne, Christiana, and Jane.

William, the second son, was a divine, and succeeded his father in the rectory of Cullington.

George, the third son, was twice married; first, to Anne daughter of Adam Lawrence, of the county of Cambridge, but he has had no issue; secondly, to Elizabeth daughter of John Smith, alderman of London, by whom he had issue two sons, George, who died young, and William; and three daughters, Elizabeth married to Daniel Biddle, citizen of London; Jane married to Thomas Wood, citizen of London; and Anne.

Arthur, the fourth son, was twice married; first, to Elizabeth daughter of —— Green, citizen of London, by whom he had issue . . . . daughters, Elizabeth, ... and one son.

Babington, the fifth son, unmarried in 1682.

Catherine, the eldest daughter of William, was married to Francis Rost, citizen of London, by whom he had issue one son, William.

Margery died young.

Anne was married to John Keat, citizen of London, and died without issue.

Elizabeth, fourth daughter, married to Edward Harrison, citizen of London, and by him had issue two sons, Edward and William, and one daughter, Elizabeth.

Martha, the fifth daughter, married to Walter Hammersford, Esq; citizen of London, and had issue four sons, Walter, George, William, and John; and six daughters, Mary, Anne, Elizabeth, Martha, Catharine, Mary.

Mary, the sixth daughter, was married to James Tisbalds, or Cleobull in the county of Herts, clerk, and had issue . . . . sons and daughters.

Margaret, the seventh daughter, died unmarried.

X   Sir

Sir Thomas Cave, which have been already mentioned in p. 131. The younger Mr. S. Cave (an able antiquary and an eminent solicitor) who had a copy of Mr. Staveley's papers, says of them, in a MS. letter to Dr. Ducarel, March 7, 1751, " His account of the earls of Leicester, and of the " great abbey, appears to have been taken from Dugdale's Baronage and Monasticon; but as to " his sentiments in respect to the borough, I differ with him in some instances. By the charter " for erecting and establishing the court of records at Leicester, the election of the steward is granted " to the mayor and court of aldermen, who likewise have thereby a similar power in respect to a " bailiff for executing their writs. But afterwards, viz. Dec. 20, 7 Jac. I. the great earl of Hun- " tingdon having been a considerable benefactor to Leicester, the corporation came to a resolution of " granting to him and his heirs a right of nominating alternately to the office of steward and bailiff, " and executed a bond under their common seal, in the penalty of one thousand pounds, for enforcing " the execution of their grant.   And as John Major, esq. was elected by the court of aldermen to " succeed Mr. Staveley [in December 1684], I infer that Staveley was nominated by the earl of Hun- " tingdon, and confirmed by the aldermen, in pursuance of the grant abovementioned."

[G] Mr. Welsted, who was born in Leicestershire, received the rudiments of his education in West- minster school, where he wrote the celebrated little poem called " Apple Pie," which was universally attributed to the facetious Dr. King, and as such has been incorporated in the last edition of his works. Very early in life Mr. Welsted obtained a place in the secretary of state's office by the interest of his friend the earl of Clare, to whom, in 1715, he addressed a small poem, (which Jacob calls " a very " good one)" on his being created duke of Newcastle; and to whom in 1724 he dedicated an octavo volume, under the title of " Epistles, Odes, &c. written on several Subjects; with a Translation of Lon- ginus's " Treatise on the Sublime."   In 1717 he wrote " The Genius, on occasion of the Duke of Marlborough's Apoplexy;" an ode much commended by Steele, and so generally admired as to be attributed to Addison; and afterwards an Epistle to Dr. Garth, on the Duke's death.   He addressed a poem to the Countess of Warwick, on her Marriage with Mr. Addison; a Poetical Epistle to the Duke of Chandos; and an Ode to Earl Cadogan, which was highly extolled by Dean Smedley.   Sir Richard Steele was indebted to him for both the Prologue and Epilogue to " The Conscious Lovers;" and Mr. Philips for a complimentary poem on his Tragedy of " Humfrey Duke of Gloucester."   In 1718 he wrote " The Triumvirate, or a letter in verse from Palemon to Celia from Bath," which was considered as a satire against Mr. Pope.   He wrote several other occasional pieces against this gentleman, who, in recompence of his enmity, thus mentioned him in his Dunciad, In a Parody upon Denham's Cooper's Hill:

          " Flow, Welsted, flow! like thine inspirer, beer;
          " Though stale, not ripe; though thin, yet never clear;
          " So sweetly mawkish, and so smoothly dull;
          " Heady, not strong; o'erflowing, though not full."

In 1726 he published a comedy called " The Dissembled Wanton, or, My Son get Money." In the Notes on the Dunciad, II. 207. it is said, " He writ other things which we cannot remember. " Smedley, in his Metamorphosis of Scriblerus, mentions one, the Hymn of a Gentleman to his Creator: " And there was another in praise either of a cellar, or a garret.   I. W. characterized in the Half Below, " or the Art of Sinking, as a Didapper, and after as an Eel, is said to be this person, by Dennis, Daily Journal of May 11, 1728."   He was also characterized under the title of another animal, a mole, by the author of a simile, which was handed about at the same time, and which is preferred in the notes on the Dunciad. In another note, III. 169. it is recorded that he received at one time the sum of five hundred pounds for secret service, among the other excellent authors hired to write anonymously for the ministry.   See Report of the Secret Committee, &c. in 1742.   And in a piece, said, but falsely, to have been written by Mr. Welsted, called " The Characters of the Times," printed in octavo 1728, he is made to say of himself, that " he had, in his youth, raised so great expectations of his future genius, that there " was a kind of struggle between the two universities, which should have the honour of his education; " to compound this, he civilly became a member of both, and, after having passed some time at the one, " he removed to the other.   From thence he returned to town, where he became the darling expectation " of all the polite writers, whose encouragement he acknowledged in his occasional poems, in a man- " ner that will make no small part of the interest of his protectors.   It also appears from his works, that " he was happy in the patronage of the most illustrious characters of the present age.   E couraged by
                                                                                                " such

" fuch a c mbination in his favour, he publifhed a book of poems, fome in the Ovidian, fome in the
" Horatian manner, in both which the moſt exquiſite judges pronounced he even rivalled his maſters.
" His love verſes have reſcued that way of writing from contempt. In tranſlations he has given us the
" very ſoul and ſpirit of his authors. His odes, his epiſtles, his verſes, his love-tales, all are the moſt
" perfect things in all poetry." If this pleaſant repreſentation of our author's abilities were juſt, it
would from no wonder, if the two univerſities ſhould ſtrive with each other for the honour of his education ; but it is certain the world hath not coincided with this opinion. Our author, however, does
not appear to have been a mean poet ; he had certainly from nature, a good genius, but, after he
came to town, he became a votary to pleaſure; and the applauſes of his friends, which taught him to
overvalue his talents, perhaps ſlackened his diligence, and, by making him truſt ſolely to nature, ſlight
the aſſiſtance of art. Prefixed to the collection of his poems is a Diſſertation concerning the Perfection
of the Engliſh Language, the State of Poetry, &c.

Mr. Welſted married a daughter of Mr. Henry Purcell, who died in 1724; and by whom he had one
daughter, who died at the age of 18, unmarried. His ſecond wife, who ſurvived him, was ſiſter to
Sir Hoveden Walker, and to Biſhop Walker the defender of Londonderry. He had a place in the office
of ordnance, and a houſe in the Tower of London, where he died about the year 1749.

7. ANTHONY GREY, tenth Earl of KENT.

THIS worthy peer, who ſucceeded to the title of earl of Kent whilſt rector of
Burbach, was born at Brancepeth, in the biſhoprick of Durham, his grandfather
Anthony Grey, eſq. being invited thither to enjoy the company of his friend and
kinſman the earl of Weſtmorland, as Dr. Fuller relates in his Worthies of England.
And when he became rector of Burbach *, he preached conſtantly, and kept an
hoſpitable houſe for the poor, according to his eſtate ; and after his acceſſion to
the title of earl of Kent, he did not in the leaſt degree diſdain the ſociety of the
clergy, neither did he abate in the conſtancy of his preaching, ſo long as he was
able to be led up into the pulpit. He was ſummoned as a peer to parliament, but
excuſed himſelf by reaſon of indiſpoſition and age. Such was his humility and
ſanctity, that he was truly reverenced by all who knew him. He married Magdalen, daughter of William Purefoy, of Caldecote in Warwickſhire, eſq. by whom
he had iſſue five ſons, viz. Henry, John, Job, a divine, who had a daughter
Mary †, married to Thomas Bearcroft of Coventry, gent. whoſe widow ſhe died
29 July, 1717, aged 60, and is buried in St. Michael's church, Coventry ; Theophilus ‡, who died 30 March 1679, aged 74, and is buried at Flitton ; and Nathaniel : as alſo five daughters, Lady Grace, married to James Ward, of Huckle-
ſcot Grange, in Leiceſterſhire, eſq. Lady Magdalen to John Brown, of Stretton,
in Derbyſhire, eſq. Lady Chriſtian, to the reverend Mr. Bearcroft, rector of the
church of Burton Noverey, in Leiceſterſhire ; Lady Patience, to ———— Wood,
of Lubenham, in the ſaid county of Leiceſter ; and Lady Priſcilla. And his lord-

* " Anthony, grandſon of Anthony, third ſon of George earl of Kent, is drawn in black [at Wreſt
houſe], with his hand on a book: a meagre perſonage. He was ſurprized with the peerage at his parſonage
of Burbach, in the county of Leiceſter, where he lived in hoſpitality, and the full diſcharge of that great
character, a good pariſh prieſt. He was ſummoned to parliament, but preferred the duty to which he was
firſt called ; never would forſake his flock, and was buried among them in 1643. His wife, Magdalen
Purefoy, is repreſented a half-length, fitting with a book in her hand, and a long motherly black peaked coif
on her head." Peacock's Journey from Cheſter, p. 380 ; and ſee Fuller, Worthies, p. 299.
‡ Thomas's edition of Dugdale's Warwickſhire, I. fol. 169.
‡ Le Neve's Monaſticon Anglicanum, vol. V. p. 142.

X 2

ſhip

ship departing this life, 1643, was buried in the chancel of his church at Burbach, where the following epitaph perpetuates his memory:

" Hoc

To the pious memory of
the Right Honble ANTHONY GREY late Earle of KENT, Lord HASTINGS,
WEISFORD, and Lord GREY of RUTHIN, Lord of this Manor, Parson and
Patron of this Parish; eminent for Pietie, Charity, Humilitie, Contempt
of the World, and a blamelesse Conversation, a constant and faithfull
Preacher of the Gospell of JESVS CHRIST even to his extreame old
age, and for some yeares after he was Earle of KENT, by discent from
EDMOND GREY, first of that name Earle of KENT, (vi.) sonn and
heire of GEORGE GREY, sonn and heire of ANTHONY GREY, sonn of
GEORGE late Earle of KENT, sonn and heire of the same Earle EDMOND:
And to the religious memory of
The Right Honble MAGDALEN Countesse of KENT his relict, daughter
of WILLIAM PURFFOY of Caldecote in com' Warwick, esquire.
He died the 9th day of November, anno D'ni 1643, in
the 86 yeare of his age:
She died the 16 day of April, anno D'ni 1653, in
the 81 yeare of her age:
and lie both underneath interr'd.
They had yssue living at his death HENRY, since deceased; who succeeded
him in all his honours, JOHN, THEOPHILUS, and
NATHANIEL and five daughters, GRACE, MAGDALEN,
CHRISTIAN, PATIENCE, and PRISCILLA.

By AMABELLA * Countesse Dowager of KENT, relict of
the said Earle HENRY sonn and heire of this earle ANTHONY,

Devotum."

* Amabella, surnamed, from her supereminent virtues, *The good Countesse of Kent*, was daughter of Sir Anthony Ben, of Surrey, knt. Recorder of London. She was first married to Anthony Fane, esq. third son of Francis earl of Westmorland; and was afterwards the second lady of Henry earl of Kent, who died in 1651, and to whom she caused a monument to be erected at Flitton in Bedfordshire. There is a picture of her at Wrest, in black and ermine, full curled hair, and a kerchief over her neck, æt. 60, 1665, by Lely. Her husband is in his robes with a small beard and whiskers, painted by Clostermans; æt. 53, 1643. Sir Anthony Ben, in heavy short hair, quilted ruff, red dress laced with black. His lady in black, a kerchief, and curled hair. The mausoleum of the Greys adjoins to the church of Flitton, about a mile and a half from the house. It consists of a center and four wings. In one is the tomb of Henry the fifth earl of Kent, and his countess Mary, daughter of Sir George Cotton of Cumbermere, Cheshire: both are in robes, and painted; both recumbent, with uplifted hands: his beard long and square, his ruff quill'd. Henry earl of Kent, and his second lady, the good countess, repose in another wing, with Justice, Temperance, and other Virtues, on each side. Both are represented in white marble, recumbent, and both in robes. His beard is small, his lip whiskered: one hand is on his breast, the other on his sword. She is dressed in an ungraceful pair of stays; her hands before, holding her robes; her neck naked; her hair curled, and commonly bushy. He died in 1651; she finished her excellent life in 1698, aged ninety-two. Her epitaph speaks her deserts: "Here lyes the Right Honble AMABELLA, late countess dowager of KENT, entombed by
" her dear lord HENRY earl of KENT, to signifie her resolution to dye with him to the rest of ye world, and to love after
" so great a loss only to God, & the interest of this noble family. This she made good, by her exemplary piety & regu-
" lar devotion in her chappell; whereto she obliged all her domesticks, every morning & evening, to attend her. And,
" surviving her own monument 45 years, she had time to raise to herself a more lasting one, by restoring the fortune of
" this illustrious family, which she found under an eclipse, to near the height of it's ancient splendour. This she effected
" by her wise counsel & large acquisitions, & by the advantageous disposal of her only son ANTHONY earl of KENT, in
" marriage with Mary, sole daughter and heiress of the Rt Honble John lord Lucas, baron of Shenfield, in Essex. To
" the concerns of her children & grandchildren she confined her thoughts; & fixed her residence at Wrest, their usual
" seat; which she wonderfully improved & imbellished; continually adding to the profit or ornament of the place, until
" death gently seiz'd her, Aug 17th, 1698, in the 91st year of her age; & was here interred by the Rt Honble Anthony
" earl of Kent, her most dutiful son; who would have caused this to be engraven, had not a sudden death prevented him;
" but it was afterwards performed, in due acknowledgement of her great benefacence, & to perpetuate his memory to all
" his posterity, by her grandsor, HENRY Duke of KENT." Pennant's Journey from Chester, pp 386, 388, 391 &c.

8. Sir Henry Firebrace.

THE anceſtors of this family are ſuppoſed to be Normans, and it is preſumed, derived their name from *Fier à bras*, which is, ſtrong of arm. When they firſt came into England, or under what reign, cannot now be determined; but by the following extracts out of the records in the Tower *, it appears they were very early ſeated in this kingdom:

Clauſ. 33 H. III. m. 2.

Rex conceſſit Waltero Ferebras, quod quandocunq; contigerit tallagium aſſideri in civitate London. non tallietur ultra dimidiam marcam ſine ſpeciali precepto regis: et mandatum eſt majori & vic. London. quod prediⱡum Walterum ultra dimidiam marcam non tallierit vel talliari permittant: teſte rege apud Weſtin. xxviij die Decembris, anno, &c. xxxiij°.

Clauſ. 28 E. I. m. 6. in Cedula.

Rex juſticiariis ſuis de banco ſalutem. Sciatis quod Robertus Ferebras, de Wylington, fuit in ſervicio noſtro, per preceptum noſtrum, die Sabbati in craſtino S. Johis Baptiſtæ proximo præterito, ita quod eo die intereſſe non potuit loquela quæ eſt coram vobis per breve noſtrum, inter Nicholaum filium Johis de Hullecrombe petentem, & præfatum Robertum tenentem, de uno meſſuagio quinq; virgatis & quindecim acris terræ cum ptinentiis in Wylington: et ideo vobis mandamus, quod prediⱡus Robertus, propter abſentiam ſuam, quoad diem illum, quoad hoc warantizamus: teſte rege apud . . . . . . vi° die Novembris.

Pat. 1 H. IV. p. 8. m. 41. p Inſpex.

Ric' Dei gra rex Angliæ & Franc' & dñus Hiberniæ omnibus in ſalutem. Sciatis quod de gratia noſtra ſpeciali, & pro bono ſervicio quod dilectos armiger noſter Fierebras, de Vertainge, tam progenitoribus noſtris quam nobis impendit & nobis impendet in futurum, conceſſimus eidem Fierebras quadraginta marcas percipiendas ſingulis annis ad ſcaccariũ noſtrũ, ad terminos S. Michis & Paſche p equales portiones, ad terminum vicæ predicti Fierebras. In cujus—T. meipſo, apud Weſtm', vij° die Julii, a° regni ñri xx°.

In the Viſitation of Leiceſterſhire, anno 1682 †, the pedigree begins with Robert Firebrace, of the town and borough of Derby, gent. who died 1645, having iſſue by Suſanna, daughter of John Hierome, of London, merchant, ſix ſons and a daughter, Rebecca, married to Thomas Moſeley, of Loughborough, in com. Leiceſt. gent. Of the ſons, Robert died unmarried; Bryan without iſſue; Samuel

---

* Communicated to Mr. Collins by the late Sir Cordell Firebrace, bart.

† From the information of the late Sir Cordell Firebrace, Bart. which is exactly the ſame with the pedigree in Le Neve's MSS. vol. III. p. 305. which he ſays is copied from that under the hand of Henry Ball, eſq. Windſor herald', 1682.

died unmarried; John died also unmarried; Benjamin died without issue; and Henry was the sixth and youngest son.

Henry Firebrace, Esq. was chief clerk of the kitchen to King Charles I. He was a gentleman very faithful and serviceable to his majesty in his greatest distresses; who, when the king was confined in Carisbrook Castle, in the Isle of Wight, engaged with Mr. Barrow, Mr. Titus, and Mr. Cresset, to deliver his majesty from that noisome confinement, and for that purpose provided a vessel, and laid horses in proper places, and used their utmost endeavours to effect it, though without success. The particulars of this memorable affair we find related in the Life of Dr. Barwick *; and as it is curious in itself, and does honour to the family, we shall here give it at large: " Mr. Henry Firebrace, a gentleman of a very ancient family, of Stoke " Gohling, in Leicestershire, at least that was afterwards his seat. How remarka- " bly serviceable he was to his majesty, in his greatest distress, appears both from " the several letters which passed between them, on the subject of his majesty's in- " tended escape, which are inserted at the end of this narrative, and particularly " from his majesty's giving it in charge to Bishop Juxon, the very day before he " was murthered, to recommend him to the prince, afterwards King Charles II. as " having been a person very faithful and serviceable to him in his greatest extre- " mities and most strict imprisonments, and therefore fit to be employed and en- " trusted by him; which was certified under that good bishop's own hand, when " afterwards archbishop of Canterbury, Nov. 25, 1661, as appears by a copy of " that certificate, also printed after the letters; which, at the instance of my " worthy friends, William Hurton, of Long Melford, in Suffolk, Esq. since then " deceased, and the Rev. Mr. John Jeffery, was most obligingly communicated to " me, together with copies of the letters above mentioned, by Charles Firebrace, " of Melford Hall, Esq. the worthy grandson of Sir Henry, faithfully transcribed " by Mr. Jeffery from the originals in Mr. Firebrace's hands. It was no doubt " upon this royal recommendation, that long before this certificate thereof. bears " date, that loyal gentleman attended upon King Charles II. in his exile: upon " the Restoration he was made Sir Henry Firebrace, and clerk of the kitchen to his " majesty, which post he enjoyed all that and the next reign; but not complying " with the Revolution, retired then from court, and died about four years after; " leaving two sons, Dr. Henry Firebrace, sometime fellow of Trinity College in " Cambridge, and Sir Basil Firebrace, Bart. now living, father of the right hon. " the countess dowager of Denbigh, and of Charles Firebrace, Esq. above men- " tioned, who had the honour to have King Charles II. for his godfather, and to " whom I take this opportunity of returning my humble thanks, not only for the " communication of those invaluable letters, which he had from the doctor, his un- " cle, who made him his heir; but for that most obliging manner in which he " was pleased to do it, sending a servant up to London, on purpose to fetch " them down from among his papers here, and have them transcribed for my use.

* English Life of Dr. Barwick, pp. 87 to 92.

" The

" The account of this attempt, and the unhappy occasion of its miscarriage, will
" from his majefty's own letters, and that worthy gentleman's, concerned therein,
" (letters I. II. &c.) appear in fomewhat a different light from what we have in
" my lord Clarendon's Hiftory and others that were wrote from him. The fum of
" that noble hiftorian's account is this, that captain Rolph, one of the agitators,
" and a creature of Cromwell's, having imparted to Mr. Ofborne, the king's gen-
" tleman ufher, his defign againft his majefty's life; and in order to the execu-
" tion of it, which he defpaired of during the king's confinement in the Ifle of
" Wight, invited Ofborne to affift him in contriving his majefty's efcape, and Of-
" borne, by the king's approbation, joining with Rolph to contrive it, when his ma-
" jefty had privately fawed the bar of the window in funder, and all things being now
" ready, the night was appointed for executing the defign: his majefty coming to the
" window, at midnight, and putting himfelf out, difcerned more perfons to ftand
" thereabout than ufed to do, and thence fufpected fome difcovery, fhut the win-
" dow, and retired to bed. And this (fays his lordfhip) was all the ground of a dif-
" courfe, which then flew abroad, as if the king had got half out at the window,
" and could neither draw his body after nor get his head back, and fo was com-
" pelled to call out for help; which was a mere fiction. (Hift. vol. III. p. 233.)
" How far that report was a mere fiction, will be feen by and by: it is true, the
" king's letters fay nothing of his majefty's fticking in the window; but for all
" that it is moft evident from thofe letters, that my lord Clarendon's account of this
" matter was not all the ground of that report; for in the firft of them, the king
" fays exprefsly, that the narrownefs of the window was the only impediment of
" his efcape; and Mr. Echard fays as exprefsly, that his majefty endeavoured to
" get out of his window by a cord, but unfortunately ftuck in the window, and
" that it was with great difficulty he got back again, as Firebrace (fays he) informs
" us in his memoirs. (Hift. vol. II. book 2. ch. 5. p. 647.) But then he fays no-
" thing of fawing the bar of the window; but makes this a different attempt from
" that wherein Rolph was concerned, and the bar cut; and in his account of the
" mifcarriage of this latter, follows my lord Clarendon, faying that fome difco-
" very was made by thofe concerned in it, fo that if his majefty had proceeded,
" he would have been fhot dead by one Rolph, a bloody captain, got ready for
" that purpofe. The memoirs quoted by Mr. Echard are Sir Henry Firebrace's,
" directed by way of a letter to Sir George Lane, Knt. fecretary to the duke of
" Ormond, faid in the title (I know not by what blunder) to be written by Mr. Tho-
" mas Firebrace, clerk of the kitchen to his majefty King Charles II. and to bear
" date at Whitehall, July 21, 1675, though the name fubfcribed to the letter
" be Henry Firebrace, and the date July 24, 1675. The running title of the
" letter, indeed, is partly Mr. Thomas, and partly Mr. Henry Firebrace's memoirs;
" but in the general title of that collection of memoirs, viz. Sir Thomas Herbert's,
" Major Huntington's, and Colonel Edward Coke's, with which this letter was
" publifhed, in 8vo. 1702; this is called Mr. Henry Firebrace's Memoirs: I fup-
" pofe it fhould be Sir Henry, for that gentleman muft have been knighted long
" before the date of this letter. The account he gives therein of this matter is,

" he

" he fays, what his eyes and ears were acquainted with, for that he then attended
" his majefty as one of the pages of his bed-chamber. He had the honour, it feems,
" to be known to the king, by feveral fervices he had done him in the time of
" the treaty at Uxbridge, at Oxford, and other places; and, being at Newcaftle
" when the Scots delivered his majefty to the Englifh, and new fervants were put
" about him, by his majefty's direction he applied to fome of the commiffioners,
" and prevailed to be admitted to that poft; in which, attending his majefty in
" his confinement, be found means to concert with him feveral methods of efcape.
" One, he fays, was, that his majefty fhould come out of his bed chamber win-
" dow, which having found wide enough for his head, his majefty concluded
" would not be too narrow for his body, and therefore rejected his propofal of
" making it a little wider, for fear that fhould occafion a difcovery. Mr. Wor-
" ley (the late Sir Edward), Mr. Richard Ofborne, above mentioned, and Mr.
" John Newland, of Newport, were all engaged in the fecret, and very faithful,
" the two former waiting on horfeback beyond the counterfcarp, with a good
" horfe, &c. for his majefty, to carry him to Newland's boat that was ready, and
" Mr. Firebrace prepared to receive him, as he was to let himfelf down by a cord
" from the window, and conduct him crofs the court (no centinel being in the
" way) to the great wall of the caftle, and thence let him down on a ftick by a
" long cord. The fignal given, his majefty put himfelf forward, but then too
" late found himfelf miftaken, he fticking faft between his breaft and fhoulders,
" and not able to get forward or backward ; but that at the inftant before he en-
" deavoured to get out, he miftrufted, and tied a piece of his cord to a bar of
" the window within, by means whereof he forced himfelf back. This is the ac-
" count of an ear-witnefs, one that was near enough to hear the king groan while
" he ftuck, and when by a light, which his majefty, on his retiring, fet in the
" window, he faw what he had heard, that the defign was broken, he gave notice
" thereof to thofe without, by throwing ftones to them from the high wall, by
" which he was to have let his majefty down, fo that they went off, and no difco-
" very was made. This attempt thus failing, Mr. Firebrace fent for files and aqua
" fortis, from London, to make the paffage more eafy, and to help in other de-
" figns which he propofed ; his majefty, in the fame letter to him where he men-
" tioned the narrownefs of the window to have been the only impediment of his ef-
" cape, having added that therefore fome inftrument muft he had to remove the
" bar; the profecution of which defign is the chief fubject of the following letters,
" till in that Nº VII. his majefty acquaints Mr. Firebrace, that nothing could be done
" without taking away the middle bar; and while they were concerting that and
" other methods for his efcape, Hammond was directed from above to have a
" careful eye on thofe about the king, which occafioned Mr. Firebrace and others
" to be difmiffed; and in Mr. Firebrace's abfence that other attempt was made,
" of which my lord Clarendon gives account, and confounds it with the former, of
" which it feems he had never heard. Yet Dr. Perrinchief, in his Life of that
" Prince, p. 72, exprefly mentions two attempts for his deliverance, by thofe
" fervants whom the parliament had placed about him, the laft, that in which
                        " Rolph

" Rolph was concerned, who waited to kill his majesty as he should descend from
" his chamber. Indeed that author seems to have taken the account from their
" memoirs of Sir Henry Firebrace, to which he gave so much credit, as to men-
" tion several other particulars from thence; when yet their authority seems to
" have wanted that support which his worthy grandson has now enabled me to give
" them from the king's own original letters.

" Here follow the letters between King Charles I. under his confinement in the
" Isle of Wight, and Mr. (afterwards Sir Henry) Firebrace, before referred to [a].

Number I.

" D [b].

" SINCE I see that A [c]. cannot stay, you must take the more care to settle
" the intelligence between my friends and me at London; to which end I hope
" you have shewn the packet to F [d]. I have written to W [e]. but it is only to re-
" fer him to you: wherefore let him know that the narrowness of the window was
" the only impediment of my escape, and therefore that some instrument must be
" had to remove the bar, which I believe is not hard to get; for I have seen
" many, and so portable that a man might put them in his pocket, and yet of
" force sufficient to do more than this comes to; I think it is called the endless
" screw, or the great force. Likewise acquaint him with those other ways that
" were in discourse among us; desiring him upon the whole matter (as well upon
" his own as other men's inventions) to give his judgement, which is the most pro-
" bable way to effect this business.

" I shall dispatch all my letters this night, to wit, four: that with the French
" superscription is for my wife, and you are only to deliver it into Withering's of-
" fice, before Thursday at night, as a merchant's letter for France: that which is
" directed to Mr. John Pile, is for W [f]. that all in cyphers is for Dr. Fraiser; and
" the fourth is for Low the merchant, to whom also you must give those things
" that I have signed, and tell him, that he must not make use of them but ac-
" cording to such directions as he will find in my letter to him.

" Except you have more than I, there is no need of altering more letters than
" I have done; if you can, let me speak with you this night at the chink. J [g].

" You see that I am better than my word; but, however, I desire to speak with
" you; if it were but to know, whether or not you understand all my directions."

Number II.

" D [b].

" I Shall not fail to make L [h]. finish the bar; and you shall have a full dis-
" patch from to-morrow: I have the aqua fortis, but can find no stockings; where-
" fore do not forget to give me them to-morrow. J [h]."

[a] Appendix to Dr. Barwick's Life, p. 380, and following pages.   [b] Henry Firebrace.
[c] Mr. Francis Cresset.   [d] Mr. Abraham Doucett.   [e] Captain Titus.   [f] Ibid.
[g] The King.   [h] Henry Firebrace.   [i] Mr. Richard Osborne.   [k] The King.

Y   Num-

Number III.
" Mr. Firebrace's letter to the King.

" SIR,

" THE duke of York is gone away, whither it is not known; but he is cer-
" tainly gone, on Friday night laft: I hope you will not he long after him. This,
" night I have thought of a new projeſt, which, by the grace of God, will effeſt
" your bufinefs. It is this: in the back ſtairs window are two cafements, in each
" two bars; one of the bars in that next the door ſhall be cut, which will give
" you way enough to go out. I am certain the top of the hill comes within a yard
" of the cafement; fo that you may eafily ſtep out, and creep clofe to the wall, till
" you come to a hollow place (which you may obferve as you walk to-morrow),
" where with eafe you may go down, and fo over the out-works. If you like this
" way, it ſhall be carried on thus: Hen. C. ſhall cut the bar, and do up the gap
" with wax or clay, fo that it cannot be perceived; I have already made it loofe
" at the top; fo that, when you intend your bufinefs, you ſhall only pull it, and it
" will come forth. You muſt fup late, and come up fo foon as you have fupped.
" Put off your Geo. and on your grey ſtockings; and upon notice to be given you,
" by H. C. come into the back ſtairs, and fo ſtep out. We ſhall meet you, and
" conduſt you to your horfes, and from thence to the boat. I have told him of it,
" and he will undertake it; therefore pray leave fome of your files, that he may
" try to-morrow when you are at bowls. If you think to try this way, I believe
" it not neceſſary to tell any elfe of it befides Z [a].

" You keep intelligence with fomebody that betrays you; for there is a letter of
" yours fent to the governor, from Derby houfe (in characters), wherein you ex-
" prefs in words at length, that though they do remove Titus, Doucett, and Fire-
" brace, yet you defpair not of your bufinefs, or to that purpofe. Therefore pray
" think to whom you writ fuch a letter, and be careful: God knows what hurt
" this may do. I ſhall have a note to you from W [b]. to-morrow.   D [c].

" If you like this way, return the note with your fenfe."

The King's anfwer at the bottom.

" Let none know of this way, but only Z [d]. only we muſt be fure that horfes
" be ready on the other fide of the water.   J [e]."

Number IV.

" D [f].

" I Do extremely like of your neweſt way; for if you can make me room enough
" to go out at the window you mention, I warrant you, by the grace of God, that
" I ſhall get down the hill, and over the works, well enough. But I pray, for my
" fatisfaſtion, give me the breadth of it when one bar will be taken away, that
" I may be fure not to ſtick: and great care muſt be had that the filing be not

[a] Mr. Ed. Worſley, late Sir Edward, in the Iſle of Wight.   [b] Captain Titus.
[c] Henry Firebrace.   [d] Ed. Worſley.   [e] The King.   [f] Henry Firebrace.

" dif-

" difcovered; which if you do, I fhall not much fear any thing elfe. I have
" begun my bar, and make no doubt to effect it without being perceived; but for
" the time, I cannot yet tell. As for that fuppofed letter of mine, which has been
" fent to the governor, there can be no fuch: for firft, I never fufpected that W[d].
" D[b]. nor F[c]. fhould be fent away before Sunday was fevennight, fince when I
" made but one difpatch, wherein I remember I wrote two letters in cyphers, in
" one of which I made no mention at all of any one of you; and in the other,
" which was to my wife, if I faid any thing of W[d]. or D[c]. (for I am fure I faid
" nothing of F[f].) it was in cypher, and not to that purpofe that you are told.
" But it is poffible that the rogue Witherings hath difcovered how I fuperfcribe
" to my wife, and hath fent one of them to the committee: wherefore I defire you
" to enquire, to fee if I have not guefled right, and not to fend that letter you have
" of mine for any wife to the poft-houfe, but either to Dr. Fraifer or my lady Car-
" lifle, with a caution not to truft the poftmafters. For the duke of York's journey,
" ferioufly I know nothing of it, but what you have told me; but I pray God fend
" him a happy journey.   J[s].

" If you can cut the bar unperceived, queftionlefs this laft way is the beft; and
" therefore I have returned your paper and fome files; but I keep fome for my
" bar: give me an anfwer to this by night if you can."

Number V.

" D[b].   23 April.
" I Pray what's the reafon I had nothing this night from W[i]. nor you? for I
" would be glad to know in what order he hath left bufinefs; at leaft, if he have
" forgotten, I defire you to remember to let me know what directions are left
" with Q. F[k]. and Z[l]. that I may govern myfelf accordingly.

" I hope this day at dinner you underftood my looks; for the foldier I told
" you of, whofe looks I like, was then there in a white night-cap, and, as I
" thought, you took notice of him. To-morrow I will begin to try the bar, and
" at night I will give you fome account of it. In the mean time I hope to find
" fomething from you to-morrow morning, when I come in from walking, in an-
" fwer to this note.   J[m]."

Number VI.

" D[n].
" I Defire you firft to remember to leave perfect inftructions with L[o]. and
" F[p]. how to fend my letters to London, and to receive anfwers from thence,

[a] Captain Titus.	[b] Henry Firebrace.	[c] Abraham Doucett.
[d] Captain Titus.	[e] Henry Firebrace.	[f] Abraham Doucett.	[g] The King.
[h] Henry Firebrace.	[i] Captain Titus.	[k] Abraham Doucett.
[l] Ed. Worfley.	[m] The King.	
[n] Henry Firebrace.	[o] Richard Ofborne.	[p] Abraham Doucett.

" without

" without fufpicion; to this end I think it beft, that the outward covers of all
" your difpatches fhould be directed to fome honeft townfman of Newport, that
" may be trufted with fo much as the conveyance of letters, and he to advertife
" hither when he has any letters; and by this means our packets will never run
" the hazard of falling into the governor's fingers. Befides, when you fend any ex-
" prefs, agree of fome token, either by word or writing, whereby to know him
" from a knave.

" Of my letters to carry to London (with thofe that I give you this day) you
" will have one to my wife, one to my lady Carlifle, one to W. L. one to A[a].
" two to N[b]. and two to O[c]. For the firft, you fhall do well to afk advice how
" it may be fafely fent over to France, and enquire well whether or not Wither-
" ings hath played the knave. Thofe to O[d]. concern yourfelf; wherefore none
" elfe muft deliver them. I would alfo have yourfelf the deliverer of thofe to
" N[e]. becaufe they are of fome concernment, and demand an anfwer, efpeci-
" ally to the laft. For the reft, fo that the parties have them, it matters not much
" by whom; yet it were not amifs, if yourfelf gave them to my lady Carlifle.

" Now as to my main bufinefs; be careful to make L[f]. rightly to underftand
" the defign of the back-ftairs window, as likewife that other of my window, that
" I may leave or chufe as I fee occafion. Alfo you muft remember W[g]. to lay
" horfes on the other fide the water, and let me know when and where; nor
" let that be long a-doing; for it were a woeful thing to lofe an opportunity here
" for want of preparation there. As for thofe other defigns you told me of, I leave
" thofe to your managing, only promifing you exact fecrecy therein, and expecting
" an account from you. So much for the affirmative: now for the negative. You
" muft not let A[h]. nor O[i]. know of any prefent defign; but give them leave to
" believe, that your difmiffions have made us lay afide all fuch thoughts for a time.

" If any, with whom I keep correfpondence, does betray me, it muft be O[k].
" yet he bragged to me in his laft letter, that he furnifhed the duke of York
" with an hundred and fifty pound for his journey; but the truth is, that N[l].
" (for whofe fidelity I will anfwer) doth fufpect him, and in the laft packet hath
" given me warning of him: concerning whom my conclufion is, do no difhearten
" him, get what money you can of him, but do not truft him. Let me tell you,
" that it was not I that acquainted him with the greater bufinefs, for I found his
" name at the joint letter you fent me, before ever I imagined he knew of any fuch
" thing; and I affure you I never wrote any thing of moment to him, but only
" made ufe of him for conveyance of letters, and fending me news: in a word, be
" as confident of my difcretion as honefty; for I can juftly brag, that yet neither
" man nor woman ever fuffered by my tongue or pen, for any fecret that I
" have been trufted withal.

---

[a] Francis Creffet.   [b] Mrs. Whorwood, wife of Broom Whorwood.
[c] Mr. Low, a merchant in London.   [d] Ibid.   [e] Mrs. Whorwood.
[f] Richard Osborne.   [g] Captain Titus.   [h] Francis Creffet.   [i] Mr. Low.
[k] Ibid.   [l] Mrs. Whorwood.

" Here

" Here I send you my answer to Z[a]. unsealed, that you may read it; because
" I refer him to you, to impart unto him all our several designs; for he is the
" only man who of necessity must know all. It was not amiss that you returned
" me back my little packet to W[b]. for I had sent him a letter in it, which now
" I find directed to you; so that now I have mended an error, which I had almost
" made: for now you have what you ought to have, and W[c]. no more than his
" own; to whom I have written very freely, wherefore you must deliver your let-
" ter to him yourself, yet I have imparted nothing to him, either concerning Z's[d]
" design, or that of W. L.'s, but that of the back stairs window, referring him to
" you for the particulars. As for the conveying my letters to my wife, you may
" advise with Dr. Fraiser, or my lady Carlisle: I have now no more to say; but
" give me an account how you have performed all these directions of mine, and be
" confident that I am, your constant friend, J[e].

Number VII.

" D[f]. 26 Ap. 1648.

" I Have now made a perfect trial, and find it impossible to be done; for my
" body is much too thick for the breadth of the window; so that, unless the middle
" bar be taken away, I cannot get through. I have also looked upon the other two,
" and find the one much too little, and the other so high that I know not how to
" reach it without a ladder; besides, I do not believe it so much wider than the
" other, as that it will serve; wherefore it is absolutely impossible to do any thing
" to-morrow at night: but I command you heartily and particularly to thank, in
" my name, A[g]. C[h]. F[i]. Z[k]. and him who stayed for me beyond the works,
" for their hearty and industrious endeavours in this my service, the which I shall
" always remember to their advantage; being likewise confident that they will not
" faint in so good a work; and therefore expect their farther advice herein.
" J[l].

Number VIII.

" Mr. Firebrace to the King.

" SIR, Wednesday night.

" IT is not ill to have more ways than one to effect your business; to which
" purpose, I have thought of this. If the fellow that waits on me could be made
" (which I think no hard matter), the business might be ordered thus: a fellow pro-
" vided on purpose shall come in a false beard, a perriwig, a white cap on, a coun-
" try grey or blue coat, a pair of coloured fustian drawers to come over his bree-
" ches, white cloth stockings, great shoes, an old broad hat, to be touched of the
" evil. He shall make his addresses to this man of ours to get him touched, and
" pretend commendations, or a letter from some especial friend. When he is

[a] Ed. Worsley.   [b] Captain Titus.   [c] Ibid.   [d] Ed. Worsley.   [e] The King.
[f] Henry Firebrace.   [g] Francis Cresset.   [h] Colonel William Legg, groom of the bed-chamber.
[i] Abraham Dowcett.   [k] Ed. Worsley.   [l] The King.

" touched.

" touched (which muſt be at ſupper-time), the other ſhall take him into the cellar,
" and make him drink (pretending joy to ſee him), and carry him about that the
" ſoldiers may take notice of him.   You ſhall have the like diſguiſe conveyed into
" your bed-chamber (which you may ſoon ſlip on), coming up ſo ſoon as you
" have ſupped; then my man ſhall by a ſign give you notice when you may come·
" forth, and ſafely ſlip up ſtairs in a little room there (ſhutting the bed-chamber
" door after you, which may be done with eaſe and without noiſe), where you
" may remain a little, till he ſees the beſt opportunity to bring you down in his
" friend's diſguiſe, and conduct you out of the gates, and from thence to your
" horſes (which he may do with much eaſe, being well beloved by the ſoldiers).
" His friend ſhall (in ſome bye place of the caſtle to be appointed) put off his
" diſguiſe and leave it, and go away in his own habit.   This I conceive feaſible,
" if this fellow can be made, which I doubt not; he having been a long time
" ſervant to the pages of the back ſtairs, and with you at Oxford.   This is only
" to hint this way to you, which, if you like it, ſhall be put in execution.   If
" you like it, and read it before you go forth this morning, pray leave an an-
" ſwer, that I may acquaint the reſt with it at our meeting, which will be at nine
" this morning.

" I writ this in haſte, and could come at no more paper."

Number IX.

The King's anſwer.

" D*.

" HAVING well thought of your new deſign, I can think but of one ob-
" jection againſt it, which is, leſt the guards ſhould examine me as I go out; but
" I conceive a trial of this may be had, without any danger of diſcovery: for it is
" but making He. Chap. bring in and carry out ſome new acquaintance of his, ſo
" clothed as you intend I ſhould be, to ſee with what freedom he can make ſuch
" a man paſs and repaſs the guards.   But in this trial there muſt be no falſe beard,
" upon which a clear judgement is eaſily made.   As for the contriving of it, I like
" it extremely well, and therefore give you back your note again; as alſo this for
" W*, who I find is not fully ſatisfied with your deſign, becauſe of the danger of
" diſcovery; but take no notice of this.   J*."

" The following is the certificate of the Right Rev. Dr. William Juxon, Lord
" Archbiſhop of Canterbury, of the ſervices of this gentleman, and the re-
" commendation of him by King Charles I. to his ſon:

" Theſe are to certify, that our late dread Sovereign, of bleſſed memory, upon
" the 29th day of January, 1648, being the day immediately before that horrid
" and execrable murder was committed upon the perſon of his ſacred Majeſty,
" did give me in charge to recommend to his ſon, our gracious Sovereign that now
" is, Mr. Henry Firebrace, as having been a perſon very faithful and ſerviceable

---

¹ Henry Firebrace,   ² Captain Titus,   ³ The King.

" to

" to him in his greateſt extremities, and moſt ſtrict impriſonments, and therefore
" fit to be employed and entruſted by his Majeſty that now is. Given under my
" hand, this five and twentieth day of November, 1661. W. Cant."

This Sir Henry Firebrace, Knt. was appointed by King Charles II. chief clerk
of the kitchen, alſo clerk-comptroller-ſupernumerary of his majeſty's houſhold,
and aſſiſtant to his majeſty's officers of the green cloth: he had two wives, firſt,
Elizabeth, daughter of Daniel Davil *, of Stoke, by whom he had four ſons, and
one daughter, Suſanna, married to Thomas Hall, of Elymore Hall, in Durham,
gent. Of the ſons, 1. Henry Firebrace, fellow of Trinity College, Cambridge,
born 1650; 2. Sir Baſil, born 1653, of whom hereafter; 3. John, who died in
his infancy; and, 4. George, who died unmarried. Sir Henry married, ſecondly,
Alice, daughter of Richard Bagnall, of Reading, in Berks, widow of John Buck-
nall, of Creeke, in the county of Northampton, gent. by whom he left no
iſſue; he died Jan. 27, 1690, aged 72, and was interred in Stoke church. See
his epitaph in p. 95.

Sir Baſil Firebrace, knt. was of London, merchant, and ſheriff of the ſaid city
1687, knighted, and advanced to the dignity of a baronet, 10 Will. III. He married Elizabeth, daughter of Thomas Hough, of London, merchant, by whom he
had two ſons, Sir Charles, his ſucceſſor, born 1679, and George, born 1681
(who died without iſſue); alſo Heſter †, born 1676, married to Baſil fourth earl of
Denbigh †, by whom he had William, the fifth earl, who was father to Baſil the
preſent earl.

Sir Charles Firebrace, bart. his eldeſt ſon, and ſucceſſor in dignity and eſtate,
married Margaret, daughter and one of the coheirs of Sir John Cordell, of Long
Melford, in Suffolk, bart. and died Auguſt, 1727, leaving one ſon, Sir Cordell
Firebrace, who in 1735 was elected one of the knights of the ſhire for Suffolk, in
the room of Sir Robert Kemp, bart. deceaſed, and was re-choſen for that county
in every ſucceſſive parliament till his death. He married, 1. Aug. 20, 1736, Miſs
Daſhwood, an heireſs; and, 2. Oct. 26, 1737, Bridget; relict of Edward Evers, of
Ipſwich, in the county of Suffolk, eſq. who was third daughter of Philip Bacon,
of the ſame town, eſq. Sir Cordell dying without iſſue, March 28, 1759, the
title became extinct, and the ancient manſion at Long Melford devolved to his widow,
who was again married, April 7. 1762, to William Campbell, eſq. uncle to the
preſent duke of Argyle, who is ſtill living. She died July 3, 1782.

The arms of Firebrace (Azure, on a bend, Or, three creſcents, Sable, between two
roſes, Argent, ſeeded, Or, bearded Vert) are engraved in plate IV. fig. 4.—Creſt, On
a wreath, a dexter arm, armed, and couped at the ſhoulder, Azure, holding a
Portcullis, Or.—Motto, Fideli quid obſtat.

* " Thomas Davil, gent. died April 11, 1746, aged 65." Epitaph at Stoke.
† Thus far the Viſitation.
‡ This lady, who ſurvived her lord nine years, died Jan. 1, 1715-6.

8. Captain

9. Captain WILLIAM TRYMNELL [*].

OF this gentleman little more is known than has been related in p. 96. from his epitaph in Stoke church, where he was buried in 1693, at the age of 67. He had two daughters:

1. Dorothy, married to Nathanael Wyatt, gent. who died Nov. 29, 1703, aged 48; his wife Jan. 27, 1693, aged 42; and Sarah, their daughter, Sept. 1, 1655, aged 3 years [†].

2. Anne, second daughter to Captain Trymnell, was married to Mr. William Johnson, of London, merchant. He died Sept. 21, 1709, aged 51; Mrs. Johnson, Nov. 2, 1737, aged 78. They had a son, Trymnell Johnson, who died Aug. 12, 1714, aged 20; and a daughter, Anna Maria Saunders, who died June 20, 1757, aged 58 [†].

10. Rev. WILLIAM STANLEY, D. D. Master of Corpus Christi College [‡], Cambridge.

THIS learned Divine was the son of William Stanley, Gentleman, of Hinckley, where he was baptized Aug. 22, 1647 [‖]. His father dying whilst he was very young, he was left to the sole care of his mother, who put him to school at Ashley in Lancashire, and afterwards sent him to St. John's College in Cambridge, in 1663, at the age of sixteen. It might be because Bp. Beveridge, who married his aunt, was of that college; though perhaps from a stronger motive, as Mr. Villers afterwards earl of Jersey (of a Leicestershire family in his neighbourhood) went thither about the same time under the tuition of the learned and worthy Dr. Gower, who is said never to have had any other pupils but these two. He stayed there till he was chosen into a fellowship of Corpus Christi college, upon the expulsion of Scargill, in 1669, and this upon the joint recommendation of his tutor and Bp. Gunning, then master of St. John's; who, knowing his merit, were loth he should quit the university so soon as he must otherwise have done, his own county (to use the language of their college) being at that time full.

He was ordained priest by Bishop Compton in 1672, became an University preacher in 1676, and commenced B. D. 1678. His first step out of the university into the world was the curacy of Much-Haddam in Hertfordshire, and a very fortunate one it was, as it placed him not only under the eye and direction of that excellent divine Dr. Goodman, but as it gave him an opportunity of being known to the earl of Essex (whose seat was there), who made him his chaplain, and then presented him to the rectory of Raine-Parva in Essex, October 20, 1681. But this he vacated soon after by cession for St. Mary Magdalen, in Old Fish-street, London, Oct. 30, 1682, which he quitted in like

[*] A family of Trimnell is mentioned in Dr. Nash's Worcestershire, vol. II. p. 317. as seated formerly at Ockley in that county; of which family Thomas founded a school, and gave other charities to the parishes of Sew, Claines, and elsewhere. Blomfield says, that Dr. Trimnell, bishop of Norwich and Westminster, was of that family, and bore their arms.

[†] These dates are all from flat stones in Stoke Church.

[‡] This Life is principally taken from Mr. Master's History of that College.

[‖] From the Parish Register.

man-

manner for that of Much-Hadham, before mentioned, Aug. 13, 1690, being collated thereto by Bp. Compton, upon the death of his friend Dr. Goodman. These were the only parochial benefices he ever had. As to dignities, he was preferred to the prebend of Cadington-Major, in the cathedral of St. Paul, Sept. 18, 1684, whereof he was made a refidentiary in 1685; as likewife to the archdeaconry of London, March 5, 1691-2, upon the promotion of Dr. Tenifon to the bifhopric of Lincoln, and many years after to the deanry of St. Afaph, Dec. 7, 1706: which he rather accepted to fet his uncle, Bp. Beveridge, at liberty from the powerful folicitations of others, than that it was a preferment he either fought after or defired.

I cannot fay with certainty when he went over to be chaplain to the prince of Orange, upon the difmiffion of Dr. Covel; but conjecture it might be about the year 1687. Whenever it was, a clergyman of an unexceptionable character in every refpect was to be provided by exprefs orders from Holland. Accordingly the Bifhop of London had it in charge to recommend two fuch perfons to the Archbifhop of Canterbury, who was to have the final approbation of one. The two thus recommended were Dr. Burnet, mafter of the Charterhoufe, and Mr. Stanley; to the latter of whom his Grace gave the preference, for this pleafant reafon, that although the former was a deferving man, an ingenious divine, and a good fcholar; yet as Mofes and the Doctor could not agree about making worlds, he thought it was better to chufe Mr. Stanley; who after being farther favoured by his Grace (about this time, as I conjecture) with his faculty for a doctor of divinity's degree, was forthwith fent over, and foon became a favourite both at court and with her highnefs. He likewife contracted there a particular acquaintance with the two Huygens, as well as with other perfons of learning and character; being without doubt recommended and fupported herein by his old friend and fellow collegian Mr. Villiers, who had waited on the princefs into Holland upon her marriage, and continued there till the prince's coming over into England in 1688 [*].

As foon as his royal miftrefs was feated on the throne, fhe advanced him to be clerk of the clofet, with a falary of 200l. per ann. fettled upon him for life, and always had him in fuch credit and efteem, that moft of her charities paffed through his hands, he being the inftrument commonly made ufe of in applications of this kind. She moreover offered him one or two bifhopricks, which he then declined, as thinking the refidence and duty would interfere with his conftant attendance upon her perfon and fervice; or perhaps rather (from his refufal of Lincoln upon archbifhop Tenifon's promotion) becaufe he was content with the preferment he already had and his own private fortunes, and found a ftation of lefs dignity and eclat more agreeable to his inclinations, and fuitable to his fchemes of happinefs in life.

The death of his old friend Dr. Spencer however brought him (though much againft his will) into a more public fcene of life in the Univerfity, as it occafioned his being elected (but without his knowledge) into the mafterfhip of Corpus Chrifti college; which

* Collins's Peerage, vol. III. p. 513.

Z

yet upon the firft notice of his choice he pofitively refufed to accept of, and even perfevered in this refufal, till two of the fellows went in the name of the whole fociety and importuned him to do it, for the fake of preferving the peace and welfare of the college, and of preventing an irreconcileable divifion among them, feeing they were unanimous in their votes for him, which they fhould not be for any other perfon. This motive had its defired effect; even though he forefaw the trouble that would follow, by being elected the fame year vice chancellor of the Univerfity; who, as a mark of their great efteem, were pleafed to pafs an extraordinary grace in his favour for admitting him to the degree of doctor of divinity with all its privileges among them, which an archiepifcopal faculty could not entitle him to.

Confidering from what motive, and with what reluctance, he took the mafterfhip, it might be expected he would refign it, as he did in 1698, becaufe he could not be more conftantly refident, nor confequently be of that fervice to the college he otherwife would. Whilft he held it, he fpent as much of his time there as he could, and as ufefully. For, that the world might know how great a treafure its manufcript library is ftored with, he fet himfelf to make that valuable catalogue of it [*], which he afterwards printed at his own expence: and which merits the acknowledgements of all lovers of antiquity, and efpecially of the hiftory of this church and nation; who being fenfible from their own experience of the care and pains neceffary to finifh a work of this kind (wherein the feveral volumes contain fuch a variety of tracts, fome of which are often fo imperfect, ill-wrote, or faded through length of time, that it is no eafy matter to get acquainted with their contents [†],) will not expect to find the firft attempt without defects. Thefe have been amply compenfated by the late accurate and informing Catalogue, taken of them by Mr. James Nafmith, late fellow of this houfe, now rector of Snailwell, Cambridgefhire [‡]. Mr. Mafters had before new arranged them, and caufed them to be put into better bindings.

During Dr. Stanley's mafterfhip the college was, through the negligence of their fervants, robbed of their communion plate on an Eafter-day; upon which he generoufly prefented them with a fet of filver gilt, the fame that are ftill in ufe, adorned with the arms of the illuftrious family of Orange, having belonged to the private chapel of Queen Mary, when princefs; who, upon her coming to the crown of England, gave it to him as a memorial of her favour and efteem.

This is but one article in the accompt of his very extenfive benefactions and charities. Among the many good and ufeful defigns he was from time to time concerned in, and fupported, was that of printing an edition of the Councils in 1692, with Proteftant annotations, by an annual fubfcription. Several fums were accordingly fubfcribed, by the two archbifhops 10l. per annum each, and by twelve bifhops 5l. each. Dr. Stanley not only did the fame, but by his intereft at court was chiefly inftrumental

* "Catalogus Librorum Manufcriptorum in Bibliothecæ Coll. Corp. Chrifti in Cantabrigia; quos le-. "gavit Matthæus Parkerus Archiepifcopus Cantuarienfis. Lond. 1722." Fol.
† Preface to Cafley's Catalogue of MSS. in the King's Library, p. 4.
‡ "Catalogus Librorum Manufcriptorum, quos Collegio Corporis Chrifti & B. Mariæ Virginis in Aca- "demia Cantabrigienfi, legavit reverendiffimus in Chrifto pater Matthæus Parker, Archiepifcopus Can- "tuarienfis. Edidit Jacobus Nafmith, A. M. S. A. S. ejufdem Collegii nuper focius. Cant. 1777." 4to.

in,

in obtaining a grant to import what paper fhould be wanted cuftom-free. Dr. Allix undertook the care and management of this edition : and had great quantities of paper imported for it; which, when the book was laid afide, was fold to the ftationers for private gain, to the o fence of the public, and the regret of the learned world. The doctor, when dean of St. Afaph, was at the fole expence * of that act fet parliament of the 12th of Queen Anne, which annexed prebends and finecures to the bifhopricks of Bangor, Llandaff, St. David, and St. Afaph, in order to relieve the widows and fatherlefs of the Welfh clergy from the fore diftrefs of paying mortuaries to the bifhops upon the death of every incumbent within their refpective diocefes and jurifdictions; which mortuaries (as the preamble to that act fets forth) "confifting of feveral of the beft goods of the deceafed, did oftentimes amount to "a confiderable part of his eftate, and the payment thereof did very much leffen "that fmall provifion which generally the clergy of thofe diocefes were able to "make for the fupport of their families, and tended to the great impoverifhing of "the fame." An act of generofity and goodnefs in the dean, that ought ever to be remembered with the utmoft gratitude by the clergy of Wales. — He likewife rebuilt what is now the beft part of his own deanry houfe, and made the whole of it habitable, convenient, and decent; where he often refided, and lived hofpitably fo long as he was able to take fuch a journey.—He fettled a leafehold eftate on a charity fchool in that town : and joined with Mr. Carter in augmenting the perpetual curacy of St. George in its neighbourhood.—But his gifts towards the augmentation of fmall livings by one or two hundred pounds at a time, with the aid of Queen Anne's bounty, were not confined to one county, but extended into different parts of the kingdom, as may be feen in Ecton's lift, &c.—To his own church at Hadham he gave a clock : and to the building of the Regent houfe at Cambridge, an hundred pounds. Such gifts and benefactions as thefe could not be hid; though he was, upon Chriftian principles, as fecret as he could be in doing his alms. What charities therefore he diftributed with his own hands cannot be difcovered, as he left no account of them. But fo far is known of him, that it was his conftant rule all his life long, to beftow in good works a clear tenth part of his whole income, whether from fpirituals or temporals.—I may here add, that he was not only a contributor to the Society for propagating the Gofpel in Foreign parts, and a zealous promoter of it, but was alfo the firft mover in the bufinefs of their charter †.

Dr. Stanley, confidered as an author, publifhed but few things, though probably, as he began early to take a fhare with the London clergy in the Popifh controverfy, he would have written more had he not been prevented in going on with them by being fent over to Holland in the capacity of chaplain.—However, before he went abroad, he was concerned with feveral divines in the fcheme of printing an Englifh Bible, with a plain and practical commentary, but more efpecially levelled againft the errors and corruptions of Popery.—His own province

* Willis's Survey of the Cathedral of St. Afaph, p. 107, and of Bangor, p. 345.
† Humphrey's Hiftorical Account, p. 12.

Z 2

was to write upon the minor prophets; a scheme that was superseded by the happy establishment of our church and nation at the Revolution.

What he published with his name were, 1. " A Sermon on Coloss. ii. 5. preached " Jan. 10, 1691-2, in Lambeth Chapel, at the consecration of Dr. Tenison bishop " of Lincoln." 2. " A Sermon on Matt. ix. 37, 38, preached Feb. 20, 1707-8, " at St. Mary le Bow, before the Society for propagating the Gospel." He has, as I am informed, another sermon in print, which I never saw, to recommend a public collection for the redemption of captives. The editors also of the Bodleian Catalogue have placed among his writings " The Romish Horse Leech," concerning the intolerable charge of Popery to this nation; by an obvious error of the press, that work being written by Mr. Staveley * in 1674. He was also the author of two anonymous discourses, the one concerning the Devotions of the Church of Rome, wherein they are compared with those of the Church of England, in 4to. Lond. 1685; and the other, intituled, " The Faith and Practice of a Church of England-" Man, in 12mo. Lond. 1706."

Such is the character and history of Dean Stanley, whom God was pleased to bless with a very healthful, happy, and long life; for he did not die till Oct. 9, 1731, in the 85th year of his age †; when, according to his own directions, he was buried in the vaulting of St. Paul's cathedral, under the south wing of the choir, among his old friends Bp. Beveridge, Dean Sherlock, Dean Younger, Dr. Holder, and Sir Christopher Wren: none of whom, except the last, have any monument, stone, or even inscription over them.

He married Mary second daughter of Sir Francis Pemberton, lord chief justice both of the Common Pleas and King's Bench, by whom he had three sons, all educated at Bishop Stortford school and Ben'et college; whereof William the eldest, LL.B. removed to Peter house, and settled at Warwick, and was official of the archdeaconry of London; Francis the second was fellow of the college, and afterwards vicar of St. Leonard in Shoreditch, till his father resigned to him the rectory of Hadham, Sept. 30, 1723, which he held, with a prebend of St. Paul's, till his death, 1775, when he was succeeded by Dr. Anthony Hamilton, archdeacon of Colchester; Thomas the youngest is dead.

The two sons of Francis Stanley were admitted at Ben'et college, 1755: the elder Francis is a barrister of the Inner Temple, and was elected recorder of Hertford 1780; the younger, Richard, was presented to the vicarage of North Weald in Essex, 1769, and to the rectory of Eastwick in Hertfordshire, 1781.

* See above, p. 152.
† It is scarce worth observing, that the natural tone of his voice was so remarkably loud, as to give occasion to the Tatler, in the year 1711, to exercise his wit upon him under the name and character of " Sir *****;" N° 54.

11. Rev.

II. Rev. Francis Brokesby.

OF this gentleman, grandson to the Francis whose epitaph is printed in p. 94, little is known; but that little is worth preserving. A letter from him in the sixth volume of Leland's Itinerary is thus introduced by Mr. Hearne: " This letter " was written by a very worthy friend, the reverend and learned Mr. Francis " Brokesby, formerly fellow of Trinity College, Cambridge, and afterwards rec- " tor of Rowley, in the East Riding of Yorkshire. It contains divers curious ob- " servations that were made (amongst a great many others) as he was travelling " through divers parts of England. He was induced to draw them up partly by " some letters that some time ago passed between us concerning Mr. Camden's Bri- " tannia, and partly by Dr. Plot's letter which I published in the second volume of " this Itinerary."

I find a tradition at Stoke, that Mr. Brokesby was the author of a " Life of Jesus " Christ *;" and also that he was a principal assistant † to Mr. Nelson in compiling his admirable volume on the Feasts and Fasts of the Church of England. He was certainly author of " An History of the Government of the Primitive Church, " for the three first centuries, and the beginning of the fourth; shewing that the " Church in those first ages, as it has been ever since, was governed by Bishops, " or Officers superior to Presbyters: Wherein also the Suggestions of David " Blondel to the contrary are considered, by Francis Brokesby, B. D. sometime " Fellow of Trinity College in Cambridge. Printed by W. B. 1712." 8vo. In a dedication to Mr. Francis Cherry ‡, dated Shottesbrooke, Aug. 13, 1711, the author

says,

* " An Historical Narrative of the Life and Death of our Saviour Jesus Christ," was printed at Oxford, 1685, 4to. But this, which was at first attributed to Ab. Woodhead, was written by Obadiah Walker, the master of University College. See Wood, Ath. Ox. II. 614. 916.
† It was a tradition in Mr. Brokesby's family that he wrote the whole book. But I am aware that it has
also been said that " Garth did not write his own Dispensary."
‡ In the Life of Dodwell, p. 301, Mr. Brokesby pathetically bewails the loss of this gentleman, and gives
some particulars of his character, by which it appears that he was a student at Edmund Hall §, Oxford, where
his love to learning, industry, and probity, endeared him to many eminent persons, and particularly to Mr.
Fenton, then principal of that society. Having a plentiful fortune, he purchased a good collection of books,
MSS. medals, and useful curiosities. He had the honour of being the earliest patron of Mr. Thomas Hearne,
whom he maintained at school, and at the university till he became M. A. His house was " a sanctuary for
" persons in distress; especially such as suffered for conscience sake." He died Sept. 23, 1713, in his 48th
year; and by his own directions was buried very privately at Shottesbrooke, near the remains of his friend
Mr. Dodwell, being carried to the grave by four of his poorest tenants. He ordered a brick work of two or

§ Thomas Cherry, a cousin-german to Francis, was admitted M. A. at the same Hall, June 26, 1706. To him
relates a letter from Edward Gardener to Mr. Hearne in the Bodleian Library. Mr. Cherry preached for Dr.
Adams at St Clements Danes with a rash on him, and strained himself into a perfect bath in that large church. He rode
to Uxbridge, Oct. 9, 1706, which struck it in, and brought on a fever: he was delirious when the curate of the parish
came to administer the sacrament, and died Nov. 17, about two or three o'clock in the afternoon. He was buried the
Wednesday following in the vault under St. Andrew's. His pall was supported by Mr. Shute, the curate, Mr. Broughton,
the lecturer, Mr. Fox, a relation, and Mr. Sparrow. Mr. Hincham, the deputy curate, read the service, and Mr.
Cherry of Berkshire assisted at the funeral. Concerning Mr. Thomas Cherry and his excellent kinsman Francis, see Mr.
Hearne, in his " Account of some Antiquities between Windsor and Oxford," sect. 19. at the end of the Vth vol. of
Leland's " Itinerary." See also his preface to Leland's " Collectanea," sect. 26.

three

fays, " The following treatife challenges you for its patron, and demands its de-
" dication to yourfelf, in that I wrote it under your roof, was encouraged in
" my ftudies by that refpective treatment I there found, and ftill meet with;
" and withal, as I was affifted in my work by your readinefs to fupply me, out
" of your well-replenifhed library, with fuch books as I ftood in need of in col-
" lecting this Hiftory. I efteem myfelf therefore in gratitude obliged to make
" this public acknowledgement of your favours, and to tell the world, that
" when I was by God's good Providence reduced to ftraits (in part occafioned by
" my care left I fhould make fhipwreck of a good confcience) I then found a fafe
" retreat and kind reception in your family, and there both leifure and encourage-
" ment to write this following treatife." As Mr. Brokesby's ftraits arofe from
his principles as a Nonjuror, he was of courfe patronized by the moft eminent
perfons of that perfuafion. The houfe of the benevolent Mr. Cherry, however,
was his afylum; and there he formed an intimacy with Mr. Dodwell, (a pillar
of that caufe, whofe Life* he afterwards wrote) and with Mr. Nelfon, to whom
the Life of Dodwell is dedicated.

Mr. Brokesby was faid to be the author of " Of Education, with refpect to
" Grammar-fchools and Univerfities. 1701." 8vo. He died fuddenly foon after
the publication of Dodwell's Life. See Calamy's " Account of the ejected or fi-
" lenced Minifters. 1713." vol. II. p. 299, which will receive light from New-
court's " Repertor." vol. II. pp. 314, 315.

three feet to be raifed over him, and a plain marble laid upon it, without any arms, name, or other infcription, but this which followeth:

HIC IACET PECCATORUM MAXIMUS. ANNO DOM. MDCC . . . .

leaving the year to be inferted. " Shottefbrooke," fays Brokefby, " a fmall village, is ennobled, and will
" hereafter be remembered, as it was the habitation, and is the fepulture, of two fuch eminent perfons, as
" Mr. Cherry and Mr. Dodwell. And now I return to give an account of the beginning and progrefs of the
" acquaintance and friendfhip betwixt thefe two worthy perfons and their profecution of the fame ftudies: but
" I muft here lament my lofs of Mr. Cherry, on whom I depended for this account, he being moft able to
" give it; and only acquaint the reader with what Mr. Cherry told me, as it accidentally fell from him in
" difcourfe. When Mr. Dodwell lived at Cookham, it was his chief exercife and diverfion to walk to Mai-
" denhead to hear news, and the chief of that which he defired was to know what books were newly publifh-
" ed. Mr. Cherry coming thither on the fame errand, they became acquainted: and as they difcourfed of thefe,
" fo alfo of books of ancienter date, and of the excellent and ufeful things contained in them, a fubject highly
" pleafing to each of them. This converfation was fo grateful to them both, that it was mutually agreed to
" meet there daily in the afternoon; and the very thoughts of enjoying it was to Mr. Cherry fo preferable to
" other delights, that he frequently fhortened his dinner, that he might be the fooner with his learned friend,
" and have the larger opportunity thereby to improve himfelf. I wifh I could give the reader the fubjects of
" their conferences. But the diftance of their habitations, efpecially of Mr. Cherry's, from Maidenhead, be-
" ing too great, and inconvenient in the winter feafon, Mr. Cherry invited his friend to be his neighbour,
" procured a place for him where he might be tabled, about a quarter of a mile diftant from him, till he had
" fitted up, and added to, a houfe for him, nearly adjoining to his own habitation, where Mr. Dodwell lived
" many years; and at length in another houfe near to it, and more convenient for him (his family being in-
" creafed) in which he ended his days."
    * Under the title of " The Life of Mr. Henry Dodwell; with an Account of his Works, and an Abridg-
" ment of them that are publifhed, and of feveral of his Manufcripts. By Francis Brokefby, B. D. To which
" is added, a Letter to Robert Nelfon, efq. from Dr. Edmund Halley, Savilian Profeffor of Geometry, con-
" taining an Abftract of Mr. Dodwell's Book De Cyclis. 1715." 8vo.
    † Related, probably, to Sir Ifaac Newton. See Gent. Mag. 1772, p. 510.

In

In that part of Stoke church which, (in p. 94,) I have fuppofed to have been a chantry, is an elegant recefs for holy water, and there are fome others in the church. On the outfide of the church, at the eaft end, is an old mural monument to the Brokesbys, almoft devoured by time and mofs, but on which the family name and date 1604 remain vifible. The name of *Brokesby* is alfo written over the church porch.

12. REV. ROGER COTES.

THIS excellent mathematician, philofopher, and aftronomer, was born July 10, 1682, at Burbach, where his father Robert Cotes was rector. He was firft placed at Leicefter fchool ; where, when he was between eleven and twelve years of age, he difcovered a ftrong inclination to the mathematics. This being obferved by his uncle, the reverend Mr. John Smith †, he gave him all imaginable encouragement ; and prevailed with his father to fend him for fome time to his houfe in Lincoln-fhire, that he might put him forward, and affift him in thofe ftudies. Here he laid the foundation of that deep and extenfive knowledge in mathematics, for which he was afterwards fo defervedly famous. He removed from thence to London, and was fent to St. Paul's fchool ; where, under the care of Dr. Thomas Gale and the fucceeding mafter, he made a great progrefs in claffical learning ; yet found fo much leifure as to keep a conftant correfpondence with his uncle, not only in mathematics, but alfo in metaphyfics, philofophy, and divinity. This fact is faid to have been often mentioned by profeffor Saunderfon. His next remove was to Cambridge ; where, upon the 6th of April 1699, he was admitted of Trinity college ; and, at Michaelmas in the year 1705, chofen fellow of it. He was at the fame time tutor to Anthony earl of Harold, and the lord Henry de Grey, fons to the then marquis, afterwards duke of Kent, to which noble family Mr. Cotes had the honour to be related.

In January 1705-6, he was appointed profeffor of aftronomy and experimental philofophy, upon the foundation made by Dr. Thomas Plume, archdeacon of Rochefter ; being the firft that enjoyed that office, to which he was unanimoufly chofen, on account of his high reputation and merits. He took his mafter of arts degree in the year 1706 ; and went into holy orders in the year 1713. The fame year at the defire of Dr. Bentley, he publifhed at Cambridge the fecond edition of Sir Ifaac Newton's " Mathematica Principia Philofophiæ Naturalis ;" and inferted all the improvements which the author had made to that time. To this edition he prefixed a moft admirable preface, in which he expreffed the true method of philofophifing, fhewed the foundation on which the Newtonian philofophy was built, and refuted the objections of the Cartefians and all other philofophers againft it.

The publication of this edition of Sir Ifaac Newton's Principia added greatly to the reputation Mr. Cotes had acquired among the greateft men of the age for his profound knowledge in the abftrufeft parts of mathematics : nor was the high
opinion

opinion the public now conceived of him in the least diminished, but rather much increased, by several productions of his own, which afterwards appeared. He gave a description of the great fiery meteor, that was seen on the 6th of March, 1715-16, which was published in the Philosophical Transactions a little after his death. He left behind him also some admirable and judicious tracts, part of which, since his decease, have been published by Dr. Robert Smith, his cousin and successor in his professorship, afterwards master of Trinity College in Cambridge. His "Harmonia Mensurarum," &c. that is, "Harmony of Measures; or, Ana- "lysis and Synthesis advanced by the Measures of Ratios and Angles," was pub- lished at Cambridge in the year 1722, in 4to; and dedicated to Dr. Mead by the learned editor, who, in an elegant and affectionate preface gives us a copious ac- count of the performance itself, the pieces annexed to it, and of such other of the author's works as are yet unpublished. He tells us how much this work was ad- mired by Professor Saunderson, and how dear the author of it was to Dr. Bentley. The first treatise of the miscellaneous works annexed to the "Harmonia Mensura- "rum" is "Concerning the estimation of Errors in mixed Mathematics." The second is "Concerning the differential Method;" which he handles in a manner somewhat different from Sir Isaac Newton's treatise upon that subject, having written it before he had seen that treatise. The name of the third piece is "Ca- "nonotechnia, or concerning the Construction of Tables by differences." The book concludes with three small tracts "Concerning the Descent of Bodies, the "Motion of Pendulums in the Cycloid, and the Motion of Projectiles:" which tracts, the editor informs us, were all composed by Cotes, when he was very young. He wrote also a "Compendium of Arithmetic, of the Resolutions of "Equations, of Dioptrics, and of the Nature of Curves." Besides these pieces, he drew up a course of hydrostatical and pneumatical lectures in English, which were published by Dr. Smith in the year 1737, and are held in high repute.

This uncommon genius in mathematics died, to the regret of the university, and all lovers of that science, upon the 5th of June, 1716, in the very prime of his life; for he was advanced no farther than to the thirty-third year of his age. He was buried in the chapel of Trinity College; and an inscription fixed over him, from which we learn that he had a very beautiful person. It was written by the celebrated Dr. Bentley, who was his constant friend and patron, and runs in the following terms:

H. S. E.
ROGERUS ROBERTI filius COTES,
Collegii hujus S. Trinitatis socius.
Astronomiæ & experimentalis philosophiæ
Professor Plumianus:
Qui
Immatura morte præreptus,
Tamen quidem ingenii sui pignora reliquit.
Sed egregia, sed admiranda,
Ex inaccessis mathesios penetralibus
Petita solertia tuum primum eruta.

Post magnum illum Newtonum
societatis hujus spes altera.
Et decus gemellum.
Cui ad summam doctrinæ laudem
Omnes morum virtutumque dotes
In cumulum accesserunt:
Eo magis spectabiles amabilesque,
Quod in formoso corpore gratiores venirent.

Natus Burbagii in Agro Leicestriensi
Jul. 10, 1682, obiit Jun. 5, 1716.

13. Rev. Anthony Blackwall, M. A.

THIS worthy and learned man, a native of Derbyshire, was admitted sizar in Emanuel College, Cambridge, Sept. 13, 1690; proceeded Bachelor of Arts in 1694, and went out Master in 1698. He was appointed head master of the noted free-school at Derby, and lecturer of All-Hallows there, where in 1706 he distinguished himself in the literary world by " Theognidis Megarensis Sententiæ Morales, " nova Latina Versione, Notis & Emendationibus, explanatæ & exornatæ : una " cum variis Lectionibus, &c." 8vo. Whilst at Derby he also published " An " Introduction to the Classics; containing a short Discourse on their Excellences; " and Directions how to study them to advantage; with an Essay on the Na- " ture and Use of those emphatical and beautiful Figures which give Strength " and Ornament to Writing, 1718," 12mo. in which he displayed the beau- ties of those admirable writers of antiquity, to the understanding and imitation even of common capacities; and that in so concise and clear a manner as seeme peculiar to himself *. In 1722 he was appointed head master of the free-school at Market-Bosworth in Leicestershire; and in 1725 appeared, in 4to, his greatest and most celebrated work, " The Sacred Classics defended and illustrated; or, an " Essay humbly offered towards proving the Purity, Propriety, and True Elo- " quence of the Writers of the New Testament. Vol. I. In Two Parts. In the " first of which those Divine Writings are vindicated against the Charge of barba- " rous Language, false Greek, and Solecisms. In the Second is shewn, that all " the Excellencies of Style, and sublime Beauties of Language and genuine " Eloquence, do abound in the Sacred Writers of the New Testament. With " an Account of their Style and Character, and a Representation of their Supe- " riority, in several instances, to the best Classics of Greece and Rome. To " which are subjoined proper Indexes." A second volume † (completed but a few weeks before his death) was published in 1731, under the title of " The Sa- " cred Classics defended and illustrated. The Second and Last Volume. In Three " Parts. Containing, I. A farther Demonstration of the Propriety, Purity, and " sound Eloquence of the Language of the New Testament Writers. II. An " Account of the wrong Division of Chapters and Verses, and faulty Translations " of the Divine Book, which weaken its Reasonings, and spoil its Eloquence " and Native Beauties. III. A Discourse on the Various Readings of the New " Testament. With a Preface; wherein is shewn the Necessity and Usefulness of " a New Version of the Sacred Books. By the late Reverend and Learned A. " Blackwall, M. A. Author of the First Volume. To which is annexed a very " copious Index." To this volume was prefixed a portrait of the author, by Vertue, from an original painting. Both volumes were reprinted, in 4to, under the title of " Antonii Blackwalli inclyti Magnæ Britanniæ Philologi Auctores Sa- " cri Classici defensi & illustrati; five Critica Sacra Novi Testamenti. Christo- " phorus Wollius, M. A. S. T. B. & Concion. ad D. Nic. Sabbathicus ex Anglico

* Yet Mr. Gilbert Cooper selects this very book as " one lamentable instance of able scholars having suc- " ceeded very ill in works, where they have betrayed the greatest want of taste and genius, whilst they were " unfortunately laborious in endeavouring to point out those excellences in others." Mr. Blackwall, he adds, " was what is generally called a good scholar, that is, he was grammatically master of the two dead languages, " Greek and Latin, and had read over all the ancient authors; but not having by nature or acquisi- " tion that happy taste of distinguishing beauties, nor a digestion to assimilate the sense of others into his own " understanding, his conceptions were as crude as his address and style were unpleasing." Such, and still worse, is the censure thrown on Mr. Blackwall, in the " Letters on Taste," p. 119—111.
† So valuable for its conciseness, and yet so complete for its clearness, it has been asserted, that no book of the same size ever before comprehended such rich stores of useful learning and sound criticism, or was so well fitted for the education of a Christian Scholar. See " The Present State of the Republick of Letters," 1731, vol. VIII. p. 38.

A a   " Latinè

" Latinè vertit, recenfuit, variis Obfervationibus locupletavit, & Hermeneuti-
" cam N. F. Dogmaticam adjunxit, Lipfiæ, 1736." Mr. Blackwall had the
felicity to bring up many excellent fcholars in his feminaries at Derby and Bofworth; among others, the celebrated Richard Dawes *, author of the " Mif-
" cellanea Critica," and Sir Henry Atkins +, bart. who, being patron of the
church of Clapham in Surrey, prefented him, October 12, 1726, to that rectory (then fuppofed to be worth 300l. a year), as a mark of his gratitude
and efteem. This happening late in Mr. Blackwall's life, and he having occafion to wait upon his old acquaintance Bifhop Gibfon (then Bifhop of
London, but with whom Mr. Blackwall had been intimate whilft he enjoyed
the fee of Lincoln) for ordination, a young chaplain was examining him in
the Greek Teftament, when the Bifhop entered the room, and with great good-
nature put an end to the examination by afking the chaplain if he knew what
he was about. " Mr. Blackwall," faid the Bifhop, " underftands more of the
" Greek Teftament than you do, or I to help you ‡." The Grammar whereby
Mr. Blackwall initiated the youth under his care into Latin was of his own
compofing, and fo happily fitted to the purpofe, that in 1728 he was prevailed
upon to make it public, though his modefty would not permit him to fix his
name to it, becaufe he would not be thought to prefcribe to other inftructors
of youth ||. It is intituled, " A New Latin Grammar ; being a fhort, clear, and
" eafy Introduction of young Scholars to the Knowledge of the Latin Tongue ;
" containing an exact Account of the two firft Parts of Grammar." Early in 1729
(to accommodate the families of his patrons Sir Wolftan Dixie and Sir Henry

* Born in 1708, and admitted of Emanuel College, Cambridge, in 1725. In 1736 he publifhed a fpecimen of a Greek Tranflation of Paradife Loft ; of which, in his preface to the Mifcellanea Critica, he had
candour enough to point out the imperfections himfelf. The blot of his life was taking part againft Bentley,
from whom the prefent father of Greek literature in this country, Mr. Toup, acknowledges to have learned
more than from all the critics of all the ages before. Mr. Dawes died in 1766, and left fome manufcripts, to
which Mr. Burgefs (who has lately publifhed a new and improved edition of the " Mifcellanea Critica")
had accefs. There are fome others in Dr. Afkew's collection, who bought Mr. Dawes's library. See
Maty's Review, for February, 1762.—A Dr. Dawes (the father probably of the Critic) refided fome years
at—at Stapleton, near Hinckley; and is recollected to have been a great fcholar, and a fearcher after the
philofopher's ftone.
† The family of Atkins, now extinct, were patrons of Clapham from 1642, when the king prefented to
the living in the minority of Richard Atkins, his ward. From 1641 to 1664 the regifters are loft. John
Gurgany, D. D. was prefented (by whom does not appear) foon after the Reftoration, and died Aug. 1671.
John Savile was prefented 1671 by John Baynes and Jof. Savile, hac vice, probably truftees for a minor, or
purchafers of that turn. Dr. Nicholas Brady (the immediate predeceffor of Mr. Blackwall) was prefented
to the rectory 1701-6 by Dame Rebecca Atkins, relict of Sir Richard Atkins, bart. § Mr. Goodwin (rector
of Market Bofworth, proctor for the clergy of the diocefe of Lincoln, and fon-in-law to Sir Wolftan Dixie)
was prefented by the truftees of Sir Henry Atkins, bart. a minor, grandfon of Sir Henry, in June 1749.
Mr. Goodwin died in 1753, and was fucceeded by Sir James brunhoufe, LL. B. the prefent rector, who
was prefented by Sir Richard Atkins, brother of Sir Henry.
‡ This fact is related on the authority of Dr. Johnfon, to whom it was told by Mr. Fitzherbert, one of
Blackwall's fcholars. Another ftory nearly to the fame purpoft is told of Mr. Blackwall ; but it has alfo been
told, and with more probability, of Dr. Bentley; viz. that being pertly queftioned by the chaplain as to the extent of his learning, he replied, " Boy, I have forgot more than ever you knew."
|| See " A fhort Elogium of the late Reverend and Learned Anthony Blackwall, &c." in " The Prefent
" ftate of the Republick of Letters, 1730," vol. VI, p. 71.—I have never feen a copy of this Grammar ; but
am affured by the greateft Philologer this country ever produced, that it has not much merit. By endeavouring to make the rules of Grammar more fimple than was poffible, he has only fhewn, that the " eafier any
" fubject is in its own nature, the harder it is to make it more eafy by explanation."

§ Dr. Brady held this rectory, with Richmond, till his death, which happened March 28, at the age of 67. He tranflated the Pfalms in conjunction with Tate, and Virgil's Eneid. He alfo was author of three volumes of fermons, and a
tragedy, intituled, " The Rape, or the Innocent Impoftor, 1692." See more of him in the Select Collection of Mif-
" cellany Poems, 1782," vol. V. p. 302.

Atkins,

Atkins, who were nearly related ") he refigned the rectory of Clapham; and retired to Market-Bofworth, where he was equally refpected for his abilities and conviviality. He died at his fchool there, April 8, 1730. His fon, John, who was many years an attorney at Stoke, died July 5, 1763, aged 56; and his epitaph has already appeared in p. 97. A daughter of the fchoolmafter was married to William Cantrell, bookfeller at Derby.

On a vifit to Market-Bofworth †, in May 1782, the principal object of my inquiries was the hiftory of Mr. Blackwall. Not the flightest memorial is placed in the church to this ornament of their town ‡. Some faint trace of his having exifted was all that I could learn, except that the noble free fchool was under his aufpices attended by upwards of feventy fcholars; and that the endowment, originally not more than feven pounds a year, is now fo much increafed that the mafter's falary amounts to at leaft 100l. befides 30l. for an affiftant, and 21l. for a perfon to teach writing. The predeceffor to Mr. Blackwall was Richard Smith, M. A. who died in 1722 (as appears by an altar-tomb in the church-yard, infcribed probably by Blackwall, but now almoft defaced by time). His fucceffor was Mr. Crompton; and the prefent mafter is the rev. Mr. Slade.

The church at Bofworth is large, and has a beautiful fpire. Within is a fpacious chancel, a body and two ailes, an old feptagon font, the remains of an organ which has been more than thirty years decayed, and fome remarkably handfome pews belonging to the Dixies, Mundays, and Burflems (the laft formerly belonging to General Godolphin). There is a handfome monument for Sir Beaumont Dixie, who died in 1719; and in the chancel is a flat ftone with this infcription:

" Here lies the body of	lie interred near this place.
Sara, wife of Mr. Thos Langmand,	She was dutiful towards God
de Iflington, com' Midd', and	and her neighbour to her life's
daughter of James Orton, clerk,	end, and in all her actions prudent,
A. M. and Sufanah his wife,	juft, and fincere.
who, with feveral of their children,	Ob. Jan. 3, 1730."

* Sir Wolftan Dixie, grandfather of the prefent baronet, married Rebecca, daughter of Sir Richard Atkins; by whom he had, befides other children, one daughter Rebecca-Maria, married to Sir Henry Atkins; and another, Barbara, married to the Rev. Mr. Goodwin.

† That I might omit no poffible chance of being better acquainted with the hiftory of this ingenious fcholar, the tombs at Clapham have been fearched, but with fruitlefs inquiry. An epitaph on his fucceffor in that rectory fhall, however, be here preferved, from a flat ftone formerly in the chancel of the church:

" Here lies the body of	Market Bofworth in Leicefterfhire;
The Rev. Mr. JOHN GOODWIN, M. A.	By whom he had one fon,
Twenty-three years rector of this parifh.	JOHN ¹, now Fellow of New College, Oxon.
He died Jan. 12, 1753, in the 71ft year of his age,	and one daughter,
He married BARBARA ² daughter of	REBECCA, wife of NICOLSON CALVERT, Efq.
Sir WOLSTAN DIXIE, bart. of	of Hunfdon, in the county of Hertford."

‡ The ingenious author of the Hiftory of Birmingham, after defcribing the hofpicality experienced at firft entering that town, and the general appearance of induftry which he faw there, fays, " I did not meet with " this treatment in 1770 at Bofworth, where I accompanied a gentleman with no other intent than to view " the field celebrated for the fall of Richard the Third. The inhabitants enjoyed the cruel fatisfaction of " fetting their dogs at us in the ftreet, merely becaufe we were ftrangers. Human figures, but their own, " are feldom feen in thefe inhofpitable regions. Surrounded with impaffable roads, no intercourfe with man " to humanife the mind, or commerce to fmooth their rugged manners, they continue the boors of nature." The hofpitality and induftry of Birmingham will not be difgraced by mentioning that thofe good qualities are equally ftriking at Hinckley. I cannot add, however, that the roads round Bofworth were improved in 1782; but muft fay that even there I met at leaft with kind reception and civil anfwers, though they afforded very little information.

¹ Who died July 15, 1767, aged 71.
² Afterwards rector of Paulerfpury, Northamptonfhire. He died Feb. 9, 1775, aged 52, and was buried with his father and mother.

14. Rev. Samuel Parr, Vicar of Hinckley.

AS the memory of this gentleman is recollected with much esteem by several of the old inhabitants, I am sorry I can say no more of him than that he held the vicarage in 1702, and died in 1720. His son Robert was rector of Horstead and Cottishall in Norfolk, as appears by the epitaph on his widow, printed in p. 49; and his grandson Robert is now a clergyman. Mr. John Parr, the vicar's brother, was many years an apothecary in the town of Hinckley.

15. Rev. John Carte, Vicar of Hinckley.

THIS worthy Divine (son of Samuel Carte *, vicar of St. Martin's, Leicester, and brother to Thomas Carte the Historian) was admitted a scholar of Trinity Hall, Cambridge, Jan. 9, 1707, where he took the degree of LL. B. He was chaplain to William the fifth lord Digby; and was presented by his father (who possessed the advowson in right of his prebend) to the vicarage of Tachbroke, in the county of Warwick; and afterwards by the dean and chapter of West-minster, on the recommendation of Bishop Atterbury, to that of Hinckley, where he was inducted Dec. 20, 1720, and resided till his death, Sept. 17, 1735. He seldom failed to preach twice every Sunday in the church at Hinckley, and once at Stoke. The last time he preached was the funeral sermon of his clerk James Merry, after which he never more was able to attend the duties of the church. The sermon at his funeral was preached by Dr. Jackson, of Coventry, to a crowded congregation at Hinckley, where Mr. Carte was buried in the chancel near the communion table, and where no other memorial remains to his memory than an inscription on a gallery, that it was erected in 1723 whilst he was vicar; though his surviving parishioners still speak of his learning, his probi-ty, his simplicity of manners, and his unaffected piety, with a degree of venera-tion. He was a most zealous assertor of the rites and ceremonies of the church of England, which, he justly observed, were equally remote from the extremes of Popery and Fanaticism; and his opinions were founded on the firm basis of Scrip-ture, with which he was so intimately acquainted, as to be able to repeat the greater part of the Bible. A favourite book of his was " Bysse's Beauty of Ho-" liness," which, he said, was worth its weight in gold.—Moses Emanuel, a Jew of uncommon learning, well known in that part of the country as a travelling ped-lar, received always much pleasure from the conversation of Mr. Carte, who in return took amazing pains to convince him of the truths of Christianity. Their friendly altercations were long and frequent, and turned principally upon the fifty-first and fifty-third chapters of Isaiah.—His absence of mind is recollected in many re-markable particulars. Some years before his death he paid his addresses to Miss Dugdale, of Blyth Hall near Coleshill (a lineal descendant of the illustrious An-

* Of whom, and also of his sons Thomas and Samuel, and daughter Sarah (a great benefactress to the parish of Great Wigston in Leicestershire) see the Anecdotes of Mr. Bowyer, p. 191—204, 366.

tiquary),

tiquary), and the wedding day was fixed; but he actually forgot to go till the day after that which was agreed on, when the lady with indignation refused her hand, and the match was broken off. Perpetually abforpt in thought, he was careless in his drefs, and totally deftitute of œconomy. He even carried his care-leffnefs in money matters to fuch a degree, that when the inhabitants of Stoke have brought to him the tithes, which he never took the trouble to afk for, he has not uncommonly (if he chanced to be engaged with a book) requefted them to come at a future time, though perhaps the next hour he was obliged to borrow a gui-nea for fubfiftence. The parfonage-houfe adjoins to the church-yard; yet he was frequently fo engaged in ftudy, that the fermon-bell has rung till the congregation were weary of waiting, and the clerk was under the neceffity of reminding him of his duty.—During the fifteen years in which he was vicar of Hinckley, he neg-lected to make any demand for tithes of the hamlet of The Hide; which his bro-ther Thomas (his adminiftrator) difcovering after his death, made a claim on the inhabitants of that hamlet for tithes in kind; and, to recover them, filed a bill in chancery, which came to a hearing in Eafter term, May 13, 1747. The de-fendants infifted that the vicarage was never endowed, and that a contributory payment of feventeen fhillings which had formerly been made was in lieu of all tithes; and that tithes in kind were not paid within the memory of man. Mr. Carte, being obliged to prove the endowment, as his brother was only vicar, and not rector, procured from the abbot of Lyra an attefted copy of a grant in 1209 from the abbot and convent of Lyra to the vicar of Hinckley, as evidence of endowment of all manner of tithes to the vicar of the parifh. This inftrument, however, was not admitted to be read. Mr. Carte next produced three terriers, the firft of them dated 1638; the reading of which was allowed, as being evi-dence, though not conclufive. As the impropriators (the dean and chapter of Weftminfter) did not think proper to difclaim their right to the tithes, which might have put an end to the queftion in favour of Mr. Carte, an iffue was di-rected, " to try whether the vicar of Hinckley is intitled to tithes in kind of " the hamlet of Hide, in the parifh of Hinckley ," and the plaintiff had time and

---

* I fhall here fubjoin the whole cafe, as I find it reported by Atkyns, III. 416.
The bill was brought for a fubftraction and account of tithes, againft the inhabitants and occupiers of Hinckley in Leicefterfhire. The defendants infift upon a contributory modus of feventeen fhillings for the lands which they hold of the hamlet of Hide in the fame parifh. The dean and chapter of Weftminfter, who are the rectors, do not in their anfwer difclaim the right to the tithes, but refer to thefe ladies, who appre-hended the had no right, and has never collected them.
Mr. Attorney General for the defendants. He faid, a vicar of common right is not intitled to tithes, but by virtue of an endowment or grant from thofe who were the owners of the land. An antient payment for tithes is a modus, and fuppofes an agreement originally.
Lord Chancellor. " A general charge of an endowment is fufficient to intitle the plaintiff to fhew " an endowment at the hearing, without mentioning the particular fact of endowment."
Mr. Attorney General then went on, and faid, The receipts run in this manner: " May 1702, received " then of Robert Ball the fum of eleven fhillings and four-pence for the tithe due at Lady-day, for his part " of the Hide grounds, figned John Par." Other receipts call it The Hides only.
Mr. Clark of the fame fide cited Hardcaftle verfus Smithfon, July 1744, before Lord Hardwicke, to fhew that the court will not conftrue the modus with great nicety where it is in general properly fet out by the anfwer.
Mr. Evans of the fame fide: A rector has nothing to do but to make out his title to the rectory, and the tithes will be due of courfe to him, but otherwife as to a vicar. There is no evidence arifes from ufage, for the plaintiff has not been able to fhew the tithes were even paid to the vicar. That a terrier, neither here, or at any price, has been admitted to be evidence of the vicar's right, unlefs ufage goes along with it.
Mr. Solicitor General for the plaintiff faid, that in the cafe of Berry verfus Evans, Lord Chief Baron Co-myns folemnly determined, that even againft a lay impropriator you cannot prefcribe in non decimando; and in extraparochial places the King is intitled; and if it appears the rector is not intitled, the vicar muft.

LORD

and opportunity given him to eftablifh the ancient endowment, and to examine
it by commiffion, which was not executed. This iffue was afterwards tried ;

LORD CHANCELLOR. " This is an unufual demand, as it is a bill brought by an adminiftrator of a
" vicar who was for 15 years together vicar of this parifh, and yet during all the time of his incumbency no
" tithe was paid, nor demand ever made ; but however, if the right appears, the plaintiff is intitled to a de-
" cree. His right depends on two queftions ; Firft, whether, as ftanding in the place of the vicar, he has
" fhewn a right to the tithes in kind. Secondly, whether the modus fet up by the defendant's anfwer is not
" a fufficient bar to that right. I will take up the fecond queftion firft. I am of opinion the modus, as
" ftated in the anfwers of the defendants, is not fufficiently laid in point of law. It is more correctly laid in
" the fecond anfwer, and is laid there in the following manner ; feventeen fhillings in the whole paid for The
" Hides in lieu and fatisfaction of all tithes, 5s. and 8d. for the part of Hides in the occupation of
" fuch a perfon, 4s. and 4d. for the part in the occupation of another, and 3s. for the part in the occupation
" of another. Two objections have been taken by the plaintiff's counfel, that it does not fay the time when
" it is to be paid, nor enumerates the perfons by whom it is to be paid. As to the firft, in the court of Ex-
" chequer, if a particular time was not laid, that court formerly would have over-ruled the modus, and not
" gone into the merits ; but lately they have very properly let in a greater latitude of proof, and it is fuffi-
" cient if it is laid at a particular time, or thereabouts. But the fecond is what I lay ftrefs upon, that it is
" not laid by whom it is to be paid ; and I do not know any cafe in the books, or in experience, where it is
" not alledged to be paid by fomebody ; and it is very reafonable it fhould be faid by whom, becaufe the
" perfon may then be fure to whom he muft apply, or againft whom he may have a remedy for his tithes.
" This cannot be fupplied by faying that in other parts of the anfwer they have fhewn the feventeen fhil-
" lings have been paid by thofe perfons who have held thefe lands, for that may be accidental ; and though
" it has been faid this court does not take cuftoms fo ftrictly certain as courts of law, yet this court requires
" cuftoms to be fubftantially laid. If before the court of Exchequer, where cafes of this kind are more fre-
" quent, it would have been over-ruled at once. The next queftion is upon the evidence. No proof has
" been read to fhew there ever was fuch an entire modus paid of feventeen fhillings a year ; but the defendants
" add feveral modules together, and then, by computation in arithmetick, make juft the fum of feventeen
" fhillings : In fome meafure like the Duke of Grafton's cafe of fines, where, by looking into the Lord's
" books, they found what was the largeft fine he took, and charged that fum to be the cuftomary payment.
" There is no evidence that thefe payments are applicable to the modus, and therefore I am of opinion it is
" not fufficiently made out. Upon the opinion I have given as to this part, if the plaintiff had been rector I
" fhould have decreed at once for him ; but a rector differs materially from a vicar. A rector has, and fo has
" a lay improprietor, a right to all the tithes in the parifh, and has nothing to do but to prove himfelf rector ;
" it is otherwife with regard to a vicar, for he muft fhew an actual endowment, or evidence of the ufage.
" In the firft place, there is no evidence here of payment of tithes in kind, which will be a much more ma-
" terial confideration againft a vicar than a rector. Whether the anfwer be fo formally drawn as might be,
" yet it is fufficient as to the denial of the plaintiff's right ; for though the defendants admit Carte was vicar,
" yet they fay they do not know or believe that he was intitled to the inclofed grounds of Hinckley, and to
" all or any part of the tithes. So that, by their anfwer, they infift he was not intitled ; but then it is argued
" for the plaintiff, that the defendants fetting up a modus is an implication that the vicar was intitled to
" tithes, and to be fure it is, but this does not preclude the defendants from objecting to the plaintiff's title,
" and it would be hard to preclude them ; becaufe they fail in the defence they fet up for themfelves. Sup-
" pofe a plaintiff at law declares, and the defendant pleads any thing in bar which by prefumption admits
" the demand, whereupon the plaintiff demurs, and the court holds the plea bad, yet they will ftill fee whe-
" ther the plaintiff in his declaration has made a cafe fufficient to intitle him to recover. The plaintiff is,
" unfortunately for him, precluded by the rule of this court from reading the evidence of the endowment,
" which it is faid would have put this matter out of queftion. The abbot of Lyra in Normandy has fent a
" certificate of the original agreement between the rector and the vicar in relation to the tithes ; but though
" it appears to come out of the abbot's hands, yet as it does not appear that it came out of the charter-houfe
" of the abbot, or that he was the proper officer to keep the records, it could not be admitted to be read.
" Even before the Reformation, a certificate from a foreign abbey was not allowed ; therefore, as the original
" deed relating to the endowment cannot be read, I muft take it from the evidence before me, which is, that
" no tithe has ever been paid to the vicar. The terriers are very dark, and I can hardly make any judgment
" of them ; and it is very far from being clear from thence, that tithes in kind were ever paid to the vicar.
" A vicar may not only be endowed of the tithes of a parifh, but of a penfion * likewife ; and therefore how
" can I prefume he was endowed of the tithes, when he might be endowed of this annual payment by way
" of penfion ? If it depended upon this only, I would require, whether in any cafe tithes have been decreed
" in kind to a vicar, where there is no evidence of tithes having ever been paid to him in kind. The dean
" and chapter, the rectors, do not difclaim their right to the tithes ; if they had, it might have put an end to
" the queftion in favour of the vicar ; this being the cafe, I am not fatisfied he is intitled to the tithes in
" kind, and therefore it muft be put in a method of trial. It is faid the rectors ought to be parties to the
" iffue, but it is not neceffary they fhould, for where an improprietor's right does not come in queftion, he
" need not even be made a party to a bill that is brought for fubftraction of tithes."

    * Which, however, was not the cafe at Hinckley. See the extract from Pope Nicholas's Valor, in p. 3.

when

when the jury found that the vicar in his life-time was not intitled to tithes in kind, and, July 17, 1749, the bill was difmiffed with cofts. The arrears of the modus, however, were adjudged to Mr. Carte *.

16. Rev. John Dyer.

OF this gentleman Dr. Johnfon could collect no other account than his own Letters to Mr. Duncombe, publifhed with Hughes's correfpondence, and the notes added by the editor, afforded. He was born in 1700, the fecond † fon of Robert Dyer of Aberglafney in Caermarthenfhire, a folicitor of great capacity and note. He paffed through Weftminfter fchool under the care of Dr. Freind, and was then called home to be inftructed in his father's profeffion. His father died foon, and he took no delight in the ftudy of the law, but, having always amufed himfelf with drawing, refolved to turn painter, and became pupil to Mr. Richardfon, an artift then of high reputation, but now better known by his books than his pictures. Having ftudied awhile under his mafter, he became, as he tells his friend, an itinerant painter, and wandered about South Wales and the parts adjacent; and about 1727 printed " Grongar Hill ‡." Being, probably, unfatisfied with his own proficiency, he, like other painters, travelled to Italy; and coming back in 1740, publifhed " The Ruins of Rome." If his poem was written foon after his return, he did not make much ufe of his acquifitions, whatever they might be; for decline of health, and love of ftudy, determined him to the church. He therefore entered into orders; and, it feems, married about the fame time a lady of Colefhill, named Enfor §; " whofe grandmother," fays he, " was a Shakfpeare, " defcended from a brother of every body's Shakfpeare." His ecclefiaftical provifion was a long time but flender. His firft patron, Mr. Harper, gave him, in 1741, Calthorp in Leicefterfhire of eighty pounds a year, on which he lived ten years; and, in April 1757, exchanged it for Belchford in Lincolnfhire of feventy-five, which was given him by Lord Chancellor Hardwicke, on the recommendation of a friend to Virtue and the Mufes **. His condition now began to mend. In 1752, Sir John Heathcote gave him Coningfby, of one hundred and forty pounds a year; and in 1756, when he was LL. B. without any folicitation of his own, obtained for him from the Chancellor Kirkby on Banc, of one hundred and ten. " I was glad of this," fays Mr Dyer in 1756, " on account of its nearnefs to me, though I think myfelf " a lofer by the exchange, through the expence of the feal, difpenfations ††, jour- " neys, &c. and the charge of an old houfe, half of which I am going to pull " down." The houfe, which is a very good one, though deferted by the prefent

* See Vefey's Reports, I. 3.
† Bennet Dyer, efq. of Aberglafney (probably his elder brother) was high fheriff of Cardigan in 1736.
‡ Firft printed in Lewis's Mifcellany. This poem " is not very accurately written; but the fcenes " which it difplays are fo pleafing, the images which they raife fo welcome to the mind, and the reflections " of the writer fo confonant to the general fenfe or experience of mankind, that when it is once read, it " will be read again." Dr. Johnson.
§ Sifter of Mr. Strong Enfor, who, after being clerk to Mr. Cox an attorney at Colefhill, entered into partnerfhip with Mr. Purefoy of Hinckley, whofe daughter he married; and afterwards retired to an eftate in that part of Suffolk which joins Cambridgefhire, as mentioned in p. 33.—A Mr. Thomas Enfor of Hofton (poffibly their father) was a member of the Gentlemen's Society at Spalding.
** Daniel Wray, efq. one of the deputy tellers of the Exchequer, and a Curator of the Britifh Mufeum. For this gentleman Mr. Dyer feems to have entertained the fincereft regard; as indeed every one muft do who has the honour of his acquaintance. The Writer of this Hiftory is proud of having been diftinguifhed by the friendly notice of Mr. Wray.
†† He had a difpenfation, in September 1751, to hold Belchford and Coningfby; and another, in July 1756, to hold Coningfby with Kirkby.

incumbent,

incumbent, owes much of its improvement to Mr. Dyer. His ſtudy, a little room with white walls, aſcended to by two ſteps, had a handſome window to the church-yard, which he ſtopped up, and opened a leſs that gave him a full view of the fine church and caſtle at Tateſhall, about a mile off, and of the road leading to it. He alſo improved the now neglected garden. In May 1757, he was again in mortar; rebuilding a large barn, which a fate wind had blown down, and gathering ma-terials for rebuilding above half the parſonage-houſe at Kirkby. "Theſe," he ſays, "ſome years ago, I ſhould have called trifles; but *the evil days are come;* "and the lighteſt thing, even the graſs-hopper, is a burden upon the ſhoulders "of the old and ſickly." He had then juſt publiſhed "The Fleece *,"* his greateſt poetical work; of which Dr. Johnſon relates this ludicrous ſtory. Dodſley the bookſeller was one day mentioning it to a critical viſitor, with more expectation of ſucceſs than the other could eaſily admit. In the converſation the author's age was aſked; and being repreſented as advanced in life, "He will," ſaid the critic, "be buried in woollen." He did not indeed long outlive that publication, nor long enjoy the increaſe of his preferments; for he died in 1758. Mr. Gough, who viſited Coningſby, Sept. 5, 1782, could find no memorial erected to him in the church, which is a very handſome building, with a lofty ſquare tower open at bottom with three high arches. Mrs. Dyer, on her huſband's de-ceaſe, retired to her friends in Caernarvonſhire, where ſhe is ſuppoſed to be ſtill re-ſident. In 1756 they had four children living, three girls, and a boy. Of theſe, Sarah died ſingle. The ſon, a youth of the moſt amiable diſpoſition, heir to his father's truly claſſical taſte, and to his uncle's † eſtate of three or four hundred a year in Suffolk, devoted the principal part of his time to travelling; and died in London, as he was preparing to ſet out on a tour to Italy, in April 1782, at the age of 32. This young gentleman's fortune is divided between two ſurviving ſiſters; one of them married to alderman Hewitt of Coventry; the other, Elizabeth, to the Rev. John Gaunt ‡ of Birmingham. Mr. Dyer had ſome brothers, all of whom were dead in 1756 except one, who was a clergyman, yeoman of his majeſty's almonry, lived at Marybone, and had then a numerous family.

* Of "The Fleece," ſays Dr. Johnſon, which never became popular, and is now univerſally neglected, I can ſay little that is likely to recall it to attention. The womiſomber and the poet appear to me ſuch diſcordant natures, that an attempt to bring them together is to couple the ſerpent with the fowl. When Dyer, whoſe mind was not unpoetical, has done his utmoſt, by intereſting his reader in our native commodity, by interſperſing rural imagery and inelidental digreſſions, by clothing ſmall images to great words, and by all the writer's arts of diſtinction, the meaning naturally adhering, and the irreverence habitually annexed to trade and manufacture, ſink him under inſuperable oppoſition; and the diſguſt which blank verſe, encumbering and encumbered, ſu-peradds to an unpleaſing ſubject, ſoon repels the reader, however willing to be pleaſed. Let me however ho-neſtly report whatever may counterbalance this weight of cenſure. I have been told that Akenſide, who, upon a poetical queſtion, has a right to be heard, ſaid, "That he would regulate his opinion of the reigning "taſte by Dyer's Fleece; for, if that were ill-received, he ſhould not think it any longer reaſonable to expect "fame from excellence." I may add that his "Fleece" had received many "blottings and corrections, and "ſome helps, from his kind friend Dr. Akenſide." It was "precipitated to the preſs," he adds, by the ſolicitation of Mr. Wray. The following ſhort epigram may perhaps be worth preſerving:

    Advent'rous Jaſon ſtole a Go'den Fleece;
    Dyer's own wool produced a Silver Piece.

Mr. Dyer calls "good Mr. Edwards" author of the "Canons of Criticiſm," his particular friend; and in Savage's poems are two Epiſtles to Dyer, one of them in anſwer to the beautiful little poem, which begins

    "Have my friends in the town, in the gay buſy town,
    "Forgot ſuch a man as John Dyer."

† Mr Enſor; of whom ſee p. 183.
‡ Who has been mentioned in pp. 14, 16, as leſſee of the glebe-land at Hinckley under the Dean and Chap-ter of Weſtminſter.

17. Rev. Thomas Morres [*], D D. Vicar of Hinckley,

Succeeded the Rev. Joseph Cardale, M. A. as vicar of Hinckley and rector of
Stoke, &c. This worthy gentleman was a fellow of Hertford College, Oxford,
and chaplain to the late princess dowager of Wales. He was blessed with a liberal
and manly disposition. He recommended, encouraged and promoted peace, harmony, and good neighbourhood; and was an encourager of industry and frugality.
He was naturally studious himself, and fond of promoting the same inclination
in others. He was well acquainted with the learned languages and arts and sciences, to which he had most happily and successfuly applied himself; for his diligence was great and indefatigable, and his memory very tenacious. Though he
had a general knowledge of literature, yet he was more particularly intimate with
the Grecian learning, and studiously examined both the ancient and modern sys-
tems of philosophy: there was something in his very countenance expressive of
the extent and keenness of his understanding. He had a critical knowledge of the
classic authors, and in his compositions joined their ease and elegance with the
more sublime parts of knowledge which appear in the sacred writings, to the study of which he more particularly applied himself, for he steadily attended the
sacred duties of his calling. His public discourses were grave, clear, and elegant; on well-chosen subjects, and delivered in a manner peculiar to himself,
which secured the attention of his hearers: his subtilty in distinguishing in difficult points was very extraordinary, and his judgement in making right decisions
extremely sharp and accurate, and delivered with so much judgement and propriety of language, that they were fit for the most learned audience, and yet so
intelligible as to be proper for the meanest capacity. With regard to his character as a minister, he was faithful, pious, and truly worthy the name of a Christian.
In private conversation, he was free from that reserve and austerity observable in
studious and contemplative men, after the mind has been long intent on grave and
important subjects, deep researches, or abstruse speculations; so that what rendered him still more to be admired was, he was extremely pleasant and agreeable in
private conversation. It is a very false idea that piety arises from a gloomy temper,
a chearful mind naturally produces good-will towards men, and gratitude to God;
it inclines us to receive pleasure from all the objects which surround us, and to
dwell upon what is most beautiful and most excellent; whence we are led to the
contemplation of the Divine Being, who is the source of all perfection. In short,
in him the Graces and the Sciences were happily blended and united; so that in
whatever point of view we see him, whether as the grave divine, the scholar, or
the gentleman, or collectively united in one striking point, we behold an object
worthy our most serious attention and imitation. He resided very constantly in
the vicarage-house at Hinckley; but, making an occasional visit to London in 1761,
was suddenly snatched from life, at his lodgings in Great Shire Lane, leaving his

* The materials of this article were communicated by Mr. Robinson.

B b   numberless numberlefs friends almoft inconfolable for his lofs, March 16, 1761, aged 47 years, and was buried near the font in the South aile of Hinckley church. It is remarkable that he told fome friends at Hinckley, his mind foreboded he never fhould return alive. He left iffue, by Anne his wife, one fon Robert, and one daughter Elizabeth, both young. His epitaph in the chancel, written by Dr. Freind Dean of Canterbury, has been already printed in p. 40; and in p. 47. a flight fpecimen of his own poetry may be feen, in the verfes on the family of Mr. Hurft.

18. Mr. John Dalby, Schoolmafter of Hinckley.

In p. 141 fome account has been given of Mr. Vynes, which I fhould be happy to continue with fome particulars of his fucceffors; but have been able to learn little more than the names of   ·

Mr. Joseph Woodland, a man much efteemed as a fcholar, who prefided in the Latin fchool at Hinckley about the clofe of the laft century;

The Rev. John Blakesley, who refigned the fchool on receiving church preferment; and was fucceeded by

Mr. John Ledbrook; and he by

Mr. Dalby; of whom I have received the following account from Mr. Robinfon, who was his fcholar: " He was elected fchool-mafter in 1739, principally " through the recommendation of my grandfather Sanfome *; a favour which he " always gratefully acknowledged. He was tall of ftature and well proportioned, and " in his fchool kept up a proper order and fubordination among his fcholars as they " advanced in learning. His cafting a look over the fchool was obferved with awe " and filence. His epitaph (written by a clergyman of the church of England, " with whom he was intimately acquainted) is here tranfcribed from a tomb-ftone " in the church yard of Afton Flamville, where he always expreffed a great incli- " nation to be buried.

" In memory	here interred. He died
of Mr. John Dalby, late mafter	Auguft the 16th, 1771,
of the Free Grammar School at	aged 65 years.
Hinckley in this country;	
the duties of which ufeful calling	There needs no epitaph to found his praife,
he difcharged with the ftricteft care	Or other trophies to his memory raife:
and attention upwards of forty years,	Here lies an honeft and an upright man;
and by his own particular requeft lies	Reader, go thou and imitate his plan."

It may be here obferved, that the names I have given are thofe of the Latin fchoolmafters; for there are two diftinct fchools under the patronage of the Feoffees, one called *The Free Grammar School*, the other fimply *The Free School*. The Latin language, however, has been fo little cultivated of late years at Hinckley, that Mr. Dalby had very few pupils who ftudied it. And a regular boarding academy having been in 1779 introduced by Mr. Gallaway, the prefent vicar, the office of Latin mafter at the Free fchool is become merely nominal, being filled fince the death of Mr. Dalby by Mr. William Allen, who was at firft put in only as

* This appears from an original letter to Mr. Sanfome, dated Worthington, Jan. 13, 1739; now in the poffeffion of Mr. Robinfon.

a

a temporary mafter, and whofe only employment is to teach young children to read their mother tongue. The Englifh free fchool, in which writing and arithmetic are alfo taught, is under the care of Mr. William Ward, the printer and bookfeller of the town.

There is likewife a free fchool at Stoke, of which the Rev. Mr. Brown is the prefent mafter, founded in the 30th year of the reign of King Charles the Second, anno Dom. 1678, by Mrs. Hefter Hodges of Somerfet Houfe in the Strand in the county of Middlefex. It is by the foundrefs ordered, that it be called " The Free " Grammar School of Stoke Golding, of the Foundation of Mrs. Hefter Hodges;" being intended for the education of youth in the principles of the Chriftian religion, according to the eftablifhment of the Church of England, together with the training them up in fuch human literature as may be advantageous and ufeful towards rendering them true and genuine fons of the Church, loyal and obedient fubjeᵈfs to the King.

19. Mr. Joseph Nutt, Apothecary, of Hinckley.

Of this ingenious perfon Mr. Robinfon, who knew him well, and who when a boy was diftinguifhed by him with more than ordinary attention, has obligingly furnifhed me with the following very curious memorial.

" Mr. Joseph Nutt was educated at the free grammar fchool in Hinckley, where he made a very confiderable progrefs in learning, and at a proper age was put apprentice to Mr. John Parr of Hinckley, an eminent apothecary, and brother to the then Vicar, in which ftation by his diligence and induftry he gained great confidence and refpeᵈt from his mafter and the whole family: for he was like Jofeph in Pharaoh's houfe; he had the care of domeftic affairs very much under his direᵈion, and frequently his mafter would defire that Jofeph might be called, that he might hear what he would fay upon any particular occafion. After this, he attended the hofpitals in London, that he might be properly qualified for his profeffion, and on his return to Hinckley carried on for many years a confiderable bufinefs with reputation and fuccefs, and was very much approved of in his profeffion. Some time about the middle of life he was chofen one of the furveyors of the highways for the parifh, when he adopted a new method for improving the fame, by turning over the roads the water that came from the town, which being confiderably enriched by wafhing the ftreets and public finks, what he could fpare from the roads, or rather after it had done the bufinefs there, he conveyed upon the lands of thofe who approved of his proceeding. The confequence was, the land was enriched, like ancient Egypt by the overflowings of the river Nile. The effeᵈ of the water upon the road, in that part below the town that is now the Coventry turnpike road, was, that it ferved like a boulting-mill; it wafhed and carried off the muddy foul parts upon the land; and the fandy, gravelly, and ftoney parts remaining by their own gravity, were left firm; for the road was fometimes wet, and fometimes dry, as he let it out of a refervoir for that purpofe at pleafure. By this method it became good for faddle and pack horfes; the laft of which occupied the roads very much at that time of day; for the pit-coal from the Warwickfhire mines was brought by them in confiderable quantities. It was alfo much better for the draft-horses; though when much used by these, especially in the coal business, the wheels of these carriages being at that time very narrow, and generally laying on great loads, were apt to disturb and cut these roads, for the materials used were commonly sand dug by the road side, which was done at a moderate expence. If upon this more gravelly or stony materials had been applied, there is no doubt, though the expence would have been greater, the road would have been much better. This, being a new way of proceeding, met with a difference of reception in the parish, which was at length so divided, that a party determined to put him out of his office. The party in his favour prevailing, he was continued for some time; but this raised him many enemies, who were ready on every occasion to insult and ridicule their surveyor. It has been said, by way of sarcasm, that he spent much of his time in the valuation of land, "the good-"ness or badness of which, like the celebrated Mr. Arthur Young, he partly "judged of from the taste." As he was not however himself a purchaser, it is evident some persons entertained a good opinion of his abilities in this particular; of whom Sir Dudley Ryder, when attorney general, and other respectable names, might be mentioned; but as this would be setting him up too high, his enemies rather chuse to ascribe to him the above-mentioned mode of judging of land. If this had been his method, I should doubtless have observed it, as he frequently made me visits, I being at that time young in life, and making many experiments on soils and vegetation, a subject that he took much pleasure in. But admitting this to be the case, the salts, sulphurs, &c. with which the different soils abound, are the very spirit and life of vegetation; for, extract these, or exhaust the land of them by frequent crops without manuring, and the ground soon becomes barren. If a person's taste was so exquisite as to make these distinctions, he certainly might form a very good judgement of the goodness or badness of land.

Mr. Nutt lived in terms of great friendship with the ingenious author of "The Fleece;" who thus takes occasion to celebrate his useful talents:

"Various as æther is the pastoral care:
"Through flow experience, by a patient breast,
"The whole long lesson gradual is attain'd,
"By precept after precept, oft receiv'd
"With deep attention: such as NUCEUS sings
"To the full vale near Soare's * enamour'd brook,
"While all is silence: sweet Hincklean swain!
"Whom rude obscurity severely clasps:
"The Muse, howe'er, will deck thy simple cell
"With purple violets and primrose flowers,
"Well-pleas'd thy faithful lessons to repay."

Mr. Nutt was also in continual friendship with the family of the Parrs through life. The Rev. Mr. Robert Parr, rector of Horstead and Cottishall in the county of Norfolk, let him the house where he lived many years, at a very easy rent, on

* The principal river in Leicestershire.

a lease

a leafe for life. The leafe itfelf, which I once faw in his friend's own hand-writing, was a kind of curiofity, being very fhort and expreffive, and free from the incumbrances and repetitions that generally attend thefe things.

He died Oct. 16, 1775, at the age of 75; and teftified in his laft will his defire of doing benefit to the town of Hinckley, by the ufeful legacy recorded in p. 29.

I have purpofely omitted giving his character, as that has been already done in his epitaph, p. 50, written by his intimate friend the Rev. Mr. Robert Parr, fon of the rector of Horftead, and grandfon of the vicar of Hinckley."

19. JOHN BLAIR, LL. D. Vicar of Hinckley.

OF the early part of this gentleman's life, no particulars have come to my knowledge. He was educated at Edinburgh; and came to London in company with Andrew Henderfon, a voluminous writer, who in his title-pages ftyled himfelf A. M. and for fome years kept a bookfeller's fhop in Weftminfter Hall. Henderfon's firft employment was that of an ufher at a fchool in Hedge Lane, in which he was fucceeded by his friend Blair, who in 1754 obliged the world with a valuable publication, under the title of "The Chronology and Hiftory " of the World, from the Creation to the Year of Chrift 1753. Illuftrated " in LVI Tables; of which IV are introductory and contain the Centuries prior " to the Firft Olympiad; and each of the remaining LII. contain in one ex- " panded View 50 years, or Half a Century. By the Rev. John Blair, LL. D." This volume, which is dedicated to Lord Chancellor Hardwicke, was publifhed by fubfcription, on account of the great expence of the plates, for which the author apologized in his Preface †, where he acknowledged great obligations to the Earl of Bath, and announced fome Chronological Differtations, wherein he propofed to illuftrate the difputed points, to explain the prevailing fyftems of chronology, and to eftablifh the authorities upon which fome of the particular æras depend. In January 1755 he was elected a fellow of the Royal Society, and in 1761 of the Society of Antiquaries. In 1756 he publifhed a fecond edition of his " Chronological Tables." In September 1757 he had the honour of being appointed chaplain to the Princefs Dowager of Wales, and mathematical tutor to his Royal Highnefs the Duke of York; and, on Dr. Townfhend's promotion to the deanry of Norwich, the fervices of Dr. Blair were rewarded,

† " The engraving of the tables," fays Dr. Blair, " has enabled us to render the whole more diftinct and ufeful than could have been done by common printing; becaufe the fifty faint hair lines, which run acrofs every plate, contain each of them an united view of the world for one year, and lead the eye, be a plain and clear direction, from any particular event, to the year of the reign of the different kings of particular kingdoms; and fo onwards, to the year of the particular æras correfponding to that event; or by reverfe, from the year of the æra, and through the intermediate columns to the oppofite page, where the particular event is regiftered. And this is indeed the true reafon, why the common manner of printing was thought to be lefs proper, and we have preferred that of engraving; which, from its great expence, made it neceffary to publifh by fubfcription; a method which on many other accounts we fhould moft williagly have declined."

March.

March 10, 1761, with a prebendal ftall in the collegiate church of St. Peter at Weftminfter. The vicarage of Hinckley happening to fall vacant fix days after by the death of Dr. Morres, Dr. Blair was prefented to it by the dean and chapter of Weftminfter; and in Auguft that year he obtained a difpenfation to hold with it the rectory of Burton Coggles in Lincolnfhire. In September 1763 he attended his royal pupil the duke of York in a tour to the continent; had the fatisfaction of vifiting Lifbon, Gibraltar, Minorca, moft of the principal cities in Italy, and feveral parts of France; and returned with the Duke in Auguft 1764. In 1768 he publifhed an improved edition of his " Chronological Ta " bles," which he dedicated to the Princefs of Wales, who " had expreffed her " early approbation of the former edition *." To the new edition were annexed, " Fourteen Maps of Ancient and Modern Geography, for illuftrating the Ta " bles of Chronology and Hiftory. To which is prefixed a Differtation on the " Progrefs of Geography. By John Blair, LL. D. F. R. S. and A. S. and Chap " lain in Ordinary to the Princefs Dowager of Wales, 1768." In March 1771 he was prefented by the dean and chapter of Weftminfter to the vicarage of

* " Thefe Tables were honoured upon the firft publication in 1754 with the countenance of fome of the firft perfonages in this country; particularly of the late Earls of BATH and HARDWICKE, two of the ableft and moft eminent men which the kingdom has produced; and therefore the Author hopes he will be excufed in taking this opportunity of declaring his private gratitude and veneration for two fuch characters, who are now far removed out of the reach either of flander or adulation. The Differtations upon the difficult parts of Chronology, which were preparing for the prefs at the time of the firft edition of thefe tables, has been long interrupted by a duty which the Author was called upon foon after to difcharge, which was the attendance of his late Royal Highnefs the Duke of York. And as this, for the courfe of near eleven years, engroffed without any interruption all his thoughts and leifure; it is therefore the only apology he can give for having fo long delayed the publication of this part of his work. How much that excellent young Prince deferved of the world and of his country was evident, and will be long remembered by every one who had the honour of being near his perfon, or to whom he was at all known; for amidft the gaiety of youth, enlivened by a great conftitutional vivacity, few perfonages of his high rank had a more fteady attention to bufinefs, or a firmer attachment to men whofe characters he approved. To Science in particular he was one of the warmeft friends, and took all opportunities of honouring and promoting every ufeful or ingenious improvement in knowledge. Flattered, unhappily, with an idea of having a conftitution equal to every fatigue, and poffeffed of a flow of natural chearfulnefs and animal fpirits which neither travelling nor watching feemed to leffen, he fell a victim to this ill-grounded prepoffeffion. For the too intenfe exercife he took in a fultry feafon and climate brought upon him the attack of a putrid fever, againft which he was perhaps lefs fortified than moft other perfons from his great temperance in wine, fo that its violence foon put a period to his life in the bloom and vigour of youth, and when he was juft entering with uncommon fedulity into the career of public bufinefs, where his abilities would have rendered him of the greateft fervice to the King his Royal Brother, and to his native country. Even in his laft moments he fhewed the ftrongeft proofs of a fortitude and refignation, as well as a prefence of mind, which was natural and unaffected, and would have diftinguifhed his character had he been born even in the loweft rank of human life. It was in compliance with his Royal Highnefs's defire that I have endeavoured to improve thefe Tables of Chronology, by adding Fourteen Maps, part of them containing the ancient, and part of them the modern Geography, which are fo difpofed in different places in the Tables, as to illuftrate the times and periods when the countries delineated in each map were the principal fcenes of action. For in his Royal Highnefs's application to the perufal of the Political Hiftory of the World in its various branches, to which indeed all his mornings were generally devoted, he found it of great advantage, for the clearer underftanding of any tranfaction of events, to have the country and the period of time placed before him in one view, as the proper companions to each other. And as they have been privately ufed in this manner for fome years paft, they are now publifhed to the world, with the hopes of their being found of fervice to fuch who may employ any of their leifure hours in the ftudy of ancient or modern hiftory. That the errors in other maps, and the times when they were rectified, may be the eafier traced and known, a Differtation is prefixed to the whole, on the Rife and Progrefs of Geography, which, though far from being fo complete as the Author could have wifhed, may ftill be of fome ufe to many who have hitherto been lefs converfant in this branch of fcience." Dr. BLAIR, Preface to the edition of 1768.

St.

St. Bride's in the city of London; which made it neceſſary for him to reſign Hinckley, where he had never reſided for any length of time. On the death of Mr. Sims *, in April 1776, he reſigned St. Bride's, and was preſented to the rectory of St. John the Evangeliſt in Weſtminſter; and in June that year obtained a diſpenſation to hold the rectory of St. John with that of Newton, near Colebrook,. Bucks. His brother Captain Blair † falling glorioufly in the ſervice of his country in the memorable ſea fight of April 12, 1782, the ſhock is ſaid to have been too great for the Doctor's ſenſibility, and to have accelerated his death, which happened June 24, 1782. But I am told it was the *influenza*, which he had in a ſevere degree, that put a period to his life.

* Joſeph Sims, B. D. rector of St. John the Evangeliſt in Weſtminſter, vicar of Radham, Eſſex, and prebend of Lincoln and St. Paul's. See more of him in the Anecdotes of Mr. Bowyer, p. 615.

† This able officer, for his gallant conduct in the Dolphin frigate in the engagement with the Dutch on the Dogger Bank, Aug. 5, 1781, was promoted to the command of the Anſon, a new ſhip of 64 guns. By bravely diſtinguiſhing himſelf under Sir George Rodney, he fell in the bed of honour, and became one of the three heroes to whom their country, by its repreſentatives, has voted a monument, for which an ingenious writer in the Gentleman's Magazine has propoſed the following well-adapted lines as part of an epitaph:

" This laſt juſt tribute grateful Britain pays,
That diſtant times may learn her Heroes' praiſe.
Fir'd with like zeal, fleets yet unform'd ſhall gain
Another BLAIR, a MANNERS, and a BAYNE;
And future Chiefs ſhall unrepining bleed,
When Senates thus reward and celebrate the deed."

APPENDIX, N° XVIII.

ADDENDA to p. 31.

On the diſſolution of the priory of Montgrace, the then vicar of Hinckley proved, to the ſatisfaction of King Henry the Eighth, that he and his predeceſſors had been entitled to receive annually, at the feaſt of St. Michael, a penſion of five pounds, ſix ſhillings, and eight pence, out of the revenues of that priory, and obtained a decree for the payment of the ſame ſum annually at the Exchequer; which the preſent vicar ſtill continues to receive, after ten ſhillings are deducted for fees at the Exchequer.

I am indebted to Craven Ord, Eſq; for the communication of the following authentic inſtrument from the Book of Decrees of the Court of Augmentation, N° 13. in the Exchequer, p. 103. " Memorandum, For as much as it duely pved " before the Chancellour of our Sovaign Lord the Kynges Courte of Augmentacōns " of the Revenues of his Crowne, that the pariſſhe preeſt of the pariſſhe churche " of

" of Hynkley in the countie of Leiceftr', and his pdeceffors parifshe preeftes ther,
" have contynnally had and enjoyed, and of right ought to have and enjoye, for
" ther falary and wages, one annuyte or annual pencon of v poundes vi fhillings
" and viii pence rilvng yerely, paiable and goyng out of the revenues and poffef-
" fions of the late Monafty of Monteprace in the countie of York diffolved: It is
" therefor ordered and decreed by the faid Chancellour and counfell, in the tme of
" Seynt Hillary, that is to fav, the 12th day of February, in the 37th yere of the
" reign of our Sovaign Lord Hen. VIIIth by the gce of God Kyng of Engl', France
" and Irlond, defender of the faith, and of the church of England, and alfo of
" Irlond in yerth the fujime hed, that the feyd paryffhe preeft fhall have and enjoye,
" to hym and to his fucceffours paryffhe preeftys there for the tyme beyng for ever,
" the feid annuyte or annuall pencon of fyve poundes, fyx fhillyngs, eight pence, to
" be paid yerely, by the handys of the pticuler receyvour or baylyf of the revenues
" and poffeffions of the faid late Monafty for the tyme beyng of the feid revenues
" and profyays, at the feftys of Efter and Seynt Michell tharchangell, by evyn
" porcons, together with all the arreragys of the feid annuyte or annual pencon
" now due and unpaid, iff any fuche be, to be paid alfo by the handys of the faid re-
" ceyvour or bayliff: Provided alway, that yf it happen at any tyme hereafter to be
" duely pved before the Chancellour and counfell of the faid Courte of Augmenta-
" cons for the tyme beyng, that the feid parifshe preeft and his fucceffours ought
" not of right to have and enjoye the faid annuyte or annual pencon of fyve poundys,
" fyx fhillyngs, eight pence, in fourme aforefeid, that then and from thenforth
" this prefent decree to be voide and of none effect, any thynge in the feid decree
" contayned to the contrary notwithftandyng."

In the reign of Philip and Mary there feems to have been fome interruption in
the payment of this penfion; as the then vicar obtained a decree of the Court of
Augmentation for recuvering his ftipend of v pounds, vi fhillings, and viii pence.

It appears from a memorandum-book in the poffeffion of Mr. Gallaway, that, in
1709, Mr. Parr, the then vicar, received, by order of Mr. Gerard, ten fhillings for
a mortuary, and ten fhillings for a funeral fermon. The furplice fees at that time
were, Weddings by licence, 5s.; by banns, 2s. 6d.; Chriftenings 5d.; Burials 4d.
Eafter offerings, 2d. for a man, 2d. for his wife; 1d. garden; 1d. fmoke; 2d. for
every one 16 years of age; a labourer 1d. every kind of handicraft 4d. Calves,
pigs, cows new milked, 2d.; a ftrayer 1½d.; horfes in the field 1s.

Three bottles of wine were ufed in the facramental fervice at Chriftmas, three at
Eafter, and five on Whit-funday and Trinity Sunday.

	s.	d.
Churchwardens of Hinckley allow for vifitation expences,	4	0
———— of Stoke,	2	6
———— of Dadlington,	1	6

On the inclofure of the open field in 1760, two pieces of ground called *The
Church Headland* and *The Vicar's Lees* were exchanged for an allotment of the annual value of twelve guineas.

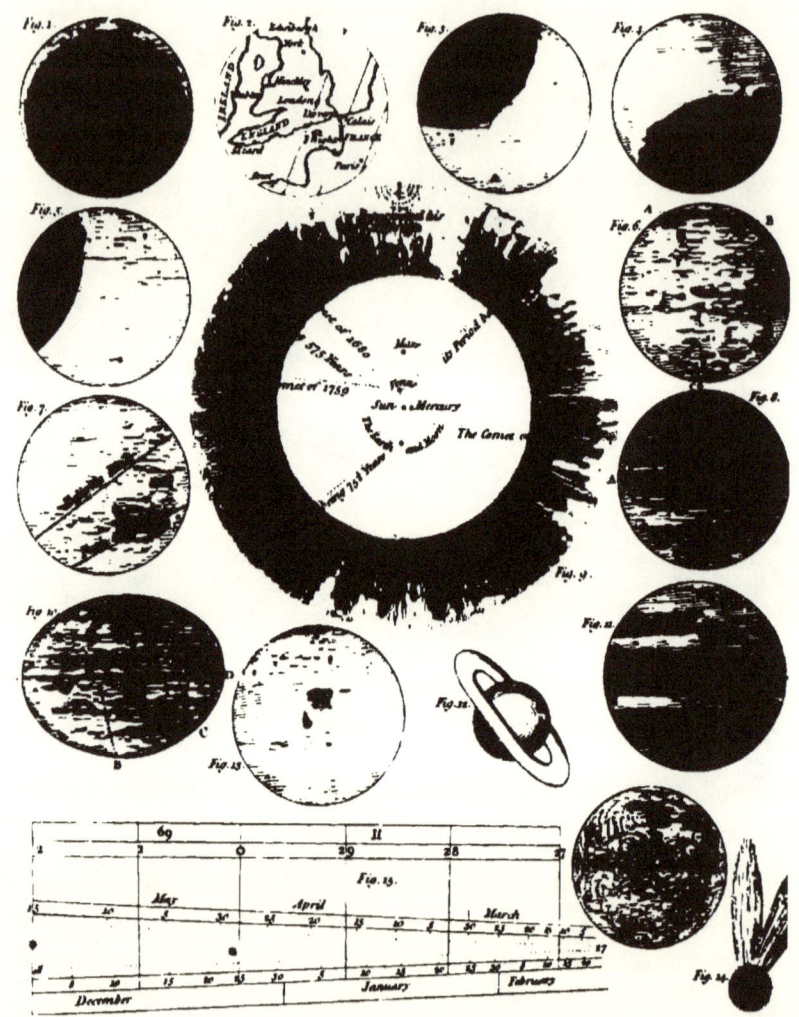

APPENDIX, N° XIX.

ASTRONOMICAL OBSERVATIONS, made at HINCKLEY, by Mr. JOHN ROBINSON.

SOLAR ECLIPSES.

1. A great and very remarkable eclipse of the Sun, on April 1, 1764, in the morning.

		h.	'	"
Began,	Apparent time	8	57	32
Visible d,		10	29	29
Middle,		10	30	11
End,		0	1	50
Duration,		3	5	18
Digits eclipsed,		11°	6'	"
The Sun's semidiameter,			16	6
The Moon's semidiameter,			14	57

This eclipse was annular in all places over which the Moon's shadow projected by the Sun passed, for there, at the time of conjunction, a bright annulus or ring of light might be observed to surround the body of the Moon on all sides. This eclipse was not annular at Hinckley. In Plate XII. fig. 1. represents the greatest obscuration there. By this observation I find that this eclipse could be no more than barely annular in London, the breadth of the path of the shadow being about 210 miles: therefore the central part of it could not pass over any part of England. Fig. 2. shews the projection of the shadow in its passage over part of England, France *, &c. and points out some places in the neighbourhood of which it was central. The shadow entered Europe upon the South West part of Portugal, in almost a North East direction, passed part of Spain, the North West parts of France, the South East parts of England, the North West parts of Holland, and through Norway into the Northern Sea; the velocity of the center of the shadow about 27 miles in one minute of time.

I have been more particular on this eclipse, as annular eclipses very rarely happen; for they can only be annular when the diameter of the Moon is less than that of the Sun at the time of a visible conjunction.

Second Solar eclipse, June 4, 1769, in the morning.

		h.		
Began,	Apparent time	6	34	30
Middle,		7	26	55
End,		8	19	20
Duration,		1	44	50
Digits eclipsed,		6°	20'	

* The French published a chart of the passage of the center of the shadow upon the Earth's surface in this remarkable eclipse.

C c

And

And here I shall mention an uncommon particular I noticed in this eclipse, which will perhaps hardly be admitted by the aftronomers of the age. In this eclipse I obferved the lunar mountains on the Moon's limb, fomewhat like what is reprefented in fig. 3, which is the type for Hinckley, at the time of the greatest obfcuration. That there are great heights or mountains in the Moon, is very evident from obfervation The ingenuous and learned Dr. Derham, in his Aftro-Theology, fays, " The mountains vifible in the Moon, although fome of them are of that " height as to reflect the light of the Sun from their lofty tops fome days before " ever it reacheth the vallies beneath them, yet on the Moon's limb we can difcern " nothing of them; but fo far from that, that on the contrary, the edge through " our beft glaffes looks like an even, fmooth, and uninterrupted circle." It cannot be denied but that this is the general appearance, though we may reafonably fuppofe that fometimes it is otherwife, for I have at times feen fome little inequalities on the limb, though never fo diftinct as in this eclipfe.

Third Solar eclipfe, June 24, 1778, in the afternoon.

		h.	'	"
Began,	Apparent time	3	34	15
Middle,		4	25	22
End,		5	16	30
Duration,		1	42	15
Digits eclipfed,		6°	10'	reprefented in fig. 4.

I shall now prefent the reader with a lift of the vifible Solar eclipfes to the end of the prefent century, calculated and adapted to the meridian and latitude of Hinckley.

		Begins			Middle			Ends			Duration		Digits
		h.	'	"	h.	'	"	h.	'	"	'	"	° '
1782	April 12, after.	6	10	21	fets eclipfed.								
1787	{ Jan. 19, morn.	9	50	19	10	20	25	10	50	31	1	0	12	1 10
	{ June 15, after.	3	59	30	4	49	26	5	39	22	1	39	52	5 41
1788	June 4, morn.	7	22	3	8	7	37	8	53	12	1	31	9	3 32
1791	April 3, afer.	0	24	51	1	47	20	3	9	50	2	44	59	7 37
1793	Sept. 5, morn.	9	30	7	11	1	41	12	33	15	3	3	8	9 19
1794	Jan. 31, morn.	10	51	39	11	42	53	12	34	7	1	42	28	3 5
1797	June 24, after.	4	45	5	5	27	51	6	10	37	1	25	32	4 25

LU-

LUNAR ECLIPSES.

1766, Feb. 24, at night.

		h.	.	.
Beginning,	apparent time,	6	22	2
Middle,		7	30	40
Ecliptic ☾,		7	40	0
End,		8	39	18
Duration,		2	17	16
Digits eclipfed,		40	12	reprefented in Fig. 5.

1776, July 30, at night.

		h.	.	.
Beginning,	apparent time,	10	2	30
Beginning of total darknefs,		11	2	0
Middle,		11	50	1
End of total darknefs,		12	38	2
End of the eclipfe,		13	38	15

Soon after this eclipfe began, a fpot or two being covered by the fhadow, they difappeared to the naked eye, but were to be feen by the telefcope. After the eclipfe became total, the principal fpots, efpecially the large ones, were vifible to the naked eye, the Moon at that time appearing with a mournful afpect, and of a rufty red colour, very vifible, but without its fhining brightnefs.

1779, Nov. 23, at night.

		h.	.	.
Beginning,	apparent time,	6	3	15
Beginning of total darknefs,		7	3	32
Middle,		7	56	8
End of total darknefs,		8	43	45
End of the eclipfe,		9	42	54

While the eclipfe remained total, feveral telefcopical ftars appeared near the Moon; alfo the Pleiades and the fmall ftars in the head of Taurus appeared very bright during the obfcuration of the Moon.

I fhall next exhibit a lift of the vifible Lunar eclipfes to the end of the prefent century, calculated and adapted to the meridian of Hinckley.

1783, March 18, at night.		h.	.	.	1783, Sept. 10, at night.		h.	.	.
Beginning,		7	32	5	Beginning,		9	43	7
Beginning of total darknefs,	8	34	6	Beginning of total darknefs,	10	42	15
Middle,		10	8	10	Middle,		11	2	33
End of total darknefs,		11	42	14	End of total darknefs,		11	22	52
End of the eclipfe,		12	44	15	End of the eclipfe,		12	22	0

3   1784,

1784, March 7, morning.

	h.	'	"
Beginning,	2	29	15
Middle,	3	45	10
End,	5	1	5
Digits eclipsed,	5°	15'	

1787, Jan. 3, at night.

	h.	'	"
Beginning,	9	11	6
Beginning of total darkness,	10	54	2
Middle,	11	45	36
End of total darkness,	12	37	10
End of the eclipse,	13	42	7

1787, Dec. 24, afternoon.

	h.	'	"
Moon rises eclipsed.			
End,	4	30	0
Digits eclipsed,	5°	30'	

1789, Nov. 2, at night.

	h.	'	"
Beginning,	11	27	8
Middle,	12	26	7
End,	13	25	6
Digits eclipsed,	2°	20'	

1790, April 28, at night.

	h.	'	"
Beginning,	10	11	15
Beginning of total darkness,	11	4	7
Middle,	11	51	39
End of total darkness,	12	40	2
End of the eclipse,	13	31	10

1790, Oct. 22, at night.

	h.	'	"
Beginning,	10	1	2
Beginning of total darkness,	11	52	10
Middle,	12	16	8
End of total darkness,	12	40	7
End of the eclipse,	14	31	15

1791, Oct. 12, morning.

	h.	'	"
Beginning,	12	4	7
Middle,	13	32	5
End,	15	0	3
Digits eclipsed,	8°	15'	

1793, Feb. 25, at night.

	h.	'	"
Beginning,	9	30	10
Middle,	10	43	37
End,	11	57	5
Digits eclipsed,	5°	7'	

1794, Feb. 14, at night.

	h.	'	"
Beginning,	8	10	15
Beginning of total darkness,	9	15	5
Middle,	10	7	7
End of total darkness,	10	59	10
End of the eclipse,	12	4	8

1795, Feb. 3, at night.

	h.	'	"
Beginning,	11	5	12
Middle,	12	25	9
End,	13	45	7
Digits eclipsed,	6°	30'	

1795, July 31, at night.

	h.	'	"
Beginning,	7	37	10
Middle,	8	8	7
End,	8	38	5
Digits eclipsed,	3°	30'	

1797, Dec. 4, morning.

	h.	'	"
Beginning,	2	29	6
Beginning of total darkness,	3	29	5
Middle,	4	12	36
End of total darkness,	5	6	8
End of the eclipse,	6	6	7

The following ASTRONOMICAL REMARKS were communicated by Mr. ROBINSON, accompanied with this rhapsodical invitation to the reader.

" Come, come with me;
" My aerial chariot mount; whose rapid wheels,
" Like sudden whirlwinds, or the bound of thought,
" Convey us high among the constellations,
" I' th' shining North, where we view Cynosura,
" That guides the seaman through the pathless deep.
" Now, listening to the music of the spheres,
" Entranc'd, we view the great Creator's works,
" How lost in wonder is the enraptur'd mind,
" And sacred love now fills the soul!"

" The use that may be made of Eclipses is very great, not only to the Astronomer and Chronologist in ascertaining more accurately the periods of the planets and fixing the ancient accounts of time, but to the Geographer and Mariner in determining the longitude of places at sea or land. By this discovery the Mariner is enabled to pass with greater safety the surface of the pathless deep, and to direct his course to the wished-for port.—But here I shall stop a moment, as sometimes in life I have been asked my private opinion of the lawfulness of the subject I am now writing upon, by unlearned but well-meaning persons; for had they been of another kind, I should have thought them much beneath my notice. These persons frequently take Astronomy and Astrology for one and the same science, and so entertain a bad opinion of it; but Astronomy is a science of itself, quite independent of the other, and consists in observing and contemplating the number, order, distances, magnitudes, periods, and appearances of the heavenly bodies. It is frequently with great justice called a *divine* science, being a knowledge which contributes to the enlargement of our ideas of the immensity, magnificence, and transcendent grandeur of God, and also affording the sublimest and most satisfactory entertainment to the understanding and mind of men. And as God hath told us, that " he ordained them for signs and for seasons, for days and for years;" it is certainly our duty to observe their stated periods, that they may answer the great end so wise and beneficent a Providence intended they should. Astronomers, therefore, in consequence of this divine appointment to determine the times and seasons, &c. have, by their repeated observations, arrived at a high degree of perfection; for, since the addition of the optical parts to the instruments required for this purpose, the improvement has been so great as almost to exceed all belief with those that are strangers to the science; but this has been the work and labour of ages to accomplish. However, the observations of the Ancients, in the more rude and early ages, have not been without their use even to the present age, in correcting our oldest accounts of time, and making our chronology more perfect; and to the Geographer and Mariner, in discovering the longitude or difference of meridians.

D d   EXAM-

E X A M P L E.

Suppose an eclipse is obferved in an unknown meridian to happen at 6ʰ 2ɛ′ 30″, and the fame eclipfe obferved at fome other place, as fuppofe London, to be at 8ʰ 4′ 30″. The difference of the times is 1ʰ 42′; which, being converted into degrees and minutes of the equator, will make 25′ 30′, the longitude of the place of obfervation to the Weſt, becaufe the time is lefs.

I ſhall now endeavour to ſhew what ufe may be made of the obfervations of the more early ages; and this I think I cannot do better than by making fome extracts from our learned countryman the great Sir Ifaac Newton, who, in his "Chronology of Ancient Kingdoms," has fixed on four remarkable periods, whereby he determines all the reſt. 1. The Return of the Heraclides into Peloponnefus. 2. The taking of Troy. 3. The Argonautic Expedition. 4. The Return of Sefoſtris into Egypt, after his wars in Thrace. Our excellent author argues from hiſtorical facts, compared and connected together in the moſt dextrous manner into a chain of invincible reafoning, and fixed to their proper periods and diſtances by a computation from the mean value of reigns and generations, founded on experience and the courfe of nature: but, as this would lead me too far from my prefent fubject, I ſhall chiefly confine myfelf to Aſtronomy, as being my proper fubject.

To prepare the way, our author gives a very curious account of the origin and progrefs of Aſtronomy; but I ſhall here take notice only of what feems directly to concern the argument. The ancient Greek calendar confiſted of twelve lunar months, and each month of thirty days. Thefe years and months they corrected from time to time, by the courfes of the Sun and Moon, omitting a day or two in the month as often as they found it too long for the courfe of the Moon, and adding a Month to the year as often as they found the twelve lunar Months too ſhort for the return of the four feafons; for the length of the folar year was difcovered by the Egyptians of Thebais no earlier than about 96 years after the death of Solomon, and not exactly then neither. Clemens Alexandrinus informs us, from the ancient author of Gigantomachia, that Mufæus, the maſter of Orpheus, and one of the Argonauts, made a fphere, and is reckoned the firſt among the Greeks that made one, and that Chiron delineated the aſterifms. Again, the fphere itfelf ſhews that it was formed at the time of the Argonautic Expedition, which is delineated in the aſterifms, together with feveral more ancient hiſtories, but not one thing later, for Antinous and Coma Berenicis are novel. It is therefore very probable that the fphere was formed by Chiron and Mufæus for the ufe of the Argonauts, for the ſhip Argo was the firſt long veffel built by the Greeks, the firſt that ventured through the deep out of the fight of land by the help of fails, and guided only by the ſtars. Eudoxus, who flouriſhed 60 years after Meton, and 100 before Aratus, in defcribing the fphere of the Ancients (i. e. the primitive fphere) placed the epuinoxes and folſtices in the middle of the conſtellations Aries, Cancer, Chelæ, and Capricorn; fo alfo did Aratus, who copied Eudoxus; and fo it appears by the fphere of Eudoxus defcribed by Hipparchus. It is plain, therefore, that, at the time of the Argonautic Expedition, the cardinal points of the equinoxes and folſtices were in the middles of the conſtellations Aries, Cancer, Chelæ, and Capricorn.

This

This main point being eſtabliſhed, the author proceeds to argue thus: 1. The equinoctial colure in the end of the year 1689 cut the ecliptic in ♉ 6° 44′; and by this reckoning the equinox was then gone back 36° 44′ ſince the Argonautic Expedition; but it recedes 50″ in a year, or one degree in 72 years, and conſequently 36° 44′ in 2645 years, which, counted backward from the end of 1689, or rather the beginning of 1690, place that expedition about 25 years after the death of Solomon.

2. It is not neceſſary to ſuppoſe, that what they called in general the middles of the conſtellations ſhould be exactly in the middle between the Prima Arietis and the Ultima Caudæ. Seeing Eudoxus deſcribed the primitive ſphere, or what was in his days called the ſphere of the ancients, as was ſhewn above, we may reaſonably fix the cardinal points at the time of that expedition by the ſtars through which he made the colures paſs in that ſphere. Thoſe ſtars which Hipparchus particularly mentions our author accurately examines, and finds that the great circle, which in the primitive ſphere according to Eudoxus (and conſequently at the time of the Argonautic Expedition) was the equinoctial colure, did, in the end of 1689, cut the ecliptic in ♉ 6° 29′ 15″ as near as can be determined by the rude obſervations of the ancients; that is, it had gone back 36° 29′ ſince Chiron's time, which amounts to 2627 years. Theſe, counted backwards as above, place the Argonautic Expedition 43 years after Solomon's death.

3. By the ſame method, the place of any ſtar in the primitive ſphere may eaſily be found, viz. by counting backward 1 ſign, 6° 29′ from its longitude at the end of 1689. The Lucida Pleiadum, for inſtance, at the time of the expedition, was in ♈ 19° 26′ 8″. Now Thales determined the Occaſus Matutinus of the Pleiades in his time to be on the 25th day after the autumnal equinox, and thence P. Patan computes the Pleiades to have been then in ♈ 23° 53′; conſequently the Lucida Pleiadum had moved from the equinox ſince the expedition 4° 26′ 52″, which anſwer to 320 years. Theſe counted back from the 41ſt Olympiad, when Thales was a young man fit for mathematical ſtudies, will place the Argonautic Expedition about 44 years after the death of Solomon. By this reaſoning, the cardinal points in the days of Thales muſt have been in the middle of the 11th degree of the ſigns, though he, perhaps leaning too much to the opinion of the ancients, places them in the 12th, for the preceſſion of the equinoxes was not yet thought of.

4. Meton and Euctemon, in order to ſettle the lunar cycle of 19 years, obſerved the Summer ſolſtice in the year of Nabonaſſar 316, and placed it in the 8th degree of ♋, that is, at leaſt 7 degrees backwarder than at firſt, which anſwer to 504 years. Count theſe back from the year of Nabonaſſar 316, and the Argonautic Expedition will fall on the 44th year after Solomon's death, or thereabout.

5. The preceſſion of the equinoxes, or their motion backward in reſpect of the fixed ſtars, was firſt diſcovered by the great Hipparchus, upon comparing his own obſervations with thoſe of former Aſtronomers. He made his obſervations between the years of Nabonaſſar 586 and 618; ſuppoſe at a medium in 602, which is 286 years after Meton and Euctemon made theirs; and in that interval the equinoxes muſt have gone back 4 degrees, that is, 11 degrees ſince the Argonautic Expedition or in 1090 years, according to the Greek chronology. Hipparchus, finding this,

D d 2

thus,

this, concluded that the equinoxes went back only one degree in about 100 years; and how indeed could he eſtabliſh any other proportion, if, as we muſt think, he believed the Greek chronology, as their falſe chronology occaſioned his error in fixing that proportion? So that error being now correcſted will rectify their chronology; for 11 degrees, at one degree in 72 years, anſwer to 792 years, which, counted backward from the year of Nabonaſſar 602, place the Argonautic Expedition about 43 years after the death of Solomon.

6. The longitude of the ſtar Arcſturus at the time of the Argonautic Expedition is found by the abovementioned method to have been ♈ 13° 24′ 52″. Heſiod tells us, that, 60 days after the Winter ſolſtice, it roſe in his time juſt at ſun-ſet. If ſo, he flouriſhed about 57 years after the Argonautic Expedition, or 100 years after the death of Solomon; that is, in the generation or age next after the Trojan war, and ſo indeed he himſelf tells us. Is it poſſible to conceive that an aſtronomical calculation of time, agreeing ſo nicely with certain matter of fact, can be falſe?

From all theſe circumſtances, ſays the author, grounded upon the coarſe obſervations of the ancients, we may reckon it certain that the Argonautic Expedition was not earlier than the reign of Solomon; and if theſe aſtronomical arguments be added to thoſe taken from the mean length of the reigns of kings, according to the courſe of nature, from the whole we may ſafely conclude that it was after the death of Solomon, and moſt probably about 43 years after it.

Sir Iſaac Newton having thus ſettled theſe four principal periods, viz. the Return of Seſoſtris into Egypt after his conqueſts about 14 years after the death of Solomon, the Argonautic Expedition about 43 years after the death of Solomon, the Deſtruction of Troy about 76 or 78 years after the death of Solomon, and the Return of the Heraclides into the Peloponneſus about 156 or 158 years after the death of Solomon; he then proceeds to fix ſome other points of ancient hiſtory. Thus far our illuſtrious Author.

I ſhall conclude theſe remarks with an ancient Lunar Eclipſe, which, having ſome things particularly remarkable, merits our notice, and carries us back almoſt 2000 years.

It is recorded by Ptolemy, from Hipparchus, that on the 22d of September, the year 201 before the Chriſtian æra, the Moon roſe eclipſed ſo much at Alexandria, that the Eclipſe muſt have begun half an hour before ſhe roſe.

Mr. Carey puts down this Eclipſe in his Chronology as follows, among ſeveral other ancient ones recorded by different authors:

Jul. Per. 4513, Sept. 22.	Ecl. ☽ Per. Calip. 2 An. 54 Hor. 7. P. M. Alexandr. Dig. ecl. 10. (Ptolem. l. iv. c. 11.	Nabonaſſar 547, Meſor 16.

Which may be read thus: In the 4513th year of the Julian period, which was the 547th year from Nabonaſſar, and the 54th year of the ſecond Calippic period, on the 16th day of the month Meſori, which anſwers to the 22d of September, the Moon was 10 digits eclipſed at Alexandria at 7 o'clock in the evening.

The

The ingenious Mr. Fergufon has beftowed fome pains in accurately defcribing this Eclipfe, which I fhall fet before the reader. " Now as our Saviour was born " (according to the Dionyfian or vulgar æra of his birth) in the 47 3:h year of " the Julian period, it is plain that the 4513th year of that period was the 200th " year before the year of Chrift's birth, and confequently 201 years before the " year of Chrift 1. And in the year 201, on the 21d of September, it appears " that the Moon was full at 26 minutes 28 feconds paft 7 in the evening, in the " meridian of Alexandria.

" At that time the Sun's place was Virgo 26° 14', according to our own tables, " fo that the Sun was then within 4 degrees of the autumnal equinox, and accor- " ding to calculation he muft have fet at Alexandria about 5 minutes after " 6, and about one degree North of the Weft. The Moon, being full at that " time, would have rifen juft at fun-fet about one degree South of the Eaft " if fhe had been in either of her nodes, and her vifible place not depreffed " by parallax. But her parallactic depreffion (as appears from her anomaly, viz. " 10° 18° nearly) muft have been 55' 17", which exceeded her whole diameter " 25' 9"; but then fhe muft have been elevated 33' 4;" by refraction, which, " fubtracted from the parallax, leaves 21' 32" for her vifible or apparent depref- " fion. And her true latitude was 30' 30" North defcending; which being contra- " ry to her apparent depreffion, and greater than the fame by 8' 58", her true " time of rifing muft have been juft about 6 o'clock. Now as the Moon rofe " about one degree South of the Eaft at Alexandria, where the vifible horizon is " land and not fea, we can hardly imagine her to be lefs than 15 or 20 minutes " of time above the true horizon before fhe was vifible. It appears that this E- " clipfe, reduced to the time at Alexandria, began at 53 minutes after 5 in the " evening, and confequently 7 minutes before the Moon was in the true horizon ; " to which if we add 20 minutes for the interval between her true rifing and her " being vifible, we fhall have 27 minutes for the time that the Eclipfe was be- " gun before the Moon was vifibly rifen. The middle of this Eclipfe was at 30 " minutes paft 7, when its quantity was almoft 10 digits, and its ending was at 6 " minutes paft 9 in the evening. This comes as near to the recorded time of this " Eclipfe as can be expected after an elapfe upwards of 1980 years."

The following account of this ancient Lunar Eclipfe is calculated for the Meri-- dian of Hinckley :

	h.		
Beginning,	3	48	45
Middle,	5	25	15
The Moon rifes eclipfed at	6	6	30
The End,	7	1	45

The SUN

is placed in the center of our fystem, and difpenfes light and heat to all the planets revolving round him. His diameter is about 893,760 miles; and he hath a rotation about his axis in the fpace of 25 days and 6 hours, and throws off from his body a fine fubtile matter that conftitutes light, which moves with fuch velocity that it paffes from the Sun to the Earth in 7 or 8 minutes of time. The Sun's motion on his axis is very evident from the fpots that frequently appear on his disk, whofe motion is very uniform and regular from the Eaftern to the Weftern limb of the Sun; and the motion of the fpots are flower towards the Sun's limb, but nearer the center of the disk larger and fwifter, and in proportion to a line of fines on each femi-diameter of the disk. Galilæus tells us, in the third dialogue of his Syftem. Mundi, that he was the firft who difcovered fpots in the Sun, in 1610. Thefe fpots appear to pafs over the disk, fometimes in a curve and fometimes in a ftrait line, according to the annual motion of the Earth round the Sun; and by this the rotation on his axis was difcovered as above, and alfo that his axis inclines to the orbit of the Earth in an angle of about 82°. By obfervation, the Sun's apparent diameter is greater in December than in June; therefore the Sun muft be proportionably nearer the Earth in Winter than in Summer, in the former of which feafons will be the Perihelion, and in the latter the Aphelion. This is confirmed by the Earth's moving fwifter in December than in June. It may be thought by fome, that when the Sun is neareft to the Earth, then the feafon fhould be the hotteft. This is fufficiently known to thofe who inhabit the Southern part of our globe, it being at that time their Summer; but with us his altitude is then fmall, and his rays coming through the atmofphere in an oblique direction, alfo paffing through a greater length of it where it is lefs rare, the rays do not ftrike us fo forcibly.

The Maculæ Solares, or fpots in the Sun, I obferve, appear moft in the parts near his equator, and are fmaller and lefs frequent towards the polar parts. They frequently arife and difappear in the middle of the Sun's disk, and undergo various alterations, with regard both to bulk, figure, and denfity, and are encompaffed as it were with atmofpheres fomewhat rarer and lefs obfcure; but the figure both of the Nuclei and entire Maculæ are variable, and commonly fubject to great changes, as increafing of bulk, changing of figure, and even quite vanifhing fometimes in a few days. Sometimes a large fpot is divided into two or more, and at other times feveral are united in one. Some take notice of Faculæ, or bright fpots in the disk of the Sun, much more lucid than the reft, as alfo that the Maculæ frequently change into Faculæ; but I have never feen any thing like them, excepting little bright fpecks in the dim clouds which encompafs the Macul e, though I have paid fome attention to this particular.

I   Of

Of MERCURY.

The firſt planet next the Sun, the fountain of light and heat, and center of our ſyſtem, is Mercury, placed at the diſtance of 36 millions of miles, and performing his revolution in his orbit in the ſpace of 87 d. 23 h. 13 min. It is but ſeldom that we ſee him with the naked eye, becauſe of his nearneſs to the Sun, being never diſtant from him more than about 28°, at which time the heavens are ſo illuminated as to render the diſcovery of ſpots on his body, by which his rotation on his axis might be diſcovered, impracticable. Neither, for the ſame reaſon, have we been able to diſcover the inclination of his axis ; ſo that the length of the day, with the variety of the ſeaſons there, is at preſent unknown to aſtronomers. The annual re-volution or year to the inhabitants of this planet (for it is the opinion of the learned that the ſeveral planets in our ſolar ſyſtem are ſo many worlds furniſhed with beings of different kinds, as our world or Earth is) is hardly equal to one quarter of ours; but in the ſituation they are placed, being almoſt three times nearer the Sun than we are, his face muſt appear three times bigger, and his light and heat almoſt nine times greater than with us. Mr. Azout pretends to prove that, though Mercury be ſo near the Sun, his light there is not capable of burning any object. But Sir Iſaac Newton makes the heat of Mercury ſo great as to be ſeven times as much as the heat of our ſummer ſun, which, he found by experiments deſignedly made with the thermoſcope, is enough to make water boil ; and therefore, if bodies will not be there enkindled by ſuch a degree of heat, it muſt be becauſe their degree of denſity is proportionably greater than of ſuch kind of bodies on our Earth. There are many things which tend to increaſe or diminiſh heat in a very conſiderable degree, as we may obſerve on this our Earth ; therefore, if Infinite Wiſdom has not made the proviſions, we may conclude that this planet is not habitable by ſuch creatures as live on our Earth : but the bodies of animals and vege-tables there may be ſo conſtructed as to require that very degree of heat to ſupport them in life, which would deſtroy beings of another texture. Through our tele-ſcopes he emits a ſparkling ſtrong light, and ſhews various phaſes in the different parts of his orbit like our Moon.

		°	′	″
The inclination of his orbit to the ecliptic,		6	54	0
Daily mean motion in the ecliptic,		4	5	32
Place of aphelion, the perihelion oppoſite ♐,		13	48	0
Place of the aſcending node, deſcending oppoſite ♉,	15	59	0	
Greateſt apparent diameter,			11	48
Leaſt apparent diameter,			4	4

To an eye placed in Mercury, and looking towards the Sun, the ſolar ſpots will appear to traverſe his diſk from Eaſt to Weſt, and ſometimes their path will ap-pear elliptical, bending one way and ſometimes another ; and the whole variety of this appearance will be exhibited in the ſpace of one revolution round the Sun : but theſe ſpots will be almoſt continually in a right line, becauſe Mercury never much declines from the plane of the Sun's equator.

The :

The phænomena of the other five planets above Mercury will be much the same as to an eye at the Earth; so that Venus and our Earth, when in opposition to the Sun, will shine with a full orb, and consequently afford a great light at night to this planet; but the superior planets will not afford him so much light as they do us.

The Sun's place, as also those of the planets and comets, may be found the same way, and after the same manner, in Mercury, and will appear as they do to us on the Earth. Mercury sometimes passes over the Sun's disk in the form of a round black spot, which is well worthy the attention of Astronomers, though not capable of affording such advantages as those of Venus; of which more will be said under that head. And as the present year afford us an opportunity, I shall give a calculation of the approaching transit for Hinckley.

1782, Nov. 12, in the afternoon.

	h.	´	˝
Beginning, apparent time,	2	46	30
Middle of the transit,	3	28	30
End,	4	10	30
Distance from the Sun's center,	15	28 North.	

Fig. 6. is a representation of this transit. The line A B is the path of Mercury on the Sun's disk, the beginning at A and the end at B.

The following is a list of Mercury's transits over the Sun to the end of the present century.

1786, May 3.

	h.	´	˝
Time of conjunction,	18	52	
Distance from the Sun's center,		12	42 North.

1789, November 5.

	h.	´	˝
Time of conjunction,	3	48	
Distance from the Sun's center,		7	20 South.

1799, May 7.

	h.	´	˝
Time of conjunction,	2	29	
Distance from the Sun's center,		4	12 South.

The

V E N U S.

The Tranſit of Venus over the Sun, June 6, 1761.

This curious and uncommon appearance had been predicted by the learned Dr. Halley, and recommended to the attention of Aſtronomers as the moſt likely means to find out the diſtance of the Sun from the Earth. In the Philoſophical Tranſactions N° 348, he has given us an accurate method, by obſervations, made of this curious phænomenon, to determine the Sun's diſtance from the Earth, true to the 500th part of it, and conſequently the Sun's parallax to a very great exactneſs. No phænomenon in the heavens was perhaps ever expected with more impatience, or obſerved with greater care; for before this there is no obſervation of the kind on record; nay, ſo far from it, that we are told ſuch an appearance was never beheld by mortal eye but once, and that by our countryman the ingenious Mr. Horrox, who, in the year 1639, had the pleaſure of beholding that moſt delightful object; but, ſince his time, the ſcience has been ſo much improved, as to enable the diligent Aſtronomer to announce to the world their future appearances.

Having prepared and adjuſted every thing for this purpoſe in the beſt manner poſſible, I made the following obſervation.

The firſt contact of Venus with the Sun, being before ſunriſe, could not be obſerved in theſe parts. As ſoon as the Sun appeared above the horizon, I perceived that Venus was advanced upon the Sun's diſk in the form of a round black ſpot, and, after the Sun had gained a little altitude, began to make a very diſtinct appearance; frequent interpoſition of clouds for ſome time, but clear air afterwards. The emerſion was obſerved as follows:

		h.	′	″
Began to emerge at,	apparent or ſolar time,	8	13	22
Venus made her total emerſion at		8	31	28
From the time the firſt part of her orb began to emerge till the whole paſſed,			18	6
The apparent diameter of Venus upon the Sun,				57½

Fig. 7. is a repreſentation of this tranſit; and the line AB ſhews the path of the planet over the Sun's diſk, the beginning at A, and the end at B.

The Hiſtorian of the Royal Academy of Sciences, for the year 1761, gives us for the reſult of the obſervations made by the French the parallax of the Sun 9½″. This, ſays he, makes the diſtance of the Sun from our Earth about a tenth part greater than it was before thought to be; 33 millions of leagues, whereas it was before computed about 30 millions. Mr. Short, taking the medium of a great number of obſervations of the Tranſit of Venus over the Sun, calculates the parallax of the Sun, at his mean diſtance, to be about 8.65″: this ſets the Sun at a ſtill greater diſtance. The diſtances of all the planets from the Sun muſt be increaſed in the ſame proportion as the diſtance of the Earth is found greater than it was before ſuppoſed to be.

E e

The

The Tranfit of VENUS over the SUN, June 3, 1769.

The former part of the day was very unpromifing, but towards the evening prefented a more favourable opportunity than might be expected, confidering the Sun's low altitude, and the tremulous motion of vapours near the horizon, &c. I made the following obfervation:

June 3, 1769, Venus's firft contact,   apparent time, 7 5 55
Totally in the difk,   7 2{ 59
From the time of the firft contact until totally in the difk,   18 4
The apparent diameter of Venus upon the Sun,   58

A reprefentation of this tranfit is given in fig. 8. AB is a line paffing through the Sun's center parallel to the horizon; C the place of Venus at the time of the firft external contact, which began near the vertical point of the limb; D the apparent pofition of Venus at her firft internal contact, and E at funfetting. The other particulars, being nearly the fame as the tranfit of 1761, need not be here repeated. One thing I fhall juft mention; the ecliptic varying its pofition in refpect to the vertical circle makes tranfits appear in a curve line.

Some Aftronomers think they have obferved a fatellite belonging to this planet, and the reafon we do not frequently fee is is owing perhaps to the unfitnefs of its furface to reflect the light fo far.

A. D. 1672 and 1686, Caffini, with a telefcope of 34 feet, believes he faw a fatellite moving round this planet, and diftant about three-fifths of Venus's diameter; it had the fame phafis with Venus, but was without any well-defigned form, and its diameter fcarce exceeded one-fourth of that of Venus. Dr. Gregory thinks it more than probable that this was a fatellite, and fuppofes the reafon why it is not ufually feen to be the unfitnefs of its furface to reflect the rays of light, as is the cafe of the fpots in the Moon, of which if the whole difk of the Moon were compofed, he thinks that the planet could not be feen in Venus. Aftron. &c. Geom. p. 472. Notwithftanding what has been advanced by former Aftronomers on this fubject, I fhall make it at leaft very probable that there is none; for, having had the opportunity of obferving two tranfits of Venus with attention to this very article, I could not perceive any thing like a fatellite during the whole obfervation of thefe tranfits: if there had been one even of much lefs magnitude than here defcribed, it muft have appeared very diftinct on the folar difk. The only thing that may be faid to the contrary is, that during the tranfit it might be between Venus and the Sun, or immerfed in her fhadow. That it fhould continue in either of thefe places during the whole time of the tranfit, I think very improbable; but that it fhould be fo during two tranfits, we can hardly fuppofe even a probability.

The diftance of the planets, deduced from the late tranfit of Venus in June 1761, in Englifh miles.

Mercury   36,841,468
Venus,   68,891,476
Earth,   95,173,000

Mars,

Mars, 145,014,148
Jupiter, 494,990,976
Saturn, 907,956,130

Having given the calculation in miles, which with some may give but a faint idea of these great diftances; I fhall endeavour to make it as intelligible as I can, by giving the meafures in time. We will therefore fuppofe a body projected from the Sun fhould continue to fly with unabated velocity at the rate of 480 miles every hour (which is much about the fwiftnefs of a cannon-ball) it would reach the orbit of

	years.	days.
Mercury in	8	276
Venus,	16	136
Earth,	22	216
Mars,	34	165
Jupiter,	117	237
Saturn,	215	287

According to the fore-mentioned diftances, the Sun's diameter is 893,760 miles; he is 1,410,200 times as big as the Earth; Mercury's diameter 3100; Venus 9360; Earth 7,970; Mars 5150; Jupiter 94,100; Saturn 77,990 Englifh miles.

The hourly motion of the planets in their orbits in miles,

Mercury,	109,699
Venus,	80,295
Earth,	68,243
Mars,	55,287
Jupiter,	29,083
Saturn,	22,101

The periodical revolution of Venus is 224 days 16 hours 49 minutes, and fhe is obferved to turn upon her axis in 23 hours. The inclination of her orbit to the ecliptic 3° 24'; her daily mean motion in the ecliptic 1° 36' 8"; greateft apparent diameter 1' 5" 58"; leaft apparent diameter 9" 34"; the place of aphelion ♈ 7° 38'; the perihelion, oppofite the place of the afcending node, ♍ 14° 35'; the defcending node, oppofite the greateft elongation of Venus, is about 48'. Venus and Mercury appearing through the telefcope fometimes horned and fometimes gibbous, like the Moon, is a proof of their going round the Sun in orbits within the Earth's orbit; on which account they are called Inferior Planets. Venus is about fix times nearer us at her inferior conjunction, when on this fide the Sun next us, than at her fuperior conjunction beyond the Sun; fhe confequently muft appear much bigger in the former fituation than in the latter, for though at her inferior conjunction fhe fhews but a fmall part of her difk, and looks through the telefcope like a Moon three days old; yet, on account of her nearnefs, that fmall part contains a greater area of light than the whole difk does when at her greateft diftance beyond the Sun. When fhe is in that part of her orbit which is Weft of the Sun, fhe rifes in the morning before him, and is called the Morning-ftar; and when fhe is on the Eaft

E e 2   fide

fide of the Sun, she fets in the evening after him, and is then the Evening-ftar.   To make thefe things more intelligible, fig. 9. is a delineation of the Solar fyftem according to the above obfervations, with the orbits that compofe our Solar fyftem, and alfo thofe Comets whofe periods are difcovered.

Great and amazing as this our folar fyftem may appear, yet this Sun with all its attendant planets, &c. admirably contrived and adapted, and every way full of magnificence, fhewing the impreffes of the Divine Hand, is but a very little part of the univerfe; for, when we are acquainted with this fubjeft, it will furnifh us with fpeculations incomparably more enlarged and amazing.

Venus may be obferved in the day-time; of which I fhall give an example or two.

1767, December 3, in the morning.

		h.		
Venus came to the meridian at,	apparent time,	9	18	32
Her apparent altitude at that time being,		27	48	55

1767, December 9, in the morning.

		h.		
Venus came to the meridian at,	apparent time,	9	7	30
Her apparent altitude at that time being,		27	10	15

1771, Jan. 6, I obferved Venus after Sun-fetting. Being near her conjunftion with the Sun, fhe appeared a flender fine crefcent; and, being near the horizon, the vapours appeared on her limb like waves, her conjunftion with the Sun being Jan. 9, at the fecond hour.

1777, March 31, I obferved Venus in the Pleiades at the tenth hour: fhe feemed to have hardly reached the center of them at that time; moft of the fmall telefcopic ftars were invifible by her great light.

In this planet the Sun will appear almoft twice as big as he does to us; his face, and confequently his light and heat, muft be almoft four times greater. They who obferve the heavens there will obferve four planets above them, viz. the Earth, Mars, Jupiter, and Saturn; and one below, viz. Mercury. When our Earth is in oppofition to the Sun, it will fhine in the night with a full face and very bright; and Mercury will accompany the Sun, and be feen as a morning and evening ftar, as Venus does to us.

As the reader may be defirous to know when this planet will again tranfit the Sun, I fhall give a fmall lift of their future appearances, calculated for the meridian of Hinckley.

		h.		
1874, December 8, Time of conjunftion,	apparent time,	16	41	
Diftance from the Sun's center,			5	3 North.
1996, June 10, Time of conjunftion,		2	8	
Diftance from the Sun's center,			13	36 South.
				2004,

		h.	,	,
2004, June 7,	Time of conjunction,	19	13	.
	Diftance from the Sun's center,		6	22 North.
		h.	,	
2109, Dec. 13,	Time of conjunction,	2	51	.
	Diftance from the Sun's center,		14	36 North.
		h.	,	.
2117, Dec. 10,	Time of conjunction,	15	58	.
	Diftance from the Sun's center,		10	5 South.

Of the EARTH and MOON.

OUR probationary planet the Earth, on which we live, together with her fatellite the Moon, performs her revolution in her orbit round the Sun, at the diftance of 95 millions of miles from the Sun, in the fpace of 365 d. 5 h. 49 min. wheh is the length of the folar year. The Earth moving round her orbit produces the feveral feafons of the year, as Spring, Summer, Autumn, Winter. And as the Earth revolves from Weft to Eaft like the reft of the planets, the Sun will appear to have an annual motion the fame way, and in the fame track, but in the oppofite point; for, when the Earth is in ♎, at which time our Spring begins, the Sun will appear in the oppofite point, viz. Aries; and fo of all the other, as fhe paffes in her annual revolution round the Sun. As I have juft obferved, the length of a folar year is 365ᵈ 5ʰ 49′; but as we in our Julian calendar, to avoid fractions, have accounted it 365 d. 6 h. which is 11 minutes too much; thefe 11 minutes, in about 134 years amount to one whole day which day being retained muft make the Sun appear to recede one day back in the calendar in that time. At the time of the general council of Nice, in the year of our Lord 325, the vernal equinox happened about the 21ft of March, and muft in 134 years happen on the 20th, and fo on. In the prefent age, the equinox was gone back to the 10th of March, viz. 11 days from its former place at the time of the faid council, and would in time have retreated through the whole calendar, and thereby have thrown all the moveable feafts into the greateft confufion. To remove this inconvenience, as alfo thofe of commerce, &c. the legiflative power, by an act paffed in 1752, threw out the 11 additional days, by calling the 3d of September the 14th, in order to bring the equinox to the place it was at at the time when that council was held; and, to keep it fixed there, ordered that the feveral years of our Lord 1800, 1900, 2100, 2200, 2300, or any other hundredth year of our Lord which fhall happen in time to come (except only every four hundredth year of our Lord, whereof the year of our Lord 2000 fhall be the firft) fhall not be efteemed or taken for Biffextile or Leap years, but fhall be taken to be common years confifting of 365 days and no more; and that the years of our Lord 2000, 2400, 2800, and every other four hundredth year of our Lord from the faid year of our Lord 2000 inclufive, and alfo all other years of our Lord which by the prefent fuputation are efteemed and taken to be Biffextile or Leap years, fhall confift of 366 days. in the fame fort and manner as is now ufed with refpect to every fourth year of our Lord.

Cur

Our times and feafons now correfpond with thofe at the calling of the firft
Chriftian council, when the affairs of the church were fettled by order of the em-
peror Conftantine the Great, in the year of Chrift 325. This correction does not
entirely remove the error, for the cardinal points ftill anticipate near two hours
in every 400 Gregorian years: but this defect is quite inconfiderable, for it does
not amount to above a day in 5000 years. Phil. Tranf. Nº 495.

I fhall now beftow a few words on the figure and magnitude of this our Earth,
the knowledge of which we may fuppofe was gradually attained with long obfervation ; for we may imagine that in the firft ages men travelled from one place to
another chiefly by the information which the inhabitants of each country gave
them, and directed their courfe by the mountains and other fixed objects. In this
manner did mankind make but flow progrefs on the face of the Earth, without
knowing its figure or bounds ; however, we may fuppofe it could not be long before they obferved that though almoft all the ftars turned round them, yet that
fome of them in that part of the heavens which we now call the polar parts remained
nearly in the fame fituation, and confequently might ferve them as fure guides
whenever they happen to lofe fight of their land-marks ; and alfo every day at
noon the Sun, when in his greateft elevation, ftood directly oppofite to the place
of thefe ftars. This is that imaginary line in the heavens called the Meridian,
which might ferve as a fixed rule to direct them when they were going to the
North or South ; and likewife they needed but to know what angle any place
formed with the meridian, to enable them to direct their courfe to the traveller under the meridian. The greateft and leaft elevations of the ftars would vary as they
moved to the North or South ; and thus they would know that the furface of the
Earth was a curve, and not a plane as they before imagined ; and if we add to
this, that to a traveller in an Eaft or Weft direction, though they obferved no variation in the elevation of the ftars, yet there was a difference in time. They might
then conclude the Earth to be fpherical, and readily call it a globe, like that of
the Sun and Moon, and fo might reckon it among the other ftars ; and they perceived that all the motion which they gave the ftars would be faved, if the Earth
performed a revolution upon her axis in 24 hours, directed to that immoveable
point that they had obferved in the heavens, and that this at once explained the
motion of the ftars. When this idea was formed, men of genius readily adopted
it : they alfo obferved, that though the Sun in his greateft elevation every day
at noon paffed in the plane of the meridian, yet he did not always pafs at the fame
diftance from the fame ftars ; and therefore could no longer fuppofe the Sun fixed
with regard to the ftars, as they obferved that he advanced in a circular zone, and
appeared to pafs one degree of it every day, and to have gone through the whole
zone in the fpace of a year, and to have returned to his firft ftation over againft
the fame ftars : they then concluded that either the Sun itfelf muft fhift his place
in the heavens and defcribe a circle round the Earth, or the Earth muft pafs in
the fame direction round the Sun ; and were therefore induced to give the Earth
this motion round the Sun which the Sun appeared to have round the Earth.
They alfo difcovered certain ftars, which they obferved did not always keep the fame
diftances, which they called Wandering ftars, as they called the other Fixed ftars.

                                                                        They

They had difcovered five ftars of this kind, called planets, viz. Mercury, Venus, Mars, Jupiter, Saturn; and found that their motion, to be regular and uniform, muft be performed round the Sun, and not round the Earth; and that the Earth, by making its revolution round the Sun, muft be between Venus and Mars. The Sun, an immenfe globe of fire, was placed by them in the center of the fyftem, without any other motion than that round his own axis, which was not difcovered till a long time after by the fpots on his difk.

The Earth, being thus reckoned among the number of the planets, was obliged to move like the reft round the Sun; and the fole prerogative referved to her was to have a planet to attend her, which performs its revolution round her every month.

The fyftem revived by Copernicus in later ages was well known to early antiquity. Many probable reafons might have induced the ancients to affign to the Earth this motion rather than to the Sun; but the ftrongeft reafons were not found out till our days, which are now fo cogent that they leave us no power to fufpend our determination.

Ariftotle, in his Second book De Cœlo, affirms that the circumference of the Earth is 400,000 furlongs; Cleomedes, book I. reckons it to be 300,000; Eratofthenes, according to Strabo, Vitruvius, Pliny, and Cenforinus, would have the whole compafs of the Earth to contain 252,000 furlongs; to which number Hipparchus, as Pliny teftifieth, added very near 25,000 more. Thefe are the accounts which the ancients have left us, which differ too widely from each other to lay ftrefs upon them; but, had they been more confiftent, the length of the mile and ftadium which they ufed in thofe days is uncertain; but what I have faid may ferve to fhew of what advantage it was thought in all ages.

Having given a fketch of the progrefs which the ancients made in the knowledge of this our Earth, with the furrounding heavens, I come now more precifely to determine its figure and magnitude, from the more exact obfervations of the prefent age. But how are we to meafure a body whofe bulk is fo difproportioned to our organs? Our eyes can command but the finalleft parts at once; our hands can grafp but atoms: but man poffeffes fomething with which the whole mafs of matter is not to be compared; that mind, by whofe will bodies are moved, and by whofe fagacity their properties are difcerned. This mind even dared to attempt to meafure the vaft body of the Earth. A much eafier undertaking had before appeared rafh and impious to one of the greateft philofophers of antiquity. Pliny, fpeaking of the catalogue of ftars which Hipparchus attempted to make, calls it *rem Deo improbam* — a difficult tafk for a Deity. But experience fhews that the human underftanding can get over greater difficulties. Therefore a more juft idea of the Divinity than the ancients had of him forbids all comparifon.

I come now to defcribe the methods ufed by the moderns; which is, to obferve the zenith diftances of the ftars at two places under the fame meridian, in order to difcover the true meafure of a degree. The ftars by whofe affiftance we meafure the Earth fhould be as near the zenith as poffible, to avoid refraction, which towards the horizon is great, and liable to variations. The diftance between the two

places

places is then to be meafured by the pole or chain, if it be a plane; but, in cafe of interruptions, a chain of triangles may be formed to the right and left, terminating in the two extremities of the diftance required.' Thus have we the length of an arch of the meridian on the Earth's furface. If the angle is but of one degree, the meafure will be the fame; and if more or lefs, we know in proportion the quantity. By thefe methods the true quantity of a degree has been very accurately determined; for our countryman Mr. Norwood found, by meafuring from London to York, in the year 1655, that one degree upon the Earth's furface contained 69½ miles; and Monf. Caffini's meafures agree with them to almoft a nicety. Caffini's were made, by the French king's command, at great diftances, with the greateft accuracy; which he divided into two arches, the one of 6°½ from Paris, to the South extremity of the kingdom; the other of 2°½ from Paris, to the North, being the whole meridian of France. According to thefe obfervations, the Earth's circumference is 25,020 miles, and its diameter, 7,970 miles. Having defcribed the bulk or magnitude of this our planetary world, with which we are fo clofely connected, I come next to confider its figure, which has been hitherto fuppofed to be that of a globe or fphere, and which we find to be nearly fo, namely fphæroidal, being a little flat towards the poles, and fhaped like an orange, which has been confirmed by experiments or gravity; but then it was fuppofed that the centrifugal force would leffen the preffure of gravity, as it is nearer to the Equator. Therefore Sir Ifaac Newton and Mr. Huygens went fo far in their calculations, as to compare the quantity of the centrifugal force under the equator, which was the 289th part of gravity; that is, every body under the equator loft the 289th part of its weight. According to Sir Ifaac Newton, the diameter of the equator muft exceed the axis of the Earth the 230th part of its length, that is, about 34 miles. If ever the Earth was in a fluid ftate, its revolution round its axis muft neceffarily make it put on fuch a figure, becaufe near the equatorial parts muft needs be the greateft centrifugal force, and confequently there the fluid would rife and fwell moft; and that it fhould be fo now, feems neceffary, to keep the fea in the equinoctial regions from overflowing the Earth thereabouts. Experiments alfo, made on pendulums which require different lengths to fwing feconds, here and at the equator, prove the fame thing; for when the pendulum of a clock departs in its motion from the perpendicular, the force which brings it back again is gravity; and this is done quicker or flower in proportion to the greater or lefs degree of gravity. The orbit of the Earth, or of any planet, is the curve that it defcribes in its revolution round its central body; thus the orbit of the Earth in its annual courfe is the ecliptick. Kepler fuppofed this orbit to be a perfect circle; but he proves it to be an ellipfis, the remoteft end of whofe tranfverfe, or longer diameter, is eight degrees diftant from the firft ftar in Aries, and having the Sun in one of its focal points.

The orbit of the Earth not being perfectly circular, but a little elliptical, the Sun will be nearer the Earth at one time of the year than at another, and the Earth will move fafter and flower, and will pafs over one half of her orbit in lefs time than the other; for, from the autumnal equinox, September 23, to the vernal equinox, March 20, is eight days lefs than from Spring to Autumn again;
and

and fo many days is our Summer half year longer when the Sun is farther off, than our Winter half when the Sun is nearer.

EXAMPLE.

	days.			days.
In March,	10$\frac{1}{2}$		In September,	7
April,	30		October,	31
May,	31		November,	30
June,	30		December,	31
July,	31		January,	31
Auguft,	31		February,	28
	———		March,	20$\frac{1}{2}$
	186$\frac{1}{2}$			———
	178$\frac{1}{2}$			178$\frac{1}{2}$

The difference 8 days.

To make thefe things more eafy, let the ellipfis, fig. 10. reprefent the orbit of the Earth (or any other planet, as they all move in elliptical orbits). A is the place of the Earth at the time of the Perihelion, when the Sun is neareft to the Earth, which in the prefent age is on the 30th of December. The Sun is reprefented in the focufes of the ellipfis at E. It is obferveable that the Earth and planets defcribe equal areas, or triangular fpaces, in equal times; therefore, fuppofing the triangular fpaces A B E, B C E, and C D E, equal, it is plain, from a bare infpection, that the Earth's motion muft be fwifteft in defcribing the curve from A to B, and muft gradually decreafe in paffing from B to C; and ftill decreafing till it arrives at D, where, being at its greateft diftance from the Sun, the motion is floweft. This in the prefent age is on the 30th of June, and is called the Apheli-on, or greateft diftance from the Sun. As I have juft obferved, the Earth, in paf-fing from A to BCD, is continually retarded in its orbit; fo in its paffage from D to A, in the other half of its orbit, it is continually accelerated. The diftance from E, the focus of the ellipfis, where the Sun is placed, to the center of the el-lipfis between the two focufes, is called the Eccentricity, and is different in the orbits of the different planets; and in all of them is fo little, that in fmall fchemes it is needlefs, and almoft impoffible, to reprefent their orbits; but, in the orbits of comets, the eccentricity is very confiderable, their orbits being very long ellipfes, and the focufes at vaft diftances from each other. If the Earth had no inclination of its axis to the plane of its orbit, the days and nights would be equal throughout the year; but, having an inclination of 23° 28', the Sun is made fometimes to vifit the Northern and at other times the Southern parts, and fo produces all the variety of feafons we enjoy. The Earth's diurnal motion in the ecliptic is 59' 8". The Earth is encompaffed with an atmofphere, up into which the vapours are carried; where being condenfed, they furnifh us with clouds, rain, &c. and alfo are, by reflecting light, the caufe of the morning and evening twilight, and alfo of the brightnefs of the fky. The height of the atmofphere is commonly eftimated at about 45 miles.

F f

THE

The MOON.

THE Moon refpects the Earth for her center of motion; and, being a fecondary planet, her globe with her orbit are, as it were, carried round the Sun with our Earth. In every revolution fhe turns once upon her own axis, and the fame face is always prefented to our view. The Moon goes through her orbit, with refpect to the fixed flars, in 27 d. 7 h. 43 min. at a mean rate; but with regard to the Sun, a lunation is 29 d. 12 h. 44 min. The Moon's orbit does not always remain the fame, but is dilated in Winter, and contracted in Summer; the greateft difference being about 22½ minutes. The Moon will be later every time in coming to her conjunction or oppofition with the Sun from December till June, and fooner from June to December. The Moon's orbit is elliptical, and the Earth is in one of its focal points, and has the fame kind of influence as I obferved the Sun's attraction had on the motion of the Earth; fo that the Moon's motion muft be continually accelerated whilft fhe is paffing from her apogee to her perigee, and as gradually retarded in moving from her perigee to her apogee. The Moon's mean diftance from the Earth is 240,000 miles, and her diameter about 2,175 miles. By the light and fhadow of the Sun upon her, it is evident that fhe has day and night in the fpace of one month. Her axis inclines to the plane of her orbit in an angle of about 6½ degrees from the perpendicular. That the Moon has mountains and deep valleys, is evident from the unevennefs of her furface, which are plainly to be feen with the telefcope. The Earth and Moon are mutually Moons to one another. When they are New Moon to us, we are Full Moon to them. The magnitude, light, and heat of the Sun are nearly the fame as with us on the Earth.

MARS.

I come now to the fuperior planets, MARS, JUPITER, and SATURN. They are fo called becaufe they move in orbits round the Sun, which are larger than that of our Earth, and fo are above us with regard to the Sun, and can never come between the Earth and Sun. The orbit of Mars is between the Earth and Jupiter, and he makes his revolution round the Sun in the fpace of 1 year, 321 days, 23 hours, and 27 minutes, at the diftance of 145 millions of miles. His diameter is about 5150 miles, and he has a rotation upon his axis, as appears from the fpots on his body, in 24 h. 40 min.; and in Mars we can difcern a great fimilitude with the Earth in its opacity and fpots, and being encompaffed with an atmofphere, which, together with the planet itfelf, reflects a glaring red light. This planet, as well as the reft, borrows its light from the Sun, and has its increafe and decreafe
like

like the Moon; and I have obferved it almoſt biſected in his quadratures with the Sun, but never horned, which is a proof that his orbit circumſcribes ours and is wholly beyond it; but I have not obferved any fatellite or Moon belonging to this planet, nor have I heard of others making fuch a difcovery; fo that, if there are any, they are fmall, or reflect too weak a light to make them viſible at a great diſtance. The axis of this planet is nearly at right angles to the plane of his orbit, as appears from the revolution of the fpots on his furface; therefore he hath a perpetual equinox. The belts or fwaths in Mars probably owe their origin to heat and cold, in the fame manner as the clouds in our atmofphere in Mars. The Sun's diameter is but little more than half what it appears on our Earth; confequently his light and heat is not half fo great as it is here. To the obfervers of the heavens in Mars, the Earth will be their morning and evening ſtar by turns, juſt as Venus is here. Mr. Flamſtead and Caffini found the paral lax of Mars to be about 25 feconds, and thence concluded the Sun's parallax was about 10 feconds.

The inclination of his orbit to the ecliptic,	1	52	0
The daily mean motion in the ecliptic,		31	27
Place of aphelion, perihelion oppofite,	♏ 1	56	0
Place of afcending node, defcending oppofite,	♉ 18	6	0
Greateſt apparent diameter,		20	50
Leaſt apparent diameter,		2	46

JUPITER.

OUR next fuperior planet is Jupiter, who performs his revolution round the Sun in 11 years, 314 days, and 12 hours, at the diſtance of 494 millions of miles. And here I fhall beſtow a few words in relating the difcoveries that we make there with our glaſſes, although at fo great a diſtance from us; for without them we could fay very little more than what I have juſt mentioned; and for this I hope I need not make any apology, efpecially as they prefent us with fuch a very noble and entertaining fcene of the great Creator's glory. For here we difcover that Jupiter is attended with a grand retinue of moons, or fecondary planets, revolving round him, and adminiſtering their light and kind influence; an admirable proviſion, he being 5 times further from the Sun than the Earth is; therefore the folar diameter is but about a fifth of what it appears to us, and his light and heat muſt confequently be 25 times lefs than ours. On the body of Jupiter I find great variation in the belts, they being fometimes more in number, fometimes fewer, as alfo broader and narrower: fometimes alfo they are darker, and at other times only like a miſt. A drawing of Jupiter's belts, as they appeared Aug. 13, 1772, at 10ʰ 30′ 0″, is given in fig. 11. Thefe belts, as I obferved, are variable, and may perhaps be owing to vapours and clouds in his atmofphere, as on our

F f 2   Earth

Earth thefe belts are commonly parallel to and near his equator; and by the fpots that appear in his belts and on his body, his rotation on his axis is difcovered to be in 9 hours and 56 minutes. The fuperior planets are much nearer to the Earth when in oppofition to the Sun than in any other part of their orbit: however, this neareft diftance of Jupiter is about 400 millions of miles from our Earth, a diftance fo great, that this planet, though of the largeft magnitude (his diameter being 94,100 miles, fo that he is in bulk 1000 times bigger than our Earth), is at this diftance reduced to the appearance of a bright ftar in the heavens. Being at fo great a diftance from the Sun, he hath four fatellites, or moons, to enlighten him, as our Earth, which is nearer, hath one. Their diftances from Jupiter, in femidiameters of his body, are as follows:

The diftance of the Firft,   5,697   in minutes and feconds of a degree is 1' 51"
            Second,   9,017   2 56
            Third,   14,384   4 42
            Fourth,   25,266   8 16

Their periodical revolutions about Jupiter with regard to the fixed ftars are,

	d.	h.	'	"
Firft,	1	18	27	34
Second,	3	13	13	42
Third,	7	3	42	36
Fourth,	16	16	32	9

The revolution of thefe planets about Jupiter with regard to the Sun is,

	d.	h.	'	"
Firft,	1	18	28	36
Second,	3	13	17	54.
Third,	7	3	59	36
Fourth,	16	18	5	13

The magnitudes of thefe planets of Jupiter are large, and I judge may be nearly as follows. The third is the largeft of them all, and may be about the bignefs of Venus. The firft is the next in fize, though fomewhat lefs than the former, and may be about the bignefs of the Earth. The fecond is a little lefs than the firft, and may be about the bignefs of Mars. The fourth is the leaft, and may perhaps be not much bigger than Mercury. Some Aftronomers make the bulk of thefe fecondary planets much greater; for the moft ingenious Mr. Huygens concludes, from their fhades upon Jupiter's difk, that there is not any of them lefs than our Earth. If we confider the vaft bulk of Jupiter himfelf, and his grand retinue of fecondary planets, which we have fuppofed to be at leaft equal to all the primary planets between himfelf and the Sun, fo that he is furnifhed with a compleat fyftem of his own, and attendant fatellites or moons exhibiting the fame phafis and figures that our Moon fhews us in the various parts of her revolution; what a variety of fcenes muft be perpetually exhibited in the heavens to an eye placed in that planet! Thefe amazing acts and indulgent provifions juftly proclaim it a work worthy the great Creator.

The fatellites of Jupiter, which were wholly unknown to the ancients, were firft difcovered by Galilæo on the 7th of January, 1610. The eclipfes of thefe fatellites are very frequent, and of great ufe on this our Earth, by enabling the mariner to find his longitude, and is frequently ufed both by fea and land.

Example

Example 1. The emerfion of Jupiter's firft fatellites at the Royal Obfervatory at Greenwich, by calculation,

		h.	,	,
1770, July 13,	apparent time,	9	5	7
By obfervation at Hinckley,		9	0	2
Difference of meridian		0	5	5 Weft.

Example 2. The emerfion of Jupiter's firft fatellites at Greenwich, by calculation.

		h.	,	,
1770, Aug. 5,	apparent time,	9	19	9
By obfervation at Hinckley,		9	13	45
Difference of meridian		0	5	24 Weft.

Example 3. The immerfion of Jupiter's firft fatellites at Greenwich, by calcu-lation.

		h.	,	,
1774, Oct. 5.	apparent time,	10	14	5
By obfervation at Hinckley,		10	8	35
Difference of meridian		0	5	30 Weft.

Thefe feveral planets, while they are gradually entering the penumbra or im-perfect fhadow of Jupiter, or emerging from it in their eclipfes diftinct from their durations within the total fhadow itfelf, are from obfervation nearly as follow, though they admit of fome variety at different times:

	,	,
Firft,	1	10
Second,	2	20
Third,	3	40
Fourth,	5	30

Thofe eclipfes of our Moon, which we call total, are not ftrictly fuch; but the eclipfes of Jupiter's planets are every one ftrictly total, they going very deep into the total fhadow of Jupiter in every one of their eclipfes, except the fourth about its greateft latitude, which cannot then come into his fhadow for a confiderable time.

The mean duration of the total eclipfes of Jupiter's planets, when they are not far from their nodes and defcribe diameters over Jupiter's fhadow, are as follows:

	h.	,
Firft,	2	12
Second,	2	49
Third,	3	32
Fourth,	4	46

The

The durations of thefe planets, while they are under occultations by the body of Jupiter either on this or the other fide, when they are not far remote from their nodes, and defcribe diameters over Jupiter's body, are as follows:

	h.	'
Firft,	2	18
Second,	2	56
Third,	3	40
Fourth,	4	54

As to the motion of thefe planets, that of the fecond is by far the moft uneven and irregular of them all; for fometimes its motion will be confiderably accelerated or retarded, which I fuppofe arifes chiefly from their mutual attraction or gravitation upon each other, as has been obferved of the Sun, Moon, and planets. The motion of the other three planets is more regular, though not entirely free from fuch inequalities. That the fecondaries of Jupiter have a rotation on their axis, I cannot pofitively affirm; but think it probable, from the great variety in their brightnefs, which may be more or lefs obfcured by fpots on their difk. Though thefe planets revolve about Jupiter's center in orbits concentrical to Jupiter; yet to us on the Earth they appear to move backward and forward along thofe diameters of their feveral orbits, and their apparent diftances will be the fine of the angles of their real motion from or to Jupiter's center.

I fhall now take notice of a remarkable difcovery made by means of the fatellites of Jupiter; and that is, the motion or progreffion of light; for light requires time to pafs fr m one place to another, and does it not in an inftant, but is of all motions the quickeft. Mr. Reaumur has demonftrated, from the obfervations of the immerfions and emerfions of the fatellites of Jupiter, that light requires the time of one fecond to move the fpace of 3000 leagues, or 9000 miles, which is near the Earth's diameter, as may be feen in the Journal des Sçavans, 1676; Phil. Tranf. Nº 136; or Sir Ifaac Newton's Philof. Nat. Math. lib. 1. Schol. prop. 96. where it is afferted that light requires about ten minutes of time to come from the Sun to the Earth; and it is moft evident, without this allowance for the time fpent in light's motion, the appearances of the fatellites, eclipfes, and emerfions, are not to be explained by any eccentricity or other hypothefis. Sir Ifaac Newton obferves, that light is propagated in time, and fuppofes about ten minutes to be taken up in its paffage from the Sun to us; but in his Optics he determines this matter more accurately. Reaumur firft, and after him others, had obferved that the eclipfes of Jupiter's fatellites happen about 7 or 8 minutes fooner than they ought to do by the tables, when the Earth is interpofed between the Sun and that planet; but as much later when the Earth is beyond the Sun in refpect of Jupiter: the reafon of which is, that the light of the fatellites hath farther to go in the latter cafe than in the former, by the diameter of the Earth's orbit. Mr. Huygens hath proved, in his Cofmotheoros, that a bullet difcharged from the mouth of a cannon, and not abating of its firft velocity, would be 25 years before it reached the Sun. Now the *via percurfa* being the fame in both, the velocities will be reciprocally as the times; that is, the velocity of light to that of a cannon-bullet perfifting in its greateft

swiftnefs

fwiftnefs will be as 25 years to 10 minutes, or as 1,314,700 is to 1 nearly; fo that the motion of light is above a million of times fwifter than that of a cannon-ball, a rapidity of motion fo great that it cannot be eafily conceived by us.

Though Jupiter is the greateft of the planets, yet his revolution about his axis is the fwifteft. His polar axis is obferved to be fhorter than his equatorial diameter, and Sir Ifaac Newton determines the differeuce to be as 8 to 9; fo that his figure is a fpheroid, and the fwiftnefs of his rota:ion occafions this fpheroidifm to be more fenfible than that of any other of the planets. Jupiter appears very illuftrious, and almoft as large as Venus, but is not altogether fo bright. If we take off his refulgent rays by viewing him through a fmall pin-hole, we fhall find his real apparent diameter very fmall. The axis of this planet inclines but very little to the plane of his orbit; therefore they will enjoy, as they do in Mars, a perpetual equinox over the whole globe throughbout the year, which is almoft 12 of ours. Their days and nights are but fhort, being about 5 hours each. The fcur fatellites, or moons, muft make a very pleafing appearance to the inhabitants of Jupiter, in their various afpeéts and revolutions, with their frequent eciipfes; and by the variety of latitude and perpetual changes of it, all parts of that vaft planet will have their due fhare in all the light and kindly fervices, and feldom or never be deprived of them. The aftronomers there will never fee Mercory, Venus, the Earth, nor perhaps Mars, unlefs in their horizon, fometimes at the beginning and end of their twilight; for, being at fo great a diftance, they will appear to accompany the Sun, and rife and fet almoft at the fame time with him. Nor will they perhaps be able to know there are fuch worlds in exiftence; for, being at fo great a diftance from them, and their diameters fmall, together with their nearnefs to the Sun, they will be as it were wholly abforbed and loft in the folar rays. But Saturn, when in oppofition to the Sun, will, with his ring and grand retinue of planets, make a fine appearance, Jupiter at that time being above 400,000,000 miles nearer than we on the Earth; but at the time of Saturn's conjunétion with the Sun, he will be wholly obfcured and loft to them for a confiderable time; and for fome before and after, he will appear very obfcure and fmall, as is plain from a bare view of the Solar Syftem, fig. 9, where thefe two planets are delineated at their greateft diftance from each other.

The inclination of his orbit to the ecliptic,	1	20	0
Daily mean motion in the ecliptic,	0	4	59
The place of aphelion,	♎ 11	15	0
The place of the afcending node,	♋ 8	45	0
Greateft apparent diameter,		24	12
Leaft apparent diameter,		14	36

SATURN.

SATURN.

IN the remote boundaries of our fyftem, at the diftance of 907 millions of miles from the Sun, Saturn makes his periodical revolution in 29 years, 174 days, and 6 hours; his diameter is 77,990 miles; fo that he is 600 times bigger than the Earth. By reafon of his vaft diftance from us, we have not been able to difcover whether this planet revolves upon his axis; but I think it very probable, as we obferve it in fo many of the heavenly bodies. However, as we have not ocular demonftration of this particular, I fhall take notice of thofe that are fo with the telefcope; for, at this great diftance from the Sun, fome provifion feems neceffary, as the Sun's diameter is there but the tenth of what it appears to us on the Earth, confequently his light and heat 100 times lefs. And here the great Creator has made fuch admirable provifion for remedying Saturn's great diftance from the Sun us muft ftrike every one that views it with aftonifhment; for here we difcover an amazing ring encompaffing him on every fide, but no where touching his body. The breadth of the ring is about 21,000 miles, and the diftance of it from Saturn on every part is much the fame; fo that the heavens may be diftinctly feen be- tween the ring and his body. The ring is judged to be about 7 or 800 miles thick, and appears to reflect the Sun's light and heat, fo as to make both itfelf and the body of Saturn to appear very illuftrious. A reprefentation of Saturn, encompaffed with his ring, is given in fig. 12. To us on the Earth, the ring puts on many dif- ferent appearances. Every 14 or 15 years, Saturn's ring hath the fame face; for, during one half of his revolution, it inclines to the Northern, and the other half to the Southern parts; all which appearances are gradually obtained by gentle progreffes from one face of the ring to the other; for at one time he appears with open Anfæ or apertures, at another time with no ring at all; and when the Anfæ are the largeft, they gradually diminifh until none are to be feen in the ring, and at laft no ring at all. The diameter of Saturn to that of his ring is as 4 to 9. When Saturn is in 20½° of Sagittarius, the Northern plane of the ring is en- lightened, and appears quite open; and when he is in 20½° of Pifces, the ring is quite fhort, or only appears as a line on his body. When he is in 20½° of Gemini, the Southern plane of the ring is enlightened, and the ring appears open again; and when he is arrived to 20½° of Libra, the ring appears fhut again. As the ufe of this ring feems to be for the reflecting of light and heat to this pla- net, we may reafonably conclude that, from the different pofitions of his ring, Saturn hath great variety of feafons. The being dignified with fuch an admirable ring, which feems intended by Providence to fupply him with light and heat, and make up for the deficiency of the Sun's rays; the prodigious fize of it; its great breadth, and vaft compafs; what an amazing arch muft it form to an eye placed in that planet! This is a thing fo peculiar to Saturn, and fo unufual in the reft of the creation, that it is a noble demonftration of the great Creator's fkill and care.

But

But this is not all. A further provision is made, by a grand retinue of secondary planets or moons; for, as I have observed that Jupiter, being at a great distance from the Sun, was attended by four Moons; so Saturn, being above 500 millions of miles more distant, besides his ring, is accommodated with five and perhaps more; for the distance between the orbits of the two outermost is so very considerable, that it is reasonable to conclude there is another lying between them, which may be invisible at so great a distance by means of some obscurity, such as is observable in the outermost itself. We may reasonably conclude that these satellites are of a prodigious bulk, for the reflecting of light and other ministrations to their primary planet; otherwise they could not be seen at so great a distance. Their distances from the center of Saturn, with periodical times, are as under:

Periodical times.				Distance in semidiameters of the ring.	Distance in semidiameters of the globe of Saturn.
	d.	h.	m.	s.		
First,	1	21	18	27	2,097	4,893
Second,	2	17	41	22	2,686	6,268
Third,	4	12	25	12	3,752	8,754
Fourth,	15	22	41	12	8,698	20,295
Fifth,	79	7	47	0	25,348	59,154

Mr. Azout asserts, that the remote distance of Saturn from the Sun doth not hinder there being light enough to see clear there, and even clearer than in our Earth in cloudy weather. The inclination of the ring of Saturn to the ecliptic is found by observation to be about 31°. Mr. Huygens first discovered the ring of Saturn and the largest of his satellites, which is the fourth, in 1665. Mr. Cassini discovered the other four, with excellent object-glasses, of 70, 90, 100, 136, 155, and 220 feet. The first and second were not seen till 1684. In fig. 15. is a representation of Saturn as traced in the heavens. The upper part of the figure represents a portion of the ecliptic divided into degrees; and in the lower part is a representation of Saturn encompassed with his ring.

Being in his retrograde motion, he came to a conjunction with a fixed star, the beginning of December 1767, 2° in Cancer, his latitude being 1° 2' South. His place is marked every fifth day, and may be progressively seen by inspection.

December 24, he comes in conjunction with another fixed star, and renders it invisible to the naked eye, though it appears in the telescope, his latitude then being 1° 0' South. He continues retrograde till Feb. 27, 1768, when he again begins his direct motion, as expressed in the figure, and comes again in conjunction a second time with the same star, April 28, and again renders it invisible, he being now above it, and his latitude 40' South; and he comes again in conjunction with the former star May 15, 1768, but in a higher situation, his latitude being 37' South.

Occultation of Saturn by the Moon, Feb. 18, 1775.

	h.	'	"			h.	'	"
Beginning, apparent time,	9	11	55	Middle of occultation,		9	36	13
Central ingress,	9	12	21	Emersion,		10	0	20
Immersion,	9	12	47	Central egress,		10	0	46
Visible conjunction,	9	35	24	End of final contact,		10	1	14

In Saturn all the planets in our system disappear, except Jupiter; and he appears to accompany the Sun, being never found either before or after him more

G g   than

than about 35°, fo that he is their Morning and Evening Star by turns, as Venus is to us; but his Moons, as I have obferved of thofe of Jupiter, muft exhibit a very great variety of appearances. At the time of conjunction with the Sun, they will be New Moons, and at the firft and laft quarter half enlightened: at the oppofition, they will be Full, fhining with their greateft brightnefs, and performing their revolutions in different times, which, together with frequent eclipfes, muft afford many curious fpeculations to an eye placed in this planet.

Inclination of his orbit to the ecliptic,	2 30	The place of the afcending node,	♋ 21 57
Daily mean motion in the ecliptic,	2	Greateft apparent diameter,	19 40
The place of aphelion,	♈ 10	Leaft apparent diameter,	14 11

GEORGIUM SIDUS

is to be the name of the newly difcovered planet (as I learn from Mr. Maty's Review) in honour of our gracious Sovereign *. This planet is of a pale colour, and of very fmall apparent diameter, it being but of about 5"; although our Earth is nearly approaching to that part of her orbit which is neareft to the planet, which is now retrograde, in the beginning of the fign Cancer, and its motion about 1' a day, with 13' of North latitude. Its apparent meridian altitude at Hinckley is 61° 23'; and this altitude will continue for fome time, with but little variation.

The Georgium Sidus is fuppofed to be at a great diftance beyond the orbit of Saturn, and will require near 80 years to compleat one revolution round the Sun. But we may hope foon to have a fatisfactory account of it from Mr. Herfchel.

MACULÆ SOLARES.

THIS remarkable appearance fhould have accompanied the Solar Obfervations, but was overlooked at the time they were printing. Before I heard of it, it had appeared, and paffed the Solar difk. On a daily examination, I difcovered the Maculæ Solares, or new appearance near the Sun's limb, July 20, 1781. From the 20th to the 24th, keeps advancing on the Sun's difk in all refpects as the common Maculæ, and has a penumbra, or kind of atmofphere, furrounding it. On the 25th, cloudy. On the 26th, advances on the difk as other Maculæ; the atmofphere very diftinct, well defined, and of a clear appearance; the fpot very dark, and will make its neareft approach to the Sun's center on the 27th at 6ʰ 30' in the morning, at the diftance of 2' 40" North. Its form was almoft fpherical, its longeft diameter being 28" 15", the fhorteft 27' 50". The atmofphere circumfcribing it appeared circular, and nearly double the fpot's mean diameter. Notwithstanding the cloudy weather, I had fome views of it before it came to the Sun's limb; but found it was divided into feveral fpots, which increafed their diftance from each other be-

---

* "The obfervations of all the firft Aftronomers of Europe concurring to prove the new ftar difcovered by Mr. Herfchel to be a primary planet: he, who, as the difcoverer, has the beft right to give it a name, wifhes it to be called the Georgium Sidus, in honour of the Prince under whofe reign it was difcovered, and as a debt due to that Prince by Aftronomy, for taking the difcoverer from a mechanical employment, and enabling him to continue to enrich fcience. Upon thefe principles, it is fuppofed, the other Aftronomers of Europe will readily concur in accepting the name. It is pleafing to reflect, that this difcovery has been made by a very natural improvement in the conftruction of Telefcopes, fo that we have a great deal more to expect from the fame diligent hands." MATY, vol. II. p. 438.

fore they came to the limb, as is obfervable of the common Maculæ, fo that there
was an entire end of this fingular obfervation.

Comparative Magnitudes.

The dark fpot's greateft diameter,	13,266 miles.
The leaft diameter,	13,c79
Mean diameter,	13,172
The diameter of the atmofphere and fpot inclufive,	26,344
The diameter of our Earth,	7,970

Fig. 13. is a reprefentation of this phænomenon.

C O M E T S.

THERE are other bodies, befides the planets already treated of, belonging
to our fyftem. Thefe, which are a kind of temporary planets, fometimes make
their appearance in the regions of the planets for a while after they return and
difappear, and are called Comets, or Blazing Stars. Modern Aftronomers have
difcovered that they are large globular bodies, moving in various directions acrofs
our fyftem, and that their orbits are very elliptical. In the diftant parts of their
orbits, they afcend to vaft heights above Saturn, and fo become a long time invifible until they again return into our part of the fyftem. The manner in which
a Comet revolves in its orbit through the planetary fyftem is reprefented in fig. 9.

I fhall now give a few obfervations on that of 1769.

Auguft 24, the Comet's direction was Eaft by South 3° in 24 hours, and
was nearly 15' South of the Pleiades, in 25' of Taurus. A line drawn from Aldebaran to Menear in the mouth of the Whale, paffes about 2° South of the Comet's body.

Sept. 5, half paft one o'clock in the morning, the Comet 2° to the South Weft
of the ftar in Orion's right fhoulder, the head or nucleus of the Comet rather obfcure, being about the bignefs of a ftar of the third magnitude, furrounded by a
hazy atmofphere; its tail pointing to that part of the heavens moft diftant from
the Sun, and its length 30°. It had juft paffed to the North of a line from the
Pleiades paffing through Aldebaran, its right afcenfion at that time being 5ʰ 20',
and declination 7' North.

Sept. 12, half paft 3 o'clock in the morning, the Comet 14° below Procyon,
the tail increafed to fomething more than 30° in length; the middle of the tail
pointed to the ftars in Orion's fword; it is now hafting to the Sun with great velocity, its motion being upwards of 4° in 24 hours Northerly, declining down-
wards Eafterly about 6° lower than it was on the 1ft of September. The Comet's
approach to the Sun, and the morning twilight, foon precluded further obfervation.

Having determined as near as poffibly I could the particular part it would make
its appearance in after its afcent from the Sun, I made the following obfervations,
which perhaps might have begun fooner had not the evenings been cloudy.

October 31, at half paft 6 o'clock in the evening, I obferved the Comet.
It made but a fmall faint appearance, fcarcely difcernible with the naked eye,

and appeared like one of the nebulous stars, with a small glare of light, but was very visible with the telescope. The head was very bright, and the tail short, and seemed divided as it were in two, within a little of the head. A representation of it is given in fig. 14. The Comet being at a great distance from the Earth, and continually increasing that distance, and being also so very near the evening twilight, it cannot be long visible. A perpendicular line passing through the bright star in the Harp to the horizon passes a little to the Westward of the Comet, the height of the Comet being 15' above the horizon.

November 5. I observed the Comet at half past 6 o'clock in the evening. It made a very faint appearance, but just discernible with the naked eye, and appeared much fainter through the telescope.

November 7. This evening, at half past 6 o'clock, the Comet appeared very faint through the telescope; it has passed on 2° to the Eastward since the evening of the 5th instant, its direction being due East.

I think it very probable that the body of this Comet is nearly as large as the Moon, and that at the beginning of September it was about 90,000,000 of miles from the Sun, and 40 millions of miles from our Earth.

We only view Comets during a small part of their revolution; for they begin to appear to us when they arrive at that part of our system which is between the orbits of Jupiter and Mars, and then only as stars of the smallest magnitude; and as they approach the Sun, they appear larger, and emit a fiery tail; and as the Comet approaches nearer, with the increase of heat the tail grows longer; and when it arrives at the perihelion, or a little beyond it, the tail is then longest; afterwards, as the Comet ascends and the heat diminishes, the tail grows less, till it becomes invisible.

The bodies of Comets must be of a very fixed and durable substance; otherwise, at their near approach to the Sun, they would be dissipated by such an intense heat. The number of the Comets was supposed to be, till the present age, between 20 and 30. But little progress was made in this part of Astronomy, and consequently few of their periods determined. Of those delineated in fig. 9, that of 1680 is 575 years, that of 1759 is 75½ years, and that of 1661 is 129 years; this last, therefore, will probably return in the year 1789, or beginning of 1790. The Comet of 1680, at the time of its perihelion, is computed to have come so near the Sun as to be within one sixth part of the Sun's diameter, and consequently must receive a degree of heat 28,000 times hotter than our Earth in Summer, which is about 2000 times hotter than red-hot iron. Aristotle and many of the Ancients would have Comets to be nothing but sublunary vapours, or airy meteors; and so far did their opinion prevail, that this difficult part of the Astronomical science lay neglected. But Seneca the Philosopher, having considered the phænomena of two remarkable Comets of his time, made no scruple to place them amongst the celestial bodies, believing them to be stars of equal duration with the world, though he owns their motions to be governed by laws not yet discovered; and at last (which was no untrue or vain prediction) he foretells that there should be ages some time hereafter, to whom Time and Diligence should unfold all these mysteries, and who should wonder that the Ancients should be ignorant of them, after some lucky Interpreter of Nature had shewn in what parts of the heavens the Comets wandered, and what and how great they were.

Upon

Upon the whole, very little was done that might be of use in this subject before the year 1577, when Tycho Brahe, that great restorer of Astronomy, being provided with proper instruments, there appeared a very remarkable Comet; which Tycho opportunely applied himself to observe. Next to Tycho, came the sagacious Kepler; and he, having the advantage of Tycho's labours and observations, found out the true physical system of the world, and much improved the Astronomical science; and after him Hevelius, who made many observations of Comets, but complained that his calculations did not agree with the matter of fact in the heavens. At length came the prodigious Comet of the year 1680, which, descending as it were from an infinite distance perpendicularly towards the Sun, arose from him again with as great a velocity. This Comet, which was seen for four months continually, by the very remarkable and peculiar curvity of its orbit above all others, gave the fittest occasion for investigating the theory of their motion; and the Royal Observatories of Paris and Greenwich having been for some time founded, and committed to the care of the most excellent Astronomers, the apparent motion of this Comet was most accurately (perhaps as far as human skill could go) observed by Messieurs Cassini and Flamstead. Not long after, that great Geometrician, the illustrious Newton, writing his Mathematical Principles of Natural Philosophy, demonstrated not only what Kepler had found did necessarily obtain in the planetary system, but also that all the phænomena of Comets would naturally follow from the same principles; which he abundantly illustrated by the example of the foresaid Comet of 1680, shewing at the same time a method of delineating the orbits of Comets geometrically, wherein he (not without the highest admiration of all men) solved a problem whose intricacy rendered it worthy of himself. This Comet he proved to move round the Sun in a parabolical orb, and to describe areas (taken at the center of the Sun) proportional to the times.

The FIXED STARS.

HAVING in the preceding pages set forth the prodigious magnitude of this our Solar System, and of the bodies therein contained; let us admire, as we justly may, the vast bulk of this our own globe, which however, as has been observed, is much surpassed by some others; so that we cannot consider them without astonishment. And were there no more of creation than the Sun and Planets, primary and secondary, it would be sufficient to manifest an almighty and all-wise Creator. But all this is a small part of the creation, compared with the Starry Heavens, which, as I shall shew presently, are an amazing, grand, and magnificent structure; and may justly be said to *declare the glory of God, and to shew his handy work.* And can we possibly view and contemplate them, and not give Him due praise? The Ancients thought the Universe was confined within far more narrow bounds than it is since found to be; for they supposed that the Fixed Stars were placed at equal distances from us, and formed a kind of arch, or boundary; but, since the invention of the telescope, such discoveries have been made, as give us a more exalted and extensive idea. As to the distance of the Fixed Stars, they are hardly

4

hardly within the reach of our methods to determine. However, I shall mention a particular or two, that will much illustrate the prodigious vastness of it. Dr. Hook, Op. Posthum. p. 109, gives very probable reasons why the Fixed Stars should be of the same nature with the Sun, which are drawn from their vast distance, and their affecting our eyes with so strong and vivid a light; which is agreed to by modern Astronomers. Therefore, since in all likelihood the Fixed Stars are Suns shining with their own native light, perhaps of a different magnitude, we may, at a reasonable medium, presume they are generally about the bigness of our Sun, and that the great variety of their magnitudes in general arises from the different distances they are placed from us. Upon such a supposition as this, Mr. Huygens supposes that the greatest, and consequently the nearest, of the Fixed Stars is Sirius; the distance of which he computes thus. The distance of the Sun to this Star is as 1 to 27,644; that is, this Star appeared so many times less than the Sun; therefore his distance must be as many times as far. He then proceeds thus: Allowing the distance of the Sun to be 12,000 diameters of the Earth, and a diameter to be 7846 miles, according to the best calculations at that time, then the nearest distance of this Star from us is at least 2,404,520,928,000 miles; which is so great, that a cannon-ball going all the way with the same velocity it had at the mouth of the gun would scarce arrive there in 700,000 years. As the Stars appear to us of different sizes, they are divided for distinction into six different magnitudes; and if we suppose each of these to be placed as far from each other as those just mentioned, what an immensurable distance must they be from us! When the eye can see no more, great numbers are yet discoverable with the telescope; and when we view them with instruments of still superior construction, we proportionally discover more and more of those starry orbs. If therefore, as we have just observed, we suppose the ball to continue its motion, how many millions of years would be spent before it could arrive at those distant bodies! And when we see ourselves surrounded with so prodigious a number of these illustrious bodies, and particularly when we take a view of the Galaxy or Milkyway, and the prodigious number that fill that part of the heavens, and cause the remarkable whiteness there, we see what is beyond the art of man to number.

The most learned of our modern Astronomers suppose that this great multitude of Fixed Stars are Suns, and that each of them is encompassed with a system of planets like our Sun. That these Stars are Suns, seems evident, because they shine by their own native light; and as to their bulk or magnitude, they are only diminished in appearance by their prodigious distances from us; and so brisk and vivid is their light, and so very small their apparent diameters, divested of their glaring rays, when we view them through our telescopes, and see their true appearance, that they then appear as shining by their own innate light as our Sun doth. And from the uniformity observable in God's works, we have great reason to conclude that every Fixed Star hath a system of natural Planets as well as the Sun; for it is certain the Sun is a Fixed Star to the Fixed Stars, as they are to the Sun. What a grand and amazing scene doth this unfold unto us, if human imagination can conceive it! Thousands of Suns ranged round us at immense distances
from

from each other, attended by ten thoufand times ten thoufand worlds! And though in rapid motion, yet we obferve them to be calm, regular, and harmonious, and that they fteadily and invariably keep the paths prefcribed them.

Since this Pythagorean fyftem of the world has been revived by Copernicus, and now by all Mathematicians accepted for the true one, there feemed ground to imagine that the diameter of the Earth's annual courfe, which, according to modern obfervation, is near 200 millions of miles, might give a fenfible parallax to the Fixed Stars, though the other could not, and thereby determine their diftance more precifely. But though we now have a foundation to build on fo vaftly exceeding the Ancients; there are fome confiderations which make us almoft fufpect that even this is hardly large enough for our purpofe; for the immenfe diftance of the Fixed Stars is fo great, that it caufeth even the great orbit which we defcribe round the Son to fink into almoft a point, or at leaft a circle of but a few feconds in diameter; therefore, as we have it not in our power to enlarge this bafe, nothing more can be done than to improve our inftruments, that we may meafure its parallax as exact as poffible. If we confider the great improvements we have of late made in inftruments, and are yet making, I hope we need not defpair in this undertaking; and that perhaps, in a few years, we may arrive at a tolerable exactnefs in this very delicate and nice difquifition.

In 1773, I endeavoured to avail myfelf in this particular, by obferving fome Double Stars that were nearly fituated; but I believe that very few Aftronomers at prefent have inftruments fit for this purpofe. I have lately had the pleafure of perufing Mr. Herfchel's Obfervations on the Parallax of the Fixed Stars; and am happy to find that he is purfuing this fubject with extraordinary inftruments, and has already given a confiderable Catalogue of Double Stars well worthy the perufal of Aftronomers.

The Fixed Stars, together with the Planets and all the Celeftial Bodies, appear every day to rife and fet, and to move with a circular motion from Eaft to Weft, parallel to the Earth's equator: all which is fairly and eafily accounted for, by fuppofing our Earth to revolve round its own axis in 24 hours from Weft to Eaft. Befides this, they have another motion (but apparent only), which is quite contrary to that; for they appear to change their longitude or diftance from the beginning of Aries forward according to the order of the Signs, or to move *in confequentia* by a flow motion of about a degree in 70 years; fo that thofe ftars which, in Hipparchus' and even in Ptolemy's time were in Aries, are now found to be in Taurus, and fo on all round the Zodiack; and thus the whole Starry Sphere appears to make one grand revolution in 25,920 years. But it hath never been obferved that they have changed their latitude. The preceffion of the terreftial equinoxes may ferve to account for the motion of the Fixed Stars, fince the quantity will be found the fame in both : for, from the Newtonian principles, it appears, the terreftrial nodes fhould go backward after the rate of about 50 every year, and juft fo much the Fixed Stars have been obferved to move forward in a year.

There is a whitifh tract, obvious to the naked eye, called the *Via Lactea*, or Milky-way, which encompaffes the whole heavens, extending itfelf in fome places with a double path, but for the moft parr with a fingle one. Some of the Ancients, as Ariftotle, &c. imagined that this path confifted only of a certain exhalation hang-

ing

ing in the air; but, by the telefcopical obfervations of this age, it hath been difcovered to confift of an innumerable quantity of Fxed Stars, different in fituation
and magnitude, from the confufed mixture of whofe light its white colour is fuppofed to be occafioned. It paffes through the conftellations of Caffiopeia, Cygnus,
Aquila, Perfeus, Andromeda, part of Orpheus, and Gemini, in the Northern he-
mifphere; and in the Southern, it takes in part of Scorpio, Sagittarius, Centau-
rus, the Argo, Navis, and the Ara. As the Galaxy is compofed of an infinity of
fmall ftars, fo it hath ufually been the region in which new ftars have appeared:
the new ftars in Caffiopeia firft feen in 1572, that in the breaft of the Swan, and
another in the knee of Serpentarius, and feveral others, which have appeared for
a while, and then became invifible again.

At prefent we have a wonderful ftar of this kind in the neck of the Whale,
which appears and difappears periodically. Its period is feven revolutions in fix
years. We have a fine view of thefe parts of the heavens in the evenings of February and March, and in thofe of Auguft and September.

There are feveral dufky or cloudy fpots in the heavens, commonly called Nebulous Stars, of a dull pale and obfcure light, as in Andromeda's girdle, Hercules's
book, Antinous's foot, Orion's fword, in the Centaur, Sagittary, &c. Thefe
ftars, viewed with good telefcopes, appear to be a number of fmall ftars. A reprefentation of thofe in Orion's fword are given in fig. 16.

Some of the Fixed Stars, efpecially thofe of the firft magnitude, may be obferved
in the day-time with a good telefcope. I have fometimes taken the meridian altitude
of Syrius, the Sun at the fame time fhining very bright.

Thus have I endeavoured to reprefent this glorious fcene of God's works, the
Heavens; plainly demonftrating infinite wifdom in the contrivance; his omnipotence
in making, and his infinite goodnefs in being fo indulgent to all his creatures, fo
nicely to adapt their motion, and to contrive their figures, to ferve to their confer-
vation and benefit. What Architect lefs than Infinite could build fo grand and
amazing a ftructure as the Heavens! And if we add to this the ftanding manifef-
tation of his will, which he has given us; we muft be ftrangely wanting to our-
felves, if we do not make a proper ufe of them, by becoming wifer and better men!

ASTRONOMICAL CHARACTERS explained.

The Twelve Signs or Conftellations of the Zodiac, in which the Planets perform
their Annual Revolutions.

♈ Aries.　♉ Taurus.　♊ Gemini.　♋ Cancer.　♌ Leo.　♍ Virgo.
♎ Libra.　♏ Scorpio.　♐ Sagittarius.　♑ Capricorn.　♒ Aquarius.　♓ Pifces.

The Seven Planets.

♄ Saturn. ♃ Jupiter. ♂ Mars. ☉ Sol. ♀ Venus. ☿ Mercury. ⊕ Earth. ☽ Luna.

☌ Conjunction. ☍ Oppofition. ☊ Afcending node. ☋ Defcending node.

° Degrees. ′ Minutes. ″ Seconds. ‴ Thirds.

APPEN-

APPENDIX, N° XX.

ADDITIONS and CORRECTIONS.

₊ This little volume having been a confiderable time in the prefs, the Author has omitted no opportunity of extending his refearches wherever it was probable to meet either with new facts, or with illuftrations of thofe he already poffeffed. The refult of his final inquiries is here made public ; and great care has been taken to advance nothing but what appears to ftand on the beft authority. Yet if any gentleman, who may honour this Hiftory with an attentive perufal, will be fo kind as to point out any errors, or fupply any deficiencies, the favour fhall be thankfully acknowledged at fome future opportunity.

P. 2. Since the firft note was printed, I have difcovered that there has been a confiderable connexion between the towns of Hinckley and Birmingham from very early time to the prefent age; and that, before the introduction of the ftocking frame, the youth of Hinckley fupplied the Birmingham traders with no fmall proportion of their apprentices.

P. 9. l. 1. In an old charter of Robert de Bellomont it is recited that Hugo de Grentefmenel was the great grand-father *(proavus)* of Petronilla, and Williclmus filius Ofberti her great grand-father's grand-father *(atavus)*.

P. 15. An unfuccefsful attempt was made in the houfe of peers, in June 1782, to revive the earldom of Leicefter in the perfon of Mrs. Perry, who now enjoys the family eftate and beautiful manfion at Penfhurft.

P. 16. It appears from Mr. Warton's admirable Hiftory of Kiddington, that Adeliza, daughter of the firft Hugh de Grentemaifnel, was married to Roger de Iveri.

P. 18. l. 8, 9. The head quarters of Richmond were at " Tamworth," not at " Coventry."

P. 19. A fimilar MS. to that mentioned in the firft note is referred to much more at large, p. 231—233.

P. 24. The great tithes of *The Wood Grounds*, and alfo of a fmall portion of land fituate in Barwell, belong to the Vicar of Hinckley by prefcriptive right.

P. 25. The *Foreign Jury* of Hinckley refembles that of Birmingham ; where, according to Mr. Hutton, " the hamlet of Deritend fends her inhabitants to the " court leet, where they perform fuit and fervice, and where the conftable is " chofen by the fame jury."

P. 26. " The high bailiff is to infpect the markets, and fee that juftice takes " place between buyer and feller ; and to rectify the weights and dry meafures ufed " in the manor." Hiftory of Birmingham, p. 88.

P. 27. The feafts in commemoration of the dedication of churches were the origin of fairs.

Ibid. By an affeffment made at Chriftmas 1781, it appears that the number of houfes, which, in p. 27, I had conjectured to be about 750, is very exact; and that,

H h   in

in the front houses, there are in general about 5 persons in each; and in the
yards and back buildings (where there are many children and apprentices) the
number is much more confiderable. On an average, it may be reckoned, there are
6 in a house, or about 4500 inhabitants in all.—I have been lately affured, however, that the collector of a levy-book took the pains to enquire particularly after
the number of inhabitants in every houfe, and found the total to exceed 7000,
which is more than 9 to a house.—A levy of fix-pence in the pound on the lands
and houfes in the parifh (exclufive of Stoke and Dadlington) amounts to about
104l. Towards this fum, Wykin contributes about a fixth part, the Hyde
nearly a twentieth, and fome lands in Barwell about a feventieth.

P. 31. l. 19, 20. r. " per manus."—note l. 1. r. " No X. p. 112."

P. 32. l. 23. r. " vacantem."

P. 33. The father and grandfather of Sir John Onebye refided at Hinckley.
Ibid. l. 24. r. " between 1740 and 1750."

P. 35. The five old bells were caft in the reign of James the Firft, in commemoration of the grant recorded in p. 55, when (as tradition expreffes itfelf) the town
was made free.

P. 45, twice, r. " BRYERLY."

P. 47. The verfes in this page were written by Dr. Morres.

P. 49. Mr. Burton the comedian ufed to ftroll about the country with his wife
and daughter, and frequently as the manager of a company. In particular, he was
often ftationed at Margate during the feafon, and was well known through the
county of Kent. The company in which he performed came to Hinckley March
14, 1774; where Mr. Burton died May 2, and was buried the next day; and on
the 6th " The Rival Queens" was performed there for the benefit of his widow.
His epitaph is printed in p. 49. The father, mother, and daughter, all died
within a fhort time of each other. Mr. Burton was a well-behaved intelligent
man, and a lover of fcience, particularly in the mathematical line. The daughter
was a promifing young actrefs, and was engaged by Mr. Garrick at Drury Lane
Theatre, where fhe appeared in December 1768 in the character of The Country
Girl, and continued to perform there through one, if not two feafons. She died at
Barnftaple in Devonfhire, where fhe is buried. The following epitaph either is,
or was intended to be, inferibed to her memory:

" Underneath the library of this church   Life's but a walking fhadow, a poor player,
            Refteth,   Who ftruts its hour or two upon the ftage,
     Until the archangel's trump   And then is heard no more,
Shall fummon her to appear on the immortal ftage,   This fmall tribute,
            The body of   To the memory of
   ELIZABETH BURTON, Comedian;   An amiable young woman,
        Formerly of Drury Lane,   An innocent chearful companion,
    But late of the Exeter theatre;   And moft excellent actrefs,
     Who exchanged time for eternity   Was placed here by J. Foote,
   On All Souls day 1771, aged 20 years.   Manager of the theatre."

P. 55. From a MS. Court Calendar * for the year 1553, it appears that the Park of Grentesmainell continued to that period an object of royal confideration. I fhall tranfcribe what relates to the county of Leicefter.

FEES and OFFICES.

Kepers, Officers, and Myniftres of Caftles, Houfes, Parkes, Forreftes, and Chafes.

		Office	Holder	Fee	
The Duchie of Lancaftr.	Leicefter.	Conftable and porter of the caftell,	Henry Duke of Suffolke.	Fee LX s. VIII d.	XVIIIl. IIIs. VId.
		Cheif forrefter, or keeper of the chace there,	Francis Earle of Huntingdon.	Fee LX s. VIII d.	
		Keper of the Wayte, als Walker, within the chace of Leicefter,	The faid Earle of Huntingdon.	Fee XXX s. IIII d.	
		Keper of Barneparke, parcell of the faid chace,	The faid Earle of Huntingdon.	Fee XLV s. VI d.	
		Keper of Hethewarde within the faid chace,	The faid Earle of Huntingdon.	Fee XLV s. VI d.	
		One of the kepers within the foreft of Leicefter,	John Elymyn.	Fee XLV s. VI d.	
	Tolowe.	Keper of the parke,	Henry Satherdell.	Fee XLV s.	
	Hinkeley, als Hinkeley Parke.	Keper of the woodes,	Robte Taylor.	Fee XXX s. IIII d.	
Augmentac'.	Bridefueft.	Keper of the houfe and lodge,	Sir John Harington, knt.	Fee LX s. VIII d.	VIIIl. XIX s.
		Keper of the parke,	The fame Sir John Harrington.	Fee LX s. VIII d. Herbage and Paynige.	
		Keper of the woodes,	....	Fee XXVI s. VIII d.	
	Abbottes Parke.	Payler there,	John Whyte.	Fee XIII s. IV d.	

* Intituled, " A Booke of Fees and Offices, primo die Augufti, Anno primo Regine Marie." Queen Mary had then filled the throne but fix-and-twenty days. For the communication of this curious MS. my beft thanks are due to the Mafter, Warden, and Fellows of Dulwich College. It is preferved in their Library, under the mark of F. 7. 1.

In another part of the MS. Sir John Harington, knight, appear to have been
"Auditor of the Honour of Leicester," and to have received for it,

Fee, c s.
Portage of every el. paid into the } iiii l.xviii s. ii d. } xiiii l. vii s. ii d.
   King's coffers, esteemed at
Allowance, lxix s.

Richard Cupper was "Auditor of the late College of
   Leicester, with the late College and Chauntry
   Lands in the South Parts;"

Fee, xxvi l. xiii s. iv d. } xxxii l. xiii s. iv d.
Portage, as before, vi l.

John Hanbie was "Auditor of the Court of Augmentacions" for the Counties
of Northampton, Warwick, Leicester, Rutland, Stafford, Salop, Hereford, and
Worcester.

Fee and allowance, cᵐᵐiii l. xv s. iiii d.

William Efelden, Efquire, "Receyvor" for all the above Counties, Fee cliiii l.

Thomas Cookes was "Woodward" of Leicestershire, with a fee of xl s. and
   "his charges in the time of the Wood-fale."

John Beamonde, "Surveior" of Leicestershire, with a Fee of xiii l. vi s viii d.
and "riding charges by difcretion of the Court," was in this year deprived
of his office.

The Hiftorian and the Antiquary will excufe my preferving the names and rewards
of a few "Artificers of fundrie kyndes," who had the honour of appearing in this
very fingular Calendar.

    Prynter, Thomas Bartlet, Fee iiii l.
    Stationer, Reynold Woolf, Fee xxvi l. viii d.
    Keper of Libraries, Bartholomew Traferon, Fee xiii l. vi s. viii d.

Paynters, {
  Anthony Tetto, Serjant Paynter, Fee xxv l. } xxxv l. } c l.
  The fame Anthony Tetto, Fee x l.
  Bartholemew Penne,   -   -   Fee xxv l.
  Levyn Tirling, payntars,   -   Fee xl l.

    Graver of Stones, Richard Atzele, Fee xx l.
    Clockemaker, Nichas Urfewe, Fee xviii l. v s.
    Clockekep, John de Moylym, Fee xii l. iii s iiii d.
    Aftronomer, Nicholas Cracher, Fee xx l.
    Mole-taker, John Whatton, Fee, with his lynes, vii l. xx d.
    Three Keepers of the Phefauntes and Partriges, Fee xxv l. ix s. ii d.
    Two Takers of Phefauntes and Partriges, Fee xiii l. v s. x d.

At the fame period the Fees to the royal band of "Mufitions and Players," including "Trumpeters, Lutars, Harpers, Rebeck, Sagbuts, Vialls, Bagpiper,
Minftrells, Drumflades, Players on the Fluyte, Players on the Virginalles, Muf-
tions Straungers (Venetians), Players of Enterludes (in nombre viii, every of them
at lxvi s. by yeare) and Makers of Inftruments, were, Mᵛⁱⁱxxviii l. v s.

The

The "Totall fumme of the Fees and Allowances to Officers and Minifters, and of all other charges," is comprifed in the following fchedule.

		l.	s.	d.		l.	s.	d.
Officers and Minifters of the Revenue in the Courts of	Thefchequire	3533	15	1				
	Thaugmentacõn — —	7249	10	3	}	13825	8	4¼
	The Duchie of Lancaftre	1148	5	7½				
	The Firfte Fruits and Tenthes	956	15	1				
	The Wardes and Lyveryes	937	2	4				
Officers and Minifters of Juftice.	The Chancery —	1597	10	11½	}			
	The Previe Seale —	365	0	0				
	The Kings Benche —	688	18	2				
	The Comõn Place —	657	12	4				
	The Kings Learned Coonfaill	289	1	0				
	The Counfaill in the North	1403	6	8	}	7406	9	6½
	The Counfaill and Officers in Wales	1808	8	4				
	The Countie Palatyne of Lancafter	110	6	8				
	The Countie Palatyne of Chefter	85	5	5				
	Juftices of Forrefts —	202	0	0				
	The White Hall —	200	0	0				
Secretaries, Clerks, Poftes, and Currors		—				1113	13	4.
The Admyraltie		—				1456	18	8
The Ordenaunce — —		—				1556	11	8
The Armorie —		—				654	5	11
Officers at Armes		—				809	1	8
The Mynt —		—				604	13	4
The Works —		—				443	14	3
The Greate Warderobe		—				246	1	2
The Butlerage of England —		—				100	0	0
The Kings Tentes —		—				79	13	2
The Revells		—				19	2	6
Officers and Mynyfters of Huntinge		—				603	14	2¼
Officers and Mynyfters of Hawkinge		—				446	11	8
Mufitions and Players — —		—				1728	5	0
Phyfitions, Surgeons, Aftronomer, and Apothecaries		—				541	2	6
The Kings Bardge		—				109	11	5
Artificers		—				432	19	8
Officers and Servaunts of Houfhold		—				16868	10	1¾
Townes and Caftelles of Warre, Fortreffe, and Bulwarkes						18051	8	5½
Keepers of Howfes, Parkes, Forrefts, and Chafes		—				5268	1	3¾
					Total,	72364	19	10¼

P. 58.

P. 58. note, l. 2. r. " begins in 1554."

P. 61. note, l. 2. for " p. 44," r. " p. 50." This is a material correction, as two diftinct facts, each remarkably confirming the other, are otherwise confounded. The fea-fight alluded to by Mr. Robinfon was not that of 1672, but fome one that happened about 30 years later. Q. the exact time?

P. 62. The Holywell being dried up about fix and twenty years ago, by digging for gravel, a new one was opened on the other fide of the road, where now ftands a neat brick pillar, inscribed, " Rebuilt 1757."

P. 64. *Corallita* are perhaps rather a fpecies of *Zoophytes*, or animals with ftone incruftations, foffil corals.

P. 68. l. 13. Strike out the *Severn*, which was inferted by miftake.

P. 69. The banner of Hinckley is in plate VII. fig. 6.

P. 79. " There is a manor oven (fourteen feet diameter) at Melton Mowbray, which " hath full bufinefs; but the baker, in Sir Matthew Lamb's time, was for obliging " every one to make ufe of it, though he could not ferve all. The inhabitants in- " timated, that though they allowed Sir Matthew to have fuch an ancient grant, " yet they were informed, that the old price for baking was alfo ftipulated, on " which Sir Matthew defifted from his claim." I owe this note to the Honourable Mr. Juftice Barrington's very excellent Obfervations on the Statutes, 1775, p. 212.

P. 80. note. The like has been obferved of Birmingham. The year of the great plague, which reached Birmingham, made no addition to the regifter of burials, as the unhappy victims were conveyed to *Ladywood* for interment. The dead bodies at Hinckley were probably depofited in the *Aflwoods.*

P. 89. The bill for making a new cut from Griff to Woodland's Farm did not fucceed in the laft feffion of parliament, and is expected to be warmly oppofed in the enfuing feffion.

P. 93. after " roof," add, " which is well leaded."

P. 94. l. 20. after " chantry," add, " where there ftill remains an elegant niche " for holy water."——l. 28. r. " viciffim amatis."

P. 95. l. 1. r. " in terris."—l. 10. " Elizabetha."

P. 100. I have feen a picture of Richmond, after he was king, in which the device of the thorn is entwined with his crown in memory of that regal ornament's being found after the battle in a thorn-bufh.

P. 102. The verfes on Mr. Ballard having been printed from an incorrect copy, not a little of the pathos is unfortunately loft. They are here preferved entire:

" I lov'd my honour'd parents dear,
I lov'd my wife and children dear,
And hope in Heaven to meet them there:
I lov'd my brothers and fifters too;
And hope I fhall them in Heaven view:
I lov'd my uncles, aunts, and coufins too,
I pray God to give my children grace the fame to do."

Ibid. l. 25. r. " aged 71."

P. 103.

P. 103. The manor of Wykin was in 1638 the property of Mr. *Watts*; and afterwards belonged to three fisters of the name of *Trotman*, from whom it came by descent to their nephew *William Burleton*, esq. the present owner of the lordship, and lessee of the great tithes *.

P. 120. On the monument of Richard Wightman at Burbach is his figure at full length, with those of his two wives (one of them named Constance), and their arms quartered. He died in 1578.

P. 129. l. 15. Sir John Cotton, of Stratton in Bedfordshire, died at Mr. Hanbury's in North Street, Red Lion Square, in Feb. 1730; and was succeeded in honours and estate by his uncle (Sir Robert) a gentleman whose extraordinary fidelity, firmness, and friendship, had made him the darling of all those of his acquaintance. Political State, vol. XLI. p. 213. Mary third daughter and coheiress of the last Sir John Cotton was married in 1757 to the present earl of Denbigh, and died at East Sheen, Oct. 14, 1782.

P. 140. Since the enumeration of Cleiveland's Works was printed off, I have seen an edition of 1661, under the title of " Poems by John Cleavland. With Ad-" ditions never before printed ;" and also one of 1662, with the same title as those of 1659 and 1660, viz. " J. Cleaveland revived," &c. This third edition, besides " many other never before publisht Additions, is enriched with the Author's Mid-" summer Vows, or Lunacy Rampant. Being an University Character, a short " Survey of the late Fellows of the Colledges." His bust, crowned with laurel, and prefixed to the editions of 1659, 1660, and 1662, is called " *Vera Effigies* " *J. Cleavlandi.*

" For weighty numbers, fense, misterious wayes
" Of happie wit, great Cleavland claimes his baies.
                    " *Sepultus Colleg. Whitintonii*, 1 *Mau, anno* 1658."
The portrait with a band is dated 1653; and that in a clerical habit, with the life of the author, were first prefixed to the edition of 1667.

P. 142. Kerenkappuch Onebye was daughter of Henry Turvile, esq. of Af- ton Flamville, the last person mentioned in Burton's pedigree of that ancient Norman family. One of them has been mentioned in p. 73, as a benefactor to Croyland Abbey, so early as 833; and they had lands at Hinckley in 1330 (see p. 20.) Their principal residence was at *Normanton Turvile*, whence *Sir William* removed to Aston Flamville, where he died in 1549 †.

                                                              P. 150.

---

* In 1724 Joseph Ward claimed exemption from tithes for lands in Wykin called *Spiceleys*, as formerly belonging to the monastery of Nuneaton ; but the plea was of course over-ruled. The whole lordship was once the property of that religious society, and might with equal reason have claimed exemption.

† The " fair-railed tomb of stone," mentioned by Burton, still remains (October 1782,) in the chancel at Aston Flamville. On it are the effigies of Sir William and his lady, and at their feet five children. On the sides six coats of arms, now nearly effaced, one of them, *Turvile*, Gules, 3 chevrons vairy, impaling *War-burton*, a chevron between 3 Crows Sable, and the crest of Turvile, a Turtle proper, holding in his beak an Olive-branch. The inscription, not exactly given by Burton, is this : " Here lye the bodyes of Sir William " Turvil, knyght, lord of thys lordship, and Dame Jane hys wyfe, doughter of Syr John Wirbytton; the " whyche said Sir Wyllim dyed the second daye of July in the years of our Lord God MDXLIX; the said " Jane died . . . ."

The other monuments mentioned by Burton are all gone, but there remains the stone figure of a warrior in armour, without any inscription. There is also a flat stone for a *Turvile* of the present century, marked
                                                              with

P. 152. Since the account of Sir Nathan Wright was printed, I have seen his monument in the church at Caldecote * ; an elegant tablet of white marble, with his arms finely blazoned, motto UNICA VIRTUS NOBILITAS, and this inscription:

M. S.	Sedecim propè annos, quot exinde vixit,
Prænobilis Viri	Famæ satur, & quam modicè compos voti,
D. NATHAN WRIGHT, Eq. Aur,	ex animo rura coluit vicina,
Qui quinque annos & menses septem	Pius & humanus,
Magistratû functus	A quoque bono & prudenti
D'ni Custodis M. Sigilli	Desideratissimus,
Angliæ,	Obiit Augusti 4°,
Æquus & integer,	Anno D'ni 1721,
Ac tanto mihi impar muneri;	Æt. suæ 68.

The communications of a friend have also enabled me to add some further particulars to the memoirs of Lord Keeper Wright. On the 27th of April, 1692, he appeared at the Chancery-bar, before the lords commissioners of the great seal, with thirteen

---

with a ✠. Another Roman Catholic is also buried here, with this short epitaph, ✠ " Hic jacet Francisca " Fortescue, uxor Caroli Fortescue de Husbands Bosworth armigeri, Obiit 4° Aprilis, an. D'ni 1697. Requi-" escat in pace." A flat stone to the memory of John Pratt, who died 1733, his two wives and one son, closes the list of monumental inscriptions in the church; where the Cradock family have a spacious vault, in which the late Mr. Cradock and Mr. Bunny of Leicester are buried, but no epitaph as yet appears to either. In the churchyard are only two inscriptions, that on Mr. Dalby (see p. 186.) which was written by the Rev. Mr. Newman, then curate of Aston Flamville and Burbach; and one to the memory of Thomas Hunt, a farmer, who died Feb. 14, 1769, aged 56; and his wife Anne, Jan. 13, 1767, aged 57.

* In this neat little church the monuments of the Purefoys from 1570 to 1629, and of Abbott 1648, as engraved in Dugdale's Warwickshire, continue in excellent preservation. Mr. Abbott's has this remarkable inscription:

" Here lieth the body of GEORGE ABBOTT, late of Caldecote in Warwickshire, Esq. whose eminent Partes, Vertues, and Graces, drawne forth to life in his exemplarie walking with God, his tenderness to all the members of Christ, who frequently fled to his charity in their wants, and councell in cases of conscience, his exact observation of the sabbath, which he vindicated by his pen, and on which, Aug. 15, 1642. God honored him in the memorable and unparalleled Defence of this adjoyning House, with 8 men (besides his mother and her maids) against the furious and fierie assault of Prince Rupert and Maurice with 18 troops of horse and dragooners †, his perspicuous Paraphrases of the Bookes of Job and Psalmes, his judicious Tracts of publicke affaires then emergent, his knowne integritie in publicke imployment, rendered him one of a thousand for singular piety, wisdome, learning, gravity, courage, fidelitie to his countrey, which he served in two parliaments, the former and this present, whereof he died a member Febru. the 2d, 1648, in the 44 yeare of his age.

This monument was erected to his memorie by his deare Mother and executrix Johane Purefoy, the wife of Colonell William Purefoy, his beloved father in law, the 28 day of August, anno Domini 1649."

Anthony Wood, in his Life of Abp. Abbot, mentions this gentleman as author of, 1, " The whole Book " of Job paraphrased, &c. Lond. 1640," 4to; dedicated to his father-in-law William Purefoy, Esq. 2. " Vindiciæ Sabbathi, or an Answer to two Treatises of Mr. Broad, concerning the Lord's Day, or Still of the " Week, 1641," 4to. 3. " Brief Notes upon the whole Book of Psalms, &c." 4to; besides other things. —Wood mentions also another George Abbot (son of Sir Maurice Abbot, lord mayor of London in 1638, and nephew to the Archbishop), who was elected probationer fellow of Merton College, 1622, and admitted I.L. B. 1630; but this latter is probably the same with the former, the son-in-law of Purefoy, and the defender of his house.

Caldecote Hall has been lately purchased by Thomas Fisher, esq.; who, with great judgement and exquisite taste, has built an elegant modern mansion, without destroying the convenience of the venerable manorhouse of the Purefoys. I will add also, to the no small credit of this respectable gentleman, that he has been equally attentive to the convenience of his tenants, by demolishing their straggling cottages, and collecting them in a comfortable little village built purposely for their reception.

† No traces of this rencontre occur in Clarendon. Tradition says, the dishes and plates were melted into bullets.

Plate XIII

S.ᴿ NATHAN WRIGHT KN.ᵀ
Lord Keeper 1700.

other gentlemen * ; whose appearance being recorded, they took the usual oaths; after which the lord chancellor Trevor made a speech to them; when the new serjeants delivered to his lordship two rings to be presented to their Majesties, with their duty and most humble thanks for the great honour conferred on them.   Mr. Wright, having been counsel for the King against Sir John Fenwick in the house of peers, was, before the beginning of Hilary Term 1696, called within the bar, being made king's serjeant, and knighted.   March 19, 1699, he made a speech in the house of commons, on behalf of Henry duke of Norfolk, in a committee of that house, on the second reading of the bill for a divorce between his Grace and the Dutchess †.   March 28, 1699, he opened the indictment, on behalf of the King, on the trial of Edward earl of Warwick and Holland, for the murder of Richard Coote, esq.; and made a learned reply to the argument of counsel as to the competency of a witness ‡.   Oct. 12, 1699, he in like manner opened the indictment, on the trial of Mary Butler, alias Strickland, at the Old Bailey, for forging a bond of 40,000 l. in the name of Robert Clayton §.   May 21, 1700, the King in council delivered the great seal (some time after the lord chancellor Somers had given it up) to Sir Nathan Wright §; and on the day King William died, March 8, 1701-2, Sir Nathan delivered into the hands of Queen Anne, then sitting in council; and had the honour of receiving it again **.   One of the most remarkable events that happened while he was in office was his sentence for dissolving *The Savoy* ††, July 31, 1702; and it may also be mentioned that in the same

---

* Mr. Serjeant Wright always took place of Serjeant Bomithon, to whom he was junior by admittance, because his writ bore *Teste* before that of Bonithon, though they were returnable at the same time. R. Raym. 601. Notwithstanding, when he came to be lord keeper, and a question of seniority was in judgment before him which turned on the very same point, he determined just contrary to what he asked himself towards Bonithon. But perhaps Wright would say, in the language of old Plowden, that " when he was to determine " for *another*, not for *himself*, then the case was altered."

† State Trials, V. 279.   ‡ Ib. V. 143, 169. || Ib. V. 233.   § R. Raym. 562.
** 1 R. Raym. 742.   Sir Nathan kept the great seal till 1705, and was succeeded by lord keeper Cowper.   Mr. Grove, in his " Life of the First Duke of Devonshire, 1764," p. 248, has given a character of Lord Keeper Wright, from a MS. copy of " Macky's Characters," containing some variations worth pointing out.
  The printed copy of Macky has, " Sir Nathan Wright, lord keeper, is son of a clergyman; a good " common Lawyer, a slow Chancellor, and no Civilian. Chance more than choice brought him the Seals: the " lords chief justices Holt and Treby refusing to succeed so great a man as the lord Somers, they fell into " the hands of this gentleman; who, being recommended by the opposite party, proved their faithful tool ever " since. He is a plain man, both in person and conversation; of middle stature, inclining to fat; hath a fat " broad face, much marked with the small-pox "—Swift's MS. adds, " Very covetous."
  Mr. Grove's copy runs thus, " He is a good common Lawyer, a slow Equity-man, but no Civilian. Chance " more than choice brought him to the Seals. Being recommended by the Tory party, he has proved their " faithful tool ever since. He is a plain man both in person and conversation, of middle stature, inclining " to be fat, broad-faced, and much marked with the small pox. He has done a great deal of good to his " private family, married his son and daughter to very good fortunes. He gave the employment of the " Clerk of the Crown to his son, and some good livings to a great many of his poor relations in the country." See also Grove's Life of Cardinal Wolsey, vol. IV. p. 150.
  †† The following curious papers relative to this transaction, unnoticed by any of our Historians, have been kindly communicated by Dr. Ducarel, from his MS. Collection of English Antiquities, Vol. AA. 1. N° 61.
                                                C° le of the SAVOY.
  " Peter Earl of Savoy, coming into England, to visit his niece Queen of Henry III. an house was built re appointed for him on the Thames, called The Savoy, which soon after became the possession of the Dukes of Lancaster, and fell to the Earl of Richmond afterwards Henry VII. who was of that line. Hence the name.
  Henry VII. by will, ordered an Hospital to be built there, which was performed by Henry VIII. in the 11th year of his reign, for the maintenance of a Master and Chaplains (who were incorporated), and several Poor. Statutes were made; the Abbot of Westminster made Visitor. Their business to pray for the souls of Henry VII. and the Royal Family.
  1 Edward VI. it was seized on by law, as directed to superstitious uses; the lands given to Bridewell and St. Bartholomew's Hospital.

I i   4 Philip

fame year, on the 19th of November, he reverfed a decree of his great predeceffor Lord Somers. [*Lawrence* and *Lawrence*, originally heard in Michaelmas
Term

4 Philip and Mary, it was re-founded to the fame ufe, the fame ftatutes continued; but after what manner the hofpital was governed does not appear at this diftance (for fo the Commiffioners in 1730 report to King
William). But the Report fays, that after the Holland war, Charles II. put in wounded foldiers and feamen;
and James II. put in Jefuits.

July 21, 1702, Lord Keeper Wright, as Vifitor of Royal Foundations, diffolved it; and a Bill afterwards
paffed the Commons, (inter al.) to confirm the diffolution; but it was rejected by the Lords.

T. living on the fpot for feveral years, and obferving what paffed, picked up fome papers and remarks
relating to the Savoy, and laid them before Lord Cowper, praying him to aid, in order to get the Mafterfhip
for himfelf. The Lord natured Lord advifed T. to get a petition (which petition his Lordfhip in a friendly
manner modelled) figned by the tenants of the Hofpital. T. did fo; and brought it to the Lord on a Thurfday. His Lordfhip delivered it the fame night to the King in Council, and a reference was got the next
Saturday. The reference Mr. Oaker had. It was referred to the Attorney and Solicitor General. They
were to report their opinion to Lord Chancellor Cowper, which, by the way, was in a manner referring it to
himfelf, fo fixed was his Lordfhip to ferve T. in this affair.

T. knowing Mr. Oaker to be early in his Lordfhip's fervice, and ready at bufinefs, defired leave to go
home for a while, and leave the foliciting part to Mr. Oaker. But his Lordfhip throwing up the feal the fecond time, and that dying, T's hopes died with him. What has been done fince that time, T. knows
not. If any thing has been done, Mr. Oaker is a likely perfon to know."

The Sentence of Diffolution.

" Die Veneris, tricefimo primo die menfis Julii, anno D'ni milefimo feptingentefimo fecundo, coram præ-
honorando viro Domino Nathan Wright milite, Domino Cuftode Magni Sigilli Angliæ, e aque intuitu Hof-
pitalium Regiæ fundationis per eorum Regnum Angliæ Vifitatore; in Vifitatione hac fua Hofpitalis de le
Savoy, prope le Strand, in com' Midd'æie, vocati Hofpitale Henrici Regis Angliæ feptimi de Savoy, feu
quocunque alio nomine idem Hofpitale nuncupatur, tento in Aula publica dicti Hofpitalis, præfente Roberto
Wilmer Notario Publico, Richardi Crawley Armigeri Regiftrarii Regii hac in Vifitatione Deputato.

Negotium Vifitationis tunc Magiftri fi quis fit, quam Johanis Hooke Clerici, Johannis Lamb S. T. P.
Nicholai Only S. T. P, et Lyonelli Coles Clerici, Capellanorum, necnon Officiariorum, Servientium, et quo-
rumcunque aliorum ejufdem Hofpitalis, aut infra idem Hofpitale, vel alibi, hujufmodi Vifitationi fubjectorum.

Moniti funt iidem Johannes Hooke, Johannes Lamb, Nicholaus Only, et Lyonellus Coles, necnon Johannes
Nedeham, ad danda fua refponfa; et prorogata eft Vifitatio ad hunc diem.

Quo die, facta proclamatione uti moris eft, comparuerunt iidem Johannes Hooke, Johannes Lamb, Nicholaus
Only, et Lyonellus Coles, necnon Johannes Nedeham, et juxta affignationem prædictam exhibuerunt refponfa fua perfonalia, in vim eorum refpective juramenti aliis præftiti, articulis aliis contra eos vicefimo octavo
die inftantis menfis datis, quæ refpective pro veris cognoverunt.

Deinde, ex mandato Domini Vifitatoris, eadem refponfa per me publice perlecta fuerunt. Quibus perlectis,
D'nus Vifitator detulit juran tentum cuidam Jacobo Balderfton Janitori ejufdem Hofpitalis, præfentis in judicio,
de fideliter refpondendo quibufcunque quæftionibus per Dominationem fuam interrogandis. Qui quidem
Balderfton interrogatus vigore juramenti fui depofuit, " That the profit of the burying-place belonging to
" the faid Hofpital do, one year with another, amount unto about 15 pounds per annum."

His ita geftis, Dominus Vifitator antedictus, perlectis refponfis prædictis, et infpectis ftatutis dicti Hofpitalis,
ac auditis Johanne Cooke milite Legum Doctore, Advocato Regio, necnon Nathanaele Lloyd Legum Doctore Advocato membrorum affertorum dicti Hofpitalis, habitaque matura confideratione totius negotii, unaliter
interloquendo declaravit,

Quod per refponfa prædicta fibi manifefte liquet, ipfos eofdem Johannem Hooke, Johannem Lamb, Nicholaum Only, et Lyonellum Coles, de facto tantum et non per Capellanos perpetuos ejufdem Hofpitalis fuiffe
et effe; ex eo quod ipfi tempore admiffionum fuarum ad officium Capellanorum perpetuorum Hofpitalis prædicti juramentum per ftatuta ejufdem Hofpitalis fua parte requifitum non præftiterunt nec fubfcripferunt, nec
eorum aliquis præftitit nec fubfcripfit; fui ipfi iidem Johannes Hooke, Johannes Lamb, Nicholaus Only, et
Lyonellus Coles, in officium Capellanorum perpetuorum ejufdem Hofpitalis debito modo jurati et admiffi
nunquam fuerunt. Ipfos tamen Johannem Hooke, Johannem Lamb, Nicholaum Only, et Lyonellum Coles,
pœnam amiffionis officii fui Capellani perpetui Hofpitalis prædicti incurriffe, idem Dominus Vifitator declaravit, ex eo quod ipfi ordinationes et ftatuta ejufdem Hofpitalis non obfervaverunt nec perimpleverunt,
nec eorum aliquis obfervavit t.a. perimplevit; fed eadem ordinationes et ftatuta, et debitum officii, juxta
et eandem exigentiam, penitus neglexerunt et omiferunt; et præcipue in hoc, quod ipfi in Hofpitale prædicto
non vixerunt et refiderunt, nec eorum aliquis vixit et refedit, juxta exigentiam ftatutorum prædictorum, fed
continue a tempore admiffionum fuarum refpectivarum ad officium Capellanorum perpetuorum Hofpitalis
prædicti hucufque extra Hofpitale prædictum vixerunt et refiderunt, et eorum quilibet vixit et moram fuam
traxit.

Idem igitur Dominus Vifitator, ratione præmifforum, eofdem Johannem Hooke, Johannem Lamb, Nicholaum
Only, et Lyonellum Coles, et eorum quemlibet, ab officio Capellanorum perpetuorum, feu Capellani perpetui,
ejufdem Hofpitalis amovendos et deprivandos fore, fecundum ordinationes et ftatuta ejufdem Hofpitalis, pro-
nuntiavit; ipfofque et quemlibet eorum ab officio Capellani perpetui Hofpitalis prædicti amovit et deprivavit.

Et

Term 1639.] Sir Nathan's daughter Lady Sambrook died in December 1775 (not 1777, as mentioned by mistake pp. 143, 150 *.)   P. 155.

Et quia modo nec Magister nec Capellanus perpetuus ejusdem Hospitalis exiflit, idem Dominus Victor Il-se-se prædictum diffolutum esse declaravit; et Domine Regine in Curia sua Scacea ei Domino Thefaurario Anglie defuper certificandum fore decrevit. Interim vero in mandatis dedit dictis Johanni Sellam et Jacebo Balderston, ut curam agant de omnibus ad Hospitale prædictum pertinentibus; ac quibustiam de cura est capellæ, et eidem quoque modo pertinentium, eis eandem adhibere curam de eifdem manua ..., et omnia et fingula munimenta, &c. penes Registrum modo remanentia ibidem, donec aliter per Dominam Reginam ordinatum fuerit, custodiri jussit.   Ita teflor, Ro. Wilmer, Notarius Publicus."

Remarks touching the Savoy.

" Lord Keeper difsolves, by his Visitatorial Power, a Royal foundation, 31 July, 1702; which was wrong, as may be guessed by this:

1. That he applied to the Parliament to get his sentence confirmed; which was needless if the sentence had been good in law. When that Bill was brought into the Commons, where it passed, T. alarmed Fowler Bishop of Gloucester, who expected to hold the Savoy in commendam; Fowler alarms Lord Halifax his friend; Halifax alarmed the Dukes of Somerset and Ormond, the Chancellors of the two Universities, who made head against it ftrenuously; infomuch that it was rejected with indignation, and sharp words passed about ' fending Wright to the Lions.' The fate was cut out into Wright street, Nathan street, Nathan Lane, &c.

2. The reason of the thing, and laws of our country, to encourage industry, give a man entire power over his property. This property he may dispose of as he pleases, provided he does not injure the Polity. Giving a property in alms is a moral act; Gift in perpetuas eleemosya never reverts, because the Giver cuts off all that claimed under him for ever. The gift is ever to descend to some use, and the local flatutes only ascertain the modus of the duty to which the reward is annexed. If people will not do the duty in that manner the Donor designed, put them out, and put others in that will. Local flatutes depend upon circumstances of His and Nunc; and are therefore variable. But beneficence is of intrinsic and antecedent worth— good in itself, and therefore not to be annihilated. For instance,

Saol, an Episcopalian Scot, founds two Fellowships in Oxford (Baliol College, I think) that they should be maintained there some years, and then, fide data, to return into Scotland, and there become afferters of Episcopacy. In King William's time, Episcopacy was abolished by law in Scotland. Such heirs at law cuter upon the estate, because the uses were incompatible. The College died into Chancery; Lord Somers decreed the Estate to the College.

St. Katharine's by the Tower is a Royal Hospital, or College (built by King Stephen, I think). Sir James Butler, the master, was complained of for mis-feazance. Lord Chancellor Somers, by his visitatorial power, visits, turns out Butler, fuspends the Brethren for a while, but he does not annihilate or difsolve; sic the Earl of Feversham was made Master, and the Brethren reftored by him.

A Man took a fancy to a Tree, kept it shorn and cropped, dies, and leaves the Poor of the Parish some Lands while they trimmed the Tree and kept it in that form he left it. The Heir at Law, in a dark night, cuts down the Tree, and ejects the Tenant; the Parish fled in Chancery. Lord Cowper decreed for the Parish. That great Man distinguished betwixt the whim and the virtue of the Testator. I had it from his own mouth, when we were talking of the Savoy.

The Sentence of Diffolution fays, " Et quia modo nec Magister nec Capellanus perpetuus ejufdem Hof-" pitalis exiftit, idem Dominus Vifitator Hofpitale prædictum diffolutum effe declaravit."

Dr. Killigrew, the laft Mafter, died in 1699 (in March, I think). This was July, 1702. The Vifitor was all this intermediate while Keeper of the Royal Confcience and Privy Counfellor. Why did not he advife King William and Queen Anne better? If they omitted what was in their power (I'll put it fafely) fhall that omiffion be conftrued to amount to a caufe of Diffolution? The King makes the Mafter of Trinity College, Cambridge, and Dean of Chrift Church, Oxford.—No man will think, that he'll put in no Head over thofe two Colleges, and then feize on the Lands. A Courtier, in King Edward IV's time, had a mind to have the Lands belonging to the Bifhoprick of Durham; that Bifhoprick was extinguifhed by Act of Parliament, not by a Vifitatorial Power.

Lord Cowper did not think the Sentence valid; yet he thought the beft way to fet it right was by Act of Parliament, becaufe, fince the Diffolution, feveral miftakes might arife, which a new Law might redrefs at once; and accordingly defigned to get fuch a Law. That Lord ordered T. to draw up a new fcheme how the new Hofpital fhould be modelled; which T. did; and as to the main it was liked.

When Lord Keeper Wright diffolved the Hofpital, Mr. Robert Wilmer, Notary Public of the Commons, acted as Regiftrar, and took the cuftody of the Foundation-charter, Rental, &c. When Mr. Oaker was Gentleman to Lord Chancellor Harcourt, he was fent to Wilmer for thofe papers, and had them. When Lord Chancellor Harcourt was out, he re-delivered them to Mr. Oaker. Mr. O. had all his light from T.

N. B. Thofe papers are to follow the Seal when fent for, they being property to no man."

Memorandum. The above mentioned papers are copied from fome original papers, which at this time (Sept. 16, 1754) belong to Dr. Richard Rawlinson †. At the back of them is the following Memorandum in the Doctor's own hand-writing: " Savoy—Aug. 1754. Received this Paper as a prefent " from John Locker, Efq; to me R. † R."

* In the Genealogy of Cleiveland, under Nichols, add, " 3. Martha, born Nov. 10, 1781;" and in p. 146, under Mervis, read, " Three fons, and two daughters, died infants: Eliza, born 1782, and still living."

† Dr. Rawlinfon's MSS. are now (1764) in the Bodleian Library.

P. 155. Mr. Welfted has feveral fongs in the " Mufical Mifcellany, 1729," 6 vols. 8vo. particularly in vol. I. p. 18. " While in the bower, with beauty bleft, &c." and in vol. IV. p. 17. " The Genius;" which is highly commended by Mr. Hughes in two letters to Earl Cowper. " It was written," he adds, " by Mr. Weifted, a " gentleman I have heard mentioned by Mr. Steele, as a promifing genius;" and the noble Earl fays, they are " excellent verfes of an uncommon kind *." In another place Mr. Hughes calls him " a young man, whom Sir Richard Steele fome time " ago profeffed to patronize and encourage, and ufed to recommend among his ac- " quaintance." He was a commiffioner of the Lottery in 1731.

P. 156. l. 11. and 13. r. " EDMUND;" and l. 22, 23, r. " HENRY, who fuc- " ceeded him in all his honours, fince deceafed."

P. 189. Dr. Blair's acknowledgements of obligation, in the firft edition, are not confined to the Earl of Bath; they are paid alfo " to fome of the moft eminent " men of Great Britain, for rank, abilities, and learning." His fubfcribers were 337.

" I have tranfcribed thefe papers faithfully, and find upon enquiry that this Sentence is of the hand-writing of Robert Wilmer. The faid Robert Wilmer was an Attorney and a Notary Public, who lived in Doc- tors Commons. The Remarks were written by Sir NATH. LLOYD, Knt. LL. D. as I am informed by perfons well acquainted with his hand-writing.—This learned and able Civilian became fellow of All fouls College, Oxford, in or about the year 1691, being then I.L. B. ; and taking his degree of I.L. D. June 30, 1696, was admitted an Advocate in Doctors Commons, the 11ft of November, that year. On his ap- pointment to the office of Judge Advocate, he was knighted ; and became afterwards ~~the King's Advocate in~~ ~~Doctors Commons, and~~ Commiffary of Surrey. In 1710 he was elected Mafter of Trinity Hall, upon the death of George Bramfton, I.L. D. and for fome time kept his abovenamed Fellowfhip with his Mafterfhip, which laft, together with all his other preferments, he voluntarily refigned in 1735, when he retired to Rich- mond in Surrey, where he died, at the age of 70, March 10, 1741. AND. COLTEE DUCAREL." He lies buried in the Chapel of Trinity Hall (to which Houfe, as well as to All fouls College, he was a confiderable Benefactor), where a very handfome monument is erected to his memory, with the following epitaph drawn up by himfelf :

" Ego   Fui
NATHANIEL LLOYD   Officialis Surriæ
Miles & LL. D.   R. R.
Filius   Annæ & Georg. I.
RICHARDI (& ELIZ.) LLOYD   Advocatus generalis
Militis & I.L. D.   &
Cancellarii Dunelm',   Hujus Collegii Cuftos,
Jud. S. Cur. Admiralit' Angliæ,   Quibus Muneribus
Et Decani de Arcubus,   Et fponte ceffi.
(In Cœmiterio S. Bened.   Fuiffe fat!
D. Pauli ad Ripas,   Iam Deo Trino & Uni.
In Jefu   Epitaphia funto vera!
Una dormicntium   Ementiti Nefas!
Tamulo fupereffeto)   Sacer eft locus ;
Cœtelis & Frater   Extra mentiamini.
RICHARDI fuperftitis,   1736."

* See Letters of Eminent Perfons, vol. I. Lett. LI. LII. LIII. In the fame collection is a letter from Mr. Welfted, dated from his office in the Tower, which he feems to have then newly obtained, expreffive of the utmoft gratitude to Bifhop Hoadly.

DIRECTIONS for placing the PLATES.